T0247785

THE MACHIAVELLI TRILOGY
BOOK ONE

THE THRONE

Franco Bernini

THE MACHIAVELLI TRILOGY
BOOK ONE

THE THRONE

Translated from the Italian
by Oonagh Stransky

Europa
editions

Europa Editions
27 Union Square West, Suite 302
New York NY 10003
www.europaeditions.com
info@europaeditions.com

This book is a work of fiction. Any references to historical events,
real people, or real locales are used fictitiously.

*This book has been translated with the generous support from the
Italian Ministry of Foreign Affairs and International Cooperation.
Questo libro è stato tradotto grazie a un contributo per la traduzione assegnato dal
Ministero degli Affari Esteri e della Cooperazione Internazionale italiano.*

Translation by Oonagh Stransky
Original title: *Il trono*
Translation copyright © 2024 by Europa Editions

Library of Congress Cataloging in Publication Data is available
ISBN 979-8-88966-014-9

Bernini, Franco
The Throne

Cover design and illustration by Ginevra Rapisardi

Prepress by Grafica Punto Print – Rome

Printed in USA

C O N T E N T S

For some time now I have never said what I believe or never believed what I said. If sometimes I have told the truth, I hide it among so many lies that it is hard to find.
—NICCOLÒ MACHIAVELLI, from a letter to Francesco Guicciardini, May 17, 1521

THE THRONE

In 1502 the Republic of Florence controlled an area that was less than half the size of current-day Tuscany.

The Republic was surrounded by enemies on all sides: it was at a standoff with Lucca to the west and had been at war with Pisa for years; Siena, to the south, had long been hostile to Florence.

The Republic's worst enemy lay to the north and east, possessed the strongest army in Italy, and had already attempted to invade the Republic twice. This enemy was Cesare Borgia: Duke of Valentinois, Duke of Romagna, son of the Pope, Captain General of the military forces of the Church, and familiarly known as Valentino.

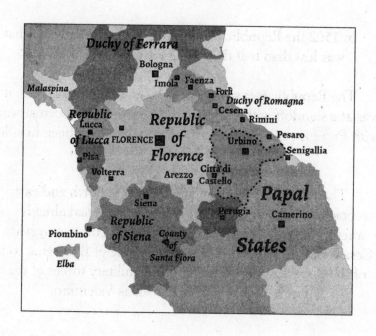

Duchy of Ferrara

Bologna

Imola Faenza

Malaspina

Forlì

Duchy of Romagna

Cesena

Rimini

Republic
of Lucca

Lucca

Republic
of
Florence

Urbino

Pesaro

Senigallia

FLORENCE

Pisa

Volterra

Arezzo

Città di
Castello

Papal

Siena

Perugia

Camerino

Piombino

Republic
of Siena

County
of
Santa Fiora

States

Elba

FLORENCE, OCTOBER 5, 1502

CHAPTER ONE

Lying in bed, he perceives movement out in the street. He opens his eyes; there's the sound of footsteps directed toward his building.

It's that bastard Magaldi. He's sent his thugs. It had to happen sooner or later, he thinks to himself, a knot forming in his stomach.

He throws off his threadbare blanket, gets up, and strains his ears to listen.

Silence from the vegetable garden. The larks are quiet; the sun still hasn't risen.

He tiptoes to the window. Through the lower slats of the shutter he sees the glow of a lantern. He would like to look closer but stops himself. They're probably looking up at his windows. It would be better if they think he's not at home.

He remembers the stories about how they came for Rinaldo Cresci, at that same time of day. Cresci owed Magaldi much less and they broke both his legs, he thinks to himself. They wouldn't dare hurt the women but they will beat me to a pulp.

His breath comes quickly. He hurries to get dressed.

His wife wakes up and looks at him in confusion. He gestures for her to be silent, then whispers in her ear that they're here, that she should go downstairs and open the door for them before they break it down, that she should say he didn't come home last night.

She nods, ashen with fear.

He kisses his wife, then leans over a wooden cradle and strokes his baby daughter's cheek as she starts to wake up.

The men bang hard on the door with their fists.

The baby starts to cry, he picks her up and passes her to Marietta, who makes her way downstairs with the little one in her arms. Their knocking grows stronger.

"I'm coming! What's the rush?" he hears her say, which is followed by a flurry of loud voices. In the meantime, he walks into a small closet and opens a window. Slender and agile, he climbs out, pausing momentarily in the void. They live on the second floor, he is about six arm's length from the ground, facing the alley behind the house. He feels a gust of cold night air.

Below him is darkness and silence. He climbs out the window, nimbly placing his feet in the cracks of the stone wall, then lets himself drop down, skinning his hands along the way. He gets to his feet and starts running, slipping on some food that their neighbors had thrown out the window the night before, almost losing his balance, regaining it, never stopping.

As he rounds the corner, they nab him. He tries to wriggle free, then crouches down to protect himself from their fists. But they don't hit him. They just hold him still.

"Got him," hollers one of the men, who stinks like sweat and has foul breath.

The glow from the lantern turns the corner, partially illuminating the faces and bodies that advance in his direction. The rest is lost in the dark of night.

There are three of them, they carry swords, and they're wearing leather jerkins embossed with the red lily of Florence. He then notices that the two men who hold him steady are also dressed that way.

"You're Gonfalonier guards!" he exclaims with relief.

"Were you expecting someone else?" their leader says. A man of around forty, he has a cruel face but a melancholy expression, and his pitch-black eyes glisten in the dark.

The prisoner recognizes him: it's the head of the constabulary guards, Dino Gherardi. He's brought in only for the most important matters, never for minor affairs. Further cause for worry.

"What's going on? Why are you here? And why so early in the morning?" he asks, his voice cracking.

No one says a thing. A cold gust of wind makes him shiver.

Gherardi nods and the men lead him down the road in the direction of Ponte Vecchio. The sound of their footsteps is barely audible. One guard holds the lantern up high. They skirt puddles of horse urine, mud, and scattered scraps of waste. The north wind continues to blow down from the mountains, whipping between the buildings, swirling around them.

"Where are we going?" the prisoner asks, trying to sound calm.

Gherardi turns around and looks at him sadly. "You'll find out soon enough, Machiavelli."

CHAPTER TWO

N iccolò knows those streets well. He used to play on them when he was a boy, throwing rocks, punching and getting punched, chasing girls who grew up to become women. He knows every shortcut and side street, where they all lead. They walk along the river. The guards, who no longer grip his arms but merely surround him, guide him down a curved street that could either lead to the Palazzo della Signoria or to the jail—either to the seat of power or the place of punishment—depending if they veer left or continue straight.

He has nothing in particular to worry about but he knows that even slander can dig a grave for an honest man. It doesn't take much to fall out of favor if, as was his case, you're a member of the Second Chancery of the Republic and you get involved in matters of State. He has always been careful not to make enemies. Had he done so without intending to? Who could have accused him? And of what?

Ever since becoming a chancellor, Niccolò has worked tirelessly and carefully, but even that could be seen by some as a flaw. People who do their work well can be problematic. He knows how envious, bitter, and competitive men can be. It's easy to point a finger and calumniate someone; all you have to do is appear before a *notaio* with your face covered, register a complaint, and the gears of an enquiry are set into motion, the millstone starts to turn, grinding up even the toughest grain. He will put up a fight, of course, but against whom?

They have almost reached the end of the street. Soon they will push him in one of the two directions. He imagines the worst. He's been to the prison before to observe interrogations. Just being there for a few hours was disturbing; he never saw anyone being tortured but he heard them screaming. He often wondered how he would react if he was ever accused of a crime and imprisoned in the Bargello; maybe he'd confess to crimes he hadn't even committed. Would he be able to resist?

The street comes to an end. They go to the left.

He begins to breathe normally again.

Somewhere in the distance a lark sings.

They step into Piazza della Signoria. A young baker's assistant with a basket of fresh bread on his head crosses their path; the boy averts his gaze.

Someone watching from a window closes their shutters.

They walk past the façade of the Palazzo della Signoria, imposing and dark in the dawn of a new day. The main portal is closed.

They head down one side of the building. Niccolò knows the street well: at the end is the service entrance, which he uses every day, climbing the stairs that lead to the vast and gelid Chancery hall. He wishes it were a normal day. Are they going to ask him about some specific paperwork? Do they want to search his desk in his presence?

They come to a stop long before his usual entrance and go through a door protected by other guards. It leads to an area of the Palazzo that is off limits to Niccolò.

It's warm inside. The foyer is large and square, it has high vaulted ceilings and a marble staircase. A sentry sits at a table with a register open in front of him. He is about to make note of the arrival of the soldiers and Niccolò, but Dino Gherardi murmurs something and the man puts down his quill.

The marble steps lead to a second staircase, this one made of brick. They climb at length, passing a few windows on the way. Outside, Niccolò sees the buildings grow smaller and smaller, rosy pink in the early morning light.

A few more narrow steps and they reach a closed door. Here, too, guards stand on either side. Gherardi knocks discreetly.

"Enter," says a deep voice that Niccolò immediately recognizes. It's the gonfalonier.

Pier Soderini sits at his desk, surrounded by piles of documents, intent on finishing a letter. A man of about fifty, he wears a new dark green robe and black flat cap, his grey hair poking out above his ears. Slightly hunchbacked, his face is lined with deep wrinkles and he has a prominent nose. He does not look up.

Niccolò considers him weak, ill-suited to the most important office in the Republic. And yet he knows one must adapt to whomever is in charge, like him, whether he likes him or not. This is the first time Niccolò has set foot in the man's office, the walls of which are lined with bookshelves that are crowded with papers, folders, and documents. It's rather dark, only a few candles are lit. Two windows look out onto the city and the air is stuffy.

"Here he is, as you ordered," Gherardi says to the gonfalonier, going on to relay how Machiavelli tried to escape.

Soderini nods with amusement and continues to write, as if listening to something of little value. He finishes his letter, raises his grey-brown eyes—at which point Niccolò bows slightly—and waves away the guards.

The gonfalonier waits to speak until the door has closed behind them. "So, you thought they had come to have a little fun with you?" He peers down at some papers. "I hear you owe quite a sum of money to Jacopo Magaldi. You're right to be afraid; that man doesn't joke around."

It's pointless to wonder how he found out. The Republic has eyes everywhere.

Niccolò replies with surprising dignity. "Yes, this is not an easy time for me but I will sort things out soon."

The gonfalonier looks at him skeptically.

"And, if I may be so bold, I would like to point out," Niccolò goes on, concealing his irritation, "that a portion of my debts are from expenses incurred for missions carried out beyond the border on behalf of the Republic."

"And yet the vast majority of your debts come from chasing women," his interlocutor points out, getting to his feet.

Niccolò continues. "I have yet to be reimbursed for my travel expenses. And, as you also surely know, I do not have a personal estate that I can dip into."

Soderini says nothing, walks over to a small door, and opens it. It leads to a narrow terrace. He gestures for Niccolò to follow him. They step outside and climb a narrow wooden staircase that takes them to the chemin de ronde.

Below them, over the parapets, silently lies the city of Florence,. The tall towers, majestic buildings, and myriad reddish rooftops are illuminated by the dawn. Because of the wind, the sky is clear, and the clouds have all been swept away. Distant hills stand out like the spikes on a crown, with the river Arno wending its way between distant villages and on through the valley.

"I find this is the best time of day to get work done. When the city is still sleeping, everything seems so calm," the gonfalonier says quietly, almost to himself. Then, without turning around, he continues. "You've been in the Chancery four years now. Overall you're a trustworthy man—if we are to ignore the time and energy you waste on your dreams of becoming a poet," he adds with some derision.

"We all have our weaknesses," Niccolò says. Inside he's seething.

"Unfortunately, it would appear that you have a few too many."

"I write for myself and only when I am not in service."

"Not always. And I know this for a fact." Niccolò is about to rebut when the gonfalonier holds up his hand, truncating any possible reply. "It's a venial sin, really. And anyway, people say that in terms of artistry you have little to offer."

"Might I ask, with all due respect, who these 'people' are? Some people think they know everything, and yet that is all they really know," Niccolò replies testily.

Soderini ignores Niccolò's comment but turns around to examine him. "However, judging from the things in which you do show acumen, you manage to see where others do not. My brother Francesco assures me of this."

"If you are referring to the honor I had in late June when I accompanied him to Urbino to meet Cesare Borgia—"

"Yes, precisely. I know that you wrote up the report about the legation in Francesco's place. And I must say that I deeply appreciated your work."

The gonfalonier shivers and turns to go back inside. Niccolò follows him, a series of questions rushing through his head. What did I do to annoy him? What does he want from me? Occupying one of the lowest ranks in the administrative hierarchy, Niccolò is used to looking up: he knows how much weight the words of the powerful carry, he knows that nothing is ever left to chance, that even their facial expressions are important. But so far, Soderini has been impassible and Niccolò hasn't been able to glean a single thing from his face.

"That devil is insatiable," the gonfalonier says, making his way over to a wall that has been frescoed with a map of Italy.

Niccolò understands without needing to ask that he is referring to Valentino, as Cesare Borgia is familiarly known.

"He's not satisfied with having conquered Romagna," Soderini says, pointing to the region and then indicating Imola. "Now he's set up camp here, only a two-day ride from Florence. With money from his father, the Pope, he's putting together an army the likes of which has never been seen before."

"So I've heard."

"Many here in Florence are under the illusion that he wants to lay siege on Bologna, and although he manages to convince many that it is so, it is not." The gonfalonier's finger moves down the map from Imola, through the Apennines mountains, and toward the valleys around Florence. "He wants to come after us once again. If he annexes our lands, he could create a vast kingdom with the states he already possesses."

Like all Florentines, Niccolò recalls the fear and frenzy of the year before, when, in May, 1501, Borgia—Prince, Captain General of the Church, son of the Pope, and cousin of the King of France—crossed into the Republic at the head of a great army, bolstered by the most powerful condottieri, Paolo and Francesco Orsini, and commandeered by Vitellozzo Vitelli, one of the ablest military leaders in Italy.

Niccolò was supposed to have gotten married that May, but the wedding had to be postponed because of his work as secretary to the Dieci di Libertà e di Balìa, the council of ten members in charge of dealing with the threat together with the thoroughly inept gonfalonier of the time, Lorenzo di Lotto Salviati. Niccolò realized that his superiors had unclear and conflicting thoughts, that they were incapable of handling the issue. Valentino's army crossed the border from the north through the Val di Marina, a narrow strip of land where it would have been easy enough to block them, if only the Dieci had sent in an army of soldiers.

At the time, Niccolò and Marietta discussed the idea of her temporarily relocating to the small farm he owned in Albergaccio, in the open countryside about seven miles from the city. But then it occurred to them that she would be even more vulnerable to enemy raids there, and far less safe than in their Florentine home with its thick walls. They had made the right decision; Vitelli's troops passed near Albergaccio, through the town of Malmantile, where they had sacked and pillaged homes and kidnapped girls and women who were then forced to work as prostitutes in Rome. Borgia advanced swiftly all the way to Campi, only eight miles away from the Palazzo della Signoria.

The people of Florence lived through those days in utter terror. Niccolò found himself greasing an old sword that had belonged to an ancestor and had been stored away in the attic for years. If forced, he would have fought to defend his family and his betrothed, but he also knew that he didn't stand much of a chance against soldiers like that. And while he practiced wielding his newly sharpened weapon, he, who had never seriously trained for battle, his wrist aching from the effort, tried to imagine what Valentino's next moves would be. That was what he enjoyed: trying to get into his opponent's head. Nothing had ever been handed to Niccolò. Trying to understand an interlocutor or adversary's strategy was the best way he had of protecting himself and moving forward.

Niccolò was not at all surprised to later learn that Borgia was a gifted liar, and that he had managed to make it look like he was performing an act of justice and not abusing his power. This prince often said one thing but did something else entirely. From that first incursion into their land, Borgia brought back Piero de' Medici, the oldest member of the noble family that the people had chased out in favor of the Republic. Borgia even manipulated Giuliano, Piero's younger brother, claiming that his goal was to return Florence to the Medici family. In so doing, he made it seem like he wasn't acting in his own interest but merely repairing a wrong that they had suffered.

They were days of great turmoil and anger. Indeed, many Florentines were convinced that the Republic had been betrayed by its own leaders. Niccolò didn't think that. Why? To what end? No, he imagined that the Dieci and the gonfalonier, realizing that they were unable to save the city with weapons, would end the upheaval by relying on their innate talents as merchants, and use money. Buying out an enemy always costs less than going to war with him. And that's exactly what happened. To gain time, they offered Valentino the position of Captain General of Florence with a purse of thirty thousand ducats a year for three years for his mercenary services. Of course they knew they didn't have that kind of money and that Borgia would probably say no, but it kept him quiet long enough for them to offer all the money they did have to his cousin Louis XII, King of France—who had recently been named Lord of Milan, a man keen on all matters related to Italy—in exchange for his protection.

It was a brilliant move, and one that Niccolò admired deeply. Pier Soderini stood out in the negotiations, even earning himself the nickname of "I-have-faith," which derived from his penchant for that phrase. And, as a matter of fact, the faith he placed in Louis XII was soon compensated. The Very Christian King did not want his cousin to extend his reach too far and preferred to maintain a balance of power. Swayed by the gold florins, Louis XII ordered Valentino to take his army and leave.

But Niccolò knew it wouldn't end there. Borgia had decided that one day he would take Tuscany and, although he couldn't openly challenge Louis at that particular time, he wouldn't stop trying. Machiavelli was one of the few to continue to fear him; the rest of Florence went back to business as usual, as if nothing had ever happened. He and Marietta took advantage of the truce and were married in September, 1501.

At the beginning of the following summer, on the hottest days of June—Marietta was already six months pregnant—Valentino struck again, this time with subterfuge, encouraging Arezzo and other lands in the State to rebel against Florence, which allowed Vitelli and Paolo and Francesco Orsini, together with Piero and Giuliano de' Medici close behind, to step in. Borgia pretended to have nothing to do with it. On the contrary, he professed to be against this new invasion. No one believed him of course, but nor did anyone contradict him.

The strike was so violent that, initially, many Florentines doubted that the news was true. The city was thrown into a panic. Niccolò spent his days and nights at the Chancery writing letters to the commanders of the Florentine army in the war against Pisa, urging them to redirect troops from that front to Arezzo, and swiftly. But it was practically impossible to stop Borgia. That same June, and this time openly, the prince invaded Urbino and the surrounding towns and banished Duke Guidobaldo da Montefeltro.

That was when the Florentine legation, headed by Francesco Soderini, bishop of Volterra, was rapidly sent to initiate diplomatic contact. Although Francesco was arrogant and shrewd, just like all members of the Soderini family, he was also nervous about the delicacy required of such a mission. Niccolò accompanied him in the role of scribe, although he was concerned for Marietta: she had started to bleed and needed to stay in bed or risked losing the baby. It was difficult for him to leave her, and yet the thought of meeting Borgia filled him with a strange curiosity, like the feeling of wanting to peer into a deep abyss.

They traveled without stopping, encountering all kinds of militia and troops, always protected by letters of safe conduct. They arrived in Urbino late at night. The ducal palace was surrounded by soldiers, the doors bolted shut and heavily guarded. They were ushered in through a back door and led to a grand hall that was filled with so many candles that it seemed day.

Niccolò was immediately struck by Cesare: his long brown hair, thick beard, his height, brawn, and surprising vigor. He seemed to be filled with an uncontainable energy. Niccolò expected him to have a foreign accent, since his family originally came from Valencia—even in the papal court they spoke Spanish—but his Italian was devoid of any accent whatsoever.

Valentino did not address Niccolò directly and only spoke to bishop-ambassador Soderini but the first time the duke set eyes on Niccolò, he peered at him closely and coldly for a long moment.

He then went on to tell lie after lie as if he truly believed them. He accused the Republic of threatening his safety along their shared border. Despite that, he said he still wanted to be their friend and that Vitellozzo Vitelli had acted on his own initiative to get back at Florence for executing his brother, who had been a member of the Dieci and was accused of betraying the city in the war against Pisa some three years earlier.

At the same time, Valentino openly threatened them. If the Florentines didn't accept him as a friend, they would be forced to accept him as a foe, and he would go on to conquer their State whatever it took. As he spoke those words, his eyes gleamed.

He's shown his cards, Niccolò thought.

Cesare seemed to be able to read their minds. He grew irascible and spoke loudly. He knew well, he said, that Florence considered him to be duplicitous, an assassin. But actually it was he who couldn't trust them; he didn't approve of the republican government. He said they ought to change it, and fast, or else they would be sorry.

The bishop behaved the way ambassadors do: he replied with courtesy, pointed things out cautiously, made promises, spoke in flattering terms, and bought time.

On its own, this did not save the Republic.

It was once again the new King of France who sent in his knights and infantry to stop his cousin from gaining too much power. He didn't trust Borgia's evil ways and knew that the Pope would back him. When the French arrived, Vitelli, the condottieri, and the Medicis, none of whom wanted to make an enemy of His Majesty the Very Christian King, vanished without engaging in battle.

"This time Louis XII will not save us. He's more interested in wresting away the Kingdom of Naples from the Spanish and now he needs Valentino. They have signed a pact, we know as much," I-have-faith reveals to Machiavelli.

For the gonfalonier to be worried, the situation must be dire, Niccolò tells himself while offering a consideration on the matter. "But we are not alone in fearing the duke; he has many enemies who are all rallying their forces against him. Bologna,

Perugia . . . Even Vitelli himself has turned against him. And Paolo and Francesco Orsini, too."

"They're still not strong enough. And they'll never be able to convince him to forget about us. We'll be forced to go to battle. We just need to find out when and where he'll attack."

Niccolò stares at the gonfalonier. If he's just been told all this, it's because they want to entrust him with a mission. But what kind of mission?

The gonfalonier walks over to Niccolò and looks him straight in the eye. "You will be reimbursed for your expenses immediately, I promise. And I'll make sure that the money-lender is patient with you . . . You'll be able to pay him back with the salary that I am now offering you and which will arrive regularly. I want to send you on diplomatic legation to Borgia. You will leave tomorrow for Imola as an envoy of the Republic."

An envoy. Not as an orator or ambassador. A job that pays less. He will have the power to represent the Republic but not to sign pacts. Niccolò is filled with bitterness and anger. Once again, they have not asked him to take on an important duty. No, that will be given to someone else, someone born into a more important family but also far less capable. He reproaches himself for going into debt to serve the State.

And yet, at the same time, he is flattered and not a little curious. Being able to spend time with Valentino means being close to real power.

"When dealing with a fox, we need to act like foxes," Soderini continues. "Even if the duke is planning on invading us, you need to propose that he sign a pact with us against Vitelli, the Orsinis, and the others."

"In order to buy time?"

"Yes. This is a critical issue. We need all the time we can get to try and unite as many armies as possible, and even a few days can save us. I have faith that you will succeed."

"Borgia might pretend to accept the alliance."

"He definitely will. He'll say he's interested, and then we'll string him along for as long as we can."

Niccolò can't resist making a snide comment. "And of course, since an envoy can't sign a pact, and because it takes time for an orator to come from Florence, even when he's ready to sign, Borgia will just have to hold his horses, with me being the proverbial horse . . ."

Soderini doesn't appreciate Niccolò's tone. "It's common knowledge that you have a sharp tongue, Machiavelli, but may I suggest that you use it only with your enemies. Of course, it will also be dangerous; that's why we're sending you."

Why hadn't he kept quiet? "I'll do my best."

"I would expect as much. We will send you instructions regularly. You will go in depth into all the details of an alliance that will never get signed. And when we are on the verge of formalizing it, we'll say that we can't make a move without the approval of the Very Christian King, our protector . . ."

"Letters will come and go, always buying more time . . ."

"Exactly. If Louis XII approves the alliance, he'll be disgraced when war breaks out and he doesn't step in to defend us; if he does not approve it, it will be clear to the entire world that he sides with our aggressor."

To his surprise, Niccolò admires the savvy strategy and wonders whether perhaps he has underestimated the gonfalonier.

"Above all, Machiavelli, we expect that once you're there, you'll use all means necessary to find out the duke's weaknesses, the composition of his armed forces, and his plans."

So he is being sent to spy. It's part and parcel of being an envoy, of course. No need to even say as much. Niccolò hesitates a few moments before replying. The fact that Soderini said it clearly means that the mission is dangerous: they are sending him because no one else wants to take the risk. Valentino can be unpredictable. Daggers, poison . . . People he doesn't like have been known to vanish.

Whenever the Republic has a problem, they send him. Just like two years ago when they quickly sent him to France, which was still besieged by the plague. They didn't even grant him time to say farewell to his father, who was on his deathbed. He went as an envoy then, too.

Niccolò's silence irritates the gonfalonier, who had expected an immediate reply.

"Have you seen Duccio Del Briga recently?" Soderini asks coldly.

Niccolò runs his hands nervously through his short, black hair. He had indeed seen that husky and dangerous man. Two days earlier, out in the street. In fact, he had even wondered why he was there. It had almost seemed like Del Briga was following him.

Many people thought that Duccio Del Briga was a paid assassin. But the lords who oversee the Bargello prison hadn't been able to prove it yet and, consequently, he has never been punished for it. They say he's killed at least five people, but possibly more.

When Niccolò saw him in the street, he immediately picked up his pace and then ducked into a church. Del Briga stood outside and waited. Was it chance? Or was the killer waiting for him?

"You can probably guess why Duccio Del Briga is looking for you. Apparently, among your many lovers, there's someone you would have done well to leave alone," the gonfalonier said.

Niccolò knows exactly who he's talking about. He remembers everything about the moments he shared with Bianca in the alcove. She was taller and older than him and it felt like he could lose himself in her body. He recalls the warmth of her skin and her moans of pleasure; unfortunately, that amorous pursuit was now marked by despair.

"While I concur that Nicia's wife deserves to be visited by every possible sin, it turns out that he is impotent and he suffers greatly because of it. When he found out about you, he swore that he would get his revenge."

Niccolò looks despondently at Pier Soderini, who continues with all-knowing smugness.

"The killer has clear instructions: cut off your member, stick it in your mouth, and then cut your throat."

"But you can defend me . . . " Niccolò starts to say. "Can't you?"

Soderini interrupts him. "The powers of the Signoria are not infinite. We have to choose how and when to use them. And an important banker like Nicia has many precious connections. People like him are, you could say, the stomach of this city."

It's true. Niccolò knows it well. He knew just how dangerous it was when he got involved with her. To avoid an encounter with Duccio Del Briga that day, he had to leave the church together with a small confraternity of penitents. He, who always kept his distance from priests! He even helped two parishioners shoulder a very large cross.

When he turned around and peeked over the feet of Christ, he saw Duccio Del Briga staring at him. And then he crossed himself: a devout criminal . . . just like so many others.

"That man will hunt you down until he completes his task. If I were you, I would leap at the chance to leave Florence," Soderini says, staring at him long and hard.

"I can't wait, Gonfalonier," Niccolò says, his face revealing a smirk.

"Do you find it funny?" Soderini asks.

Niccolò knew that sometimes, when his face relaxed, it looked like he was sneering or laughing at something. In actual fact, it was just his personal way of detaching from reality.

"Not at all," he says, clenching his jaw to look serious. "Thank you for the opportunity to leave the city."

Pier Soderini exhales. He looks reassured.

Niccolò realizes he's about to utter his famous phrase.

"I have faith that you'll do us great honor. In the report

that you'll send the Dieci di Libertà e di Balìa, which I will also read, you shall only provide information of a general nature regarding Borgia. I want you to address the more serious news to me alone. I will decide how and when to communicate it to them."

Niccolò can't possibly say no to this request, but it occurs to him that it is highly unusual. It would appear that the gonfalonier doesn't trust anyone, even within the Palazzo della Signoria. What is he hiding from Niccolò?

Soderini walks over to his desk, unlocks a drawer, takes out a piece of paper and passes it to Niccolò. "Memorize these code numbers immediately. Use them when you write to me."

Niccolò has a sharp mind and it doesn't take him long to memorize the codes. He hands the paper back to the gonfalonier who then holds it up to a candle and tosses the flaming paper onto a metal dish.

Soderini goes on to inform Niccolò that the Republic has a spy in Imola by the name of Attilio Farneti. He comes from Romagna and works as a tailor in a fabric shop near the duomo; Niccolò should use extreme caution when approaching him.

He then hands Niccolò a black hood with two holes for eyes and asks him to put it on. He rings a bell.

"The man who will now join us," he explains, "will teach you the secret password for the informer and how to use invisible ink to write between the lines of the letter that you address to me. Do not say a word in his presence. No one must hear the sound of your voice."

A door opens. An elderly but nimble man dressed all in black comes in. He holds a small glass jar of a clear liquid. His expression is tense.

"Now I must return to my work. Good luck with the mission," the gonfalonier says, going back to sit down at his desk. The man in black approaches. Niccolò watches the paper with the secret codes turn to ash.

Marietta tries hard to stay calm, but she's clearly worried. Niccolò feels all the burden of his imminent departure and slowly fills his two travel bags, packing his good red velvet robe as it is the only one he owns that is somewhat elegant.

Envoy. Spy.

That's another secret he can't reveal to her. He has kept her in the dark about so much . . .

"They say terrible things about those Borgias," Marietta says, her eyes revealing the depth of her concern as she holds little Primerana tightly to her chest.

"Just like other lords in other states across Italy," he replies. At least this is true. All kingdoms have their share of criminals, and they boast of them when it suits them.

"And such a low salary," his wife continues to complain. "Who knows when the money will arrive. They still owe you for the June mission."

"The money will arrive soon," he says reassuringly. "It was an honor to be chosen, and you'll see, when I get back . . . " He doesn't finish the sentence so that she will imagine a vast recompense. Beyond his initial concern, he's starting to feel quite pleased that he was chosen to represent the Republic.

Marietta sits down on their bed, still holding Primerana. Her eyes are shiny with tears. The little one doesn't realize that her mother is sad and turns to look at her father.

"How long will you be gone?" Marietta asks, her voice breaking.

"A few weeks, I would think."

"You always say that. And then it turns into months."

Niccolò sits down next to her. "This time it will be different. I have no desire to be in that man's court any longer than absolutely necessary." She wipes away the tears that now stream down her cheeks and Niccolò embraces her. "Marietta, it's a big opportunity for me. Really. I have never been able to prove my worth, but now . . . Sometimes . . . I've never confessed it to you but I fear I count for very little . . . "

"How can you possibly say that?" she says sharply, holding back her tears in order to bolster his strength.

"It's true," Niccolò says, his hand on his heart, his face expressing deep bitterness. "It's like there's a moth in here and it's eating away at me. I feel such pain. How can this be all there is to life?"

His wife realizes the intensity of his unhappiness and caresses his cheek. "We lack for nothing . . . We love each other," she says, indicating Primerana, who is now staring quietly at the two of them. "And we have her. I know you want to be recognized for your writing, Niccolò, and you will be. I'm sure of it."

Niccolò stands up, unable to sit still any longer. "It's not just that. Try and understand. I want to have an impact on the history of the Republic, I want to leave a trace. I'm already thirty-three years old. So many younger men have already accomplished far greater things than I have."

"That's because they come from more important families than yours."

"I know, but it doesn't change the situation. I don't have a lot of time left, Marietta."

He wonders why he is complaining so much and immediately regrets it. On the other hand, now that she has stopped crying, his wife begins to reveal that keen and perky spirit that he likes so much.

"When you get something in your head, it's a waste of time trying to convince you otherwise," Marietta says, drying her eyes. "You're always in some kind of trouble! Never a dull moment with you!" she laughs.

Without a word Niccolò gratefully embraces her, breathes in her scent, gently pats their daughter's soft face, and absorbs all her warmth.

It's early morning. The north wind is still blowing, the sky is clear.

Marietta stands in the doorway with Primerana resting on

her hip. She holds out a sack which she has filled with bread, hard-boiled eggs, and a form of pecorino cheese so he won't have to spend the little money the Republic gave him as an advance in an osteria along the way. She also hands him a goatskin with red wine from their farm in Albergaccio. Strong and tart, it will keep him company for the first leg of the journey.

Niccolò, wearing his old travelling clothes, hastily takes all she offers him, impatient to be on his way. One of the guards brings him a horse. The poor old beast ought to be out to pasture, but instead they pile her high with baggage.

Dino Gherardi is among the men present. He pulls Niccolò over and hands him a pouch of coins. It's not the entire amount the gonfalonier promised, and this does not bode well for the future, but there's no point complaining now. Niccolò hands most of it to his wife and then turns back to the head of the constabulary guards.

Gherardi tells him that he has been assigned Baccino, a trustworthy and able steward, for the duration of his stay. Niccolò knows him from some years earlier when he had been sent to follow the military commissars in the war against Pisa; he had relied on Baccino for all his practical needs. He has gone ahead and left for Imola the day before, both to inform the court of Machiavelli's imminent arrival and to procure lodgings. Also already in Imola is Ardingo, the messenger, to whom Niccolò can entrust his first letters, both for the Dieci di Libertà e di Balìa and—Gherardi looks meaningfully at Niccolò—for the gonfalonier. Other messengers will arrive on horseback in due course to carry subsequent letters.

The Republic is clearly in a hurry to find out what's going on, Niccolò thinks to himself.

Gherardi hands him a letter of safe conduct and his credentials, which are sealed with wax and stamped with the Marzocco, the symbol of the Republic, a heraldic lion with one paw resting on a shield embossed with the Florentine lily.

Niccolò looks at the seal and feels a surge of pride. While

the Republic may indeed have some inadequate people in its service, its ideals transcend all mankind. Niccolò's heart is filled with that idealism.

The two guards step away discreetly. Before getting on his horse, Niccolò pulls his wife close, feels her large, beautiful breasts press up against his chest, and kisses her quickly on the neck. They spent the night making love and only slept for two hours. He'll be tempted to bed the first woman he encounters, but Niccolò always desires Marietta. He sees no contradiction in this. For him, it's easier to count the hairs on a person's head than understand the impulses of passion.

He then kisses Primerana, who smells of milk. The love he feels for the little one, his flesh and blood, is so strong he can't find words to describe it.

He rides off without turning back for one last look. The burden of saying farewell is alleviated by his keen desire to see new lands, meet new people, and find out if he is up to the challenge that Pier Soderini has set before him.

Once past the city walls, the wind drops. The road starts to climb toward Fiesole and into the Apennines. A raffish young man dressed in bright colors passes him on a splendid and lively steed.

"A big old ewe would have been faster than that nag!" the man calls out rudely.

"Ha! You're right!" Niccolò laughs, then waits until the man is some distance ahead and adds, "Or your wife."

CHAPTER THREE

Niccolò rides slowly, making his way up the mountainside and through a beech forest. The trees lessen the impact of the north wind but still it blows sharply. He pulls a peasant-style black woolen tabard out of his sack. It used to belong to his father, Bernardo, and to his grandfather before that; it's not much to look at but very warm, and Niccolò always wears it when he's on the farm. As he slips it over his head he notices something shiny: a flat medallion of the Virgin Mary that Marietta has stitched to the fabric without telling him. He tries to pick it off but needs his knife to cut the thread and it's in the sack with the food. He's too cold now to go looking for it and doesn't want to stop.

He pulls the tabard tightly around him and imagines his arrival at the court of Borgia.

"Your most excellent Lordship," he will begin. Or perhaps it would be better to say "Your Excellency, Duke . . . " Every word is the start of a path. Niccolò knows that what he says will either lead him far or toward a dead end. Everything he's achieved to date has been thanks to his ability with words, both written and spoken, but this time, if he wants everything to go smoothly, he will have to excel and use language impeccably, without committing a single error. It will be like walking along the edge of a cliff, he thinks to himself, much like the one he is riding along.

He doesn't look out at the vast, green landscape or distant mountains, which are so beautiful and worthy of admiration. He doesn't hear the sound of the river flowing down into the valley. He just keeps on mentally drafting the words of his opening speech. "Most Excellent Duke" is the best way to begin. That way he doesn't have to specify whether he means of Valentinois or Romagna. Indeed, if he mentions the latter, which the man only recently acquired with the help of France and in the name of the Church, and which the Pope immediately signed over to his son, it might make Borgia just want more.

On the other hand, what wouldn't trigger that man's voracious appetite? In the past three years, while trying to devour the Florentine Republic and in addition to Urbino, he also seized the Duchy of Camerino and the Principality of Piombino. He even received the insignia of the Golden Rose from his father, an honor that officially recognized him as representative of Christ on earth.

And to think that Borgia is six years Niccolò's junior . . . Of course, it's easy to reach those heights when you're born into a wealthy family, one that, even before your own father is named Pope, has a pontiff in its ranks. Cesare was raised on his mother's milk and shrewdness. He's already seen and done so much: archbishop at the age of eighteen, then cardinal, after which he abandoned the priesthood so he could focus on increasing his wealth and power through all means possible, doing whatever crime or misdeed was required—and always succeeding.

A small fort sits along the mountain pass, marking the border between the territories. Niccolò gets off his horse and shares his pecorino with the few soldiers stationed at the garrison. In his head, he continues to refine his speech for Borgia. It seems strong but he knows that a good night's rest will bring new ideas.

The soldiers, who come from small villages that dot the mountains, offer him some wine that's worse than the one he has in his goatskin, but he thanks them and accepts. He talks and jokes with them, and asks about their homes and families. Although he's relatively uninterested in nature, he's fascinated by mankind. He relishes watching people do routine tasks in new ways, he likes analyzing people's characters, finding out if they're taciturn, imaginative, artificial, peevish, hopeful, or resigned.

Although the soldiers appreciate that Niccolò is different from them, they also perceive his sincerity and welcome him into their midst with warmth. After dinner, they clear the table and start playing with an old deck of cards; they laugh and place bets and poke fun at each other; they argue for a farthing and yell so loudly that it feels like their voices might carry all the way to Imola.

At dawn, Niccolò sets out on his path again. They give him a new horse, older and wearier than the first. He doesn't care. He's caught up in his thoughts. As he calculated, a night's rest has brought him new words and a different way of presenting his message, one that he finds far more convincing than his earlier one.

Valentino's lands begin just beyond the fort. It's hard to see exactly where the borderline is in the thick beech forest around him, but on the path itself there is a clear marker: a large house built of dark stone. At the sound of the approaching rider, three soldiers come out. They wear black hose and leather jerkins decorated in red, yellow, and blue, Borgia's colors, making Niccolò feel as though the prince is somewhere nearby; the duke is very exacting when it comes to the uniforms his men wear.

As they are checking his letters of safe conduct, Niccolò observes Valentino's coat of arms on a marble plaque that's been affixed to the façade. The white stands out clearly, as if expressing just how tightly Cesare intends to hold onto Romagna.

They grant him passage. The road begins to descend shortly after, continuing to wend through the forest. A boar runs across his path and into the valley. The wind picks up again.

He goes back to thinking about his speech and decides to practice saying it out loud, so he can judge the effect it might have on his audience.

He comes to a halt when he sees something white in the distance between the trees: a military encampment. Niccolò rides off the main path and into the woods, the leaves muffling the sound of his horse's hooves. There's no undergrowth, so it's easy to make his way. He heads down into a gully, then climbs up again, noticing a boundary stone embossed with the sign of the lily. He's still in an area where it's easy to confuse one state with the other; the irregular border line that shifts with the continuous power struggles follows the rising and falling land. One wrong step takes him from one territory into another.

In fact, once he is beyond the gully, he is back in Romagna. He has gotten very close to the camp. A standard waves from the largest tent with colors that he recognizes, that of the Marquis of Torrenotte, a condottiere recently hired by Valentino, along with others, to fill the gap left by those who have broken their contracts with him. Niccolò has heard that the Marquis and his mercenaries are well paid, that Borgia doesn't scrimp when it comes to getting ready for war. With all the soldiers he has hired across Italy, he has effectively made it much more expensive for everyone.

Better not get too close, there are surely watchmen on patrol. Niccolò hears reveille and sees the dark shapes of soldiers coming out of their tents. He heads back the way he came and returns to the path. He already has something to refer back to the Republic: troops have set up camp in that particular place so they can attack the fort where he played cards the night before.

The road descends for a long stretch until it is flanked by the river Santerno, which comes crashing downhill between huge boulders. Amidst the thinning trees he catches glimpses of the plain below and notices how it has been carefully divided into cultivated plots of land.

He has stopped drafting his introductory speech. The substance is there; now he just needs to polish it.

At a switchback in the path, he encounters a variegated

troop of about a hundred mercenaries marching toward him. They carry long halberds and swords, and walk in no precise formation towards the border.

No one else is around. It's just them and him.

He freezes, instinctively bringing his hand to his pouch of money. He realizes it would be far more dangerous to turn back than press on. They're already sizing him up. He takes in their sunburnt, lined faces and mean eyes. These men wouldn't think twice about robbing him and dumping his body in the river.

He sits up confidently in his saddle, salutes the first soldiers elegantly, and announces his mission. "Greetings, I am the Florentine ambassador on my way to meet with Duke Valentino, who awaits me in his court."

They do not reply, but their leader, the tallest and most stalwart of them, issues an order to his men with a strong northern accent. "Let him pass."

They step aside so he can ride between them. Their stench reaches him on a gust of wind; clearly they haven't been able to wash or change their clothes in a very long time. He salutes the leader but the man does not reply.

As Niccolò passes in their midst, he notices how carefully they look at him. Trying to appear casual, he observes them, too. He realizes that they are part of Naldi's army, founded by a family that hails from the Ravenna area. They have been in the service of the Borgia family for quite some time and they, too, are paid handsomely. They were in the front lines when Borgia attacked and conquered Arezzo.

Another switchback and he disappears from their sight. He continues to hear the sound of their armor clanging as they march while he continues in his descent.

The sun begins to set. The dark rooftops of Imola are visible in the distance. Outside the city walls is a military encampment, a sign that there isn't enough room in the city to hold all the soldiers that Borgia has assembled. Niccolò sees men pitching even more tents. They must be expecting more troops soon.

A canal lined with windmills, olive mills, and spinning mills leads from the Santerno to the deep moat that runs around the city walls.

The main road that leads into the city runs parallel to the canal. Niccolò studies his wavering reflection in the current, then observes the men and women laboring nearby. He examines their clothes and is fascinated by their different manner of dress and their unusual way of speaking.

Four massive iron cannons, the likes of which he has never seen before, are being hauled by oxen toward the fortified city gate. The men who drive the animals speak to each other in French; it would appear they're complaining about the local food. He passes the cannons, observes their breeches and barrels, and notices that they're decorated with the crest of the King of France. The gun carriages have also recently been emblazoned with the Borgia motto, *Aut Caesar aut nihil*. Niccolò can still see the burn marks.

Two guards step in front of him, blocking his way. He shows his papers and they let him through the gate. As he is riding down a long street between the buildings, he sees Baccino, his steward, walking toward him. Around thirty, short and wiry, the man is all muscle and nerves.

"Welcome. I was on my way to the gate to wait for you. I have found us lodgings."

Niccolò thanks him, glad to get off his horse and walk for a bit. There is less wind between the houses, so he takes off his black tabard and tosses it onto his saddle, folding one end of the fabric over the medallion of the Virgin Mary.

Swiss foot soldiers, dressed in their black and red coats, are everywhere. Two prostitutes try and entice him with their favors.

Niccolò smiles at them. "I'm sorry, dear ladies, but I have no money to spend." For once it's the truth and he doesn't enjoy saying it.

Baccino leads him to the inn, a derelict-looking place with a dingy entrance.

"I imagine it's even worse inside," Niccolò says.

"There was nothing else available. The city is full of soldiers and they have requisitioned all the more comfortable places. And with what we can pay . . . But this place has its advantages, you'll see."

They turn down a nearby alley, leave his exhausted horse in a stall next to the stronger steeds belonging to Baccino and Ardingo, the messenger, and enter the lodging house through a side door. A heavy woman of about forty with a terse, matter-of-fact manner hands them a key.

Baccino helps Niccolò carry his bags up to a small room, furnished more or less as he expected: with a tiny window and small desk. Although he says nothing, his displeasure is evident. He throws his sack down on the straw mattress and a cloud of dust rises into the air.

To soothe his tired feet, he takes off his boots but hangs them up high, over the staves, knowing from experience that these kinds of places are full of mice.

"I need to wash up," he says, suddenly realizing just how tired he is.

There's the sound of heavy footsteps on the stairs: two messengers sent by the duke's secretary. Borgia heard that Machiavelli had arrived and wants to see him.

"Now? I thought I would ask for an audience tomorrow morning."

"His Excellency said now."

"Let me change. I can't come like this, in my traveling clothes."

CHAPTER FOUR

A t the end of the long, narrow street that runs through the center of Imola, Niccolò catches sight of the thick walls of the Rocca stronghold, amber yellow in the late afternoon light. A few steps further and he sees one of its rounded corner towers, cannons poking out the embrasures.

The road opens onto a wide empty space in front of the stronghold, designed so that attackers would be vulnerable to artillery fire.

The Rocca is square in shape and safely built into the corners of the city walls. The defensive moat that runs around Imola also cuts through the open space, providing the fortress with a second level of protection.

On the far right is a grassy field, about a hundred arms long and wide, where a crew of men are busily working on what may once have been a stable, repairing and reinforcing demolished walls. Niccolò notices that they have dug a deep hole in the center, and squared it off with strong chestnut posts that are as tall as a four-story house and eight lances long. Are they building a second fortress?

With the duke's two men leading the way, they cross the drawbridge, enter the heavily guarded Rocca, and climb a staircase. Suddenly, the stark military architecture softens into a sumptuous wing with frescoed walls. This is the Palazzetto del Paradiso, one of the two guards says.

Waiting for him in an antechamber, together with two soldiers carrying swords, is don Miguel Corella, the duke's lieutenant and private executioner. A Spaniard, around thirty, he's dressed in black and has a cruel face, olive skin, and a disturbing gaze. He peers closely at Niccolò. Although it is not customary to search an envoy, Corella pats him down while greeting him, verifying that the only thing that Niccolò is carrying under his red robe is a near-empty money pouch. He even looks carefully at Niccolò's black velvet flat cap before leading him into a grand tapestry-lined hall.

Cesare Borgia is sitting on a chair that resembles a throne. Leaning on one elbow, he is deeply engaged in conversation, speaking drily to a dark-haired military man. Just like when Niccolò saw him in Urbino, Borgia appears to be exploding with energy. He's wearing an ochre robe—embroidered with figures that Niccolò has a difficult time deciphering—over a white shirt and black gloves. Sitting by his side is a giant grey mastiff in a metal-studded leather collar.

A young damsel with very fair skin sits reading on a stone bench off to one side, facing a roaring fireplace. She has blond hair that has been elaborately braided at the nape of her neck and wears a lavender dress decorated with elegant arabesques.

Trying to appear casual, Niccolò looks her up and down and then glances around the room while Valentino concludes his conversation. He notices two windows and a large balcony that looks out onto the surrounding countryside. On the far side of the room, a heavy oak door leads to a short corridor, which clearly leads farther into the Palazzetto. He feels the eyes of the duke upon him. He bows and hands him his papers. Borgia takes them but doesn't bother looking at them.

"Machiavelli, I remember you well. It was the end of June. You had an impertinence about you, not like those other diplomatic eunuchs . . . "

Initially Niccolò is caught off guard but then he begins the speech he artfully composed along the way. It flows easily. Soon he reaches the offer that he has been sent to communicate. "The Republic of Florence, through me, offers its respects . . . "

When he mentions Florence, the young lady turns around,

tips her head delicately to one side, and glances up at him with clear blue eyes.

Niccolò is surprised by the intensity of her gaze but pretends not to notice. She can't be more than twenty years old. He's startled by her beauty, but there's something else, too, something dignified and mournful. He desired her as soon as he set eyes on her.

She goes back to looking at her book. Borgia realizes that they've exchanged looks but doesn't bother introducing her. It's as if she doesn't exist. It all happened so quickly.

" . . . and proposes forming an alliance with you against your enemies," Niccolò says. He is about to continue, but the duke raises his hand to interrupt him.

"Back in June, I mentioned how difficult it is for me to trust your Republic. Too many people are in charge of making decisions, and these people change their minds far too often. I still feel this way. As for my enemies, I can take care of them on my own." He appears to be in a bad mood, annoyed, tense. "And yet . . . "

"And yet?"

"You know how keen I am on forging a strong relationship with Florence. I will examine your proposal carefully." The duke's mood has changed. He now seems almost friendly and welcoming.

Niccolò nods. The Prince got to the crux of the matter immediately. None of the phrases Niccolò prepared are of any use to him anymore; he hurriedly tries to invent others, but Valentino precedes him.

"Friendship with your Republic means a great deal to me. I have not been able to build a relationship with you until now because of the cruelty of the Orsini and Vitelli families. They have repeatedly, and in all ways imaginable, tried to convince me to engage in battle with you. But I have always defended you Florentines, and this is one of the reasons they've turned against me. I am fully aware that, at this very minute, they are putting together an army with the goal of taking Urbino away from me and reinstating the old duke. This doesn't worry me though; their efforts are pointless."

"They have their sights set on Urbino?"

"Of course they do. Conquering it was easy, and if I lose it, it won't be hard to get it back."

Was Borgia telling Niccolò this so that he would think that all the duke's concerns and worries had to do with Urbino?

"I have shown too much clemency with those lands already, and it has not served me well. Do you know that two days ago they recaptured the fortress of San Leo?"

Niccolò hadn't heard this and he looks at Borgia in surprise. The duke looks more annoyed than displeased.

"The castellan was fortifying a wall when some local peasants took advantage of the situation. Apparently they hid and waited until some long beams were being carried over the drawbridge and, precisely when it couldn't be raised, they stormed across and massacred the garrison stationed there. Some say they relied on the Vitelli and Orsini families for help, but this is not yet clear."

Why is he talking about a loss? He's just stirring up dust, trying to distract him.

Niccolò focuses on the figures embroidered on the duke's robe and realizes that they represent the signs of the zodiac.

Borgia waves away his thoughts, his mood changes, and he becomes almost likeable. "I know that you're a gifted writer. They say that your reports for the Dieci are well-written, eagerly anticipated, read and commented on by all. You've won over quite a circle of admirers."

Clearly, he's heard this from his spies. The gonfalonier is wise not to trust anyone in the Palazzo della Signoria, Niccolò thinks to himself with some alarm, while also feeling somewhat flattered by the compliment.

"I was curious and so I enquired about you. You nurture ambitions of becoming a historian. You excel in prose, and only prose, because your poems, well . . . " Valentino rubs the fingertips of one hand together as if to indicate something flimsy, while also appearing to take pleasure in Niccolò's disappointed expression.

"With all modesty, I consider my poems to be quite strong," Machiavelli says.

The damsel glances at him again, this time with curiosity. Flattered, he stares back and tries to make eye contact with her, but she quickly looks away.

"Why do you persist with what you lack, Envoy? Leave poetry to the poets and focus on your strengths. Rely on your talents with prose," the duke says.

Niccolò is speechless. No one ever has ever said as much to him, criticizing and praising him simultaneously. Naturally, the words of praise feel better than the criticism, and so he holds onto them tightly; if he allowed himself to be wounded by all the criticism he has received over the years, he never would have persisted.

"Why are you smiling, Machiavelli? I remember that smirk, I wondered about it even back in June. Are you laughing at your interlocutor?"

"Absolutely not, your Excellency. It just happens. It may be . . . " He hesitates, but Valentino nods, encouraging him to go on. "It may derive from my way of looking at the world, the way writers do."

"That's exactly what I thought," Borgia says, stepping down from his throne and turning politely to the young lady. "I know how much you enjoy sitting by the fire and reading poetry, but I must ask you to leave now."

The damsel obeys coldly and silently, disappearing down the corridor that leads into the Palazzetto. Maybe she will go to the duke's chambers, Niccolò thinks.

Valentino walks up to Niccolò and looks him straight in the eye. "I'm glad they sent you to spy on me. Go ahead and try—if you can. At the same time, I think it's too bad that you can't put your talent as a writer to work. I could actually use someone like you," he says, walking over to a table made from a stone splay, with two seats carved into the wall on either side. The dog trails after his master. Borgia beckons to Niccolò to follow him and points to a stack of books on the table. "You see those? Slanderous volumes, each and every one of them, all published to hurt me. I keep them here so I see them every day; it keeps my rage alive. There are so many of them, and you have surely read them. Lies, every single one. And they will last in perpetuity."

He then walks toward the balcony, again gesturing to Niccolò to follow him. They step outside, the dog behind them. Two men with crossbows keep watch, one on either side, ready for surprise attacks. Niccolò stares at them apprehensively but Valentino ignores them. The vast plain, luminous in the setting sun, stretches out before them.

"What do you see out there? Farmhouses, the country-side . . . Reality as it truly is." He then taps his index and middle finger of his gloved hand on his chest, between Taurus and Gemini. "And when you look at me, what do you see? Everything those books say: a man who arranged to have his brother killed so that he could take his place as Captain General of the Church, a man who sleeps with his sister, a man who will do anything to extend his dominion."

Niccolò is embarrassed.

"And yet none of it is true," Cesare says firmly. "Allow me to make you an offer: help me write my reality. My story. I will tell you all my secrets, and you will give them shape with words."

"But I work for the Republic."

"You will continue to do so! This assignment will not in-terfere with what they have asked you to do. You will, in fact, write anonymously. And you will earn so much money from it that you'll be able to pay off all your debts and live without worries."

Again Niccolò is shocked—how many spies does Valentino have in Florence to know about his debts?

Borgia smiles with artificial modesty. "I have eyes and ears everywhere in your beautiful city. Think it over. You have until tomorrow evening. I will wait for you at the *vigilia secunda* to know your reply. I trust you will accept."

"Thank you for your high regard, Your Excellency, but how can you make me this offer if you've never read anything I have written?"

Borgia's eyes shine with delight. He returns inside and Niccolò follows him. The mastiff stretches out on the balcony. Valentino removes a piece of paper from one of the pockets of his robe, unfolds it, and begins to read aloud.

"In one of your reports from last June for the Dieci you called me 'splendid and magnificent . . . So fierce in battle that there's no great enterprise that he won't take lightly.'"

Niccolò tries to hide his shock. Even if he could speak, he doesn't know what he could possibly say. Those were his exact words. Who in the Dieci or the Chancery made a copy of his report?

The duke goes on. "'. . . In the pursuit of glory and reputation he never rests, and recognizes neither weariness nor danger; he has arrived at a new position before anyone understands that he has left the old one. He is well liked by his soldiers, and he has enrolled the best men in Italy. These qualities make him both victorious and dangerous for the future; added to which he is always lucky.'"

Cesare smugly folds up the piece of paper. "Your words show that you understand me, but, at the same time, they are somewhat excessive. If you accept the task, I will ask you to praise me in more measured terms. I also do not want you to hide my flaws. Everything must be done with great care. In this way, the result will be balanced."

As Niccolò leaves the Rocca, he reflects on the offer. Is it a trap? Why would it be? No, Valentino seemed sincere. Accepting the task would mean spending more time with the duke and could be a good way of gleaning something of his plans. It aligns with his role of spy. Soderini himself suggested he take advantage of all opportunities.

Of course, he would also have to be extremely careful: Borgia will only reveal things that suit him and he will try and manipulate Niccolò to act against the Republic. He's certainly very capable of doing that. His manner of alternating threats with flattery was surprising. In fact, Niccolò is reminded of a talented actor he knew back when he used to frequent a traveling theater troupe—Niccolò feels a deep pang of desire for Tullia, one of the troupe's singers and his lover for a few weeks—who was capable of capturing the audience's attention even when silent, stealing the scene merely with his presence, as if he were some kind of otherworldly messenger.

In any case, the meeting with the duke confirmed Niccolò's memory of him from June: Borgia emanates great vitality. He seems unconquerable, far stronger than Louis XII, whom Niccolò met while on mission in France for the Republic two years earlier, chasing after the king as he traveled through town after town, fearful of coming into contact with the plague. His Majesty the Very Christian King had lively, uneasy eyes but a simple face, he resembled an ironmonger or farmer, and he looked exhausted from being in power.

And what about that young lady? She must be a lover but there was nothing submissive about her. He thinks back to the look in her eyes and finds himself longing for her again. The more time he spends with Valentino, the more he will be able to see her, and who knows, one thing always leads to another . . . Then he remembers his fling with Bianca and the hired assassin. Maybe he ought to steer clear of women connected to powerful men.

Niccolò walks back to the lodging house in the final light of day. He's certain he's being followed, but that doesn't trouble him. When he reaches the inn, he climbs the stairs to his room. As previously agreed, Baccino is waiting for him. They look at each other complicitly. Niccolò takes off his long red robe and hands it to the steward, who puts it on, together with his master's black cap. Niccolò, meanwhile, dons his old black tabard. The two men go downstairs in silence.

The entrance is empty. The steward walks swiftly out the front door, his head down, while Niccolò leaves via the side door, through the stables, past the horses, and out into the alley without anyone noticing him, thanks to the long evening shadows.

The duke's men, who followed Niccolò there from the Rocca, will now tail Baccino, who will take them on a long, roundabout stroll.

A dusky light hangs in the sky. In the piazza in front of the Duomo, people rush homeward. Niccolò periodically glances over his shoulder to make sure he is not being followed.

On the corner of one of the streets, he sees the tailor's fabric shop that the gonfalonier mentioned. It's large and has only one entrance. A heavy bald man is folding and putting away large, colorful samples of cloth in the candlelight.

Niccolò glances around. When the street is empty, he walks in.

The shopkeeper peers at him suspiciously while continuing to fold the fabric.

"Greetings," the man says in a heavy Romagnolo accent, his warm smile contrasting sharply with his keen eyes.

"Greetings to you. Do you just sell fabric or are you also a tailor?"

"I'm also a tailor, if you can afford me," the man replies rudely, glancing at Niccolò's tabard. "But I'm closing up shop now. Come back tomorrow."

"It's an expense I can't forego," Niccolò says. "They say it's going to be very cold this winter."

"No worse than the winter of two years ago," the shopkeeper replies and then hesitates.

"Or that of the year before. But even if it's cold, it will pass. Sooner or later summer always returns."

"Indeed, summer always returns," Attilio Farneti says, staring at him meaningfully. "You can speak freely. We are alone."

"I am the envoy sent by the Republic."

"I noticed your Florentine accent. Welcome."

"Thank you. I saw some large new cannons by the front gate."

"Military equipment has been arriving from France for days now. The duke has accumulated as much artillery as the rest of Italy has all together. I heard they're expecting more French soldiers, four hundred spearmen, and their helpers."

"That many? Did you hear it from the troops themselves?"

Farneti doesn't reply. He probably has a paid informer in Borgia's army but prefers not to reveal any more than that.

"What can you tell me about the soldiers marching toward the border with the Republic?"

"It's not easy to get news from up in the mountains. People are being extremely cautious," Farneti says.

"When will the duke's troops move?"

"It's impossible to know. Valentino is terribly secretive. Only he knows his next moves."

"And what about Vitelli and the others? Are they making progress?" Niccolò tries to get Farneti to speak.

"It would seem so. The news that the mercenaries want to go to battle against Borgia fills the people who hate the duke with hope, such as the people of Urbino. They can't stand him because his soldiers sack, steal, and rape. Apparently, the people of San Leo managed to fight back."

"Yes, I heard. It's true. And what about here? Are the people ready to rise up against him?"

"It's different here. The cities of Romagna are well governed. Many people like him. And those who do not like him keep silent about it," the shopkeeper says.

"So you do not think he will lose Romagna?"

"It's highly unlikely."

"Who's the blonde lady with him?"

"Dianora Mambelli, from Forlì. Spoils of war."

Ah, spoils of war, so I was wrong, Niccolò says to himself. She is under his control. And yet her gaze was not that of a prisoner. "Did he take her when he captured Forlì?"

Outside someone walks by holding a lantern. Farneti holds a sample of fabric up to the candle and pretends to show it to Niccolò while replying, "Yes. As you may recall, most of Forlì surrendered immediately, but some noble families hid inside the fortress and tried to resist. The girl's father was an advisor to the Countess. He wanted to fight back at all costs."

"Mambelli, of course! Valerio Mambelli. I believe I met him when I was sent on legation to the court of Caterina Sforza, a few months before the siege . . . A tall man? With a reddish beard?"

"I can't say."

"He was one of the secretaries. A man of great valor. I imagine he met with an unpleasant end."

Farneti nods and puts down the piece of fabric. The street is empty again. "Valentino executed him and his family, and he raped the girl."

Niccolò feels great sorrow for her and shudders at the thought. The longing he felt for her now seems very wrong. Of course, there was no way that he could know it, but even so, he feels ashamed.

"Some people say that he's been charmed by her," the tailor adds.

"Charmed?"

"Initially he wanted to show her off, to remind people that those who resist get killed and the women end up belonging to him. But he's kept her around for too long now. He hasn't made her disappear as he has done in the past with others."

Niccolò ponders this. "Even Achilles was infatuated with his slave, Briseis."

"Who?"

"No one, never mind. And how is she taking it?"

"What can she do? She has to submit to him."

Clearly, the young lady detests the situation she finds herself in. She didn't seem at all resigned and must despise Valentino. Maybe, Niccolò thinks as he slowly walks back toward the inn, she knows some of his secrets, seeing how she is forced to spend time with him. He needs to speak to her alone. But would it be fair to complicate things any further for—what was her name?—Dianora? After all she's been through? He certainly doesn't want to add to her troubles.

Back in his room, he sits down at the small desk and, under the weak light of a candle of poor quality, he writes up a report for Pier Soderini until he's numb with cold.

Magnificent and Distinguished Vexillifer of the People of the Republic of Florence: today I arrived in Imola and was received with great courtesy by His Lordship. He said that he has always desired friendly relations with us and that any interruption in them is due to the malice of others, and not his own.

Niccolò goes on to summarize his conversation with Valentino, while reflecting on the fact that he should also relay this same information to the Dieci. He will paraphrase the very lines he is writing. He describes Cesare Borgia's attitude and his tone of voice. He conceals everything that has to do with him personally.

This is, in effect, all that I can write to Your Lordships at this time; and though it's part of my assignment to write you how many visitors are at this nobleman's court, where they are staying, and other local particulars, since I just arrived today, I can't be sure of the truth of what I have learned, and thus I will save it for another occasion.

With the modest coffers given to me before leaving, I have procured lodgings that are far below the standards of an Envoy of Florence, and therefore I respectfully ask for further . . .

The goose quill pen scrapes the paper. Niccolò dips it in the ink. He adds the word "money," his salutations, the date, and then blows gently on the paper so the ink dries. He then takes out the bottle of secret ink, opens it, picks up a brand new quill pen and cuts off the tip.

Before beginning to write, he thinks back to the codes given to him by the gonfalonier.

Numbers 1 to 10 stand for the border towns between the Republic and the Duchy of Romagna where the enemy army might pass, from north to south;

12 is the Lily, which is to say Florence, which needs to be referred to as if it were a male noun, and not like a city, a female noun, to avoid being deciphered;

58 and 59 both indicate Valentino, and should be used randomly to give the idea that he is referring to two different people;

Numbers 21 to 28 are code for Borgia's enemies who have joined forces and who have sworn to defend each other and fight as one unit.

He dips the pen into the ink and begins to write his secret message, the words disappearing immediately. He needs to know exactly what he wants to express before setting the words down on the page. He writes about what he saw when he crossed the border at 3. He writes about the duke's powerful new cannons, and the large number of French spearmen who will soon be arriving.

He holds the paper up to the light: he sees no trace whatsoever of the mysterious ink. He thinks about how meaning always gets buried between the lines anyway, even in a letter not written in code.

He concludes the letter and seals it with wax. Then he focuses on the letter for the Dieci di Libertà e di Balìa, filling it with vague and scintillating words about Borgia and Imola. It comes easily because he already knows what he wants to say, but even so, he chooses his words carefully. He's practically certain they will get back to the duke.

Shortly after dawn, slender and agile Ardingo takes the two letters and swiftly mounts his horse.

"Zerino will be here soon," the messenger says. "He's already on his way. He can sleep in my room. After him will come Mancino, then Campriano, and then I will be back. To mobilize this many riders, the Republic is clearly hungry for news."

"I hope I can gather information quickly enough for them. Good luck," Niccolò says.

CHAPTER FIVE

L ate that night, just before the *vigilia secunda*, Niccolò returns to the Rocca. There are still men working on the site next door, even at that hour, illuminated by torches. For the most part, the city walls look as though they have been repaired. He notices that the workers have planted even longer wooden poles in the center section of the worksite, and they are laboring around them. It looks as though they have already laid some cross beams and a portion of a roof. Whatever this building will be, it clearly needs to be finished with great urgency.

Niccolò enters the stronghold and goes up the stairs to the Palazzetto del Paradiso. Once again, Corella pats him down, especially carefully in the area where he keeps his money pouch, this time by pretending to dust off Niccolò's robe. Then he leads him into the grand hall where flames from the fireplace brighten the room.

Dianora is not there. Valentino is busy examining a number of papers tucked inside a red leather folder stamped with his coat of arms. He's wearing a doublet and ivory colored shirt, and still has on his black gloves. Niccolò wonders why. A heavy pouch rests on the stone table under the window.

Don Miguel Corella takes it and hands it to Niccolò. "This is an advance for your work," he says courteously. It's heavy. "Open it," don Miguel says. Borgia pays them no mind, he's absorbed with other matters.

Niccolò unties the cord of the pouch and peers inside. Gold florins sparkle in the firelight. This is the first money he will have earned solely from writing. He doesn't try and count how

much is there but he can tell from the weight that it's a signifi-
cant amount.

"Thank you," he says.

"No need for thanks. It's payment for your art." Corella
lights a candelabra that is sitting on the stone table, pushes the
libelous writings up against the wall to make some room, and
invites Niccolò to take a seat. "Is this enough light for you?" he
asks considerately.

"Yes, it is."

Then don Miguel sets down some ink, paper, quill pens, and
the portrait of a young man whom Niccolò has never seen before, after which he leaves the room.

Niccolò looks around, his eyes gradually becoming accus-
tomed to the shadows. He notices that the corridor that leads
into the palace actually ends in a bedroom. Sitting on the bed,
illuminated by the flickering flames of another fireplace, is
Dianora. She's peering at him carefully. Perhaps because he
now knows what has befallen her, it seems to Niccolò as though
her eyes are begging for help. I must find a way of speaking to
her, he thinks, but how? And what could I possibly say to her?
It's hard to imagine what she might be feeling and experiencing. He will need to be very delicate with her; he doesn't want
to wound her any further. He will find a way of taking one small
step toward her and will then wait for her to take a step in his
direction, if she so desires. In the meantime, he peers closely
into the room. Suddenly, a thin, elegant, and almost spectral
woman dressed in black appears. She glares at him and walks
over to close the door. Dianora continues to look at him, even
more intensely than before, until the door shuts and she disappears entirely from his view.

Niccolò turns to Valentino, who is walking toward him with
evident pleasure on his face, holding the red folder close to his
chest. The duke gestures for Niccolò to sit down at the stone
table. He also takes a seat and leans in.

"We will call it *Res gestæ Cæsaris*," he says. "A Latin title is always convincing." He sees a look of surprise cross Niccolò's face. "After all, it's my story, and I am Cesare."

"But by saying *Res gestæ Cæsaris*, people will inevitably think of Julius Caesar."

"That's exactly what I want. You will write it in the third person. It must appear to be an objective account of my achievements."

"Like *De Bello Gallico*, which everyone knows Julius Caesar wrote."

"I won't mind if people think I wrote it," the duke says with a smile. "You have the responsibility of making me look good. I will tell you what I went through, but it will be up to you to turn it into literature. You can take all the time you need. We will work on it at night, since during the day I am busy with endless other matters."

He takes a piece of paper out of the folder and hands it to Niccolò.

It's a brief list of six paragraphs, each one beginning with a year, from 1497 to 1502. The words and numbers have been written emphatically, the ink markings are heavy.

"This will be the order of the chapters," he explains.

"We will divide the narrative into years?"

"Yes, to make it easier to read. You will begin with 1497, when the most odious fact attributed to me took place." Cesare points to the portrait of the young man. "They brought back the body of my brother Giovanni, Duke of Gandía, to the Vatican, on June 15. He had been stabbed nine times. I was desperate, we all were, especially my father, whom I had never seen in such a state. He loved Giovanni the most, he was the first-born, and he forgave him all his misdemeanors. My brother's body had been thrown into the Tiber by his killers. After floating in the water for so long, his body was swollen, the most ghastly color, filthy with mud, and covered in horrendous wounds, the worst of which practically severed his head from his body."

"Forgive me if I ask, but when he was found, is it true that he was carrying a pouch of golden ducats in his pocket? That's what people say."

Valentino nods. "Yes, he was not robbed; he was murdered. Of course, he did have countless enemies." He picks up a piece of paper from the ones on the table and hands it to Niccolò. "This is a list of the names of people we suspected during the investigation. I want you to include their names, every single one of them. The night before his death, we attended a dinner that our mother had arranged for us in a vineyard we own, near the church of Santi Silvestro e Martino ai Monti. Have you ever been to Rome? No? Well then, you don't know the place. It's in a beautiful position, up on a hill, cool on summer evenings thanks to the breeze that blows in from the sea. Many of our friends were there. Late at night a man in a mask arrived, and went to speak with Giovanni. I saw them talking together, but there was nothing hostile in their conversation. I can still recall his gait; if I ever see that man again, he won't get away from me. It all seemed very normal because my brother was the heart of a band of merry-makers. I was sure they were talking about women, or some secret rendezvous planned for later that night. When the party was over, I was not surprised to see the man ride off with Giovanni, on the same horse. Giovanni's groom was the only one to accompany them."

"I don't want to bring up unpleasant memories, but what kind of mask was the man wearing?"

"Simple. Black. No frills or decorations. Why do you ask?"

"Details like that stay with readers even more than the actual story; they make the reader feel present."

"Very true. Use them. The man was dressed all in black. Even his hair was black, although I can't tell you how long it was because it was tied back, and he wore a leather hat, which was decorated with a peacock feather. After dinner, we went back to our lodgings at the Vatican. But Giovanni continued on to Piazza degli Ebrei, where he told the groom to wait for an hour, and if he wasn't back, he should go home. Giovanni then went off with this mysterious figure. None of us were alarmed until late the following morning. We started searching for him. That afternoon they found the groom in an alley that leads to the river, practically dead, unable to speak. A man who slept in a boat docked on the river's edge to guard a shipment of wood told us that he had seen a small group of people lead a white horse down to the river, and that a lifeless body lay across its saddle."

"Was your brother's horse white?"

"No, it was bay and it, too, disappeared into thin air. According to the witness, the people threw the cadaver into the water but its cape kept floating up to the surface, so they threw rocks at the body until it sank. We had the Tiber dredged and searched until Giovanni's body was found, but by then the current had already dragged him out of the city."

Valentino hesitates and takes a deep breath.

Niccolò glances at the page with the names on it.

"I know the guilty party is one of those people," the duke continues. "Write about the branch of the Orsinis that has always been hostile to the Borgia family: I always thought it was them. But, because people love to gossip, a rumor started that said I had the most to benefit from my brother's killing."

"We'll write that this is not the case."

"Yes, but be sure to leave a hint of doubt in the reader."

"Why?"

"Because fear is stronger than all cannons."

"But then you'll create an image of yourself that is cruel . . . You said our narration would speak of reality."

A smile crosses Valentino face. "Half of reality is image; maybe even more."

Niccolò is shocked, he had never thought about things like that.

Borgia goes on. "Believe me, it's just the way things are. To reign is to have people believe."

To reign is to have people believe. The duke certainly has a unique mind, Niccolò thinks to himself as he walks out of the Rocca, the church bells ringing midnight. He explained things in a way that had never crossed Niccolò's mind before.

He is glad he has accepted to write for Valentino. He would have done it for free if he had known that he would learn all these hidden facts. He holds the money pouch tightly and feels even more enthusiastic because of its tangible weight. A few soldiers sit around a bonfire in the corner of a small piazza. In the light from the flames he sees three prostitutes standing in the doorway of a two-story house.

He doesn't hesitate. He's attracted by the biggest and tallest of them, a woman with thick thighs and a prosperous bosom, a direct gaze, and long, dark hair. She's laughing about something. Now, thanks to Valentino's money, he can afford to do as he pleases. He doesn't even negotiate with her. He's certain he's being watched and imagines that tomorrow morning Borgia will know all about it, but it won't be considered odd. Actually they say that Cesare and his father regularly invited prostitutes to dinner at the Vatican, and that his sister even enjoyed watching them.

He follows the woman upstairs to a small room with a narrow bed. Her name is Licia and she comes from a small village not far from Cesena that surrendered to Valentino two years earlier without even fighting. The army had been led by Corella. Besides requisitioning food and livestock, the men behaved quite decently, she tells him.

She decided to follow them to Imola because they paid her well, just as Niccolò had. Rivers of money flowed among the soldiers because the duke was always generous with those who fought to protect him. She was making the kind of money that would have taken her years of backbreaking farm work to earn. Once she saved a little more, she'd quit that line of work, move to a quiet town, far away from everyone she knows, find someone to marry her, and settle down.

He tells her that he hopes she succeeds and he keeps her

talking. He does it artfully, because everyone knows that prostitutes and constabulary guards are in cahoots, managing to get her to talk about Borgia and how the people of Romagna feel about him. She has only good things to say: Valentino brought order where before there was none. Prior to his arrival, her region was controlled by a number of capricious lords who imposed outrageous taxes. Today the taxes are lower and everything is decided by law. It's all very clear.

As he listens to her, he thinks back to Dianora's pained gaze and the story of her awful suffering.

He points out that the duke also brought war and that cities and castles are now battling each other to death.

Well, some people always go looking for trouble, don't they? Licia replies.

CHAPTER SIX

Niccolò returns to his room at daybreak and throws himself down on his straw-filled mattress. It occurs to him that Zerino, the new messenger, will arrive later today and he has nothing to communicate to the gonfalonier. He sleeps a couple of hours and by mid-morning is up and about. He leaves his room to hunt for news.

The sun is warm and the wind has died down. He walks between the market stalls and admires the wares on display in the piazza around the duomo, stopping to haggle over some fried fish, which he then eats while meandering up and down the surrounding streets and looking in one shop after another.

Although he never turns around, he knows that the duke's men are following him. He is putting on this act for their benefit. When he and Tullia, the singer from the theater troupe, were lovers, she taught him a key element to acting: if you want to be believed, do less rather than more. So he doesn't overdo it. He acts like a man out for a walk. He finds he enjoys it. Indeed, it occurs to him that being an actor and being an envoy are quite similar; both roles require simulation and dissimulation.

Slowly, he makes his way to Farneti's shop, where he stops to feel the swathes of fabric as if he had never felt them before. He can't keep trading clothes with Baccino or waiting for the cover of darkness to go out. He needs to establish a connection with the shopkeeper that seems casual but that also has a purpose. As soon as the merchant comes out to greet him, Niccolò asks him about prices and which fabric would be best for a mantle. It's not an excuse: soon it really will be cold and he definitely can't wear his old country tabard to the court.

The shopkeeper points out a few different rolls of fabric and tells him that they're well-priced and warm but that if he comes inside he would gladly show him others. Niccolò pretends to hesitate before entering.

"Do you really need a mantle?" Farneti asks once they are inside and alone.

Niccolò nods, reaching out to feel a soft, brownish fabric with reddish hues. "This one is nice. How much is it?"

"It's costly, I'm not sure with what they pay us . . . "

"Yes, of course. While it's never a good idea to throw away money, I actually got lucky at cards. Is it warm?"

"If you can afford it, yes. It's the best there is."

They quickly come to an agreement on the mantle as Farneti has more important news to share. Two new militias, recently arrived from Lombardy, have been deployed at the border. They didn't even enter the city but went directly up into the mountains. They've increased the surveillance in the area making it practically inaccessible; it will take time to find informers among the new troops, all of whom are foreigners, which complicates things even further. Farneti also found out that Borgia's military commander, who has been busy reinforcing Imola and constructing new weapons, has just returned from a reconnoiter in Tuscany, done in the greatest of secrecy.

"Leonardo da Vinci went to Florence?" Niccolò asked in alarm.

"Yes, and we have no idea why. He was there for two or three weeks. We realized it only now that he's back: a carpenter in his bottega found out."

Niccolò wonders if he went there for personal matters. Probably. Da Vinci is originally from a town outside of Florence and would never betray his city . . . Or would he? After all, he does work for Borgia. What if he went to draw maps of the city's walls? He definitely knows the city well enough and even lived there once.

"We have never met in person; perhaps I could try to sound him out," Niccolò says.

Farneti shakes his head with skepticism. It's a well-known fact that to get a word out of da Vinci you need red-hot pliers. But maybe he could try getting Saladino to talk. No, not the great Turkish sultan. Saladino, or Salaì as he's familiarly known, is a boy from Lombardy, a scoundrel really, who Leonardo likes having around. Niccolò might find the young man outside his master's workshop, on Via di Santo Spirito.

Someone walks in the shop, a woman of about forty and her daughter, who is around twenty. Farneti changes the topic.

"Excellent choice of fabric. Allow me to take a few measurements for your mantle," the tailor says, extending a measuring tape across Niccolò's back.

Afterwards, Niccolò walks down Via di Santo Spirito, cautiously observing Leonardo's bottega from the outside, through the open door. He sees several piles of wooden arches and wonders what they're for. They're made of aged chestnut, like those being used at the worksite near the Rocca. Will they be taken there? Is that one of da Vinci's projects? What kind of contraption is he building?

He goes and sits down in an osteria across the street. The list of foods and wines and their prices are written on a wooden board: they're not cheap. If he sits at one of the tables outside, he can keep an eye on the entrance to the bottega. He orders a goat-meat *pastello* and some house wine, and savors the food while planning his next move, gradually identifying the ingredients of the dish: in addition to the flaky pastry and goat meat, there's lard, fragrant herbs, a soft cheese, eggs, and something else that he can't quite place.

Out of the corner of his eye, some distance away, he notices two men whom he is certain he saw the day before. They're pretending to carry on a conversation and are acting the part rather well. Up until now, he hasn't given them anything special to report: I took a walk, placed an order for a mantle, now I'm having lunch, all reasonable activities. But how will I find out more about da Vinci? Saffron—that's what's in the *pastello*. Delicious. This wine, on the other hand, is awful.

Suddenly, there's the sound of raised voices from da Vinci's workshop. A man with a heavy Tuscan accent is accusing someone of being a thief; this person, deeply offended, replies harshly in a Milanese accent.

A young man walks out. He has longish hair, a somewhat feminine face, and an insolent look. He continues to deny the accusations being slung at him from within, and with a grand show of disdain, he strides out and crosses over to the osteria, sits down at a table near Niccolò, and orders some food and wine, making sure the host knows he should charge Maestro da Vinci.

"I'm not sure you did well to order the wine," Niccolò says casually to him as soon as the host walks off. "It's not very good at all."

"Maybe the wine they served you is bad. But I always come here and I get special treatment," the young man shamelessly counters.

"Well, then, if that's the case, kindly let me taste a bit of yours so that I might order some for myself," Niccolò says with an agreeable smile.

After tasting it, he pretends to like it, and even goes as far as to say it's extraordinary, suggesting that he buys a fiasco for the two of them to show his thanks to the man for his suggestion.

It's hard for Salaì to refuse a gift. Two glasses later, Niccolò invites him to come sit at his table. He introduces himself as a traveling merchant and starts to talk about all the cities he has visited for work.

"In Tuscany, the city I like best is Pisa, and I have seen them all," he says, topping up the young man's glass.

"Enough, enough," the young man says, feebly holding his hand over his glass.

"Just one more," Niccolò says, encouraging him. "As I was saying about Pisa . . . not even Florence can compare." He pauses for a second. "Have you ever been to Florence?"

"I just got back, actually," Salaì says, taking a drink of the wine.

"Did you visit the whole city?"

"Yes, I even traveled to some of the surrounding towns."

"So then, you surely went to Fiesole, up on the hill. You can see all of Florence from there . . . " An ideal position for drawing a map of the city.

Salaì looks at him suspiciously. "Fiesole . . . yes. I was there. But why all the questions?"

Niccolò shrugs. "I miss home, I suppose. I enjoy talking about it." He raises his glass in a toast. Salaì relaxes and refills his glass.

"There you are! I should've guessed as much," a man calls out, approaching them from behind. Niccolò instantly detects hints of a Florentine accent in the man's speech. He's around fifty years old and has long hair and a long beard, both streaked with white. He glares at Salaì, then at Niccolò, then back at the young man. "Time to get back to work."

Niccolò, who perceives that da Vinci was driven by jealousy to come over to them, doesn't relinquish right away. "Please, come sit with us," he says kindly.

"Now why on earth would I do that?" the man replies sharply. "My time is precious."

Niccolò looks at him with a mixture of hostility and envy: da Vinci has a reputation not only as an engineer but as a painter and man of many talents. "As is mine."

"Then use it more wisely."

"Who do you think you are, talking to me like that?"

"This is my master," Salaì says meekly, tail between his legs.

"Master of what?" Niccolò scornfully and rudely asks.

"None of your business," da Vinci replies and motions to the young man to get to his feet.

Salaì obeys immediately. Leonardo throws some coins down on the table for whatever the boy ordered, as well as some additional ones.

"That's too much," Niccolò says sharply.

Da Vinci mumbles something and goes back to the workshop, followed by Salaì, who turns around and waves his farewell.

Niccolò doesn't even bother replying. He knows he will never be able to talk to him again. He finishes off the contents of his glass. Another day is almost done and he still hasn't learned anything about Valentino's plans for Florence.

Later that afternoon, Niccolò writes first to the gonfalonier, informing him that two armies have gathered at the border and that da Vinci traveled to Florence on behalf of Borgia. Afterwards, he writes a letter to the Dieci filled with vague, impressionistic details. He then goes back to working on *Res gestæ Cæsaris*, giving shape to the intimacies the duke confided in him the night before, while reflecting on the notion of power. He feels as though the work is coming along nicely. He finds it easy to alter his style to suit his audience, it's a skill he has honed over the years. Whatever task Niccolò has before him, he throws himself into it with zeal.

Later that evening Zerino arrives, covered in dust from the journey. Niccolò hands him the two letters, which he has already sealed. The messenger will depart the following morning, after which a third rider will arrive.

Niccolò dines with Baccino. The innkeeper offers them an unappealing dish so they decide to go out. As they walk up and down the city streets looking for an osteria someone had suggested, they plan quietly.

"I can't leave Imola now, Baccino, but no one will notice if you go up into the hills and find out what's going on."

"On the border with the Republic?"

"Exactly."

Although Niccolò feels he can trust Farneti, it would be good to get confirmation of the news from a second source.

"I know that they've increased the surveillance," Niccolò says. "To pass without being noticed, you'll need to take a different road each time and pretend that you are either on your way to Florence or coming back from it."

Baccino nods. "I'll set out tomorrow."

"If anyone asks, tell them you're a merchant."

"I wish I were! I'd live a grand life," the steward says with a chuckle.

CHAPTER SEVEN

A t the sound of the *vigilia secunda*, Niccolò hurries back to the Rocca. He brings with him the pages he's written about the killing of the Duke of Gandía. He's willing to do whatever it takes to set foot inside Valentino's secret world. He also hopes to see Dianora again. He recalls the way she looked at him, the desperation and anger in her eyes. What is really going on in her mind?

There are twice as many workers on the construction site as the night before. The roof is almost complete. On one side it is supported by the city's external walls and elsewhere by a number of the wooden arches that Niccolò saw in da Vinci's bottega on Via di Santo Spirito. United together, they form a dome or cupola. Niccolò sees the Maestro up high, Salaì is there, too, holding a burning torch while da Vinci hammers the wood, inspecting it probably, testing its quality.

The duke waits impatiently.

Dianora sits next to the fireplace, a small book in her hands. As soon as Niccolò walks in, she gets to her feet to leave, as if the duke had forewarned her. Her blue eyes glimmer in the flickering light. She's wearing a mauve dress and her hair has been braided into a crown.

Cesare doesn't even bother introducing her. He grabs the pages out of Niccolò's hands and starts reading them attentively. The young woman approaches Niccolò, looks at him meaningfully, and bows her head ever so slightly, as on the prior occasion.

"Milady . . . "

"Milord . . . " Her voice is sweet and the Romagnolo cadence gives it a pleasant musicality.

Borgia continues to read. He begins to frown, his face growing darker by the minute. Niccolò musters up the courage and speaks to Dianora with great courtesy, whispering so as not to disturb the duke, while she passes by.

"Are you reading a collection of *strambotti*?"

She slows down and delicately whispers her reply. "How did you know?" Her hand automatically goes to the back of her neck.

"I recognize the publisher's imprint, from Venice . . . " he replies softly. He would have continued but Dianora glances quickly at Valentino and gestures for him to be quiet.

The duke, bothered by their voices, looks up at them and then goes back to concentrating on the text before him.

Dianora walks away, down the corridor, casting a backwards glance at Niccolò that expresses so much: pain, dignity, strength. He stares at her, wishing he could talk to her further, help her. He hopes that the look in his eyes relays this, since saying it with words is impossible. He watches her walk away; in the silence he hears the soft rustle of her dress.

Borgia puts down the papers. "You've disappointed me."

"Why? What's wrong?" Niccolò asks unhappily.

The duke replies scornfully. "There's not enough malice in your writing. And yet I was very clear with you about my expectations. And take that smirk off your face!" He throws the pages down on the table.

Niccolò grows serious, picks up a sheet of paper and reads a passage out loud: "'People say that the death of the Duke of Gandía was desired by his brother, that he had a great deal to gain from it . . . ' That doesn't seem malicious to you?"

The duke shakes his head vehemently. "It should say, 'People are convinced that the Duke of Gandía's death was desired by his brother . . . ' That I would understand."

"But what reasons can I give for this certainty?"

"Invent them! I don't know, you could say something like, 'The two brothers were heard arguing and threatening each other only the day before about who would lead the pontifical armies.' Of course, I know this is not true, but no one believes me anyway."

"By doing that, you'll never separate yourself from the gossip. It's important to rely on undeniable facts. We could say, 'The two brothers were heard arguing about who would lead the pontifical armies, a role better suited to Valentino because of his acumen and courage . . . '"

"Yes, exactly. When truth is mixed with falsehood it becomes stronger. Acumen, courage . . . " Borgia savors the words. He clears his throat. "I like that. Although one day these walls will fall, words will remain. The power you writers have is far greater than that of us warriors." He stares at Niccolò with sincere warmth. "I wasn't wrong about you, no. Rewrite it. Do it better. I want you to surprise even yourself. How much time do you need?"

"One or two days at the most."

"Fine. I will have them set up a study for you here, so that you can work in greater comfort."

"Thank you but that's not necessary."

"I insist. That way I will also be able to observe you while you work."

"As you wish."

Valentino nods and then stares at Niccolò for a moment before continuing. "My men in Florence have informed me that Duccio Del Briga has been ordered to kill you. I have relied on his skills in the past; he always carries through."

Niccolò suddenly finds it hard to breathe. "But I'm here, far away, safe . . . "

"So you haven't heard that Nicia told him to teach you a lesson nonetheless? If the assassin can't strike you directly, which for the moment is impossible, he will take it out on your wife or daughter."

"What?" Niccolò cries out, deeply shaken.

"I'm certain of it."

"The gonfalonier didn't tell me about that!" he says inadvertently.

"Ah, so he only gave you part of the information? He was probably more interested in sending you here."

When Niccolò finally speaks, his voice cracks with emotion. "I request your permission to leave. I must return to Florence immediately."

Cesare raises his hand to interrupt him. "There's no need. You have nothing to fear. I will stop the assassin." Although he speaks with utter confidence, Niccolò continues to look at him nervously.

"I would be infinitely grateful, but why would you?"

"I need you to stay concentrated. You can rest assured that I will take care of the problem."

"But how? Will you pay him? Or . . . ?" Niccolò does not complete his sentence.

Valentino replies curtly. "I will find a way."

"If you do not mind, allow me to return to the inn so that I can at least write to my wife and warn her."

"Write her from here. Do it now. I will send one of my messengers with your letter with both discretion and speed. You certainly can't use the messengers of State for such a message."

"But I can't possibly accept . . . "

"Are you worried about what they might think in Florence? I assure you that no one will even notice."

As soon as Niccolò finishes his letter, he hands it to one of the duke's messengers, a youthful and energetic man who assures the envoy he will leave at dawn and change horses often to get there as fast as possible.

Even so, it will take more than a day for his wife to receive his letter. What if the killer comes to their house before then? He thinks about Marietta and the baby. He would give everything to be certain that the messenger will reach his house in time. He is overcome by a feeling of his own impotence mixed with anger for Soderini, who never mentioned a word of this. He curses the lust that led him to pursue Bianca and swears to himself that if everything goes well he will never be unfaithful to Marietta again.

Valentino, completely ignoring Niccolò's state of mind, starts to tell him how, three years earlier, he traveled to the court of the King of France to procure a wife. Niccolò makes every effort to listen but is in a state of shock and despair; hearing the duke talk about conjugal bliss makes all the concern he feels for Marietta even harder to bear. He notices a glint in the Prince's eyes, as if the man were deriving pleasure from bringing the envoy this grief. Some people do enjoy tormenting others, Niccolò tells himself.

The story is not a new one: Cesare, after unsuccessfully trying to marry the daughter of the King of Naples so that he could enter into that line of succession and gain access to the throne, instead decided to join families with Louis XII. But Niccolò hadn't heard the part that Cesare was now taking great pleasure in recounting: how he appeared in court with jewels sewn to his clothing, silver spurs, gold baubles on his bridle and saddle. Although he knew that the French would find it excessive, he was pleased nonetheless to be the source of envy.

Speaking as if it were all very obvious, Valentino explains that he was certain of success because of what he brought with him to the court of the Very Christian King: a letter of annulment from the Pope, so that Louis could get remarried. In exchange, Cesare received Charlotte of Albret, a seventeen-year-old relative of the monarch. Of course, Borgia also had to bring gifts for the girl's family and promise her brother a cardinalship.

Niccolò can't stop the duke from talking. Debilitated, he reflects on how he married Marietta for love, how paltry her dowry was, how they never really had much money.

Cesare keeps on talking about his wily marriage negotiations, which continued for months. Niccolò realizes that he's telling him all this not only because he considers it an achievement, but so that he will include it in *Res gestæ Cæsaris*. In the way he wants Niccolò to write it, it should reveal how his choice of a bride was not dictated by love—highly unusual in such situations—but part of a careful strategy of increasing his grip on power. Charlotte was prey and he caught her. Perhaps this was why he had intercourse with her four times on their wedding night, a fact that was widely commented on, the duke says with pride. By becoming the cousin of the King, Cesare received the title of Count of Valence and Diois and was given a castle in Issoudun, which was not in the best of condition. He also received forty-thousand francs a year, an army of one hundred of the King's spearmen available to him at all times, and was named Knight of the Order of Saint Michael. Valence was immediately elevated to a Duchy, and thus Cesare became the Duke of Valentinois, thereby earning himself the new nickname of Valentino.

Effectively he had made a good deal; he was now connected to a rich and powerful king. Of course, this also meant he had to send in his militia and condottieri whenever France's interests in Italy were under threat, whether it was against the Duchy of Milan or the Kingdom of Spain, the only enemy that posed a true threat to the Very Christian King. But the advantages far outweighed the disadvantages, and Charlotte soon gave birth to a daughter.

"Luisa will marry a man from the House of Gonzaga," he concludes with great satisfaction.

"But she's only two years old . . . "

"So?"

Niccolò's thoughts go to little Primerana and he is overcome with anguish once more. The heaviness in his heart makes it hard to breathe.

He doesn't sleep at all well that night. He gets up, lies back down, over and over. With the passing hours his thoughts begin to blur, he is reminded of mistakes he made in the past, and feels deep bitterness at his too many weaknesses.

As the duke's stories about his marriage echo through him, Niccolò feels drained of both energy and mental acuity. If he could, he would chase away all those thoughts from his mind. Unfortunately, though, the words have sunk deep down inside, such is their power. In order to expel them completely, he needs to write, but he simply doesn't have the strength.

At dawn, he hears a horse trot past. He looks out the window and sees the duke's messenger riding toward the city walls under a drizzly and cloudy sky.

As he's closing the shutters, he hears an even louder clatter of hooves coming from the Rocca. It's a group of knights, with Valentino leading the way. They're wearing armor and moving swiftly; clearly they are not going hunting. Where could they be going? Riding alongside Cesare is don Miguel, as well as other members of his army, all of them talking animatedly. They don't notice Niccolò, who instinctively retreats within.

He knows that the duke never announces his movements in advance. He disappears and reappears whenever he wants, unexpectedly, like lightning. But why were they in such a hurry?

As soon as the city wakes up, he walks down to the main gate, hoping to hear some news. No one knows a thing. The rain has stopped. Once beyond the city walls, he realizes that the tents they had been setting up when he arrived, and many others that were since added, are still empty. Apparently, the troops the Prince was waiting for have not yet arrived. There's a buzz of activity: he sees an entire troop of soldiers gallop off down the road that leads to the sea. Are they going to catch up with Valentino?

Baccino is off reconnoitering in the mountains and won't be back for two or three days, so Niccolò can't send him to follow the soldiers who have just left.

He decides, instead, to go talk to Farneti, who tells him everything he knows. Borgia received a message by carrier pigeon at dawn and set out shortly after. About a thousand men left with him. They didn't head into the mountains, this much is certain. Farneti has an informer in their midst and hopes to receive more news soon.

That night, unable to sit idly by, he heads to the Rocca in the hopes of learning something, and possibly some news from Florence.

The domed roof has been completed. Now the workers come and go through the front door carrying beams. He hears a furious hammering from within but doesn't have time to explore it. He promises himself that he will, as soon as he can.

When Niccolò reaches the entrance of the Rocca, he pretends not to know that the duke has left. He says he is expected. They make him wait. Eventually a heavy-set, middle-aged man arrives. He has a thick beard, dark hair, and rheumy but keen eyes. He's wearing a black tippet with a crimson border and a golden cross hangs around his neck.

He introduces himself as Agapito Geraldini, First Secretary to Valentino. Niccolò saw the man in Urbino, but never up close. An Umbrian archbishop, he is sharp, erudite, extremely eloquent, and deeply faithful to Borgia, who periodically uses him as an ambassador.

Geraldini, who moves slowly because of his weight, escorts him up to the Palazzetto del Paradiso and informs him that His Excellency left Imola for matters of state, that he does not know when he will return, but that Niccolò was indeed expected. The duke instructed his men to prepare a study for Niccolò and bring him some documents from the archives, leaving word for Niccolò that he should start writing immediately.

Niccolò frowns at the archbishop, annoyed. Do others know of his agreement with Borgia?

As if capable of reading his thoughts, Geraldini reassures

him that he knows nothing more than what he just mentioned, that he has no idea why his lordship made those decisions, and that he certainly will not discuss them with anyone. Indeed, he came out to greet Niccolò personally in order to maintain the highest level of secrecy possible.

"We secretaries are held to utmost discretion," he says complicitly.

A narrow spiral staircase leads them to an isolated room that has been decorated in a simple fashion, with windows that face the inner courtyard. A fire burns in the small fireplace. Various papers and scrolls rest on the desk, as well as writing implements, a bell, a tray with some grapes, a pitcher of water, some biscuits, a carafe of wine, and a glass.

"You can come here at any hour of the day or night. The soldiers know they should grant you access to the Rocca and you can find your way up here on your own. No one will disturb you," he says, somewhat out of breath, while lighting a number of candles. He points to a door and explains with a complex web of words that beyond it lies a privy. "Whatever you may need, all you have to do is ring the bell and a servant who doesn't know who you are will arrive."

Niccolò nods and thanks him. He has never been given such a luxurious room for writing. The Chancery is always cold and crowded with noisy colleagues. He writes his historical and poetic compositions at home, at the dining table. Even so, tonight he just can't bring himself to write. His thoughts are focused on his wife and daughter. He sees them before him, more alive than the people around him. Geraldini notices this, says nothing, and leaves him alone.

Niccolò's despair worsens. It seems fathomless.

CHAPTER EIGHT

Holding Primerana in her arms, Marietta reads the letter from her husband and is deeply troubled by the news. He has learned of a serious threat to their little family; he is safe where he is but they should shut themselves in and open the door to no one. She should rely only on their neighbors to bring them food, and do absolutely nothing until he sends an update.

Mother Mary of God, what has that blessed man gotten himself into this time? Matters of state, to be sure, but what do we have to do with it, Marietta wonders, her chest constricting with anxiety.

Borgia's messenger, dressed in a non-descript manner, stands waiting before her. He made his way into the city by mixing in with other travelers and carries false papers that say he's from Bologna. In his letter, Niccolò urges Marietta not to tell anyone about the messenger, not to ask him any questions, and to entrust him with a verbal message which he will then relay back to Niccolò.

"Tell my husband that I will be careful. He mustn't worry about us. Tell him to dress warmly and not get sick, it's getting cold out now. If you can take him a few things, I would like to send some clothes: a doublet, two shirts, and some handkerchiefs that I sewed."

The messenger nods. Marietta offers him some food and drink, which he refuses graciously telling her he is in a hurry to start back and will eat along the way. He does not mention that before leaving Florence he has another urgent message to deliver on behalf of his lordship.

As soon as the messenger takes the clothes and leaves, Marietta cautiously walks over to the window and peers out. She sees quite a few people milling about, but in particular she sees a man with a sinister look standing in a doorway not far away. He watches the messenger ride off, looks up at their shutters, then turns away when he catches sight of Marietta at the window.

What an ugly face that man has! What could he have possibly been looking at? Holy Virgin, keep us safe, Marietta says, crossing herself. She closes the shutters firmly, tiptoes downstairs while saying a prayer, bolts the door, and rushes back upstairs.

Duccio Del Briga continues to stare at the house, looking for a weak spot that will be his way in.

CHAPTER NINE

Niccolò can handle the anxiety during the day, but at night it's impossible. He imagines every twist and turn in the route that he took from Florence to Imola, recalling all the challenges and dangers he encountered. How long will it take Valentino's man to ride it? What if something happens to him on the way there? Or on the way back?

He goes to the Rocca even though he knows the messenger won't be back that day, but if there's any news at all, it will arrive there, and he simply cannot stay away. When Geraldini walks into the study, initially Niccolò is struck with fear but quickly learns it is only because the duke wrote to find out how his writing was coming along, and to remind Niccolò that he expects to see the corrected pages. Niccolò lies and says that everything is proceeding well. He's exhausted and jittery. He tries to go back to writing but cannot.

On the afternoon of the day that the messenger is expected to return, Niccolò is terribly restless. It occurs to him that for deliverance to come, Borgia would have to pay an assassin to kill Duccio Del Briga, at which point Niccolò will be forever indebted to Valentino and obliged to write better than he has ever written before.

To cancel out this debt, as well as to distract himself, he forces himself to focus on the manuscript. It's a struggle at first but then he starts to find his way. He makes notes and formulates ideas, jots down phrases and sentences, and the work temporarily takes his mind off his troubles.

While puzzling over phrases and rhetorical devices, he walks to the window for some air. It has stopped raining and the sun is going down. He peers out across the inner courtyard for the first time. It's hard to tell what lies behind the ten or so windows that he sees. All of them are dark except a corner one, in which he sees the weak glow of a fireplace.

He notices that a ledge runs under the window and all around the courtyard; it's old and narrower than the crowning element, which is higher up. Clearly an additional floor was added onto the upper part of the Rocca some years earlier. Judging from the color of the stones, this happened long before Valentino arrived.

The courtyard itself is paved with cobblestones, has a central drain for rainwater runoff, and is surrounded by a portico. There's no one around.

He sits back down and starts to write quickly. He has just finished when he hears someone knocking softly at the door. He rushes to open it, hoping to see the messenger but it is only Geraldini.

The secretary asks how the work is proceeding, congratulates Niccolò when he learns that he has finished, takes a step back, and reassures the guest that the Prince will return the following day and will be happy to receive him. Niccolò quickly calculates that for a message to have arrived in a single day, Valentino can't be more than thirty miles away.

As he descends the staircase with Geraldini, he sees the messenger coming slowly toward them. He wears a tense expression; Niccolò fears the worst. But it is only fatigue. Even though he's a young man, riding fast for so many hours at a time takes its toll. The messenger says that Niccolò's wife and child are well, he relays her message word for word, and hands Niccolò the clothes that she entrusted to him. Life has meaning again.

Niccolò walks out of the Rocca and heads directly toward the whorehouse, hoping to spend a little time with Licia, but she's busy with another client. So he goes upstairs with another woman. He doesn't mind. In his state, anyone will do.

CHAPTER TEN

S ee how well the mantle falls?"
"Yes, I do, but don't you think it should be a little tighter around the shoulders?"
"I advise against it, it would be much less comfortable."

Niccolò and Farneti stand in front of a mirror. Even though they're alone in the shop, people passing by can see inside, so they need to behave like a tailor and his client.

While Farneti makes a few minor adjustments to the already basted mantle so that it fits Niccolò's body even better, he mentions news he has gleaned from his spies and from listening to conversations at the taverns frequented by soldiers and merchants. It's incredible how much people talk, even when they have received precise orders to keep their mouths shut, because everyone knows that gossip can cause armies to lose battles.

With all the information in circulation, it is hard to distinguish what is true from what has been invented. The duke is still afield, no one knows exactly where, but he left a number of troops and guards behind to defend the city. It may be that after the loss of San Leo he wants to defend Urbino at all costs, and yet he does not want to leave the rest of Romagna vulnerable to attack. Consequently, he gave orders to the governor of the region, Ramiro de Lorqua, a man known for his swift and exacting cruelty, who often sets up base in Cesena, to make the rounds of all the fortresses and prepare them for battle.

The soldiers that Valentino was waiting for from France have not yet arrived, but many envoys have been sent to recruit new ones: foot-soldiers from Val di Lamone, gascons from Lombardy, pikemen from Switzerland. Messengers were even

sent to Rome and France in the hopes that they would rapidly
send help, in the form of both troops and money. There's no
doubt the duke will receive both from the Pope, and probably
from the Very Christian King, too.

The troops commanded by Vitelli and the Orsini brothers,
not to mention the others, are well-armed, but it doesn't appear
as though they're advancing with great haste toward Urbino.
Only Giovanni Bentivoglio, lord of Bologna, ordered his four
companies of foot-soldiers to attack, but then had them retreat.
The Venetians have stayed on their side of the border and don't
seem to harbor any hostile intentions toward Valentino.

No one seems to know where the duke is. Apparently, don
Miguel, the commander of Borgia's infantry, was forced to rush
off and help the castellans of Pergola and Fossombrone, two
towns near Urbino, who were struggling with popular upris-
ings. As a result, many of the inhabitants were killed. In other
words, it would seem that things were going well for Borgia,
Farneti concludes.

This means that Florence is still in danger, Niccolò thinks
to himself. "Did you learn anything further about the troops
positioned at the border with the Republic?"

"Borgia is indeed gathering many men there," Farneti says,
going on to inform him precisely of where and how many. It's
a very numerous army. Even though he might be busy on other
fronts, clearly Borgia still has his sights set on Tuscany.

When Niccolò returns to the inn, he finds Baccino waiting
for him. The steward greets his master with a worried expression on his face, then holds a finger up to his mouth. They
mustn't talk indoors, they need to be wary of the innkeeper as
she may be one of Borgia's spies.

They head out into the streets as if going for a stroll. They
talk only when they are alone.

While traveling up and down the Apennines, Baccino saw
Valentino's men camped everywhere.

"How many soldiers does the fiend have?" Baccino wonders aloud. "There are more soldiers in those mountains than trees."

"Give me the facts, Baccino. Numbers. How many infantrymen? How many knights? I need to know precisely where they are."

Baccino gives him the information, confirming and completing what Farneti had already mentioned. It's a worrisome scenario.

Niccolò decides he must write to the gonfalonier immediately. They return to their lodgings and he rushes up to his room. Baccino stops on the ground floor to ask the innkeeper for something to eat: he's exhausted and ravenous, and simply doesn't have the strength to go out again.

To his surprise, the woman puts some rather good food on the table. Apparently, when she wants to, she knows how to cook well. Baccino eats voraciously and then starts to flirt with her. The innkeeper may well be one of Valentino's spies, but that doesn't stop the steward from desiring her.

Niccolò is busy calculating the messenger's timing—the one who left with the letter for the gonfalonier must have reached Florence by now—when he hears the sound of approaching hooves and drummers. He leans out his window and sees crowds lining the street. A large group of men on horseback are advancing up the main road. They're dressed in armor and carry their weapons, but their helmets are off. It's a show of force. They're preceded by drummers, who announce their arrival.

A herald leading the way announces that the rebels of Pergola and Fossombrone have been punished and that Valentino has returned to Imola. Celebrations will take place the following day: there will be a bullfight in the piazza outside the monastery of the Poor Clares, which His Excellency the Duke will attend in person.

The townspeople cheer enthusiastically.

Borgia's bodyguards lead the procession, their eyes darting this way and that over the exulting crowds, ready to intervene at the slightest threat. They're experts at it: only soldiers who have received at least one battle wound are allowed to protect the Prince.

These men are followed by soldiers on horseback. At their center is Cesare. His left hand is closed in a fist and rests on his thigh; he holds the reins with his right hand. A few wounded soldiers have bloodied bandages. Don Miguel is not among them.

Marching behind them are hundreds of strapping young men whom Valentino recruited in various parts of Romagna on his way back to Imola. The herald informs the townsfolk that other men will soon arrive, forming a new militia of six thousand soldiers who all hail from the duke's territories. They don't know how to march in formation yet, nor do they have uniforms, so they don't look much like an army, but their resolve is steadfast.

Niccolò immediately understands why the Prince recruited them: he wants to form his own army. He conquered Romagna with help from his father's men and the French, and later he used the Orsini and Vitelli militias, but they have since rebelled. He wants to be the lord of his own armed forces and, if this muddle of farmers can be transformed into real soldiers, he will succeed in his goal.

When Borgia passes beneath the window, he looks up and salutes Niccolò with his gloved hand.

Niccolò responds with the same courtesy.

CHAPTER ELEVEN

I'm pleased to see you and am eager to get back to work," Borgia says, turning away from the fireplace in the grand room and facing Niccolò. The *vigilia secunda* has rung. The grey mastiff rubs up against the duke's leg and receives a pat in reply. "I read the corrected version of the manuscript. This time I can say that you were sufficiently malicious."

"I'm pleased to hear that."

"There's just one thing that still does not convince me. Your style varies too much, even on the same page."

"We must always try and imitate nature, which itself is varied. If I did the same thing over and over, I don't think it would be strong."

"This is true. You are right. Continue, then, in this manner. Did you hear how efficiently don Miguel punished the rebels? And that's not all: Vitelli can barely stand on his two feet, he's sick with the French disease, and Paolo Orsini is covered with scabies. The planets are truly not aligned this year for those who chose to revolt."

Niccolò nods politely.

Dianora is sitting next to the fireplace. She is reading a different book this time. It's as if she's invisible.

"Perhaps," the duke continues, "in their desperation, those two men will move their soldiers towards my lands. They may even cross the border into territories belonging to Florence. It's happened before, you know."

Why is he telling Niccolò this? What is he trying to say?

"Let's not forget that they're my enemies as much as they are yours. Vitelli hates you Florentines. And the Orsini army goes wherever the wind blows. I do believe that the alliance you propose might actually suit both of us."

Cesare, the dog at his heels, walks away from the fireplace and over to the table on which lays a map. He bends down to examine it, then beckons to Niccolò to join him.

As he does, Dianora turns her head and gives him a piercing look, signaling both alarm and dismay. He scrutinizes her face for more clues while listening to Borgia, whose back is turned to him.

"And we have other shared enemies . . . It would be wise to fight them together, too. I know it and so does the Dieci. But the term we really ought to be using is 'go to war' and not just 'fight.' For some reason, your Republic is always afraid of calling things by their proper names . . . "

The damsel subtly shakes her head from side to side. Even though she says nothing, Niccolò intuits that she is trying to tell him something. He nods to show that he understands.

"Come over here and look," Borgia says. He indicates the map, which shows the Italian peninsula in its entirety.

Niccolò has never seen anything like it before. It's as if the person who drew it had flown overhead and had an eagle-eye view of what lay below: every single state is carefully outlined in black; the mountains are shades of green, depending on their height; the main thoroughfares are white; the rivers are blue, with the most important ones a darker hue; the names of the cities are in varying shades of red, with the larger the city, the darker the color. A sense of balance and harmony prevails over all. This is not the work of a mere cartographer but a true artist, someone skilled at blending and using colors. It must have been done by da Vinci, Niccolò quickly realizes.

The duke points at Città di Castello. "Look, Vitelli's home town is only five miles from your border. At this very moment, I know that he is moving artillery. Is he doing it against me or against you? It would be in both our interests if you were to send troops to your nearby town of Borgo San Sepolcro, there." He indicates a spot on the map. "You could keep an eye on him and on the surrounding roads."

"I will relay your observation and request to the Dieci in the hopes they accept it," Niccolò says. It occurs to him that what Borgia is saying has some logic to it, but sending troops to Borgo San Sepolcro would mean taking them away from the garrison in Arezzo, where there may be further acts of rebellion, or from the ongoing war against Pisa. Is this what the duke is actually trying to achieve?

"Machiavelli, it is in situations like these that one learns who one's friends truly are. The Republic would only have to move fifty soldiers on horseback, three or four hundred infantrymen, a few cannons . . . If necessary, I'll gladly assist with the expense."

How keen he is on the plan. Too keen.

"My city wants nothing more than to form a pact with you, Your Excellency, but we must, of course, ask permission from the Most Christian King."

"Naturally. And I will do the same. But you can be as sure as death that His Majesty will want the Florentines to come to my assistance. And I would be exceedingly grateful for it. Also, because, mere days from now, I will receive reinforcements of men and artillery from France, at which point I plan on attacking Bologna." He points to Bologna on the map as if it were already his.

That makes sense, Niccolò thinks. He has already laid siege on part of that city and now he wants to deliver the final blow. But it is well known that the duke often does the exact opposite of what he says.

"Bologna has forged an alliance with Vitelli and the Orsini brothers, who have sworn to defend the city . . . " Niccolò says cautiously.

"I'm not worried about fighting on two fronts at the same time."

Unfortunately, he is also in a position to do so, Niccolò says to himself.

"This evening, though, I would like to tell you the story behind the tragic death of my brother-in-law, Alfonso d'Aragona, Duke of Bisceglie, whom I was unfairly accused of killing. As usual."

"The second point on your list."

The Prince nods and is about to say something when there's a knock on the door. He spins around to see who it is. A soldier approaches and whispers something in his ear.

"I must resolve a problem that has arisen between the soldiers. I will not be long. Wait for me," he says.

"Shall I return to the study that you graciously prepared for me?"

"You may remain here. In the meantime, read what they wrote about me and that crime," Borgia says, pointing to the pile of slanderous writings. He pulls out one of the books. "Here, this one is particularly offensive," he says, tossing it to Niccolò, who catches it.

The duke turns and looks at Dianora. He doesn't have to say a word. She gets to her feet, goes down the corridor, and closes the door behind her. The key turns drily in the lock.

With the mastiff close behind, Valentino walks out, without locking the door to the grand hall. Niccolò sits down at the table but instead of reading the book he starts to mentally compose the letter that he will later write to Soderini to inform him of Borgia's proposal. He will also have to communicate as much to the Dieci. But then he stops. He tips his head to one side. He thinks he heard something. Someone is tapping softly on the door that leads to the inner chambers.

He walks over cautiously, holding up a candle. From behind the heavy door comes the muffled voice of Dianora.

"Are you alone, Envoy? If so, speak quietly."

"Yes, I am alone," Niccolò whispers. He bends down, peers through the bronze keyhole, and sees Dianora's face. She looks at him cautiously, her face wan in the weak light.

"Why did you agree to write for him?" she asks.

She's reprimanding him for having accepted to write on commission. What does she know about his needs, duties, or his shortage of money? He has to provide for his family, make sure they can buy food to eat. He also has to protect the Republic, for it finds itself in a dangerous position, which justifies all possible actions. He certainly doesn't deserve to be chided. He knows he shouldn't be offended but nonetheless her words disappoint him.

"The best way of understanding a person's intentions is to spend time with them," he replies.

"I figured as much. And why did you propose an alliance with him after all he has done to the Republic?"

"For the very same reason."

"But he'll always be your enemy!"

"We know it well."

The young lady is silent. She looks somewhat reassured but is still hesitant.

Niccolò feels the need to add more. "I'm here to save my city."

"Then don't trust what he says!" Dianora blurts out. "He's not interested in Bologna. He is going to attack Florence when the moon is full. He has a spy who will open the gate at Porta al Prato—that's what it's called, isn't it?—in the middle of the night. The name of his spy is Andrea Ulivieri."

Niccolò knows the man. He's one of the guards responsible for protecting the city walls.

"Andrea Ulivieri?" Niccolò repeats for confirmation from Dianora. And yet Ulivieri swore allegiance to the Republic . . . How long has he been pretending? Why would he betray them? What did Borgia promise him? And why is this young lady telling him all this? "Why are you revealing Borgia's secrets to me?" he asks.

Even in the dark, he can see her face flush red with anger: two dark splotches appear on her cheeks. "I hate the man. I want someone to kill him. You Florentines could do it. I certainly won't be able to."

Niccolò is inclined not to trust her. It's not in his nature and he has been shaped by experience. "How did you obtain this news?"

"Sometimes I listen in when he's making plans with his men. He pays more attention to his dog than he does to me."

"That's not true!"

She sighs and says nothing, but he notices that her eyes are shiny with tears for the humiliation she has to withstand.

He peers at her closely, perceiving her pain. "Frequently there's a way out of even the most difficult situations," he says to her.

Dianora doesn't say a thing. She would like to believe him but does not.

Niccolò understands the intensity of her pain and is tempted to show his respect for her with silence but also feels forced to press her for more information out of a sense of duty. "Can you open the door? We could speak better that way. You have the key."

"It's too dangerous. Even talking like this is risky."

"Do you know anything else about the attack on Florence?"

"No, but if I hear anything I'll let you know."

"It will be hard to speak again."

"We'll have to wait for the right occasion. You'd better go now. He could be back any minute. And the woman who guards me might return soon, too."

Troubled, he walks over to the window and stares up at the new moon. It's a mere sliver now, hardly there, but it will be full in eleven—no, twelve—days. He knows Porta al Prato well, and unfortunately it is an ideal place for a surprise attack. It doesn't have any side towers for extra defense and only has a single gate, no second entrance with a portcullis that could be lowered to fend off attackers. Its walls are low and should have been better fortified with a bastion. And then there's the river Mugnone that flows nearby, which ought to have been closed off with a dyke to make it less easy to cross. He has to sound the alarm, he has to let Florence know how and when the traitor will act, he will have to send Mancino with a letter at dawn. But what if it's all a ruse? What if Borgia is using her? It's possible but it doesn't seem probable. Dianora's tears were sincere.

Dianora.

Despite his apprehension, he likes the way her name feels on his lips.

CHAPTER TWELVE

I can't let Valentino suspect that I know anything; the future of Florence depends on me, Niccolò says to himself, hearing the scuffling of paws followed by Borgia's footsteps. He rushes over to the table, sits down, and pretends to be studying the booklet the duke tossed him before leaving.

The door opens and Valentino walks in, preceded by the dog. The duke is frowning, as if still troubled by the issue he went to resolve. He sees Niccolò at work and peers at him closely.

"What's the matter? You look worried," the duke says.

Niccolò is deeply concerned but tries to remain calm. "I'm concentrating on this, wondering how best to reply to the calumny . . . " he says easily. But then he flinches nervously when the dog, who has since gotten used to him, comes and rests his head in his lap.

The two men stare at each other. Borgia scrutinizes him. Niccolò realizes that he must distract his attention.

" . . . to put you in the best light possible." Niccolò knows that people in power enjoy being adulated and, in fact, Borgia immediately relaxes and nods.

"Do you think you can find the right words?"

"I'll try my hardest," Niccolò says. He's doing fine, he has to keep placating him, mollifying him, he has to get Valentino to speak. The dog whimpers for attention. Niccolò is forced to pat his head.

"When you write about the death of Alfonso, my beloved brother-in-law, I want you to do it the same way you did before, with details, observations, insinuations, and malice."

Niccolò replies that he will do so gladly and then asks Borgia where he can get more information.

Valentino says that he will provide everything needed. He remembers those days well, even though two years have already passed. He suggests that Niccolò take notes and he begins to tell the story.

Niccolò listens, aware that the more he gets the duke to talk, the less he himself risks making a mistake. In his tense state, Borgia's words feel like a scalpel on his skin.

Although it was the middle of July, Valentino begins, a series of thunderstorms had brought some cooler weather. Alfonso of Aragon, the Duke of Bisceglie, had dined with the Pope at the Vatican. Lucrezia, Alfonso's wife, and Sancia, Alfonso's sister, were also present; the two women had become good friends. It was an enjoyable dinner. They had fish from Civitavecchia, eels from Lake Bolsena, and an icy dessert made with zabaglione and fruit, something they call Florentine cream.

Niccolò notices how much pleasure Borgia derives from telling the story. Soon he is talking rapidly.

After dinner, Alfonso left the Vatican for a palace he owned not far away, to go to bed, while Sancia and Lucrezia stayed on. The clouds had lifted, the night sky was luminous. The duke set out by foot with two of his courtiers and Tommaso Albanese, a gentleman who was part of his close circle.

I've heard that name before, Niccolò says.

That may well be, but I doubt anyone has ever told you the truth about him, Valentino replies. Tommaso was strong, dashing, dark-skinned, and a skilled fencer. Alfonso was tall and so fair-skinned that he looked almost effeminate, with long dark hair and greenish eyes. They walked past Saint Peter's. As usual, a number of pilgrims were sleeping on the ground. Alfonso's assailants were hiding among them. At someone's signal six or seven of them jumped out and attacked. Alfonso's two courtiers ran off, calling for help. Alfonso unsheathed his sword and defended himself ably and courageously and Albanese did the same.

The duke was stabbed deeply in his shoulder and thigh, for a total of eight wounds. Eventually, he fell to the ground, covered in blood. The assailants tried to finish him off and dragged him toward some whinnying horses that were being held by a few accomplices.

Horses? No one ever mentioned horses, Niccolò observes in silence. Did Borgia just reveal something new? If so, he seems unaware of it.

Maybe they wanted to throw Alfonso into the Tiber, Valentino continues, like they did with his own poor brother, the Duke of Gandía. But Albanese stepped up and managed to strike three of the aggressors. In the meantime, the two courtiers who had run to get help returned with the Pope's soldiers, who rushed into the piazza. The attackers jumped on their horses and galloped off. Alfonso was carried back to the Vatican. Lucrezia came running to him in great despair. While a surgeon tended to his wounds, she leaned over her husband, who whispered something in her ear. She promptly fainted.

"Did he say who attacked him?" Niccolò asks but immediately regrets doing so. Bad timing. He feels a sharp pain in his gut.

In fact, the question bothers Borgia, and a hint of anger crosses his face. They never found out, he replies sharply. When she came to her senses, Lucrezia couldn't recall a thing.

Naturally. Her husband probably told her that he had recognized don Miguel among the assailants; she couldn't possibly say that.

Valentino looks at Niccolò as if reading his thoughts. Niccolò brushes away his fear, it's senseless, he can't allow himself to feel it. He does everything he can to look innocent, he must, he has to keep Borgia talking. He feels the mastiff drooling on his leg and tries to push him away but the dog stays put.

Alfonso was taken to a room in the chambers of the Pope, who was so disturbed by the event that he immediately summoned the ambassador to the King of Naples so that he would call for the best masters of medicine. Lucrezia, meanwhile, asked for permission to call in the best surgeons from Naples and her father granted it immediately. Pontifical guards kept watch outside the room all night. They were joined by a few men from the House of Aragon. Lucrezia and Sancia slept by Alfonso's side and prepared his food for him themselves.

It occurs to Niccolò that none of this was ever mentioned in any of the writings he had ever read. Clearly, Alfonso's wife and sister were afraid that someone was going to try and poison him. Valentino was offering up new details, in perfect keeping with his malicious spirit.

The dog finally leaves Niccolò's side and lies down at his master's feet.

The surgeons arrived from Naples. Slowly and gradually, Alfonso's condition started to improve. He was only nineteen years old, he was strong, and the medical care he received was excellent, the duke says emphatically. As soon as the duke's brother-in-law was well enough, he went to see him, to show his support.

Valentino then feigns a look of deep offense. In Rome a rumor was about that he'd said, "Things that don't go well at lunch often go well at dinner." When they ought to have been looking for the attackers among the many enemies of Alfonso of Aragon, they instead started heaping suspicion on him, fomented by Tommaso Albanese, who had since healed from his own wounds at the house of a poet friend. A few other noble families also started hinting that Cesare was behind the ambush.

Not a few, Niccolò thinks to himself. All of them.

It was those calumnious comments that were the root cause of the tragedy that followed, Valentino says. The men from the House of Aragon, who had come to protect Alfonso, believed the rumors and started to plan accordingly. Even his own brother-in-law must have been convinced that Cesare had ordered the attack. By then it was August. Alfonso would periodically get up and make his way over to the window and look down on the gardens. One day, when he saw Cesare out walking among the trees, he took up his crossbow and shot an arrow at him.

Niccolò looks at him in surprise. "No one ever mentioned that," he says softly.

"That's why I'm telling you," Borgia replies. He goes on to say that somewhere among his things he still has the arrowhead that Alfonso used to try and kill him. He had it examined and discovered it was poisoned. Obviously, after such an act of open hostility, he had every right to defend himself. He took on more guards and investigated a conspiracy set in motion by the faithful servants of the House of Aragon. When he had enough proof, he sent don Miguel and a troop of soldiers to arrest them. It was an act of justice, Valentino explains.

The more Borgia speaks, the weaker Niccolò begins to feel. It's as if he's bleeding out, as if he's dying. The effort that Borgia puts into lying is so strong that it forces Niccolò to relinquish. He wishes he could leave the room but cannot. He nods, yes, an act of justice. Of course. He looks down at the piece of paper where he is scribbling his notes.

Valentino goes on. Lucrezia put up a fight, she tried to oppose the arrest of the guards, and Sancia stood by her side, not allowing their men to be taken to jail. Don Miguel told them with all the graciousness he could muster that he was merely obeying orders. He suggested that Lucrezia and Sancia ask the Pope to intervene; he wasn't far away, just in another wing of the Vatican. If the Pope decided to liberate the men of the House of Aragon, don Miguel would do so without hesitation. Alfonso's wife and his sister went to speak to His Holiness.

Niccolò feels like he was there in the room as a crime was about to be committed. His nerves are shot, his quill pen trembles in his hand. He's scared: if Borgia asks him once more what's troubling him, he might break down and admit everything.

But the Prince is galvanized by his own telling of the tale, inspired by his own fervor. It was at that point that his brother-in-law, alarmed by all the shouting and yelling, got up from bed and, in the excitement of the moment and not entirely healed, suddenly felt dizzy and fell to the ground awkwardly. Don Miguel, who went to see what had happened after he heard him fall—and not before, as those ignoble slanderers claimed—tried in vain to assist him. Alfonso died a few minutes later from internal bleeding. By the time Lucrezia and Sancia came back, he was already dead. And that is what happened, Cesare says. He sits up in his throne, proud and silent.

Niccolò is also silent, sapped of energy but safe.

The night air helps Niccolò regain his strength. He returns to the lodging house slowly, making his way through town like an elderly man. He then lights all the candles he can find and quickly writes a letter in code to the gonfalonier with details about the date of the attack and the name of the traitor.

Composing sentences that are his alone is a restorative act; it helps him think clearly. The world returns to its usual order.

He wonders whether he should warn Marietta, too. He could write her in private but then refrains from doing so. Where could she and the baby go? Certainly not to Albergaccio. His wife and child's destinies are tied to that of the city of Florence.

Afterwards, in his report for the Dieci, he doesn't mention the information he learned from Dianora, and instead refers in great detail to Valentino's proposed alliance, which is as false as the words he used to describe the assassination of his brother-in-law.

He can't sleep. He doesn't even try. At dawn, he calls for Campriano, a solid and industrious messenger. He hands him the two letters and orders him to set out immediately, telling him to travel swiftly and safely.

Just in case something happens to the courier, Niccolò writes two similar letters to Soderini and the Dieci, which he will entrust the following day to the new messenger.

CHAPTER THIRTEEN

D
ianora said that if she finds out anything else, she'll tell me. Maybe she'll be at the bullfight, maybe I'll be able to talk to her there, but we'll have to be careful that no one sees us, Niccolò thinks as he sets out to look for the piazza and the monastery of the Poor Clares.

Crowds of excited people indicate the way.

The streets that lead to the piazza are blocked off by carts that have been tipped over onto their sides, with people pressing up against them to be able to see. Important guests, like himself, have seats on the two loggias that look out onto the piazza, one for the clergy and one for the accredited ambassadors to the court. Although he is not of the same rank, he has been given a spot there. While this gesture reveals how highly the duke considers him, the ambassadors and orators from other cities find it somewhat offensive and hardly even acknowledge his presence when he arrives in their midst.

He looks around for Dianora but doesn't see her. Agapito Geraldini greets him cordially.

People with homes around the piazza lean out their windows to watch. Even the Poor Clares are watching through the grate of the convent, drawn to the unusual spectacle.

There's a cruel excitement in the air.

Suddenly, there's shouting from a nearby alley. A bull comes charging out of a narrow space between a wall and an overturned cart, bolting into the piazza. Its exit is immediately blocked off. The animal veers sharply to the right, then runs in a circle, trying to escape. As it rushes about, men dressed in Borgia's colors either jump out of the way or press up against

the walls; they carry short poles with sharp metal tips. A few
of them hide for safety behind a gate held in place thanks to
robust oak beams.

The bull continues to circle wildly. Soon Valentino's mastiff starts chasing it, barking aggressively. A knight in armor on
horseback rides into the piazza from the inner courtyard of a
building. He carries a lance and his steed wears a leather harness, as if ready for battle. He waits until the bull slows down,
then charges it, striking it twice with his weapon, driving the
lance deep into the animal's neck. The mastiff barks crazily. The
bull quivers with pain and tries to charge, but the horse is protected by its leather harness.

Niccolò is horrified and fascinated at the same time.

The ambassador to the Marquis of Mantua, a rotund man
with rosy cheeks who apparently attended a bullfight while on
legation in Spain, explains to everyone sitting nearby that piercing the animal with the lance enrages and weakens the beast, cutting the muscles and tendons the animal needs to raise its head.

The duke appears, also on horseback, from the doorway of
a different building. He's dressed in heavy violet brocade and
carries a long sword. He approaches the bull from the side,
spears it before it can even react, then rides off, turns around,
and comes back for a second attack.

The Mantuan ambassador says to the Venetian ambassador,
a thin man with a hooked nose, that this is not Borgia's first
bullfight. He has already slayed bulls in Saint Peter's Square in
Rome. And yet it's odd, he remarks, to see him attack an animal
that is the symbol of his own noble family; it's as if he were furious with his own bloodline. Perhaps, in some way, he feels compelled to slay the animal in order to achieve even greater things.

Although the men speak quietly, Niccolò overhears everything. He has trained his ear to decipher what the powerful
utter in a whisper. They, meanwhile, don't even register his
presence. His humble birth is like an invisible border that can't
be crossed.

He watches the events unfold in the piazza. The bull, now covered with wounds, enraged and confused, is approached by a man carrying two spears. The beast charges him, head low, but the man sidesteps it easily, and drives the spears into its rump. The animal spins around and chases the man, who is forced to hide behind the gate, while other men enter the piazza. Cesare studies the movements of the bull: it's losing blood, it's trying to defend himself, and it's bothered by the dog that continues to snap at its heels. The duke jumps off his horse, bands together with his men, throws down his sword, grabs two spears, and drives them into the beast in one smooth movement.

Niccolò feels an involuntary rush of excitement. It's as if everyone around him feels it, too. He's happy that Dianora is not there; the spectacle would unquestionably upset her.

This bull is a true fighter, the Mantuan ambassador says to his neighbor. "With each strike it receives, it gets closer to death. They're cutting through its muscles, nerves, and blood vessels, and yet notice how it doesn't give up. This bull truly has strength and character."

The Venetian ambassador wonders out loud why the duke chooses to risk his life in such a way. Geraldini replies that His Lordship has so much energy that he has to release it somehow, and so much good fortune that he never really risks anything.

Cesare picks up his sword, takes two steps back, and avoids the charging bull, which is still being chased by the mastiff.

One of the men armed with a lance waits for the bull to face him so that he can sidestep it and stab it, but this time the animal is ready and, with a rapid flick of his horns, wounds the man, gouging his side. He falls to the ground. The crowd cries out in concern, the sound echoes through the piazza, followed by a tense silence. The mastiff barks even harder.

A few men step in and distract the bull by waving colorful wooden shields while others grab the wounded man and drag him away. The dog goes back to snapping at the bull, but now the beast, in its desperation, turns around and spears the dog with its horns, tearing out the dog's guts. A howl of pain makes Borgia rush forward with his sword raised.

"It's too soon! The bull is still dangerous," the Mantuan ambassador says with deep concern. "The animal has to be rendered weak before it can be killed; more time needs to pass between one charge and the next." Everyone is silent, including Geraldini. The spectators realize that the situation has grown dangerous.

Niccolò can't stop watching. His eyes go from the bull to Cesare and back again, over and over.

The bull moves away from the dying dog and rushes Cesare, who dodges it with agility. The beast retreats, stands still for a moment, then charges Valentino again, who once again side-steps it.

Three soldiers rush in with long, heavy, iron spears and ask their lord if they can kill the bull. They speak in Valencian Spanish, but everyone understands what they are saying.

"No," Cesare replies.

As soon as he says that, the bull charges him again: he bows deeply and twists his torso to one side to avoid the animal's horns.

For one long second it looks as though he's been struck. A gasp rises up from the crowd. Someone screams. A young woman faints. Cries ring out from deep inside the monastery. Soldiers rush in. The duke waves them away, raises both his hands to the sky, turns around to show everyone that he's not injured. The Mantuan ambassador applauds.

Cesare then grabs a spear with his left hand, takes up his sword with his right, and strides toward the bull. The animal's mouth hangs open, tongue lolling, exhausted but still standing, confused, devastated by pain.

Valentino approaches it, insulting it and goading it loudly, making noises with his tongue. The beast charges him again, but Cesare steps to one side and drives the spear into the animal's flesh between his front legs, causing the exhausted bull to trip, break a leg, and fall to the ground, face down.

Cesare climbs on top of it and sinks his sword deep into its side, all the way to the hilt, looking for the beast's lungs and heart.

The bull groans in pain, blood gushing from mouth and nose. Then, with a final shudder, it stops moving.

Niccolò is deeply shaken and yet also overcome with a kind of fever. Together with the rest of the crowd, he lets out a great cheer. Everyone feels the same ferocious passion. While they applaud and holler and yell, the duke merely raises an arm in a kind of salute, then rushes over to his dog, who is already dead.

The crowd continues to cheer and chant his name. After closing the mastiff's eyes, Cesare saunters slowly around the piazza, reveling in the frenzy, absorbing the people's energy. In the meantime, Cesare's men cut off the bull's penis and present it to him as a trophy. They tie ropes around the animal's hooves and two horses begin dragging away the corpse: the meat will be given to the poor. Rivers of blood flow out of the beast's mouth and line the cobblestone streets.

CHAPTER FOURTEEN

Niccolò studies himself in the mirror of the tailor's shop, noticing how the color of the fabric changes in the light, depending how the mantle falls; it's truly an article of clothing fit for a gentleman and he likes the way he looks in it. At the same time, he listens carefully as Farneti, who peers out the window now and then to see who is walking by, informs him that one of the duke's armies never made it to Urbino. Some say it was because of poor weather, others say because Vitellozzo's infantry blocked their passage. Either way, the two armies will soon go to battle.

He turns to see how the mantle falls behind him. "Truly excellent craftmanship. But wouldn't it have been better to take a little longer to finish it, allowing us a pretext for additional meetings?"

"That would have raised eyebrows. Everyone knows that I work quickly. We've already been seen together too much. We'll have to find another way to meet up. Or perhaps I should leave you written messages in a secret place."

"Yes, that might be more prudent."

Farneti picks up a piece of paper and sketches a map. "If you walk a half mile out of Porta Montanara gate, you'll come to a fork in the road where the oak forest begins. One of the oak trees, just inside the forest, has been struck by lightning." He draws the shape of the tree for Niccolò and then points to a spot on it. "Just here, two arms' length up, there's a hole in the trunk. We can leave messages for each other there."

"Fine. Let's not forget to burn the messages after we have read them."

Farneti nods, looks around to make sure no one is watching, and promptly burns the map.

Niccolò looks at himself in the mirror again. "Have you heard anything about the French spearmen?"

"They're on their way, but I do not know when they'll arrive. The young men that Valentino recruited in Romagna are camped just outside the city walls. There are six hundred of them. They're already being trained."

"Does the duke always keep Lady Mambelli close by?"

"He allows her to go to confession at San Michele in the early hours of the morning. Other than that, she is not allowed to leave the Rocca."

"Do you think I might talk to her on such occasions?"

"Valentino's personal guards and a woman dressed in black accompany her to the church. Whenever she leaves the fortress, that woman is with her."

"Yes, I saw her once. Who is she?"

"Her name is Lucina, but I don't know her last name. She comes from Valencia, like most of the duke's trusted servants. She keeps a close watch on Mambelli. The only moment the damsel is on her own is when she goes into the confessional."

"Who's the priest? What kind of man is he?"

They say that Brother Timoteo, the prior of the Osservanza monastery, is very holy and even performed a miracle, but it happened in Germany, so no one can say for sure if it really took place. Apparently he has connections from Milan to Rome, as well as nimble fingers, adept at pilfering money, food, and drink.

He's around sixty, has white hair and a beard, and grey inscrutable eyes; he's portly, disheveled, and takes great pleasure in deceiving people.

He oversees thirty-three friars, including a young and angelic looking one who often visits him in his spacious, thick-walled cell around midnight.

Niccolò is extremely cautious about contacting the prior. He leaves the inn through the stable after exchanging outfits with Baccino, then wanders for a long time up and down side streets and alleys to make sure he is not being followed. Eventually he makes his way to San Michele, which is connected to the monastery, wondering each step of the way if he is doing the right thing.

He enters the church as sly as a fox and kneels down in a pew to wait for Brother Timoteo to celebrate mass. After the service, Niccolò follows him into the cloister.

He tells him that he is a traveling wool merchant and that he urgently needs to confess his sins. His guilt is so heinous that he needs to speak to a friar who is close to God, such as the prior. In saying as much, he hopes to be able to corrupt the man in privacy.

Brother Timoteo looks at him with great amusement, saying that he didn't realize that the Florentine envoy also dealt in wool. The prior goes on to explain that he saw him at the bullfight with the other diplomatic delegations, and enquired who he was. The fox has met an even bigger fox.

With his cards out in the open, Niccolò asks the prior where they can talk safely. The friar takes him to the campanile, where the bell pull hangs. Then he starts to ring the bells for a funeral, which will be the next mass he celebrates. The poor man was quite well-off, the prior says, may his soul rest in peace. Luckily the family of the deceased will be giving the prior a nice, shiny obol, he whispers into Niccolò's ear, and he then invites the envoy to tell him what is weighing so heavily on his heart.

Between one toll of the bell and the next, Niccolò explains that he has to perform an act of Christian charity: he has to bring lady Mambelli news of her only surviving brother, who has found refuge in Florence. He is sure the prior will understand that it must be done with the greatest discretion.

Brother Timoteo looks at him slyly. While continuing to ring the bells for the dead, he says that although it is indeed a noble goal—dong—and that the Lord will surely appreciate the gesture—dong—of all the women here in Imola—dong—she's the only one that Machiavelli should never approach—dong.

Niccolò drops a florin on the stone floor—ding. The friar pulls the bell—dong. Another florin—ding. Niccolò is spending the money that Borgia gave him because the funds from Florence have already run out.

Ding. Dong. Ding, ding. Ding, ding, ding.

The friar looks at the coins greedily. After a few more pulls of the bell and just as many florins, they reach an agreement.

CHAPTER FIFTEEN

It's early morning in Florence. A tall, slender man, around fifty years old, leaves his home and walks toward the Arno. It's the shortest route to get to Porta al Prato, where he will put on his uniform and take up duty.

He walks past a woman on her way to do her food shopping and three men who are standing around, chatting. Suddenly, the three men throw a dark cape over him and hold him tightly while he kicks and punches trying to get free. They then tie a rope tightly around him at waist height to immobilize him. Other guards appear on both sides of the street, encouraging the passerby to move on, while the three men lead him away.

"Who are you? What do you want? I haven't done anything," comes the muffled voice of the prisoner.

"Silence, Andrea Ulivieri. You will speak when spoken to," one of the three men says. It is Dino Gherardi, the head of the gonfalonier's guards.

Ulivieri tries to wriggle free, kicks out, and calls for help. To silence him, Gherardi punches him hard in the direction of his voice; there's a cracking sound. His nose is broken.

CHAPTER SIXTEEN

Escorted by three of the duke's guards and the woman in black, Dianora approaches the church door. Two of the soldiers wait outside, while the third enters with the two women.

Embedded in the paving stone of the central nave is a sundial which Dianora crosses with the woman in black on one side and the guard on the other. The day has hardly begun and morning sunlight illuminates Dianora's dark red velvet skirt.

There is no one else in the church. The guard looks around and then nods at Lucina. The woman gestures to Dianora that she can enter the sacristy for her confession. They watch her carefully as she strides off.

Confession is the only time she's free. Borgia concedes it to her to alleviate her dark moods.

Dianora opens the door and walks into a large room. Light enters from windows positioned high up, but the walls are lined with dark wooden cabinets. Sitting in an oak chair that looks as though it's about to give out under his weight, is Brother Timoteo. Next to him is a prie-dieu.

The prior gets to his feet and walks toward her and greets her warmly. While he is a man of experience, the horrors she has relayed to him have affected him deeply, and he feels something akin to compassion for her.

While Dianora kneels down on the prie-dieu, the friar walks to the door, greets the guard and the woman in black, and closes the door almost all the way, so that only the young lady is visible from the nave. Even though Timoteo's proclivities are well-known, it's never a good idea to be alone in a closed room with a damsel.

Then, instead of going and sitting down in the oak chair as he usually does to hear her confession, the prior walks to a far end of the sacristy.

Dianora watches him uneasily. She does not realize that one of the cabinet doors on her side of the room is slightly open. It's not actually a cabinet, she quickly learns, but a secret passageway that leads to the monastery garden.

Standing in its shadows is Niccolò. Through the semi-shut door he can see Dianora from the back, kneeling on her prie-dieu. If he cracks opens the door a little further, he can also see a portion of the nave: Lucina is sitting in a pew with a bored look on her face. The guard is nearby, leaning against a column. From where Lucina sits, she can easily see her ward, but she currently only appears interested in the guard, with whom she's engaged in conversation.

Niccolò looks at Dianora. Now that the moment has come to talk to her, he hesitates. Maybe he is exaggerating. Yes, he could remain silent, but the future of his city is at stake. He tells himself that he will never have another opportunity like this, so he begins to whisper to her in a soothing manner.

"Do not be startled, but it is I, the envoy from Florence. Do you recognize my voice? I assure you that you are not in danger; the woman who watches over you is not looking at us."

Dianora winces and goes pale. She's on the verge of turning around but refrains from doing so. Instead, she stays calm and glances at Lucina instead.

"See? From where I am, I can observe her without her noticing me," Niccolò says reassuringly. "I had no other way of seeing you and didn't know how to warn you. If you speak to me as if you were in confession, no one will suspect a thing. But, if you'd prefer, I'll leave immediately."

Dianora glances uneasily at Brother Timoteo. He is sitting in the far corner, his back to her. He opens a cabinet and casually takes out some wine and a chalice for Mass.

"I have an agreement with the prior. He has been well paid. He can't hear us from where he is," Niccolò adds.

She glances into the nave, then twists around and catches sight of Niccolò in the doorway. She quickly turns back and looks straight ahead again, tucking a lock of hair behind one ear. "This is dangerous," she says softly.

"No more dangerous than how we spoke before. I thought about it for a long time . . . "

"And yet you did it all the same."

"We don't ever have to meet again, if you don't want."

Dianora doesn't speak, she is deeply uncertain. Niccolò realizes that this meeting creates yet an additional burden on her. Maybe he has done wrong. But there's no going back now, no way to make it right again.

"I put my life in your hands, like you put yours in mine, when we first spoke. We have to trust each other," he says to her.

"Did you warn Florence?" she asks.

"Yes, the messenger arrived yesterday at the latest. I'm sure they've taken all the right steps."

"Thank the Lord. Now that beast of a man will be trapped," she says. Niccolò notices that the thought of Valentino's death visibly eases her tension. "He'll never guess that your armies will be waiting for him."

"He'll get what he deserves," Niccolò says decisively although he knows he can't promise her anything. What will the gonfalonier decide to do? Will they actually wait for Borgia's attack and set a trap for him? Will they kill Borgia, as Dianora hopes? He doubts it. If anything, they will try and capture him in order to negotiate better. Nothing is ever certain in war.

"I don't want to stay here long. It's too risky," Dianora says.

"Stay only as long as your usual confession would last. It would be odd if you left too soon."

She looks over at the prior, who is beatifically gulping down wine, his lips and mouth red with the stuff, and ostentatiously looking away.

"Do you know if the duke is moving his troops toward Florence?" Niccolò asks.

"Yes. He gave clear orders: three hundred men each night, so as not to draw attention. Despite the loss, he presses on."

"What loss?"

"You don't know? The armies of Vitelli and the Orsini brothers overcame don Miguel and Ramiro de Lorqua near Urbino. Corella was wounded but not seriously."

"Did they lose many soldiers?"

"Not more than five hundred."

Too few.

"When did this happen?"

"At the beginning of last week. Two days later, Borgia lost Urbino."

"Are you sure? Did you hear him say as much?"

"Yes."

This information is well worth the risk they are running and all the florins he gave the friar. So this is why Valentino came back to Imola; how skilled he was at dissimulating.

"Did Valentino seem worried?"

"No. He's convinced he'll defeat them next time. He's trying to split up the alliance between his enemies. He even sent a message to Paolo Orsini."

So he reached out to the most malleable of them . . .

"Does he suspect you at all? Are you in any danger?"

"He doesn't fear me at all. He thinks I belong to him, like some kind of object. He's felt that way ever since he raped me."

"Raped you . . . ?"

"But you knew that already, didn't you? He has told everyone, he's proud of it. We . . . " Dianora's voice cracks, tears spring to her eyes.

"Hush, don't talk about it," Niccolò interrupts her. "Not if it's too difficult for you."

" . . . We thought we could stop him," she says, trying to go on, but she begins to weep. Who knows what tragic memories are buried deep inside. It is hard for her to find the words to express her suffering. She changes the subject. "They fired their cannons at the walls of the fortress for weeks on end, without stopping, day and night . . . And finally they broke through." Dianora wipes away her tears.

"Don't, please."

"I'm always thinking about it. Talking helps."

She sobs. Brother Timoteo glances over and then away again. He's both worried and embarrassed. Niccolò leans in.

"I wish I could help you."

"Then kill him when he attacks Florence. That way I can die in peace."

"Die, Milady? But why?"

"I live for that moment only. I haven't taken my own life because it would be a sin against God, unforgiveable. If I can be avenged, my survival will have meaning."

If Niccolò could see her face, he would see it filled with hope for a future without Valentino.

"I must go now. I can't stay any longer," she says quickly. "But I would like to see you again. Perhaps here? Is that possible?"

"Yes. I will make it happen."

Dianora wipes her eyes and gets to her feet. She feels considerably lighter. Brother Timoteo, despite his large belly, nimbly rushes over and takes his place in the oak chair.

When Dianora opens the door to the sacristy with her usual elegant composure and dignity, the prior is comfortably seated in his chair.

Lucina gets to her feet.

The two women together walk toward the soldier.

The three of them cross back over the sundial and exit the church door.

Niccolò watches her as she leaves. He lets out a heavy sigh, disturbed by what she told him and what he imagines she has experienced. He would like to assist her but realizes that he is completely powerless. The fact that she told him that talking helps her assuages him somewhat, as does the thought that he will see her again. Suddenly, he realizes why the gonfalonier sent him and not someone else, and why he didn't tell him about the danger that Marietta and Primerana were in. Soderini knew that Dianora was here with Valentino, he supposed she knew some of the duke's secrets, and he calculated that Niccolò would be keen on talking to her. No one else would dare do what Niccolò has just done and what he will continue to do. It would appear that I-have-faith is no idiot after all.

CHAPTER SEVENTEEN

B ack in his room at the lodging house, Niccolò works on the chapter devoted to the death of Alfonso d'Aragona. Valentino will certainly appreciate the results, but the act of writing so many lies gives Niccolò a somewhat strange and disturbing sensation. The sadness he feels after meeting with Dianora finds its way into his sentences and thoughts. And yet he cannot stop; working on the manuscript is also a way of remaining by her side. A man in his position has to do whatever it takes, he knows. The fact that he has no choice in the matter is somehow reassuring. Even so, he finds a moment to put down his pen and decides to go have lunch in an osteria where they serve delicious soups and eggs stuffed with pecorino cheese. He pulls his new mantle tight, protecting himself from the cold wind that started to blow in full force the night before.

Niccolò sees don Miguel walking toward him, his arm lightly bandaged. When did he get back to Imola? Niccolò is surprised to see him. Corella looks at him with an obscure expression.

"Greetings, Envoy."

"Salutations, don Miguel."

"Nice mantle," Corella says, stopping him in his tracks to feel the fabric and rub Niccolò's arm. "I was on my way to find you. The duke has asked to see you."

"Now? At this time of day?"

"He has something he wants to show you."

The bastion in the city walls facing Bologna clearly was recently rebuilt and reinforced and the smell of lime still lingers in the air. Niccolò, escorted by Corella, steps out onto the windy terrace and sees four cannons pointed at the countryside. He also notices troops of infantrymen marching down below, creating a cloud of dust.

He had me come here so that I would see the soldiers, so that I write to Florence and tell them that he is moving part of the army toward Bologna, Niccolò thinks.

Valentino is supervising the work of a number of soldiers who are shifting the direction of a long cannon. He catches sight of Niccolò and turns to face him.

"Come, I want you to understand the kind of problems that I have to face every single day. I have the best military engineer in the world. He built this bastion so that it is unassailable, and yet the stupidity of an artilleryman who misdirected the cannon . . . " A soldier standing nearby looks down in embarrassment. "A mistake like this could ruin everything. All it takes is a minor mistake to lose a battle." He directs his attention to a group of men. "Now, push! More to the right! More! Now, stop!" He bends over the breech, brings his eye up to the vent field to check the sight line, seems satisfied, and motions for Niccolò to approach. "Now it's in the right position," he says, inviting him to have a look.

The cannon is pointing directly at the road below, where a few men are riding. The wind whistles ominously through the bore.

Valentino waves away the soldier responsible for the mistake. "Throw him in a cell with bread and water for a month." While they drag off the man, the duke checks the position again and nods. "See? If I hadn't thought of it," he says, tapping his forehead, "I wouldn't have been able to fix the problem. Potential mishaps can be corrected; those to which we fall prey, cannot."

He moves away from the cannon and invites Niccolò to follow him to an area that is protected from the wind. Don Miguel follows a few steps behind.

"Are you always prepared for everything?" Niccolò asks as they take their distance from the soldiers.

"I try to be. Naturally, Fortune is always a decisive factor, but I think we are responsible for at least half of what happens."

"Half . . . " Niccolò repeats. The duke certainly likes dividing things in two. This time it's Fortune and personal strength, while before it was the image a person projects and reality.

"It's not enough, really. If we don't take all precautions, a disaster can happen at any time. When a river breaks its banks, it destroys everything around it. When I make military plans, I exaggerate all the risks. I stay up nights musing over all my decisions very carefully. But you mustn't write that! I never let anyone see that side of me. On the contrary, I want people to notice how calm I am. As soon as I make my final decision, all doubts vanish; I sacrifice everything for the success of the campaign."

A table for two has been set in an area that is protected from the wind.

"Would you care to dine with me?"

"It would be an honor."

"I was hoping you would say yes. I've already given instructions to the kitchen. How is the chapter on the final days of the Duke of Bisceglie coming along?"

"I'm making swift progress but I need more time."

Borgia sits down and invites Niccolò to do the same.

"When it comes to writing, you know better than I do. But remember that I await it eagerly."

They are served bread, water, and wine. Valentino doesn't touch a thing. A taster steps forward and takes a few sips of wine. Another one chews the bread. The duke doesn't even seem to notice them.

Even Corella, who has remained standing, seems to find the situation perfectly normal.

"I asked my cook to prepare some hare and boar. I hope they are to your liking," Borgia says.

A servant brings a dish with some chunks of meat in an aromatic sauce. Niccolò, who is very hungry, looks at the dish, his mouth watering. A third taster takes a piece of bread, some meat and sauce, chews them up, and swallows.

"Now we have to wait thirty minutes," Valentino says.

Just enough time to make sure the food isn't poisoned.

"In the meantime, allow me to tell you about Urbino. Did you hear the news that it fell? No? Well, you will in due course. They put the entire garrison in prison and hung my governor, as well as many of my men. But I will have my revenge," he says as if it is a certain thing. "They brought back the old duke, who was hiding under the protective wing of the Venetians. But, as I said, it won't be hard to chase them out again—" He interrupts himself and looks at something behind Niccolò, who instinctively turns to see. A messenger in riding clothes comes forward with a pail covered with a cloth.

"Another dish prepared by your cook?"

"Something far better, if it is what I think."

Corella approaches the messenger, softly asks him a question, and the man nods. Don Miguel takes the pail and brings it over to the table.

"Is it news from Florence, Miguel?" Borgia asks.

Corella nods. "Yes, it has just arrived."

Niccolò must be strong and contain his nerves. Did they hear that Andrea Ulivieri had been arrested? Of course, the traitor couldn't possibly have been on his own; someone else may have raised the alarm . . . What if Dianora had set a trap for him? What if she and Valentino had a plan? After all, she is in the duke's hands. Oh, why on earth did he ever trust her?

Borgia smiles at don Miguel.

Niccolò looks off into the distance, far beyond the bastion. For a moment he thinks he would rather throw himself off the edge than be taken prisoner, but he knows he wouldn't have the courage. It's better to live, whatever the cost.

Borgia motions for his private executioner to show the contents of the pail to Niccolò. "A gift for you. Have a look."

Corella approaches. Niccolò raises the cloth. Inside, covered with salt, is the head of Duccio Del Briga. He's been beaten and his face is covered with congealed blood. Niccolò feels his stomach constrict: he's horrified and relieved at the same time.

"A man, a problem. No man, no problem. Your family is now safe."

"But Nicia, the banker, might find another way," he says in a hoarse voice that doesn't sound like his own.

"Del Briga's body was left in front of Nicia's house. I think he'll let it go after a warning like that."

Niccolò feels as though he is about to vomit. He covers the head with the cloth and takes a deep breath. "Thank you, Your Excellency." The horror has passed. He now feels surprisingly content. "From the bottom of my heart."

Valentino nods benevolently.

CHAPTER EIGHTEEN

The cell in which Andrea Ulivieri was thrown after being tortured was pitch dark except for three lanterns hanging on the wall.

He managed to resist for a long time. Gherardi and his men interrogated him for hours without touching him, just to tire him out. He denied being a traitor and swore that he had always been faithful to the Republic. He had a long answer for each of their questions, he retraced his steps over the past several months, he listed friends and relatives—all of whom were arrested immediately—who could testify in his favor.

At midday, officers from the Bargello came to ask for news. Gherardi had none to give. They wondered whether perhaps Ulivieri was innocent. No, Gherardi said, he's lying. His suspicion was confirmed not long after when guards from the garrison that protected Porta al Prato caught a twenty-year-old soldier under Ulivieri's command as he was fleeing for Lucca. The boy was terrified and confessed immediately.

They beat Ulivieri hard, but he still didn't talk. So they took him to the torture chamber where they gave him five pulls of the rope. Despite the terrible pain in his flayed muscles and dislocated shoulders, which were reset each time, he didn't talk. Hanging in the air from his wrists, arms twisted behind his back, sweating heavily, he continued to scream that he had nothing to confess. Below and across from him sat a judge and a chancellor.

With a gesture from the head executioner, one of the jailers released the rope and Ulivieri dropped sharply four arm lengths. The cord grew taut, his body spun around, his shoulders were dislocated, he screamed loudly, and then he fainted.

They brought him almost all the way down to the ground but held him up by the legs so he couldn't touch the pavement with his feet.

A second jailer threw a pail of water in his face, bringing him back to his senses. Ulivieri moaned loudly. A doctor examined him, pulling and pushing and relocating his shoulder. "You may continue," the doctor declared.

"Increase the pain," the judge ordered.

This time the executioner had his men attach iron weights to the prisoner's feet, then ordered for him to be raised up once more. Ulivieri couldn't think straight but he was also very stubborn.

"I never betrayed anyone!"

He knew that if he confessed he would be put to death. Slowly, this option was starting to appear less painful than what he was going through.

They hauled him up to the ceiling and then let him drop again, again almost all the way to the ground. His body came to a sudden halt, the weights yanking him down, his arms twisted in an unnatural and violent manner, his shoulders dislocated once more. He screamed, this time longer but weaker, and then fainted.

They lowered him down yet again, threw water on him, the doctor visited him and reset his dislocated limbs. "You may continue."

Blood and snot flowed from the prisoner's nose, he was drooling, his glassy eyes stared at the executioner as they approached him, grabbed his hair, and looked deep into his eyes.

"Shall we continue?"

"No," Ulivieri croaked.

"Then speak."

"No."

"Increase the pain," the judge said.

They added more weights, hauled him back up to the ceiling, and released him one more time. His arm bones broke, his body twisted through the air. Every single movement added to the intolerable pain.

"Stop! I'll talk!" he screamed in agony.

CHAPTER NINETEEN

N iccolò Machiavelli
Envoy of Florence at the Court of Duke Valentino
Greetings,
Since being elected Gonfalonier by our people,
12 is safe thanks to your swift action, for which I am very grateful.
I have not written any missives or letters, neither to Lords or
acquaintances, unless
*The man you wrote about acted in the name of money. He was
not alone,*
somehow related to the honorable office I have been asked
to fulfill: for this reason
*the poisoned plant has secretly been uprooted, but soon 58
will realize it.*
I have not even written to the most Illustrious Prince.
Try and find out if 59 has a backup plan. Also, communicate to us
I now write on behalf of Marco and Iacopo Brinciassi, two
of our wagon drivers
*and with great haste, how many men, both riders and infantry,
he has in his command*
who were robbed of six mules in the past months in Castel
Durante
and where they are located; send a list.
by men in the employ of His Excellency.
*The messenger who brings you this missive will give you ad-
ditional invisible ink*
Kindly speak with his Illustrious Lordship about this matter
and relay to him
*and all florins available to us at this time. We have no additional
money at our disposal.*

how much it would mean to me if he would return the mules to the Brinciassi brothers.

With sincere regards to His Lordship, and may God only increase his happiness.

Be well.

Florence, 26 October 1502

Pietro Soderini
Vexillifer of the People of the Florentine Republic

* * *

Niccolò Machiavelli

Secretary, Envoy of Florence at the Court of Duke Valentino

Greetings,

That which His Excellency the Prince has asked of the Dieci di Libertà e di Balìa regarding troops to be sent to Borgo San Sepolcro is not possible; we need to use them to protect our borders, from high to low. Make all efforts to explain this to His Lordship in the best way possible so that no shadows are cast on us. We understand that the prince would like more, but we have no choice.

Tarry as long as you can; try and discover what his intentions are for our Republic.

We have written to the Very Christian King three times already and await his response. We include the letters sent to His Majesty here, so that you may share them with the Duke as proof of our noble sentiments.

The information you have sent is useful but we have nothing to offer in exchange.

On behalf of the Republic, ask the Prince for a letter of safe conduct for our merchants traveling through his towns and states on their way to and from the East, a route that is of great importance to the prosperity of our city.

Farewell.

Palagio Fiorentino, 28 October 1502
Dieci di Libertà e di Balìa of the Florentine Republic.
Marcellus.

* * *

Magnificent Vexillifer of the People of the Florentine Republic
Your Illustrious Lordship,
In addition to this missive, to be delivered by Ardingo, I will make all efforts to send you
I received the ink and florins, for which I am very grateful.
additional letters but I must point out that I am dealing with a Prince
I provide the list that you asked me for, based on the information I have gathered. I can
who governs his matters personally, and it is impossible to know his next move.
personally only attest to what I see around the city; for all else I rely on others.
I spoke to His Excellency about the mules of wagon drivers Marco and Iacopo Brinciassi,
58 is here now, and will not leave until the French spearmen arrive; they
and he immediately called for his First Secretary so that the matter would be swiftly handled.
are expected this week. Also soon to arrive are the Swiss, whom they say will number
Yesterday, Lord Paolo Orsini arrived in these parts dressed as a messenger to
around 3000. Infantry and captains around Imola: Dionigi from Naldo, 600 men;
explain himself to His Lordship. He had been urgently called for by
Marcantonio from Fano, 600; Comandantore, 600; Romolino, 500;
Valentino and came to justify what had taken place in Urbino
Master di Sala, 400; Sgalla, 300; Grechetto, 200; the Spaniard Salzeto, 300;

and to find out the Duke's intentions so that he can refer to the others. Today he sent

Giambattista Mancino, 400; Mangiares, 200; Giannetto from Seville, 150.

one of his men to those with whom he is allied to find out their decision.

Armed soldiers: the Spaniard Don Ugo, 50; the Spaniard Monsignore d'Allegri, 50;

I could not find out anything further, nor do I expect to be able to do so,

Don Giovanni from Cardona, 50. These last three companies are smaller because

as His Lordship is extremely secretive. What he harbors in his soul towards Lord Orsini,

of the onslaught they suffered at the hands of the Vitelli forces and the resulting retreat.

I cannot verily judge.

They said Conte Lodovico della Mirandola had 60, but I discovered there were 40.

His First Secretary approached me to discuss the matter and explain the arrival

He and his forces are 6 miles away from here now.

of Lord Paolo and said, "They merely want the Duke to reassure them,

Rinieri della Sassetta, 100 crossbowmen. Master Francesco da Luna,

but it remains to be seen how this will be done."

50 musketeers on horseback. Other men from Lombardy will be arriving soon.

They speak of peace but prepare for war. There is no

They say that three troops of mounted soldiers have set up camp in Faenza.

movement of the allies, neither coming nor going: this truce is very ambiguous,

How many others are spread out around Romagna remains to be seen. I will be ever vigilant.

and the winner will be he who best deceives the other, the one with more men and allies.

Imola, 31 October, 1502

Your Servant, Niccolò Machiavelli, Secretary

CHAPTER TWENTY

The moon is full tonight. Right about now, Florence would have been under attack, Niccolò thinks as he walks to the Rocca. He is proud of what he managed to do and feels deep gratitude for Dianora.

He hasn't seen her in some time. He didn't see her when he brought Valentino the gonfalonier's request about the mules or when he asked for papers of safe conduct on behalf of the Dieci for the merchants. At his last encounter with Borgia, he handed over the chapter on the death of the Duke of Bisceglie.

His thoughts have often gone to Dianora. She must have realized by now that things did not go exactly as she hoped: Valentino did not leave for Tuscany before the full moon, and if he were to leave now he would never catch up to his army at the border. She is probably wondering what actually happened. Surely she is upset. But she also knows how even the best intentions can go askew and produce results that run contrary to all expectations. By telling him about Ulivieri, Dianora managed to save Florence, at least for now. But she didn't obtain what she truly wanted, which was Borgia's death.

Had she heard anything new in the meantime? Had there been recriminations? Accusations? New plans?

When he steps out into the open area in front of the Rocca, he sees men still hard at work on the building and its cupola, using mules to transport large pieces of machinery full of gears and teeth.

Standing in front of the entrance is da Vinci. He examines the parts one by one before letting the men carry them inside. Niccolò would like to approach and observe him closer but he

134 · FRANCO BERNINI

recalls the man's cantankerous manner and decides against it. Even so, it's hard not to be curious.

Upstairs, Dianora is standing in front of the fireplace, facing the flames, her back to him. She neither turns around nor greets him when he walks in.

The duke is seated on his throne. He is wearing his black gloves and now even a black mask. He does this from time to time. It's one of his odd ways, like how he takes leopards with him when he goes hunting. While it doesn't shock Niccolò, it is a disturbing sight nonetheless. He also notices with some surprise that a thin, middle-aged archbishop is leaning over Valentino and applying leeches to him. This must be Gaspar Torrella: in addition to being a man of the church, he is also Borgia's master physician. Cesare holds out his arm casually so the man can continue bleeding him and scrutinizes Niccolò intently from behind the eyeholes of the mask.

"There has been a good deal of coming and going of messengers these past few days. Any news of import?" he asks coldly and gruffly.

"Nothing I haven't communicated to you in our meetings."

The duke continues to glare at him. "Can you tell me if there have been any executions in your city of late?"

"Not that I am aware of. Why do you ask?" Niccolò says, forcing himself not to look at Dianora. The interrogation is hard to sustain.

Valentino waves his hand as if to say that it's nothing, a minor matter, and then points to the pages that Niccolò had left him. "I read them and am satisfied. You have proved to be a strong writer. I would only like to add a few comments of a more general nature. You can decide where to insert them. Would you like to take notes?"

"With pleasure."

"The first consideration is this, and it stems from experience. Everyone confuses desire with reality—people thrive on hopes and dreams—but the fact of the matter is that people need to act in the world as it is."

Niccolò writes this down. "Well said. I'll find a good place to add this," he says reassuringly.

"I don't doubt it. Do you know Andrea Ulivieri?"

Niccolò stops writing, his hand hovering over the page. When he looks up, his eyes are clear. He knows that the slightest mistake could cost him his life. Dianora knows it, too. She turns a page of the book she is reading.

"Andrea . . . What was the last name again?"

"Ulivieri. He's a member of the guards that protect the city walls."

"It's a large unit. No, I don't know him. Why do you ask?"

"He wounded one of my men. I would like to find out more about him so that I can decide what actions to take."

"If you'd like I can enquire about him."

"I would be grateful. Another consideration that I would like to appear in *Res gestæ Cæsaris* is this: when men commit minor offenses they should either be thanked or ignored, but this is not so for serious offenses. When a serious offense is committed, it should be of such intensity that the person does not fear vendetta. Did you write all that down?"

"One moment . . . yes."

"As far as I'm concerned, I'm only cruel when strictly necessary. How strange, I was certain that you knew this Ulivieri man."

"I assure you that I do not. Why would you think that?"

"I was told that you did."

No one could have said as much. The Dieci do not know what has conspired and a leak could only have come from there. The gonfalonier surely maintained his secrecy.

"By whom?"

Borgia waves his hand casually in the air again to show that it is a negligible matter.

"There's far too much tongue-wagging in this world," Niccolò adds.

"This is true."

"You were saying that you are only cruel when strictly necessary . . . "

The duke nods. "Ulivieri has disappeared; my men in Florence can find no trace of him."

"How can a member of the armed guards disappear? Did he desert?"

"That's one hypothesis."

"If so, I can easily find out. How did he harm your man?"

"Ulivieri found out that he worked for me, so my man had to flee Florence. He was precious to me. He was the one who eliminated Duccio del Briga."

"Then I owe your man a debt of gratitude; I'll try to find out more."

"I'm counting on it. Yes, I'm only cruel when necessary. In Romagna, for example, I spilt rivers of blood."

Dianora gasps. The duke glances casually at her.

Niccolò realizes that he's intentionally torturing her. Somehow he has to stop him. "But in that instance, you had a clear plan. We could use your comment about acting on reality as a way of introducing that accomplishment."

A muscle in Dianora's neck relaxes. She breathes deeper, grateful for the diversion.

"You're right, Machiavelli. That campaign was more or less a bloodletting," Valentino says, gesturing at the leeches. "Sometimes it's necessary to do so in order to acquire new strength. Those lands needed law and order, and that was the only way to bring it about. Now, in fact, almost all of them are at peace."

Dianora shudders almost imperceptibly. Valentino stops his cruel rant. His mood has changed; talking about his successful campaigns has lifted his spirits.

"Almost all?"

"The task is not yet complete but it soon will be. I crushed the inept despots and thieves that ran those cities and I have built a single and fair state. The inhabitants are grateful to me. I would like you to write about this. Actually I would like you to go and see what is happening in the duchy with your own eyes. Would you enjoy that? That way you can write about it with firsthand knowledge of the facts."

Niccolò hesitates. Why is Borgia trying to send him away from Imola? Is it because he doesn't want to have inquisitive people around? Does he want to be free to attack Florence from a new direction? Does he have other spies in his city besides Andrea Ulivieri? Or does he know what transpired and want to kill Niccolò while he is traveling? Is the suggested journey actually a death sentence? And why was he so keen for Dianora to listen in to this conversation?

"Of course you want to," Borgia insists. "Like all writers, more than anything else, you are deeply curious."

Now Borgia is trying to flatter him. And Niccolò can't refuse the invitation.

"Will I be free to go wherever I want? And talk to anyone I please?"

Valentino nods. The archbishop-physician begins to detach the leeches from his body. "Wherever you travel, you will be safe. In this way, you'll begin to understand what I have in mind: a new Italy."

"Did you say 'Italy'?"

"Of course."

Niccolò looks at him; all concerns have vanished. "That word, for me . . . well . . . I might be Florentine by birth but I suffer deeply at seeing Italy divided into a myriad of small states . . . "

"And governed by idiots! Constantly bickering among themselves!"

"Yes, unfortunately. I would like nothing more than to see Italy united under a single fair and sovereign leader."

The prince nods in approval but is also quick to offer a sarcastic comment. "This is the first time I've seen you animated by something, Machiavelli. Tell me: do you think your city could actually be this leader?" He turns to the physician and dismisses him after saying a few words to him softly in Valencian.

Niccolò replies with verve. "Yes, I do. Florence is not just powerful, its foundation rests on all the virtues of the first Roman republic."

"Ah, our virtuous ancestors . . . Did you know that your gonfalonier is seeking to extend his position for life? Did you know that?"

Niccolò stares at him in silence. He had heard it mentioned before he left, but only in the vaguest of terms, in order to protect Soderini from the factious opposition. He understood the rationale behind it and could appreciate its advantages, and he almost agreed with the notion, but he saw how dangerous it could be, too. He had been pleased when people stopped talking about it.

"I know that it has been discussed," he says cautiously. "But, if it were to happen, Soderini's reach would be controlled by other magistrates of the Republic. In this, my city has established an excellent balance of power, guaranteeing the will of the people."

"For now, perhaps. Even though what you call balance of power is really just confusion . . . You're too intelligent not to understand that power does not tolerate limitations of any kind; that is its nature. I find it healthy while you do not. And yet you surely know that this is how the Republican era of ancient Rome ended. You must accept that ours is an era of emperors, kings, and princes," Borgia says, indicating himself.

Niccolò is silent. The comment has affected him deeply but he tries hard not to show it.

"Do you think he suspects us?" Niccolò whispers to Dianora from the passageway that leads to the church garden. She is kneeling on the prie-dieu, while Brother Timoteo rustles around in the cabinet at the far end of the sacristy and pulls out a form of cheese.

"The duke is suspicious of everyone. He asked you those questions because he wanted to put you to the test. He interrogated me, too. What happened to the man who was supposed to open the gate at Porta al Prato? Why did he ask you about him?"

"I do not know. The duke must have news that I do not. It may be that Ulivieri actually escaped; maybe the man realized that he was involved in something far too dangerous."

"Why did he ask you if there had been any executions recently in Florence?"

"It was his way of finding out what I know."

"And why did he decide not to carry through with the attack?"

"For now he has not, but who knows what will happen in the future."

Dianora is skeptical. She looks behind her, into the nave. Lucina is staring at something and the soldier who's been assigned to her is nowhere to be seen. Dianora turns all the way around and looks long and hard at Niccolò.

"This is not what I expected to happen. Maybe I was wrong to trust you but I had no choice. I still don't."

What can he possibly say in response? He can't tell her the truth, of course. And yet the lie weighs heavily on him. He shifts the conversation onto another topic.

"Believe me when I say that the duke is as much your enemy as ours."

The prior coughs. He motions to remind them that Dianora shouldn't risk drawing attention to herself by constantly turning around. She goes back to staring at the confessor's empty chair and is silent, uncertain if she should continue or not.

The friar glances nervously at Niccolò. He had wanted a hefty sum of florins for this second encounter; it had not been easy to convince him to do it.

"Have you heard anything new, Milady?"

She hesitates before answering, then shakes her head. "He hasn't met with his men in the throne room to give orders recently. As of yesterday, he has cancelled all audiences. He's in a terrible mood and more violent than usual. Every so often it happens."

"Florence is ready for battle, thanks to you."

"Are you saying that he'll declare war all the same?"

"Yes. I don't know when, but he definitely will. And we won't back down."

Dianora's face lights up. Even though Niccolò can't see it, he notices how her shoulders soften. He looks away from her and into the nave to see what the guard and Lucina are doing. They are standing together and chatting, they're not looking at the sacristy.

"Why do you have to go and visit Romagna?"

"He didn't give me a choice. You heard him yourself."

"He often talks about my land. He takes pleasure in making me suffer. I appreciated the fact that you interrupted him and changed the topic. But then he got his hooks into you by talking about Italy." Dianora's tone has grown hard. "He really does not care about it at all, but he knows from his spies that you yearn for unity. Don't you realize that he's trying to appeal to the writer in you so that you'll forget about your task as envoy of the Republic? He did the same thing with others who came before you. He sent them around Romagna so that they would speak well of him."

"Others?"

"Yes, but he didn't like their work as much and so he dismissed them. He's satisfied with yours, at least for now. He says that you understand him."

So Borgia wants to send him away from Imola out of vanity, not to have him killed. Niccolò is silent. Dianora keeps talking.

"You don't know him like I unfortunately do. He's only strong thanks to his father, who has usurped the throne of God on earth. But the Almighty will not allow this to carry on forever. When you go to my city, remember that without the help of the Pope and the King of France, he would never have been able to conquer us." She speaks with a sense of deep pride. A person can even be proud of a terrible defeat, Niccolò thinks to himself. But then she recalls the price she had to pay and sadness overcomes her. She sighs.

She starts to speak again, this time in a feeble voice but with tired determination. "We retreated to rooms in the fortress that were located next to a chapel. In my innocence I thought that if things went badly we could hide out there, that no one would touch us because it was a holy space. When I said as much to my father, I felt so strong, as if I had found a way of saving us. He looked at me sadly, caressed my cheek, and let me believe it." Dianora brings a hand to her face and sobs softly with grief, then brings her hand back down to the other in her lap.

"I believe I met your father once, actually. Was his name Valerio?"

"Yes."

"I met him in July of that year, when the Republic sent me to your city. He was a sharp man, full of spirit." And now that he thinks about it, Dianora resembles him, not just physically but also in her manner of speaking.

"He loved to laugh. And he did, for as long as he could . . ." Dianora's voice breaks, but she finds strength to go on. "Did you really speak to him?"

"Twice, actually. I recall how he enjoyed the trust of the Countess, too."

"He tried everything to save both his Ladyship's life and our own. She was contrary to all negotiations, but even so, he initiated talks with the duke's envoy. It was the first time my father disobeyed her and he did it for us, for his family. We would've surrendered if Borgia had let us; and we would have given him all the gold we had. They even let my father believe that it was feasible. My father was deluded, just like me. How Borgia loves to lie . . . In our final days together, my father seemed serene.

We thought we would be freed, and that made everything that happened afterwards even crueler. And your 'Italy' just stood by watching."

"Everyone admired your strength and resistance."

"But no one lifted a finger to help us! Italy is not a fair or just place. It listens only to whoever is strongest."

Niccolò does not reply. She is right. He observes her in silence. If he could see her face, he would see how her pain has transformed her, making the light in her eyes even more intense.

"They came for us in the middle of the night. We were awoken by shouting and the sound of fighting. My father and brothers took up their weapons and looked at us one last time. We women shut ourselves in the chapel and locked it from the inside. In addition to my mother and me, there were two other girls with their mother. They, too, sought safety in the chapel. We prayed with all our might, but the Lord didn't hear us . . . Amidst all the shouting I recognized the voice of my father: he didn't back down, he continued to incite his men to fight, and I heard his cries of pain when he fell. I also heard Giacomo, my older brother, beg for mercy. They threw him off the bastion with Ugo, my younger brother, who pleaded for his life, too. Then they broke down the door of the chapel, there were about ten of them, French, all covered in blood and sweat, excited by the victory, like wild beasts. We ran for safety behind the altar, but before they could touch us, a voice stopped them. It was him, Borgia, that killer, that assassin. He, too, was covered in blood. I had never seen him before but I could tell he was the leader. All the soldiers obeyed him. My mother thanked him, he looked at her ferociously, and then he saw me."

She doesn't have the strength to go on. Niccolò can imagine the rest. Having chosen his prey, Borgia left the other women to the soldiers.

"Afterwards, they cut my mother's throat. But not mine. I still wonder why . . . " Dianora continues speaking, it's as if she's casting off a burden. She gasps, struggles to breathe, tries to control herself so as not to risk anything. "My life ended that day. I cry when I wake up and cry when I go to sleep. I have nightmares. Even if they give me medicine to help me sleep, I can never rest for more than a few hours. When dawn arrives, I sit up and start thinking, and the tears start rolling down my cheeks. It takes enormous effort, but I also can't sit idly by. I have to do something to chase away the terrible thoughts, thoughts that pursue me. Even writing—because now and then I write sonnets—is so deeply tiring."

"I am sorry to have made you talk about all of this."

"Talking about it with you brings me relief, as I said last time. I have no one else to confide in. If you only knew how hard it is to stay silent . . . The world has been cruel with me. I had never been with a man before. I had never left Forlì except for a short trip to Venice with my father. Oh, how my father adored me . . . " She sighs deeply. "The thing I fear most is losing my soul to that terrible man. I don't want to become the woman he wants me to be."

"It's one thing to be forced to do something but to lose one-self is an entirely different matter."

"But how long can a person continue to do something they find repugnant before they become that very thing?"

"You will never be the same as the evil done to you."

Of this, Niccolò is certain. He has never seen so much melancholy dignity in a person. Dianora sighs again, but this time it as if a weight has been lifted, at least temporarily, from her shoulders.

The prior gestures to them from the far corner. His face is livid with tension.

Dianora tries to compose herself. Niccolò glances at the nave: Lucina and the guard are sitting in a pew, talking. Now and then the woman glances at the sacristy and then back at the soldier.

Dianora starts to speak again. "I beg you, when you go to Forlì, go to my family's tomb and place your hand on it for me.

It will be as though I am there. Surely they have been buried in San Francesco Grande, in the family chapel." As she speaks she slowly reaches out her right hand.

Niccolò nods, deeply moved. "I promise."

Dianora stands up quickly. When she returns to the nave, Lucina and the soldier get to their feet and escort her out of the church.

He watches her walk off. The thought of what Dianora suffered and continues to suffer brings him a sharp pain in both his chest and gut.

CHAPTER TWENTY-ONE

The road from Imola to the coast is crowded with people, animals, carts, and merchants. It's windy and clouds of dust swirl around them. Niccolò rides a docile and strong black horse. Wrapped in his mantle, he is grateful that his profession allows him to visit new places, meet people, and take journeys which he could otherwise never afford.

It's cold but sunny, and horseback riding is a pleasure in these conditions. On the right are the hills, while the plains extend to the left in a bluish hue. From how other people look at him, his horse, and his clothes, he realizes that they think he is a wealthy man and this amuses him greatly.

He observes people, too. He sees a young woman with a Greek profile carrying a bundle on her head; a child follows behind, grabbing at her skirt. A white-haired old farmer drives a cart full of vats of strong-smelling grape must. Three men with pale, cruel faces look like they've been up all night.

Niccolò has his old tabard in his sack in case it starts to rain. Before leaving, he removed the holy medallion that Marietta had sewn on it and left it at the inn. In one of the pockets of his robe he carries the letter of safe conduct from Borgia, which obliges soldiers and subjects to let him pass without paying taxes or duties. Innkeepers at rest stops must provide him with food, lodgings, and the best horses they have. And everyone else he encounters along the way has to offer their help any way he might need.

He thinks back to what Dianora said about Valentino. It's true that without the money and military might of the Church the duke would be no one. On the other hand, he is making the most of the good Fortune that he has been dealt, as they say, and not everybody is capable of that.

Two opposing truths, side by side. The world is full of con- tradictions. None of them ever weighed heavily on him, but he finds this one a burden.

What is happening? Dianora's words have gotten under his skin. He shares her hatred for the man. At the same time, he can't ignore the relevance of everything the Prince has confided in him about power, or his keen intelligence for that matter. This troubles him and he continues to mull it over. The best preaching comes from the worst pulpits, he once heard some- one in the Chancery say, and he knew immediately what that meant.

He is startled out of his reverie when he hears someone shout at him. Without realizing it he had been riding directly toward a man leading a mule that carried a woman with pitch- black hair. He apologizes and guides his horse more carefully.

The main gate to Forlì is greyish yellow, imposing, and flanked by two defense towers. Niccolò was there six months before Borgia conquered it, sent as a simple envoy, as usual. *Humilis, minimus servitor*, he used to sign his letters. But at that time, he had reached the city via a different route, along the Castrocaro road, and he had entered through a different gate. He had been sent to negotiate the acquisition of gunpow- der and cannonballs, and to renew a mercenary contract for Florence with the son of the Countess. As such, every minute of his time was counted for. Now things are different; he can look around and observe the people freely.

Waiting for him at the gate, near the soldiers on duty, is a man dressed in bright colors. He bows to him. "Lord Machiavelli, I am the secretary to the castellan. Have you ever been to Forlì? It will be my pleasure to act as your guide."

Niccolò bows deeply in reply. "Thank you for your kind wel- come. Yes, I have been here before and, as you will read in the duke's missive, I have complete freedom to move around and see whatever I choose."

The man frowns and doesn't even glance at the papers. "As you wish, but grant me at least the privilege of having you as my guest at the fortress for dinner, and to spend the night."

"Thank the castellan for me; I will gladly join you."

"That way we'll be able to talk about everything you learn in the meantime," the secretary says sarcastically, stepping to one side, and allowing Niccolò to enter the city. But then, overcome by his own arrogance, he says, "And how exactly do you plan on getting to know the inhabitants of a city that is not your own?"

"I have my ways," Niccolò replies. "And they've never failed me."

The prostitute has luminous, olive skin. Originally from Puglia, she came to Forlì to live with a rogue of a man who was initially charming but really only wanted to take advantage of her. She realised it soon enough. And yet, she was still in love with him.

She earned the nickname La Scura because of her dark skin. She was there when Borgia invaded and conquered the city. Niccolò suavely gets her to talk about those days. It was December, it rained constantly, it was bitterly cold, and everything happened all at once. If the townspeople surrendered, Valentino promised them protection, but that's hardly what came to pass. His troops, the French and German armies, and the soldiers of the Church all started sacking houses. She, herself, was not harmed because she managed to hide in a cellar.

Things went less well in the fortress, which resisted for a month. The sound of exploding cannons was incessant and the air was practically unbreathable due to the acrid stench of gunpowder, an odor that was new to La Scura. There were countless deaths, and even more were wounded. La Scura still remembered the sound of the men yelling to defend the fortress, and then, when the fortress was breached, the sound of both men and women screaming in pain. Then came the wailing. And finally, silence.

All cities change hands now and then, she knew that well. She had seen it happen elsewhere, as she traveled up the length of Italy.

Two years have passed since then, and people complain less now. Many, the majority, are pleased with Valentino; most of the men who govern the city are far better than the ones who worked for the Countess.

The Mambelli family chapel in the church of San Francesco Grande is tucked away in a corner between the transept and the nave, not far from the main altar. It's the only one with unlit candles. Its walls are frescoed in lively colors with scenes from the Passion.

Niccolò walks over and examines the burial plaques: the oldest ones date back two hundred years while the most recent ones are from only ten years ago.

An old woman notices him. "Did you know the Mambelli family?" she asks.

"I am a distant relative from Florence."

"I thought there was no one left except the daughter, who met with a terrible fate."

"She's a cousin of mine."

The woman peers at him closely and shakes her head. "Poor girl, how I pity her. That family had everything; some of their ancestors are even buried near the reliquaries of the True Cross, under the central altar. A rare privilege. But they were stubborn people. You just can't fight some things."

"I know what you mean. I don't see the tombs for the family members who died recently; I thought they would be buried here, among their ancestors."

"Their bodies were thrown into the crypt along with every-one else when the battle ended," the old woman says, pointing to an oak trapdoor in the floor at the end of the transept. "It was practically overflowing with bodies . . . So many people died."

Niccolò imagines the bodies being carelessly dumped into the pit and sprinkled with lime: mothers, fathers, brothers, sisters; the old and young, all piling up on top of other cadavers that were already decomposing and putrefying; thieves and other wrongdoers, eventually all reduced to bone and dust.

He says nothing.

"May they rest in peace," the old woman says, crossing herself and kissing her fingers.

Niccolò walks over to the trapdoor. He bends down and gently rests his hand on it for a long moment.

Outside, he stops at a gurgling water fountain in a quiet piazza, leans over the spout, and gulps some water. He dries his mouth with the back of his hand and looks up at an elegant, three-story home across the way. Its large windows have marble sills and elegant arches. The sky is heavy with dark clouds.

"Is that where the Mambelli family used to live?" he asks a middle-aged passerby with a large mole on his face.

The man looks at him suspiciously. "Why do you want to know?"

"I sold them some fabric a while ago and they owe me money. I just arrived from France and heard what happened."

"The family was decimated. Now the building houses a Rota, a court of appeals set up by the duke."

"A court of appeals?"

"Yes, and it travels all around Romagna. When they're in Forlì, the judge holds court there. Anyone can go and ask him for justice. And he doesn't grant special consideration to the powerful, either, not like before."

Niccolò looks up at the house, and points to where the sitting room must once have been. "Is that where he holds audiences?"

"Yes, there's one going on now. Anyone can go in and listen.

Did you have a contract with Mambelli? Were there witnesses to the contract?"

"Witnesses? Yes. And yes, I have a written contract."

"Then you should go in and petition for compensation from the State; they took over all the wealth and goods that belonged to the people who rebelled. I'm sure you'll get the money you're owed." The man goes on to enthusiastically explain how the new justice system is different and better than the earlier one: it used to be that the magistrates were all from Forlì, they all knew each other; now they're from other towns. They pass judgement and move on. Before Valentino took over, the judges' only job was to make sure the rich slept well at night, and they were very good at doing that. Anyone who didn't follow the rules or fought back was marginalized and left to rot, like that fellow, Baldassarre: he didn't follow anyone's rules and survived only by stealing a little here and there. Back then, when a judge ruled in favor of the rich, he received money and honors. Now the tune has changed, and everyone is deeply grateful to the duke for it."

Niccolò goes inside and walks upstairs to the stately hall: its walls are of light-colored stone, the ceiling is high, and a pearl-grey light shines through the windows. He observes the crowd, cheek to jowl: they're workers, common folk.

He goes and stands in front of a window from which he can see the room in its entirety. He continues to study the people, noticing an eagerness, a sense of expectation. He tries to hear what people around him are saying. He has always enjoyed eavesdropping: he takes in everything and retains only what is useful.

Three women are discussing a sentence that the Rota emitted the day before. A rich nobleman who had always been forgiven was forced to compensate a carpenter whom he hadn't paid for his work. Because the nobleman had his men beat the carpenter to keep him quiet, the nobleman had also been sentenced to ten beatings with a stick. The punishment would take place the following Sunday in front of the Duomo. It didn't matter that he was from an important family, who his relatives were, or that he had hired the best lawyers. The case had also been very enjoyable to watch, one of the three women says, and it sounds like the one that will take place today will be equally, if not more, entertaining. The judge will be ruling on a notable timber merchant who chopped down wood from a city-owned forest without permission.

Niccolò looks at the accused man. Heavyset, red in the face, and all dressed in black, he stands talking to his lawyer, who is tall and pale. Nearby are two guards dressed in Borgia's colors.

He tries to imagine the great hall when Dianora lived there. It must have seemed enormous to her when she was a child and then, for many years, it was probably the center of her happy world, until war forced the family to seek refuge in the fortress. She surely received guests there, banqueted, danced, and celebrated Christmas and Easter in that room. He can almost imagine her gliding nimbly between all the people.

Strolling, dancing, and smiling.

Smiling. It occurs to him that he has never seen her smile. He is overcome with such a deep emotion that he's forced to look away, outside, onto the piazza below. He sees people hurrying by, two carts cross paths, two women stop to talk at the fountain from which he had drunk not long before.

The crowd buzzes and he turns to see why: the judge has walked in. He's tall and lanky, he has a Roman nose, and his eyes shine brightly. As soon as he opens his mouth to speak, Niccolò hears someone say that, based on his accent, he must be from Rimini: an outsider, not someone who is part of local politics. They approve heartily.

The case unfolds swiftly. The court has done their research well and they have clear proof. The judge measures his words, asks careful questions, and in an artificially benevolent manner he deflates the lies that he is told. Niccolò admires his style:

he's serious, goes into detail, and is never swayed by rhetoric. The public, meanwhile, is somewhat let down. They preferred the judge from the day before, who was from Bologna, and a prodigious orator. Even so, they're satisfied with the sentence the judge emits: the timber merchant has to pay a hefty fine and spend eight months in prison. The guards take him away.

Someone yells out that justice has finally been served.

As he's walking to the fortress, with night falling fast, he sees dozens of Swiss mercenaries in their black and red doublets. Niccolò observes the stately home in which they are housed; it too must have once belonged to an important family who resisted Valentino. As he passes by, he sees about twenty soldiers standing around a bright bonfire in the court-yard, drinking and laughing while two whole pigs roast over the flickering flames.

In one corner he sees a cluster of pikes: they must be about nine arms' long. Niccolò begins to suspect that Borgia is scattering his troops all across Romagna to conceal just how many of them there actually are. The duke is aware that Niccolò will notice this; it's a display of his power and he wants Niccolò to inform Florence of it.

When he arrives at the fortress he looks for signs of the attack, but there's no trace of it, except for the bricks of a different color where the wall was breached. Clearly, reconstruction was done rapidly and carefully.

"His Excellency found Romagna to be run by incapable lords who, instead of governing their subjects, robbed and plundered them. These lands were once full of thieves and brigands, but the Prince brought order to the people. He has united them and instilled peace." The castellan, Gonzalo de Mirafuentes, speaks Italian well. A skinny man, he eats voraciously and enthusiastically, slurping down his capon skin soup and talking at the same time.

"What about the people? Do they all support him, or did the war leave some scars?" Niccolò asks, sprinkling his soup with powdered cinnamon, a delicacy he's tasted only once before.

"Did you notice any misgivings in the people you spoke to?" the secretary interrupts him to ask.

"No, but I think it is a fair question to ask."

"Yes, your Lordship, it is a fair question," Mirafuentes replies. He takes a sip of his wine then wipes his lips. "The difficulties we encountered in the recent past did indeed generate some hatred, but the duke is now purging these feelings, and soon he will win over all the inhabitants. He has instituted a court of appeals, presided over by a very capable man, so that the people will have justice."

"Yes, actually I saw the court at work."

"And what impression did it give you?"

"Admirable."

"That is not His Excellency's only reform. He is also dividing Romagna into four districts to govern it better. He has put Leonardo da Vinci in charge of rebuilding and reinforcing the fortresses that were damaged, although he knows well that this will be for naught without the support of the people, as Caterina Sforza learned at her own expense when she tried to resist him here—against the will of her own people, who instead welcomed us." As the castellan speaks he gestures proudly at the vast hall around them, as if it were a trophy.

Niccolò had been in that room before, when he was sent as an envoy and received by Caterina Sforza in the room next door. A robust and pretty blonde, Caterina was a strong and astute negotiator. She sold him infantrymen, gunpowder, and cannonballs in exchange for Florence's help in fending off Cesare Borgia, a danger she had even then perceived.

She was a courageous woman and, when needed, cruel. She revealed this side of her character when a number of conspirators killed her husband and took her children as hostages in the fortress. She chose to meet with the rogues personally. When they threatened to kill her children, she boldly raised her skirts and showed them her pudendum, saying that there were more children where they came from. She won that battle, reconquered the fortress, and then exacted her vengeance coldly. But she lost to Valentino. Mirafuentes was right: a fortress is not enough without the support of its people.

When they finish their soup, three servants rush over and clear their plates.

"The duke is well-liked because he made it safe for people to live here. Ask anyone, the majority will tell you as much," the castellan insists.

"I believe that the envoy is already doing that. He's talking to just about everyone," the secretary intervenes.

The servants bring out a dish of sturgeon, first boiled and then fried to a crisp, covered with its eggs and a slightly tart sauce.

"His Excellency has a special place in his heart for Romagna," Mirafuentes says, bringing a large forkful of the fish to his mouth and chewing noisily. "His plan is to make it a place of happiness, the center of his kingdom."

Niccolò's chambers in the fortress are located next to the chapel. It's a spacious apartment, with many rooms. He's almost certain that it's the same place where the Mambelli family sought refuge but he thinks it's probably wise not to ask.

When he's alone, he chooses a room with a single bed, wondering if this was where Dianora slept. He moves about gingerly, respectfully, as if she had indeed stayed there and he didn't want to disrupt something that had once belonged to her.

The heavy furniture is made of walnut. As he is unpacking, he takes a false step and falls onto a corner of the dresser; its sharp edge jabs him in the ribs and knocks the wind out of him for a few seconds.

When he catches his breath, he goes over to the window and

looks out at the moon. He wonders how long it takes to truly forget the scars of war and change of regime. Even Florence is peaceful in appearance, but he knows that the followers of the Medici family, who were chased out eight years earlier, are numerous and powerful, and that they continue to plot against the Republic. Forlì seems calm, but how can Valentino have won over the hearts of all its inhabitants in only two years' time?

He lies down on the bed—the moonlight shines through the window—and while the fatigue of the day begins to overcome him and his muscles begin to relax, he thinks about Dianora and how she slept there, about her inner strength despite all that she lived through. The words of Boccaccio come to mind: *bocca basciata non perde ventura, anzi rinnuova come fa la luna.*[1] She has survived, and may well be stronger because of it, but she has been forced to pay a hefty price.

And what of him? He's full of doubts and painful thoughts. The news that Pier Soderini will probably be gonfalonier for life has shaken him. Damn that ambitious man and his manipulative ways. Damn the Dieci, too, for not realizing that they have a spy in their midst, that they are being duped by a foreign Prince. Damn the people of Florence, whiners and complainers the lot of them, capable of exploding with rage but then forgetting about everything, like a passing storm.

Damn Borgia, that rapist, and his greed for other people's lands; he's cruel with the weak and cowardly with the strong; he's false, self-aggrandizing, and evil. Damn the duke's father, too, who has never done or thought of anything other than deceiving his fellow man, always finding people who are gullible.

Damn Vitellozzo, whose French sickness is driving him insane; damn all the Orsinis, whose allegiances fluctuate like a weathervane; damn the lord of Fermo who killed his relatives and took their place, damn the incestuous lord of Perugia, and damn the lord of Siena, who is weak and a turncoat; damn the lord of Bologna, who can barely take a step without sinking. Damn everyone these men are connected to, separate from, uncertain about, or cruel with. Damn even those they want to kill.

Damn the Very Christian King of France, who's just one big chicken thief, concerned only with nabbing other people's lands and defending himself from other chicken thieves. Damn the Catholic Kings of Spain, the Emperor, and even the Great Turk.

Damn all of Italy, which after all is only a name: hundreds and hundreds of cities incapable of joining together, each one wanting the death of their neighbor more than their own life, always so petty, lacking in greatness, never thinking of the future.

And damn you, too, he says to himself as he falls asleep, you poor sod, from your lowly background and fallen nobility, the offspring of ironmongers; poorer than even your poorest ancestors; so cruel with that unfortunate damsel, interested only in getting information out of her, continuing to do so even though it weighs heavily on you. You, Niccolò, with your coat of arms that depicts iron nails! Nails!

CHAPTER TWENTY-TWO

V alentino's troops spread out like a dark sea across the moonlit fields outside Florence, armor clanking and horses whinnying. Soldiers advance rapidly across fields and through hedges, footsteps muffled by the earth. Thousands of them. Every so often there's the flash of a lantern.

The troops can see where to go thanks to the light of the moon shining in the dark sky, but it's not so bright that anyone who sees them from high up on the ramparts could tell just how many of them there are.

But no one sees them. Only Niccolò, and he's paralyzed with terror. He opens his mouth to scream but no voice comes out, only a long groan.

As the wind whips down from the mountains, he feels the moisture from the rocky walls deep in his bones. He watches as a hundred or more foot soldiers rush the gate at Porta al Prato; someone sends up a flare, an intermittent signal. Ulivieri replies from up high, his skin shining white in the silvery glow. He's naked except for his unlatched helmet; a large knife is wedged deep in his belly, the blood around the wound is caked and dry.

The bastions to Niccolò's left crumble softly, as if made of sand. A long crack appears in the protective stone wall, splitting it open and extending like lightning, creating deep gouges in the earth from which shoot tall, fiery flames.

He sees the Arno to his right—even though he knows it can't possibly be there as it flows on the other side—teeming with boats crowded with Swiss mercenaries, their pikes poking forward like the quills of a porcupine, the river itself a black and bloody gash in the defenseless body of the city.

The bells toll and toll. He glances behind him: enemy forces have already entered the city, soldiers engage in battle around him. A horrifying tangle of human bodies tear at each other like snakes, fighting with spears and hatchets and swords.

He shivers, then looks down at his hands and sees he is entirely defenseless, with neither weapons nor armor. He's standing in a deep puddle of foul water. The gonfalonier lies on the ground, his throat slit, his mouth twisted in an obscene snarl. Niccolò doesn't dare approach the body as people might think he killed the man.

A woman's shrill scream makes him spin around, a girl with long red hair; she is struggling to free herself from a terrifying man in black armor who has pushed her up against the bastion and is tearing her clothes off, with the intention of raping her. To defend herself she has managed to jab a small hook into his neck and blood spurts everywhere.

Niccolò would like to step between them but he can't move, he can't react, he's in the throes of agony.

The woman tugs on the hook. She and the man tumble into the putrid water.

He doesn't have the strength to watch so he looks elsewhere. Farther down the ramparts, in a bed surrounded by green curtains, under white sheets and a red blanket, he sees Marietta and Primerana: silent, pale, and desperate. Enormous black rats scurry around the bed, in and out of the water, trying to claw their way up the blankets. He wants to run toward them but cannot.

Behind him, Florence is on fire. Flames shoot out the windows and doorways of the stately buildings, their great wooden portals smashed in. People try and put out the fires but the wind constantly revives them.

Now the man who's been stabbed with the hook turns around and stares at Niccolò, who tries to keep his distance. Suddenly, Niccolò feels a smooth rope tighten around his neck, then someone hammers a nail into his temple. He falls to the ground and is dragged by the feet through the water. He holds a sharp scythe in his right hand and swipes out at the air around him, trying to free himself. He is overcome by an unknown and invisible strength; his arm turns onto himself, the blade sinks into his ribcage, slices him open, his ribs crack, the wound grows deeper, a man screams in pain.

His own voice wakes him up, he's covered in sweat, it feels like the nightmare has not yet ended. He waves both hands in front of him to banish it, chase it away, but it overtakes him. The only thing he can use to defend himself is that tiny hook of reason. He reaches for it and yanks on it with all his might.

CHAPTER TWENTY-THREE

The vivid dream and the fear that something serious is about to happen stay with him as he gets dressed.

Sunlight distances the ghosts, but they don't disappear entirely. Only when he steps outside into the street does the cold brisk morning air chase them away for good.

As he continues on in his journey, Niccolò notices that the fields that extend between Forlì and Cesena have not been ploughed in a very long time. This means that farmers won't be able to sow new seeds, the time for which is fast approaching. Niccolò knows the names of all the plants on his land in Albergaccio. Some of them were passed down to him from his father: Little Mandolin, Always Loaded, Marvelous. He understands the soil. He gets off his horse to pick up a handful, crumbles it, and lets it fall through his fingers. It's healthy and rich in nutrients, so why aren't they working it?

He stops for lunch at the humble home of some farmers. The house sits between an oak and linden tree and is protected by a weathered wooden fence.

The head of the household is a bald man with gentle eyes, around fifty, his skin wrinkled and dark from working outdoors. His wife is younger; she has a round, wide face and her hair is still black. Three sons, their wives, and children live there too. All the family members are emaciated. Seeing such gaunt children makes Niccolò deeply sad.

The woman welcomes him warmly. She gladly sets a place for him at the table so he can regain his strength and continue onward. Her husband invites him to sit on a bench, while children and grandchildren gather around. His wife blows on the ashes in the fireplace to get the fire going, shucks some beans, and puts them on to cook.

They bring out a few small terracotta amphorae with two kinds of olives, some cheese and bread. The woman then sets down some eggs that have been cooking in the embers, together with a basket of sweet-smelling apples and grapes. They serve him water from the well. Niccolò feels like he has never eaten such good food. Time passes quickly as he engages in conversation with these good people.

"Why are the fields around here left fallow? The soil is good, I myself have a farm in Tuscany and know about such things."

"Because we don't have any grain," the man says both sadly and cautiously.

"Why not?"

"There's none to be found . . . "

Niccolò perceives that the man is both embarrassed and wary about saying too much. Someone must be hoarding grain. "But the landowners, surely they have grain . . . " he says gently.

The head of the family nods slowly. "Yes, but they pay a great deal for it and are not willing to share it."

Without saying anything specific, he has told him everything. Someone is definitely stockpiling grain and reselling it at an impossibly high price. It can only be the governor, Ramiro de Lorqua, an able soldier—and thief. Niccolò says no more. He doesn't want to embarrass these kind folk.

"Ramiro the Ogre hides the grain and only sells it to certain people," one of the sons blurts out. "Meanwhile, we're dying of hunger."

The father looks at his son uneasily and then back at Niccolò. "Please, don't say anything to anyone. We'll get in trouble."

"Of course, I promise. I know how to keep my mouth shut. Anyway, I'm only passing through."

Borgia knows how to pick his soldiers but not his administrators, he thinks.

He would like to pay for the lunch and takes some coins out

of his pouch. They look at the money, it's an immense amount for them and would make their life much easier, but they don't accept it. Niccolò tries to insist but is unsuccessful. They accompany him to his horse and say their warm goodbyes. He knows he will never see them again and yet he already feels close to them. It's hard to say farewell.

When he gets to the fence, he's tempted to leave a florin on the gate post but then he decides against it. He truly doesn't want to offend them.

The outline of Cesena lies ahead, faded yellow in the late afternoon light.

Suddenly, a cloud of dust appears ahead: three riders, galloping fast toward him, take up the entire road.

He observes them as they approach. They're wearing light armor and no helmets, their swords hang by their sides. Leading the group is a broad-shouldered man, around fifty, with long hair and a keenly intense gaze.

Niccolò is careful not to stare and rides over to the side of the road to let them pass, but they slow down and come to a brusque stop in front of him. From under the horses' hooves, pebbles shoot every which way. The cloud of dust is swept away by the wind.

The rider with the long hair hints at a salute. His face is chiseled and he has a muscular build. Niccolò notices a long scar running down his cheek.

It's Ramiro de Lorqua; he has come out to greet him. When Niccolò last changed horses, someone must have recognized him and alerted the governor. He looks bold, even brazen. His recent defeats don't seem to have disturbed him at all.

While Niccolò is pondering the reason for this encounter with Valentino's right hand man—he helped the duke conquer Romagna and is in charge of a vast territory, with much to do and steal—the knight holds out a sealed, personal message from Cesare. It has reached him via a series of messengers. Niccolò opens it and immediately recognizes the handwriting.

Niccolò, we trust you are enjoying your journey through Romagna. We kindly ask you to indulge us and grant the Governor the same trust and faith you have placed in us and spend an hour with him. Allow him to conduct you to a particular location, after which you may return to the path that most suits you.

In expectation of your news and return, and with salutations . . . .

He signs with his first name only. A swirly arabesque: the S in Cesare elongated and intersecting with a flourish on the C, which arches over his name like a scythe.

Niccolò glances at de Lorqua, who looks at him dutifully. The governor knows—he has been informed—that Niccolò doesn't want to be guided anywhere, but it would appear that de Lorqua desperately wants to show the envoy something that would otherwise be inaccessible to him, reserved only for soldiers: the stronghold of Cesena. He points up at it. It sits at the very top of the hill town and has thick new walls built in the French style, made to resist cannon balls.

From up there, he will be able to see the entire valley, the plains, the distant hills, and as far as the sea; surely such a view will be of great interest to the traveler.

De Lorqua has a playful but mischievous manner. Niccolò accepts the invitation, but continues to wonder why it is so important to Valentino.

The fortress holds a unique position from which they can see far off into the distance. The large inner courtyard is crowded with tents. It would appear that two armies of archers are camped out there, which means that Borgia also has men in Cesena. He clearly wants Niccolò to see this and the Republic to know it. But Niccolò is not there only for that.

From the highest point of the fortress, under the clear blue sky, everything looks so still and within reach. The sea shines on the horizon like a shiny strip of metal.

Niccolò takes in the recently reinforced walls. Florence can't afford such massive protection. De Lorqua informs him that not even the newest weapons can break through such walls. Cesena will become the capital of the Duchy, and the fortress will one day be the powerful heart of the city. He describes Valentino's ambitious plans: new frescoes for the churches; a university for the study of the liberal arts, engineering, and medicine; a vast library.

He points to a large building down below, which, together with several adjacent to it, is entirely covered with scaffolding. It looks like a spiderweb or an intricate forest of poles, and workers swarm across it.

"That's where His Excellency will transfer his court. His wife and daughter, Luisa, will join him there. It will be his royal palace. As you can see, he is uniting and enlarging several adjoining large homes."

De Lorqua then traces a line with his finger toward the coast, stopping at a dark spot that's barely perceptible on the horizon. "That's Cesenatico, our port city. The duke wants to make it more efficient, and Maestro da Vinci will take care of that. The entry to the canal was almost filled with sand but it is now accessible. And commerce with the East is flourishing again."

The governor touches his right shoulder and says that a scar from an old battle wound aches, a sign that tomorrow it will rain. Niccolò glances skeptically at the azure sky, it's hard to believe. De Lorqua insists, he's certain of it, he's never been wrong. The man then points to an area slightly inland and tells Niccolò to look carefully. "That, over there, is the Rubicon, which Julius Caesar crossed with his army when he set out to conquer Rome."

Niccolò stares hard at the spot. He knows about that historic moment from his studies, how it marked the end of the Republic and the beginning of the empire, but he never actually set eyes on the Rubicon. Although he doesn't believe that places have spirits, the way the ancient Romans did, he has to admit he feels a presence in the air. It must be his imagination, he thinks, and brushes away the thought.

"His Excellency went there in late summer. He spent the night on the river's edge, just thinking. He told me that he had an important dream while he was there."

"A dream?"

"Yes, he didn't say much more than that, except that it had to do with a prophesy an oracle once revealed to his father. Have you heard the story?"

"No."

"When the Pope was still a boy, the oracle told him that he would give birth to the king of Italy."

Of Italy no less, Niccolò thinks to himself.

"When my Lordship went to the Rubicon, he took a book with him which I would like to present to you as a gift."

De Lorqua hands him a volume bound in thick leather with gilt decorations. It's Plutarch's *Parallel Lives*, a text that Niccolò has long desired but could never afford.

He once saw a far less valuable copy, when he was twenty, in the library of his teacher, Marcello Adriani, now the Head Secretary of the Dieci, the man who signs their letters. He recalls the feel of the paper, how it practically crumbled in his fingers, not at all like this magnificent edition.

Niccolò holds the book in the palm of his hand. A bookmark decorated with the symbol for good fortune causes it to open to the section that has to do with Caesar and his passage across the Rubicon.

The following day Niccolò rides toward the sea in the pouring rain. He had wanted to go to Cesenatico but he lost his way during the violent thunderstorm. Then he caught sight of the sea. He stopped to remove his beautiful mantle, which he folded up and stored in his saddlebag, and put on his old black tabard, which kept him dry.

Although it is not raining that hard along the coast, the sky out at sea is as black as night, even though it's not yet midday. High waves, whipped by the wind, crash in dark metallic colors. The sound of the surf as it pounds the sand fills his ears.

Niccolò has never seen the Adriatic before, and only saw the Tyrrhenian two years earlier—he was, after all, born inland—when he was sent to oversee one of the many phases of the endless attack on Pisa. He had been impressed but not to any excessive degree: he had never been terribly swayed by the marvels of nature. But now he finds the sea truly awe inspiring.

Bobbing about on the tall waves, less than a quarter of a mile out to sea, is a small boat. Three fishermen, surprised by the storm, are struggling. He can't quite discern what they're doing. Slowly he realizes that they're trying to bail out the water that has collected in the bottom of the boat. Three small men against Nature.

Unable to do anything to help them and realizing their lives are in danger, he is distressed, but at the same time he finds their suffering fascinating to watch from where he stands at a safe distance.

He knows that sooner or later he, too, will encounter dangers, and that other people will look on who won't be able to help him. Like those fishermen, he will find himself at the mercy of something decisive, as impersonal and eternal as nature, something that decides the destiny of mankind: war, peace, the rise and fall of our lives. Will he be strong enough? Will he get by with only the virtues he possesses? Will he be lucky enough to survive?

He approaches the water's edge, which is somewhat dangerous because the wind and raging seas could easily drag him out, but he can't resist. If he could get closer to the fishermen, he feels like he might be able to save them.

He watches, holding his breath. The wind grows stronger, forcing itself deep into his lungs, the rain and saltwater splash up from the surf, slap his face and fill his mouth and nose. If he could see himself, he would perceive his tense expression, as if the future had already arrived, and it was indeed terrible, and he was struggling to survive.

The boat splits in two. He sees the two parts separating. The small figures are thrown into the water.

He cries out in horror but the sound vanishes in the howling wind.

Two of the fishermen manage to grab onto the larger portion of the boat and hold on for dear life, bobbing up and down on the waves.

The third man disappears below the waves.

The storm moves up into the Apennines, the sky clears, and soon only a few scattered clouds are left in the sky.

The luminous water of the Rubicon flows slowly past the grassy shore. Niccolò watches the river from the parapet of the three-arched Roman bridge, which was built after Julius Caesar crossed it. No, the bridge wasn't there that fateful January night when the general decided to challenge Rome and become its king.

Niccolò clambers down the banks to the water's edge, making his way between the trees and thick clusters of reeds. A water snake glides by. Two geese fly overhead. This is how it must have been in Caesar's time. He sits on a tree trunk with his copy of *Parallel Lives*. The wind blows hard, he feels the moisture in the air, and he begins to daydream.

Back then, Rome was poorly governed, bordering on anarchy. Two men grew in strength thanks to their armies, who were scattered across the lands dominated by the Republic: Caesar and Pompey. Each man wanted to kill the other. Pompey had more soldiers and was certain that he would be able to manipulate the Senate.

Caesar, then fifty years old, returning from his conquest of Gaul, reached the Rubicon with a single army. In those days, Roman generals were not allowed to cross the river with their militias; it was tantamount to insurrection. Caesar stopped by the river's edge and sent the Senate and Pompey an offer, which was moderate and balanced, at least on paper, and designed to confuse them.

It occurs to Niccolò that Borgia did the very same thing with Florence and is currently doing it with Vitelli and the other mercenaries. Perhaps Borgia has taken inspiration from the man he considers his predecessor or maybe subterfuge just comes naturally to him.

Unlike the Florentines, who pretended to welcome Valentino's offer, Caesar's enemies in Rome turned him down and chased his representatives out of the city, forcing them to flee dressed as slaves, frightened for their lives, thereby providing Caesar with the pretext he had been hoping for.

Niccolò opens the book and reads the lines of Plutarch that reach across the space of fifteen centuries.[2]

Now, Caesar had with him not more than three hundred horsemen and five thousand legionaries . . .

Less than half of what Borgia commands, Niccolò observes.

. . . for the rest of his army had been left beyond the Alps, and was to be brought up by those whom he had sent for the purpose.

Just like the reinforcements that Valentino was waiting for from France.

He saw, however . . .

However . . .

He saw, however, that his enterprise did not at first require a large force. Rather, it must take advantage of the golden moment, showing boldness and speed. He was more likely to terrify his enemies with an unexpected strike than by overwhelming them with full force.

And yet he decided to press on.

He himself spent the day in public, attending and watching the exercises of gladiators

The parades, processions, the bullfight . . .

but a little before evening he bathed and dressed and went into the banqueting hall. Here he held brief converse with those who had been invited to supper, and just as it was getting dark and went away, after addressing courteously most of his guests and bidding them await his return. To a few of his friends, however, he had previously given directions to follow him, not all by the same route, but some by one way and some by another.

... soldiers camped out all across the land.

He himself mounted one of his hired carts and drove at first along another road, then turned towards Rimini. When he came to the river which separates Cisalpine Gaul from the rest of Italy (the Rubicon), and began to reflect, now that he drew nearer to the fearful step and was agitated by the magnitude of his ventures, he checked his speed.

Then, halting in his course, he communed with himself a long time in silence as his resolution wavered back and forth, and his purpose then suffered change after change. For a long time, too, he discussed his perplexities with his friends who were present.

Who knows if Borgia is even capable of changing his mind. He certainly doesn't confide in anyone and never seems to ask advice from anyone.

.... *estimating the great evils for all mankind which would follow their passage of the river, and the wide fame of it which they would leave to posterity. But finally, with a sort of passion, as if abandoning calculation and casting himself upon the future, and uttering the phrase with which men usually prelude their plunge into desperate and daring fortunes, 'Let the die be cast,' he hastened to cross the river; and going at full speed now for the rest of the time, before daybreak he dashed into Rimini and took possession of it.*

It is said, moreover, that on the night before he crossed the river he had an unnatural dream; he thought, namely, that he was having incestuous intercourse with his own mother.

So that's why the duke said he had a dream! Such is the degree to which he identifies with the great soldier after whom he was named ...

Niccolò wonders if Borgia came to the river's edge to

consecrate his idea of becoming king of Tuscany and all of Italy. In much the same way that Julius Caesar made a peace offering while simultaneously preparing for war, perhaps Borgia thought that a surprise attack under the cover of night, aided only by the light of the moon, would be the best way to end the Republic.

CHAPTER TWENTY-FOUR

N iccolò rides swiftly back the way he came. The black horse they gave him is strong, agile, sensitive, intelligent—a true joy to ride. He sets out at a gallop. He's traveled a great deal in the name of the Republic and always in a hurry, but this time he is rushing back because he is impatient to see Dianora. Now that he has seen where she lived, he feels incredibly close to her.

In his exuberance, he rides the horse off the beaten path and across the flatlands, the black steed responding quickly to all his desires. Niccolò whoops with pleasure to ride so fast, he stands in his stirrups, then sits again; he feels at one with the sensitive steed, a centaur.

He sees a row of vines. Instead of avoiding the obstacle, he rushes toward it. The black horse gallops hard, with precision and care; in the instant that Niccolò conceives of and signals the command, the horse leaps off the ground and lightly and effortlessly clears the row of vines, landing a good distance ahead. But when the horse's front hooves sink a little into the earth, Niccolò almost loses his balance, his body still hurtling forward from the jump. He quickly realizes that he shouldn't have taken such a big risk, and his heart starts to beat wildly in his chest. Slowly, reason returns to him and he goes back to trotting safely along the path for carts and merchants.

He thinks about Dianora. He will need to meet secretly with her again to obtain further information, and this worries him because she expects so much from him. He will have to encourage her, he will have to keep deceiving her. He knows it's his duty, but it will also expose her to even greater risks than the ones she is currently running.

Should he keep his distance? It would be safer for her but more dangerous for Florence. And yet, Dianora wants nothing more than to hurt Valentino, and has every right to feel that way. Essentially, it is a race against time. Although Borgia seems to be charmed by her now, as soon as he tires of her, he might have her killed. Then again, he might not. It's hard to say. Apparently, other girls that he has captured during his sieges are still alive. He may even keep other spoils of war scattered around other cities in Romagna.

Her beauty is her condemnation. When she walks into a room, even the air itself lights up. In this, her strength is also her weakness.

As he indulges in recalling her physical traits, he notices that he has unconsciously crossed a line: he has always been careful about not getting too attached to any one woman, precisely because he is so attracted to the fairer sex. This was the case even with Marietta. He knew that he would be able to live with her, thereby guaranteeing her the stability that is expected from both husband and father, only if he were able to keep his deeper sentiments under control. But with Dianora, this is not easy. She has broken through his defenses. He doesn't desire her anymore—how could he possibly?—he feels the power of her spirit. He wishes he could protect her, but that's both impossible and dangerous. She could lead him to make a mistake, and he simply can't let himself lose control of the situation. He must remember to use her only as much as she is needed for his mission and keep his distance.

Never let your guard down, Niccolò tells himself. Valentino is always watching. He has been watching this whole time from Imola, manipulating Niccolò even though he promised him complete freedom. Borgia is like a spider weaving a web, day in and day out: first with the secretary of the castellan, who waited for him in Forlì and forced him to accept his hospitality; then through the message sent to Cesena and Ramiro de Lorqua, who addressed him by his first name; then by placing the book by Plutarch in his hands. Nothing was done by chance. Valentino was capable of manipulating Niccolò's thoughts so that he would write what the prince wanted. Dianora was right when she said to be careful and not to trust him.

The black horse is drenched with sweat; lather has formed on its shoulders, neck and even its head. Its breathing comes rapidly and raucously. Niccolò pats the horse with gratitude and it flicks its ear and nickers. Soon Niccolò arrives at the post house where he will spend the night. He dismounts, leaves the horse in the care of the stablemen, asks for some food, and continues to wonder . . . Had he been tricked into sleeping in the room where Dianora's family had stayed? Was he being tested? Had someone been following him? No, he's almost certain that this was not the case. He had been very careful, especially in Forlì. Maybe it had been a mistake to accept Borgia's invitation and travel through Romagna. There could be consequences for him later on. The letter that Valentino had sent to him in Cesena was surely copied into the archives of the Duchy, as dictated by protocol. It would come out sooner or later, and it could be used against him when he returns to Florence. If it does, he'll need to invent an excuse to give to Soderini. He'll need to say that he was indulging the Prince's whims, which also allowed him to move freely through Romagna and observe how many troops he had in the various cities.

Even worse, the people in Florence might learn that he agreed to write a biography of the duke and use this against him. If that were to happen, Niccolò would say that he played along with Borgia, and even encouraged him, so that he could gain his confidence and find out his secrets, that he was just following the gonfalonier's orders. The worst thing that could happen is that they ask him to return the money he received from the duke. While this would certainly be unfortunate, he would get over it. Once poor, always poor. The only problem was that he had already spent a fair amount of it.

Niccolò sits at a table on one side of the room. The roast veal is tasty and cooked to perfection, but he barely savors it because of his concerns. Suddenly, it dawns on him that he must leave Imola as quickly as possible. He needs to request to be summoned back to Florence.

Absorbed in his thoughts, Niccolò is unaware that a tough-looking man of about forty is watching him.

The man approaches and sits down. "How's the food, Chancellor?" he whispers.

Niccolò almost chokes on a morsel and spits it out.

"Don't worry! If I had wanted to poison you, you'd already be dead. I've been waiting for you for two days. I knew you would come through here on your way back to Imola," the man says.

Niccolò regains his composure and peers with curiosity at the stranger. The man glances around the room. The other diners are all far away, but he lowers his voice just the same.

"I need to speak to you in private. My name is Fosco Tinardeschi. I used to fight for Valentino."

Even though Niccolò has never met him, he knows the name. They say he's a soldier of exceptional courage and fights for Vitellozzo. Why is he in enemy territory?

They take their conversation outside, under a tree, where they are somewhat concealed by darkness.

"I fought hard for Borgia under the leadership of my condottiere, Vitelli. But like him and many others I have had to distance myself from Cesare. The man is a fiend, a dragon, we were afraid that he would devour us all, one after the other. Instead, we chose to band together to fight him. And now we're winning."

"You are?"

"Yes! You must have heard how he lost Urbino. We're getting stronger every day, even around here, where he thinks he's in control. You have no idea how easy it is to travel in secrecy down the backroads, how many people here in Romagna are ready to rebel . . . "

"I learned that many people appreciate him."

Tinardeschi shrugs. "It's easy to trick people, but when Valentino loses his next battle, they'll come to their senses, and shift their allegiances to our side. We'll attack him when and where he least expects it. By the end of the year he'll be gone. We already have a strong enough army to do it. He himself fears us."

"Perhaps you underestimate him."

"No. The timing is perfect. I come to you because we want to offer your Republic a second chance at joining forces with us against him. We think you'll accept when you see what we are capable of."

"Second chance? When was the first one?"

"More than a month ago. Didn't you know? Well, it doesn't matter. Write to the gonfalonier or to the Dieci and tell them you met with me today. I represent everyone fighting against Borgia."

"But Vitelli is an enemy of Florence . . . "

"Not when faced with such a danger. As I already said, this situation has been building for some time. Uniting forces would be good for both of us."

Niccolò looks at him with genuine surprise. Something else that Soderini hid from him . . . Is the gonfalonier merely using him as a pawn in the game? Will Florence unite forces with members of this alliance? If so, which ones? They're all connected somehow, either complicitly or by blood. Even the code numbers that represent them are sequential: 21, Vitellozzo Vitelli, Count of Montone, lord of Città di Castello, Monterchi, and Anghiari, son-in-law of 22; Paolo Orsini, lord of Mentana and Marquis of Atripalda, cousin of 23; Francesco Orsini, Duke of Gravina, who wanted to marry Lucrezia Borgia, Cesare's sister; 24, Oliverotto Euffreducci, lord of Fermo, brother-in-law of Vitelli; 25, Cardinal Giovanni Battista Orsini, who conspires with them from Rome; 26, Giampaolo Baglioni, Count of Bettona, lord of Perugia; 27, Pandolfo Petrucci, who rules over Siena; 28, Giovanni Bentivoglio, lord of Bologna.

Is there a weak link in the chain? Yes, 22, Paolo Orsini, but Valentino is already dealing with him. Unless Orsini is playing both sides.

"Did you hear what I said, Machiavelli?"

"Of course. I'll write to Florence."

"Why are you smiling? What's so funny?"

"Nothing. I'm not. I was just thinking."

CHAPTER TWENTY-FIVE

I n the evening shadows, the oak forest outside Porta Montanara is practically dripping with dew and the ground is soft and damp.

Niccolò makes sure that no one is around before making his way into the forest. Long before he reaches the old, lightning-split oak that Farneti told him about, his shoes are soaked. Cautiously, he places his hand in the cavity in the trunk and finds a waxed fabric bag.

Inside is a piece of paper dated two days earlier.

Yesterday, the yeomen for the French spearmen arrived in the county of Faenza and tomorrow the first five companies will arrive under the command of Montison, Fois, Miolans, Dunais, and the Marquis di Saluzzo.

Between the branches, in the dwindling light, Niccolò can see the walls of Imola and the stronghold of the Rocca. The news about the French spearmen means that he will have to meet with Valentino that evening to try and find out more. If he sees Dianora it will be in Cesare's presence, so it won't be hard to avoid contact with her. This thought fills him with strength. He starts to sing loudly: "*Cavalca il Conte Guido per la Toscana, la lanza in man che 'l porta, e la bandera, e la bandera.*" It's a popular and catchy tune that was started in Tuscany a few years earlier and has an easy, flowing melody. He often sang the ditty after celebratory dinners.

Niccolò returns to the city in an excellent mood.

"Finally! I was starting to worry about you," Baccino says when Niccolò arrives at the inn, still singing the song.

Baccino is sitting at the dining table. The innkeeper brings him some food and coyly rubs up against his arm. Niccolò perceives this new intimacy immediately, imagining that it developed during his absence. Judging from the appearance and the aroma, the food appears superb.

"I was only gone five days, Baccino."

"I know, but they came looking for you."

"Who did?"

"On Friday, a knight arrived on behalf of the Dieci. His name was Totto. He left again this morning, but then someone new arrived: a string bean of a fellow who doesn't say a word and seems more dead than alive."

"Where is he now?"

"He just went out."

"Did they bring letters?"

"Of course. Totto brought one, the string bean brought two: one from the Dieci and the other from the gonfalonier." Baccino takes them out of his satchel and, as he is handing them to Niccolò, he turns to the woman and speaks to her in an informal manner. "Gemma, how about feeding our envoy? He must be hungry and tired."

"What do you want to eat?" the innkeeper turns to Niccolò and asks.

"Whatever you've got," Niccolò replies, taking the letters.

Gemma serves him a dish of what Baccino has: veal belly stew with grated cheese, bread, and spices.

"What was that song you were singing?" she asks him.

He knows very well how catchy the tune is: as soon as people hear it, they start singing it. It spreads like the plague. That's what happened to him the first time he heard it. It got into his head. Even before he replies, Baccino starts singing it. Soon enough, Gemma is singing along with him. From the way the two of them look at each other, it's perfectly clear what's going on.

Niccolò eats quickly—the food is delicious—while reading first one and then the other letter from the Dieci, in which they express their surprise at his lack of news, especially since they sent Totto, whom he could have easily entrusted with a letter.

Write us now, they say, and give it to Iacopino, the second rider. They need to know if Valentino is really preparing for war; they need to know everything Niccolò can find out about the duke's agreement with the mercenaries.

This information is particularly important for them because they have decided to send an orator to Rome to meet with his Holiness the Pope, seeing how the duke never makes a move without involving his father. And the orator needs to know absolutely everything that Niccolò can possibly relay to him.

So, not only are they pressing him for more information, they're planning on using his findings to facilitate someone else's job.

Back in his room he reads the missive from the gonfalonier. In normal ink, I-have-faith writes that he is relying on the messenger used by the Dieci, Iacopino, to carry this letter.

In normal ink, he asks for a general update but also wants Niccolò to enquire specifically about the wellbeing of Silvestro de' Buosi, a faithful mercenary who fought for the Republic and who is now being kept prisoner in Forlì, and gravely ill. He was captured the year before in Anghiari and, at the request of Dionigi, Naldi's comrade, he was sent by Vitellozzo to see the duke. He has been in prison ever since. The gonfalonier asks Niccolò to discuss this with the Prince and plead with him to free the man.

Curiously, in his letter, Soderini uses the first person plural; Niccolò doesn't understand if he has adopted a *pluralis maiestatis* or if, by "we," he is referring to all the people of Florence and the authorities. Is it possible that power has already gone to his head? It would seem so, judging from the way he signs the letter, clarifying that, from this moment forward, Niccolò needs to address him with the title *Vexillifer Perpetuus*, which he has been given to better protect the people.

The lines written in invisible ink and code are even more direct. I-have-faith reminds him that he must, first and foremost, inform him about things related to war. It will be up to the gonfalonier to decide what to tell the Dieci, and when.

He pauses. Clearly there's a power struggle going on within the Palazzo della Signoria despite the fact that Soderini is now *Vexillifer Perpetuus,* or perhaps precisely because of that.

He goes back to reading the letter. I-have-faith orders him to obtain a copy of the articles of agreement between Valentino and his allies.

"Lord Envoy, are you there?"

He is almost done changing his clothes in preparation to go to the Rocca when he sees a light flickering under the door, out on the landing, and hears a voice he does not recognize speaking in a Valencian accent. Whoever it is climbed the stairs very quietly. Or rather, Niccolò had heard the floorboards creak and a soft step but he had been absorbed by his own thoughts.

It's surely one of Borgia's men, he thinks. They know he's back. The person is probably just verifying that he's there, he probably already asked Gemma as much. That's assuming, of course, that she's not a spy herself, in which case she may well have informed the court personally.

Before replying, he looks around. There's nothing suspicious in sight. In case anyone ever came to search the room, he marked the bottle of invisible ink with a Latin label for a cough syrup.

"Who's there?"

"It is I, Gonzalo Rodriguez, one of the duke's guards."

Worried but curious, he opens the door. A tall, thirty-year-old with a thick beard, wearing a sumptuous doublet, stands staring at him with a lantern in his hand.

"Has His Excellency asked to see me?"

"He is traveling but left instructions for you. Would you please follow me to the Rocca?"

When they are downstairs, they hear Baccino and Gemma singing. They're still sitting in the dining room, the fire blazing. "*Cavalca il Conte Guido per la Toscana la lanza in man che 'l porta, e la bandera, e la bandera.*" They sing loudly and gaily. Clearly they have been drinking.

There are more men than usual on the scaffolding around the cupola, working by the light of lanterns and torches. The large portal is now flanked by elegant wooden half-columns and connected by a triangular gable, also made of wood.

"What is that building going to be?" Niccolò asks the soldier.

"A theater. There will be a performance to celebrate the birthday of her Ladyship Dianora Mambelli."

Niccolò hides his surprise and even feels a touch of jealousy. "What kind of performance?"

"I don't know. Engineer da Vinci is taking care of it. He created something similar once for the deposed Duke of Milan."

"When will the performance be?"

"I am not sure about that either."

Niccolò continues walking with Rodriguez in the direction of the Rocca, his eyes taking in the massive walls that imprison Dianora. After just hearing it once, while they were leaving the inn, the soldier is already humming "Cavalca il Conte Guido."

Niccolò ponders this piece of news. So Valentino wants to show off Dianora. But why? He is confused.

His pace slows down as he reflects on it. Rodriguez glances at him strangely and also walks slower.

As he approaches the carefully-guarded narrow doorway to the Rocca, its walls rising up high above, Niccolò imagines Dianora far from Imola—free—and the fantasy makes him feel almost dizzy.

Why is he indulging in such boyish fantasies? The mere

thought is disturbing and destabilizing, and could potentially be very dangerous.

"What's the matter?" Rodriguez's voice brings him quickly back to reality.

Without realizing it, Niccolò has stopped walking altogether.

"Forgive me, I was thinking about something."

He sighs with frustration. He tells himself that it's natural to have moments of doubt and indecision, but he has to get over it. He has to regain his lucidity, he needs to be able to count on his inner strength, that sense of determination that has always pushed him beyond all the humiliating moments he has experienced, beyond every single mistake he has made. He doesn't know where this strength comes from, but it is his true nature. He knows that everything can be explained and resolved if he can come to an understanding of its truest essence.

This revelation brings him back to his senses. He picks up his pace, strides through the doorway and enters the citadel.

Standing in the courtyard, at the base of the stairs, is Corella. He's talking to two soldiers and holding a lantern. When he sees Niccolò arrive, he waves the soldiers away, walks over to the envoy, and tries to smile but doesn't quite succeed.

"His Excellency would like you to read some documents."

Niccolò forces himself to be natural. "The articles of the agreement that His Lordship Geraldini mentioned?"

"The First Secretary is in charge of those treatises and will give them to you when he thinks most opportune. However, my Lordship gave orders to show you, on your return to Imola, a report on the wars in Romagna."

Borgia is starting to apply pressure.

The two men climb the stairs that lead to the study, side by side, practically rubbing elbows. A soldier walks ahead of them carrying a lantern, the light of which projects their shadows on the walls and the low vaulted ceiling. Without turning to him, don Miguel asks, "His Excellency would also like to know what impression you had of the lands you visited."

"Excellent. The Prince was right to speak so highly of his governing skills."

Corella turns to look at him. "And what do you think of de Lorqua?"

Niccolò wonders why he is asking. "He seems like a man of great resolve."

"I will communicate as much to the duke. He will be pleased to hear it. Those cities are indeed beautiful. Conquering them cost us a great deal of fatigue and blood: ours, of course, but especially that of others."

"Have you been in the military for long, Signor Corella?"

"Ever since I was twenty years old. Before that I was a student at the University of Pisa."

Can this possibly be true? "What did you study?" Niccolò asks.

"I was studying to become a *notaio*. That is where I met Cesare, who was studying canonical law. That is when I offered myself to his service."

"Therefore, in addition to a soldier, you are also a scholar?"

"No one is ever just one thing. But after fighting my first campaign, I knew that my life was on the battlefield."

After the soldier lights all the candles in the study, he and Corella retreat, leaving Niccolò alone.

A pile of documents rests on the table. On top of it is a note. He recognizes the duke's handwriting and signature.

Read this report, Niccolò. It is exactly what I do not want from you. Now that you have seen my lands with your own eyes, I expect you to write about them in your own words, and quickly, as I will soon be back. For now I would ask that you begin to write persuasively about the wars we fought in Romagna. Remember to use malice where needed, which in these pages is entirely lacking. Farewell.

Dianora had told him that Borgia had relied on other writ-ers before . . . These pages must have been written by one of those people. Begrudgingly, he begins to read. The author's style and syntax emulate that of the commentaries written by Julius Caesar on the conquering of Gaul—clearly Valentino asked him to do that, too—but it was done artlessly, drily. Or rather, he did it well enough but there is something that sounds off-kilter and Niccolò has a hard time saying what it is.

There had been a first military campaign against Romagna and then a second one, both of which had been carefully pre-pared. Niccolò remembers hearing about them in Florence via the letters and reports of the Chancellor.

The hostility all started in September 1499 with the Papal bulls that stripped the Lords of Imola, Faenza, Forlì, Rimini, Pesaro, Urbino, and Camerino of their cities because they had not paid the taxes they owed the Church. In so doing, Alessandro VI gave his son, Captain General of the pontifical army, an excellent pretext to invade the lands.

Even God was brought in to the discussion; the author has the duke say that all his actions were done in His name. There's no mention at all of any of the suffering. It's as if it never ex-isted. No bloodshed. In this regard, don Miguel was far more honest than the person behind these writings.

The city of Imola surrendered without resistance at the end of November and the Rocca was taken in early December. Then came Forlì, where the inhabitants of the city opened the gates to Valentino while members of nobility tried to hold them off, taking refuge in the fortress, which fell to the duke on January 12, 1500.

There's no mention of Dianora or the people who defended her, but the author does mention Caterina Sforza, who was cap-tured, raped, and imprisoned at Castel Sant'Angelo in Rome, then freed almost a year and a half later.

The rest of Romagna was spared because the King of France had to recall his troops, who were urgently needed on other fronts, and due to the onset of bitterly cold weather and heavy snowfalls, which impeded all military efforts.

The anonymous writer describes Caterina Sforza's destiny with gratuitous pleasure, celebrating her probable rape by Valentino, declaring that it was both his right as conqueror and the result of a feral instinct that resides within all mankind. "Deep down inside our souls, aren't we all corrupt?" the author writes.

Niccolò understands why the manuscript sounds off to him: it's a celebration of the baseness of humanity. He knows of one writer who has built his whole reputation around this notion: a man of letters, a member of the court, and a poet laureate. His name is Antonio Nuffi. Handsome and slender, originally from Genoa, Nuffi dances through the chambers of the powerful, taking great pleasure in discussing the evil ways of man but only comprehending things superficially. Mainly, the man writes about himself, emulating Petrarch's *Familiares*, trying to convince people that the banalities of his life are of everyone.

Yes, that's it. Borgia must have turned to Nuffi, who enjoys a relative amount of popularity. Many important people have fallen for him, including a fair number of scholars. But of course, the herd follows the head sheep, who in turn only follows the sheepdog of gossip. To his merit, Valentino realized that Nuffi wasn't up to the task. Cesare is certainly no sheep.

With this awareness, Niccolò goes back to reading. Nuffi revels in descriptions of the second military campaign in Romagna, which Cesare initiated in October 1500, and with many more soldiers than the first. At this point in time, Paolo and Francesco Orsini had joined him, together with Vitelli and the lord of Perugia. Twelve thousand men in all and an infinite artillery.

Pesaro and Rimini surrendered immediately, but not Faenza.

The lord of that city at the time was sixteen-year-old Astorre Manfredi, an extremely handsome, intelligent, cultured, and beloved young man. He was the soul of the resistance, but in the long run the besiegers won out. In April 1501, Astorre was forced to surrender but did so only after signing a pact that promised the wellbeing of the populace and his own freedom. Valentino agreed and praised the Faentini, saying that if there had been more of them, he could have used them to form an army with which he could have conquered all of Italy.

The pages do not include the epilogue, which Niccolò knows well, as it was the subject of much talk in Florence. Astorre and his younger brother were imprisoned in Castel Sant'Angelo for one year. It was said that Astorre was repeatedly raped by one of the jailers, and possibly by Valentino himself. In early June they put ropes around the necks of the two young men and tied them to a pole which was then rotated until they strangled. Their bodies were thrown into the Tiber.

Throwing bodies into the Tiber seems to be a tradition in the Borgia family, Niccolò thinks to himself.

Before returning to Romagna, Valentino had to interrupt his campaign due to *force majeur*. He was obliged to spend much of the spring and summer of 1501 in the south, fighting for Louis XII of France, who was engaged in battle with the King of Naples, Federico d'Aragona. As lieutenant, Cesare participated in the siege on Capua, where the enemy had amassed infantry and horses. This battle was described in the manuscript.

During the siege, the French conquered Capua, which was followed by a gruesome sacking and pillaging that horrified all of Italy, but which seemed to please Nuffi to no end. As happens when a city chooses not to capitulate, women and girls, and even nuns, were raped. To avoid the violence, some women threw themselves into wells or rivers. Others were taken to Rome and sold off cheaply. Still others sought refuge in towers and fortresses and may have survived the first round of attacks but then ended up in Valentino's hands, who wanted to examine them all before choosing to keep forty of the prettiest.

Naturally, Borgia had wanted all this to be included, in order to spread fear. It was also probably true. Where did those forty women end up? Maybe they, too, had eventually been sold off in Rome.

Niccolò gets to his feet in disgust, walks over to the window that looks down into the courtyard, and opens it to breathe in some cold air.

A window opens across the way, the same one where a few nights earlier he had seen the flickering flames. Even now he sees the fire burning in the hearth. Dianora appears. She stares calmly and quietly at him, almost as if she expected to see him there.

Niccolò gasps. His decision to keep his distance instantly vanishes.

Dianora reaches out to him the same way she extended her hand in the sacristy.

He understands: she is asking him if he rested his hand on the tomb of her relatives. He nods.

Even though she is some distance away and it is almost dark, he sees her eyes grow shiny with tears. Then she turns to look at someone or something behind her, closes the window, and walks away.

"Where have my loved ones been laid to rest? In which part of the family chapel?"

Should he hide the truth? Probably not, he thinks. She will hear about it anyway. "I'm sorry to tell you that they were not buried in the family chapel but in the catacombs, with all the others who were killed during the siege."

Dianora covers her face with her hands, elbows on the prie-dieu, her shoulders heaving with sobs.

"Perhaps I shouldn't have told you but at the same time I didn't want to deceive you."

"You did well to tell me."

"It was cruel to bury them there."

"Borgia will never show me mercy. He'll kill me when he is tired of me. Who knows where my body will be thrown."

"I don't think that will happen."

"It will, and I don't care. At least I will finally be with my loved ones."

Niccolò is silent and looks away.

"Do you believe in God?" Dianora asks him.

He looks at her but doesn't say a word.

"Are you religious?" she asks again.

"I don't really know how to reply."

"Well I am, and I know I will see my parents again. They're waiting for me. I am not afraid of dying. I belong with them."

Niccolò is silent. He doesn't believe in heaven; he's only interested in humankind and what connects people on earth. The ability to decipher human connections already seems like so much to him. But who is he to take away Dianora's hopes?

She begins to whisper a prayer in Latin.

"Answer me when I call to you, my righteous God. Give me relief from my distress; have mercy on me. Allow my grief to be the source of all that will come to light . . . "

Brother Timoteo, from over in his corner, looks perplexed. What on earth is she saying?

"My Lord, I find refuge in you. Protect me from my persecutors so they do not tear me apart like lions."

Lucina, pale and shivering, watches Dianora pray. She wonders what strange penitence the prior has inflicted on her. What sins could she possibly have committed? What did she just confess to the friar?

A ray of sunlight reflects off the solar clock and onto the guardian's gold necklace, its pendant resembling a curved hook or toothpick, long and thin.

Niccolò observes the woman through the crack, hoping she will stop looking at Dianora soon. The duke's guard stands nearby and, in a pew a bit farther back, an elderly woman kneels in prayer.

"Judge me, oh Lord, in keeping with justice, in keeping with my innocence, Most High One." She then falls silent.

When Niccolò, who didn't say anything while she was praying, notices that Lucina has gone back to looking elsewhere, he speaks to Dianora again. "Do you know where he is now?" he whispers.

She shakes her head.

"We can no longer meet here, Dianora. Brother Timoteo doesn't want to risk it anymore. Where else can we meet?"

"I don't know."

"That window where I saw you . . . "

"It's one of the two rooms into which I am locked."

"What? Your chambers consist of only two rooms?"

"Yes, the other one looks out over the plains. That witch of a woman sleeps outside my door, in a small nook. She watches me constantly."

"Can you ask the duke for permission to take a walk?"

"Every so often he lets me go out, but she always comes with me and so do the guards."

"What lies beyond the room where you sleep?"

"The archives."

"The archives of the duchy?"

"No, the duke's own personal archives. And beyond that are his chambers, where he sleeps alone. I am forced to go to him whenever he wants, like that time you saw me from the great hall."

"So his chambers are adjacent to the room where he receives people?"

"Yes, they're connected by the corridor. And before I go into his rooms, they always search me. A guard, but usually Corella, sleeps in his antechamber."

Niccolò watches as Lucina makes conversation with the guard. "Does he ever let you go out for air on the terrace of the Rocca?"

"Often, but only when no one is around, and always with the witch and guards."

"We'll find a way to meet again," Niccolò promises her.

"I should leave now."

"Yes, you're right. We can't take any chances."

Niccolò continues to keep an eye on Lucina as she talks to the guard; he notices that she keeps shivering. "That woman doesn't seem to be well. Does she have a fever?"

"Yes, and even so, she felt compelled to come and keep an eye on me," Dianora says, removing a folded piece of paper from her bodice. "This is for you," she says, placing it on the floor, hidden from view by the prie-dieu.

"What is it?"

"A sonnet I wrote. You understand poetry. I want you to tell me what you think of it."

"Now?"

"Now is impossible. If and when we get a chance to talk again." She makes the sign of the cross, gets up, and walks back to the door that leads into the nave.

Brother Timoteo quickly gets up and makes his way to the confessor's chair. Dianora waits for him to take his seat before she opens the door.

Niccolò follows her with his eyes as they leave the church, the guardian on one side and the soldier on the other.

Niccolò looks at Brother Timoteo, who is staring at the piece of paper on the floor.

"If I were you, I would destroy all written documents," the prior murmurs. "And thankfully, from this day forward, I'll never see you again." The friar goes and shuts the door to the nave, then walks over, picks up the piece of paper, and passes it to Niccolò through the crack. "Leave through the garden, the usual way. You know which path to take."

A sudden knock on the door makes them both jump.

"May I come in, Father?" a woman's voice asks. It's the elderly lady who had been praying.

"Go! Hurry!" Brother Timoteo hisses as Niccolò scurries off down the corridor. The prior then walks to the door. "Of course!"

The woman, hunchbacked from old age, looks at him with rheumy eyes.

The friar opens his arms wide. "Are you here to confess your sins?"

The elderly lady nods and slowly walks in.

Niccolò strides quickly down the paths of the monastery garden, between fruit trees and herb bushes and flower beds. He sees apple trees, lemon trees, and grape vines. There are plants for decorating the church and violets for tinctures and syrups.

At the end of a row of pear trees are some fruit trees the likes of which he's never seen before. A bed of reddish leaves lays in a circle beneath them. Looking down at them, he is overcome by a strange sensation. When the prior first showed him the path out of the garden, he mentioned that the seeds for those trees had been brought there by missionaries from the Orient more than two centuries earlier. They use them to produce potent medicines.

He walks past a tool shed situated between two tall laurel bushes, then past a large stone pool of water filled with fish that will eventually be served to the monks. Only a little bit further and he will reach the wall. With ease, he climbs up and over, knowing that on the other side is an untilled field and no houses.

As he walks away from the monastery walls, he remembers his nightmare in Forlì. The girl's long hair was the same color red as those fallen leaves.

CHAPTER TWENTY-SIX

Senza pietà Fortuna qui mi serra,
né vedo alcuno ch'aiutar mi possa.
Tanta infelicità mi fa sì scossa
che pace più non trovo in questa terra.

Io sono donna, come è la Fortuna,
eppur contro di me crudel s'addossa,
e leva i ferri, e mi dà ogni percossa,
strazio m'infligge, dolori in me raduna.

Io per fuggirla nelle memorie mie
rincaso, e lì rivedo ciò che ho avuto:
e padre e madre, e le dolci anime pie

che il cielo prima del tempo ha voluto.
Mi levo contro oltraggi ed angherie,
nessun mi toglierà ciò che ho vissuto.[3]

At a safe distance from the monastery, Niccolò stops in an alley to read the poem. Then, full of admiration, he carefully refolds the piece of paper. He was around twenty when he started composing poems; Dianora is younger than he was and already writing verses that, although not entirely perfect, are graced with assonances and echoes that come to life in surprising ways. She looks to the past for consolation but also courageously mentions the hardships she has encountered and endures. Her talent can only grow in the years to come.

Nelle memorie mie rincaso [To dwell in memory] . . . How devastating to think these words were written by someone whose home was so brutally taken from them.

Mi levo contro oltraggi [And yet I rise up against these offenses] . . . Interesting to see how she used the reflexive verb in two ways: to distance herself from something and to do battle with it, both of which she actually does, escaping mentally from her prison and rebelling against Valentino.

At the same time, *levarsi* also means to get up out of bed, to rise up from the object to which she is chained, from her imprisonment, from slavery. She casts off, fights off, and rises up all at once.

Né vedo alcuno ch'aiutar mi possa [No one nearby to lessen my distress] . . . This is a cry for help, and it seems directed at him, the only one who can assist her. She is placing her trust in him, and this moves him deeply.

Suddenly, he hears a military drum roll.

Then a second one.

He turns to see what's happening.

Coming up the main artery of the city are twenty military drummers, in four rows of five across. They're all about the same height, some are blond and others are dark-haired, they march in formation, and they're dressed in the colors of the Very Christian King. They roll and beat on their snare drums energetically, and it sounds like approaching thunder.

Knights on horseback come next, dressed in full regalia as if heading into battle and grouped into squadrons. At the head of each section, on chargers, are the lance captains: they're covered in armor from head to toe, they carry their swords by their side but their helmets are strapped to their saddles; their long spears, which extend upward from their stirrups and rest on the pommels of their saddles, are reinforced with sharp iron tips. Behind them come the equerries, who are less heavily armed and carry half-pikes with standards waving from the points.

Then come either two musketeers or two crossbowmen, also on horseback, who are followed by servants on their nags, who in turn lead a number of horses yoked to carts full of gear and other weapons and lances.

One troop after the next, as far as the eye can see. The flags that flutter in the wind are of all imaginable colors. It's a grand display of power.

The sound of the horses' hooves echoes on the cobblestones in counterpoint with the drummers.

The townspeople line the street and watch in amazement. Even Niccolò, who has to push his way through the crowd to see better, is struck by the quantity of soldiers, the quality of the horses, and the variety of weapons, in particular the new muskets. Thinking back on his own experience in the war against Pisa, Niccolò notices how harmoniously the troops move together, something that happens only after much training and experience in battle. He imagines the kinds of strategies of warfare they are capable of setting in motion, in terms of both attack and defense: the musketeers and crossbowmen can either offer side support for the head spearman and equerries or defend them from enemy assault; the spearmen are trained to form squadrons and charge when needed; the musketeers and crossbowmen can also create a united front and provide a cover to the other troops.

Then, from the end of the road, comes the loud blare of trumpets, adding to the drumrolls and clattering hooves. Trumpeters ride ahead of the spearmen, who are still out of view, but the blaring sound announces their arrival.

So the troops from Gaul have finally arrived, Niccolò is tempted to think but then corrects himself, dispelling the parallel between Cesare Borgia and Julius Caesar that the former manipulated him into thinking back when he was sitting on the shores of the Rubicon. Niccolò chides himself and forces himself to judge only what he sees before him.

There must be five hundred spearmen: a formidable powerhouse that, when united with his other troops, will assure

Borgia of military supremacy over all of central Italy. And if the duke actually manages to convince the Orsini, Vitelli and their allies to join his forces, as it would appear, he will be able to do whatever he wants.

But where is Cesare? Niccolò doesn't see him anywhere. He's probably bringing up the rear, basking in the glow. If what Farneti told him is correct, the spearmen will march through Imola and go on to set up camp in Faenza.

Niccolò watches them all go by, until even the final grooms and curious onlookers who marched with the procession have passed.

No sign of Valentino.

His absence alarms Niccolò more than if he had been present.

CHAPTER TWENTY-SEVEN

N iccolò stands at the window of his study and looks out across the courtyard yet again. Night is falling. Dianora's window remains shut.

Down below, on the ground floor, there's the sound of clashing swords; he realizes there's an armory beneath the porticoes.

Two stable hands come out and dump pails of dirty water into the central drain. He quickly ducks inside so as not to be seen.

He glances once more at Dianora's room, but still no sign of her.

He goes back to his desk and rereads the draft of the new chapter of *Res gestæ Cæsaris* on the siege of Romagna in 1499. He took a decidedly different approach than Anteo Nuffi, whose twisted perspective actually helped Niccolò in finding his own, gave him wings. Reading what that buffoon had written offered a compendium of everything Niccolò didn't like and made it easier for him to choose exactly what to include.

At the same time he felt forced to do battle with another enemy: the truth. Or at least a part of it. Niccolò considered himself lucky that, so far, he has only had to deal the years leading up to 1499; he has not had to write about the siege of the fortress of Forlì. Now that Dianora has begun to tell him how things really came to pass, he would have a hard time finding just the right words.

As he finishes rereading the chapter, he notices that the sound of clashing swords has stopped. Training is over for the day.

Not long after, he hears a woman groaning in pain. He hurries to the window and looks down into the courtyard. Two men are carrying out a stretcher on which lies Lucina, trembling and coughing. Torrella, the master physician, walks behind at a safe distance, observing her carefully while holding a handkerchief up to his nose and mouth.

Niccolò looks up. Across the courtyard Dianora is watching the witch get carried off. She catches sight of him.

They communicate through gestures. He's surprised how much he understands from her facial expressions and gestures: Lucina has a sickness in the lungs, they're taking her somewhere, but she doesn't know where.

Niccolò studies the cornice that runs below their windows, it's wide and strong enough to traverse. Dianora, repressing a cough, sees where he is looking, intuits what he's thinking, and shakes her head. No, it's too dangerous, for both of them.

He nods but then glances at the sky. Soon it will be dark.

He was on the verge of climbing out the window three times, and three times he decided against it. If someone were to see him, it would mean certain death for both of them. But his eagerness to find out Valentino's secrets is stronger than his fear.

He prepares to climb out onto the parapet once again, and this time goes through with it. He presses himself up against the wall, remembering how, when he was young, he walked and then ran—ran!—along the parapets of the bridges that cross the Arno. Although that was more than twenty years ago, it feels like just the other day. He did it in response to a dare, to show off just how courageous he was; if he had backed down, he would have been ridiculed for the rest of his life.

And yet, if he had fallen into the river, full of swirling eddies and currents, he almost certainly would have died. An old bargeman once told him that if you get dragged down by the rushing water, you should never fight it but let yourself sink down to the muddy bottom and then, using all your strength, push yourself back up to the surface.

Air, however, is not water. Air won't have mercy on him. But he can't stop now, not with the destiny of his city at stake. Florence is far more important than he is, far more important than his own life.

Thanks to the memory of that watery abyss, the straight line of the cornice is relatively easy to follow. Turning the first corner is hard. He leans forward, places one foot boldly on the other side, hesitates a moment—he feels fear strike deep in his soul—and then moves on. The second corner is easier.

Dianora's window is closed. He taps softly on the glass. Nothing. He knocks, the sound almost audible in the night air. She appears, but retreats in fear. Then she comes forward and hurriedly opens the window.

"We'll be killed if we get caught!" she whispers, coughing softly.

"I know, but there might never be another chance. Allow me to enter so no one sees me."

"You're forcing me to open up for you—and that's not right."

"I beg your forgiveness."

"That's not enough."

"Then I will go back."

Dianora doesn't say anything. Niccolò starts to retreat.

"Stay," she says, opening the window for him.

He clambers inside. He's never been this close to her. He can smell her scent: violets, sweet but delicate. "Where did they take the old hag?"

"Some remote place."

"What's wrong with her? Is it the plague?" he asks with a deep shiver.

"No, I think it's her lungs. But Borgia doesn't want to take any risks. He gave orders that anyone who falls ill should be taken away."

Why did Niccolò think it was the plague? It hasn't reappeared in a long time. He remembers those days well and is still scared of the illness.

Dianora coughs again.

"Are you unwell, too?"

"No, it's nothing, just a chill."

"Is there anyone in the duke's chambers now?"

"No, no one."

He looks around her room: the frescoed ceiling, the bed and furniture of inlaid wood, a fire burning in the hearth, and a door not far from her desk, which is covered with pieces of paper.

"Is that where you composed your beautiful poem?"

"Did you read it?"

"I liked it very much. I brought it back—here—we mustn't leave behind any traces. Your words are now part of my memory. You might be a prisoner, but your soul is free."

She doesn't say anything, but her breathing comes faster, her chest rising and falling rapidly.

He speaks to her about the symmetries he noticed in the poem, and the many meanings he found. Dianora listens attentively, as if transported far away. The corners of her mouth turn up in a sad smile, far more luminous than the one Niccolò imagined in the great hall of the Mambelli household in Forlì. She stares at him with such intensity that he has to look away.

"As you know, I also write poetry. I started to write this canzone a few weeks ago." He takes out a folded-up piece of paper and hands it to her. Dianora accepts it and opens it up.

Perché la vita è brieve
e molte son le pene
che vivendo e stentando ognun sostiene;
dietro alle nostre voglie,
andiam passando e consumando gli anni,
ché chi il piacer si toglie
per viver con angosce e con affanni,
non conosce gli inganni
del mondo; o da quai mali
e da che strani casi
oppressi quasi—sian tutti i mortali.[4]

Dianora looks up at him.

"You, too, have a wound," she says.

He's shocked. What is she talking about?

"An inner wound," she clarifies.

"Like everyone else."

"But, unlike so many others, you choose not to reveal it."

A shiver runs through him as if someone had opened a door that leads to a secret chamber within him. He feels invaded by an obscure torment: not regret, but a disgust with the world and himself, a sputtering of past illusions and sorrow.

"I'm sorry if what I said makes you unhappy," Dianora says.

"No, it's nothing," he says with a heavy sigh, contradicting his words, caught up in his thoughts.

"How will you proceed with the canzone?" she asks him gently.

"I don't know yet."

She hands him back his piece of paper. "I'm certain the result will be beautiful. But please, I beg you: leave now."

He looks at her boldly. He knows he needs to force her hand, to get her to do something that will be hard for her but vital for him.

"The French spearmen have arrived," he says.

"I imagined as much. I heard the drummers, the blare of the trumpets, all the fanfare."

"Borgia is going to be a difficult adversary to beat. He is making agreements with Vitelli and the others, and will soon rise up against Florence. There will be war. I need to find out what he is plotting."

"He didn't mention anything before he left."

"May I go look in his archive? You said it was next door. Perhaps I will find something useful."

Dianora shakes her head, no.

He presses her. "The only way we can beat him is with the element of surprise. That's the only way we will be able to kill him," he insists. "It all depends on you."

She wrings her hands together the way she did in the sacristy.

"Fine, follow me," she says curtly. She walks to the door, opens it, and they step out into the cold corridor. Dianora points to a tiny nook where there's an unmade bed. "That's where the old witch sleeps."

They walk down the corridor and enter a vast, icy room. The walls are lined with bookshelves that are filled with leather folders, all neatly tied shut. There's also a desk covered with papers.

Niccolò sees some maps on the desk and walks over to them. None of them are of Florence. There are more papers beneath the map. He picks them up and quickly realizes they're the articles of the agreement between the duke and his allies. He gives them a cursory glance.

For a true and perpetual peace . . . They agree to form an alliance in union against anyone who tries to attack them . . . He skips the preamble, looking for substance. *Restitution of the city of Urbino to the Duke of Romagna . . . In exchange the duke will take them into service and pay them condottieri wages . . . One of the members of the alliance will have to be with him at all times, but not all of them: they can decide who among them it shall be . . . When the duke requests it, they must be willing to give up one of their legitimate sons to His Excellency . . .*

Dianora points to some blank pages. "Why don't you take a piece of paper and transcribe the information?"

"He might notice it's missing."

"Shall I go and get one of mine?"

"Thank you, Milady, but we must be quick. I can't stay much longer."

She rushes off and he watches her as she leaves. When he's on his own, he feels deeply anxious and yet also very excited: he has his hands on Borgia's secret documents. Once again, thanks to Dianora, he has managed to trick the duke.

He comes to the conclusion of the agreement: *whosoever disrespects this alliance will be the enemy of all those who underwrite it; all signatories agree to come to the defense of each other no matter who causes offense or for whatever reason, in the name of the Holy Father Alexander VI and His Majesty, the Very Christian King of France.*

So, 58 will form an alliance with everyone from 21 to 28.

12 is alone.

He quickly jots down everything and takes his leave of Dianora, who gazes at him sadly and ponderously as she shuts the window.

He returns to the study with the sensation of having asked her too much; his satisfaction is tinged with regret.

He then hurries out of the Rocca, makes his way back to the inn, and writes a letter to the gonfalonier.

Between the lines, in invisible ink, he informs the gonfalonier of the arrival of the French spearmen and the agreement between Borgia and his allies. He also communicates that he didn't receive the information from the duke's secretary, as he originally hoped, but through other means.

Now he understands why Valentino pretended to want an alliance with Florence and why he put off coming to an agreement: he, too, was buying time. The same way that the Dieci and I-have-faith had been doing.

Niccolò has hit his mark, he thinks to himself, and is reminded of a skilled archer he observed during the battle with Pisa: when shooting at a target that seemed too far away to reach, the man aimed much, much higher than expected, knowing that by taking that trajectory, the arrow would fall exactly where he wanted. Niccolò now feels like that archer.

He seals the letter and then picks up some blank sheets of paper. He's filled with so many emotions and images of Dianora that only by writing about her can he regain his calm. But his words all fall short. He can't capture his impressions. Each one of his rhymes seems trite.

He puts away his papers. He wishes he could return to the Rocca just to be close to her, but that would only raise suspicions.

He has to stay where he is and suffer through the anxiety and restlessness.

The night is long and filled with thoughts of Dianora. Even when, many hours later, his weary body seems close to falling asleep, he sees her face before him. He gets some rest around dawn, at which point he then feels obliged to get up, get dressed, and entrust the messenger with his missive, telling him to hurry. Luckily, it's Ardingo, one of the swiftest and most capable of the messengers. Niccolò listens to his horse's hooves clatter down the cobblestones, raising sparks.

He wonders groggily what Pier Soderini will do now.

Perhaps when faced with such a great and imminent danger, he will have to forge an alliance with the only power capable of beating France and the papacy: Spain, the enemy of the French, who controls a large swathe of southern Italy. The main thing is that the man take action and bring an end to all this meaningless prevarication.

CHAPTER TWENTY-EIGHT

This time, Niccolò hears the soft footsteps on the stairs and notices how they stop in front of his door.

"Envoy, it is I, Rodriguez. Are you still asleep?"

Niccolò nervously walks to the door. Did someone see him go in or out of Dianora's room? He doesn't think so. It was too dark. But he can't rule it out.

"I'm awake. What is the purpose of your visit?"

"His Excellency is asking for you."

There's no way out, Niccolò thinks as he quickly opens the door. Rodriguez is alone.

"Has the duke returned?"

"This morning at dawn. He asks you to bring him what you have written."

"I left it at the Rocca."

Valentino is wearing neither his mask nor his gloves. He's in his riding clothes and is covered in dust from traveling.

Dianora is nowhere to be seen. Had it all been a trap? The expression on the duke's face seems friendly enough. Can Niccolò trust him?

"Welcome, Machiavelli. I was eager to see you and read the new pages."

The duke appears to be in a good mood. He reaches out for the new chapter. Niccolò relaxes and hands him the black leather folder that contains the most recently completed section; Valentino opens it and picks up the first piece of paper.

"Before you begin reading, Your Excellency, I need to convey a message to you from the gonfalonier on behalf of the fate of Silvestro de' Buosi, whom you are keeping prisoner. Pier Soderini offers a sincere apology if he has in some way offended you."

Borgia's brow furrows as he reflects on the case. "Silvestro de' Buosi? Ah yes, Naldi's troops captured him. They were furious with him and wanted to kill him."

"The Republic would be both grateful and willing to offer a recompense if you would free him."

"It's already a great deal that he's alive. I asked Naldi to spare his life even though he didn't want to, but I certainly can't free him. What do I stand to gain by helping one and offending many? I will order that he be treated with care, this much I can do."

He looks down at the page and begins to read carefully, stopping here and there to ponder a passage, ignoring Niccolò, who stands nearby. Or perhaps he has forgotten about him entirely.

At least half an hour goes by before Cesare speaks. He seems transfixed; occasionally he nods lightly.

Outside the window, from the plains, comes the sound of soldiers training for battle under the command of military fife and drum units. The duke is so concentrated on what he is reading that he doesn't even notice.

Finally he looks up and toward Niccolò but his eyes peer far off into the distance. "Your prose has a classical ring to it. I like it. Here and there it reminds me of Sallust."

"Actually I was thinking of him while I wrote it."

"You can tell, but only a careful eye would be able to detect it. I often read Sallust. And Tacitus, and Plutarch, too, as you know. At night, before falling asleep, their chronicles keep me company. I find them instructive."

"I agree with you."

"You did a very good job this time. The only thing that occurs to me is that you're lacking in warfare experience."

"I was present at—"

"—at many battles against Pisa, I know. But you were always

in the background. You don't know what a person feels during battle. Come, sit down, take notes."

They sit down at the stone table. Valentino brusquely pushes away the stack of libelous writings, rests his forearms on the surface, and stares at Niccolò.

"It's important to take the information that our subordinates report with a margin of error. When soldiers are sent out, they tend to see the enemies as being more numerous than they actually are."

"So how do you make a decision?"

"I bring together all the information I have and then decide. On my own. If I am weak, I retreat. Otherwise I attack with a rapid offensive and always in places where the enemy doesn't expect it, where he feels strong."

"Strong?"

"Yes, although obviously not to an excessive degree. I always position my armies carefully before I go into battle. I station them in places where I can assemble them rapidly, in a single day. I can do battle against thirty thousand men with just ten thousand."

Who exactly is he talking to now? His biographer or the envoy of the Republic? Perhaps both at the same time.

"Do you know what truly decides the outcome of a battle? What really pushes the soldiers forward? It's the example of their superiors and the people alongside them. Yes, when we do battle, we're . . . like brothers. And what guarantees victory is . . . the spirit that a true commander can arouse in his soldiers."

"Spirit?"

"Yes. Spirit counts far more than weapons, which of course have to be the best. How do you think I conquered Romagna? Only with cannons? No, they would never have been enough on their own. My men were galvanized by desire. A desire for adventure and conquest that I managed to instill in them."

"But what if the troops stop and panic in the midst of a battle? What if they retreat?"

"Then I make sure that the men who bring up the rear slay them."

Niccolò continues to take notes. The fife and drums grow louder.

"Military life is the highest form of existence, believe me. In it lies the secret of power . . . "

A decisive knock at the door interrupts them.

"Enter!" Valentino says, somewhat annoyed, but sits up when he sees a tense Corella coming toward him, accompanied by a messenger covered in dust.

Don Miguel announces that there's news from the third district but before continuing he glances rapidly at Niccolò. Should he continue?

Cesare nods, he may.

Corella informs him that two villages have rebelled and chased out the garrison soldiers.

The work of Fosco Tinardeschi, Niccolò thinks to himself. While Borgia's allies are proposing peace they are simultaneously preparing for war, perhaps to procure better conditions from the treaty that they're currently negotiating.

Valentino is almost pleased by the news. "Good, Miguel! Sack and burn the villages! That will serve as an example and will rouse the soldiers' spirits."

He turns to Niccolò. As if dictating, he says, "It's healthy when a conquered town fights back, much in the same way that certain illnesses, when well cured, make the organism stronger."

He looks at Corella. "Show no pity. Raze the buildings to the ground, hang all rebel leaders, and slaughter their families."

He turns back to Niccolò. "Rebels need to be punished swiftly. That's how you keep your kingdom."

Niccolò is stunned. As Borgia goes back to issuing orders to don Miguel on how and when and where to strike, Niccolò compares the man's lucid ferocity with the dithering and irresolute conduct of the Dieci and I-have-faith, and thinks back to how especially ineffective the leaders were at the revolt of

Arezzo, the summer before. They didn't punish the city for rebelling, they left the walls intact, they sent in additional troops,
and ordered the noblemen of Arezzo to come to Florence for a
scolding. Talk instead of action. Words alone cannot keep the
Republic standing.

"Did you hear what I said?"

Niccolò is distracted. The duke finishes giving instructions
to Corella, who starts to leave, and the duke is now addressing
him again.

"We were discussing what it means to do battle when we
were interrupted. I want you to understand what I'm talking
about, and experience is the best instructor. Miguel!"

Corella, already at the door, turns back. "Yes, my lord."

"Before you leave, send me a fifer and a drummer. The best
ones."

Niccolò looks with curiosity at Valentino. What is he
thinking?

"Follow me," Cesare says and walks over to the balcony.

They step out into the bright sunshine. The two crossbowmen who stand at either end automatically raise their weapons
and point them out at the plains.

Below, beyond the dry ditch, obeying the signals relayed to
them by the fife and drum corps, are four companies of one
hundred men. They're simulating a deep attack against a hillock that is being defended, for the sake of the exercise, by two
hundred soldiers spread out in five rows. The assailants advance in close-knit ranks, one after the next.

"Those men are all subjects of mine from Romagna, they're
the same men you saw marching in a disorganized manner
under your window. They were farmers, with no experience
of weapons. I entrusted them to my best trainers and now, in
less than a month, they move as a compact unit. Look at how
they immediately recognize the signals that are being communicated to them. Can you see? Each company has its own fifer

and drummer, near the flag-bearer. Can you hear the beat of that drum? It's from that company, the one farthest away, down there. That sound means: turn to the right. And do you hear the fifer? That means: to the attack."

Niccolò watches as the troops indicated by Borgia change direction and begin to rush up the hill. Other signals directed to troops on the opposite side have them bend to the left and begin running up the hill. The two central groups maintain the pace. Then they, too, initiate a swift attack, following different signals.

"That's the flanking maneuver, and it wasn't terribly well executed. But they will improve. Soon I will be able to send them into battle and they will fight honorably."

Niccolò realizes that Valentino is capably transforming simple peasants into his own private militia. He wonders whether Florence might ever do the same.

There's the sound of footsteps behind them. The drummer and fifer have arrived.

"Do you want to try and control the troops, Niccolò? I will order them to follow the commands issued from up here. You merely have to tell the musicians where you want them to go and your commands will be translated into music."

"I truly do not think I am capable, Your Excellency."

"Try! It costs you nothing!"

Before he can even answer, Valentino has told the fifer and drummer to issue a command to the entire company: stop, listen, and prepare for commands to be executed as one unit.

"They're all yours," Cesare says, gesturing to the soldiers who have interrupted their assault exercise and are busily recomposing their ranks, only slightly ruffled after their running.

"What should I do?"

"Whatever you want."

"Are you sure?"

"Stop wasting time."

"I would like the troops to go around the hillock and approach one side of those who are defending it."

"All together or one at a time?" the drummer asks him.

"All together."

The drummer beats loudly on his drum, echoing from above, and the sound of the fife flies through the air over the plains. The four groups do an about-face, retreat about a hundred meters, shift their formation, and recompose themselves.

Then the music of the drummer and fifer changes. The four hundred soldiers obey.

Niccolò observes how the dark mass advances like a single person. He feels loftily surprised that he was the one who made it happen, almost noble. Something deeply primordial rises up inside him.

Borgia watches him attentively, judging him. "Are you beginning to understand what it means to be in command?"

Niccolò nods.

"There's nothing quite like this feeling," Valentino adds.

Niccolò, thrilled, issues another order for the musicians. "To the attack!"

The two men hesitate and glance at the duke.

"You want them to attack now?" Cesare asks to be certain and with some amusement.

"Now. Yes."

Valentino smiles and turns to the drummer and fifer. "Obey him."

There's a fast roll of the drums, a shrill whistle from the fifer, and the troops rush forward in unison. The first line sinks into the ditch. A few of them clamber out, but before they can all emerge, the second line is already on top of them. Then the third line closes in and the soldiers fall together in a shapeless heap. The men in the final row stop short and lose formation.

Borgia bursts out laughing. "Didn't you see the ditch?"

"No . . ."

At a gesture from the duke, the fifer and drummer stop. Cesare can't stop laughing. It's contagious and soon Niccolò is laughing, too. The crossbowmen and players try not to chuckle but have a hard time of it.

"Do you know that those men think that I gave the order?" Niccolò is mortified. He turns serious again.

"Don't worry! It's not serious! We'll say it was that idiot of an ambassador from Ferrara, that I let him command briefly to please my sister, the Duchess, Her Ladyship," Valentino says, laughing again. "I'm grateful for the distraction, thank you." The duke wipes away a few tears and issues terse orders to the two musicians. The drummer drums, the fifer fifes. In the blink of an eye, the soldiers retreat. Those who fell down jump to their feet, and the rows are recomposed.

"Companies in line," Borgia orders.

The men get line up.

"Half-moon formation."

The mass of soldiers assumes the shape of a scythe.

"Advance at top speed."

Dust rises from eight hundred feet running at the same time across the plain.

"Faster."

The dust cloud grows thicker.

"Bend the tip of the half-moon toward the hillock, have the rest of the army follow. At the attack."

The scythe attacks in one point only, cutting through the lines of defense. The two groups mix together.

Cesare looks over at Niccolò, who is watching in admiration.

"That's what a commander can do. If this were a real battle, from this moment on everything would depend on the soldiers, as I was saying earlier." He turns to the drummer and fifer. "Beat the retreat," he orders. Then Cesare looks at Niccolò. "And you go back to your desk; it's better for everyone."

CHAPTER TWENTY-NINE

Niccolò hurries back to his study filled with the emotion of commanding the troops. He feels like he's flying over the Rocca, over Imola, over all of Romagna, the same way he felt when he looked at Leonardo's map. His gaze takes in the lands around him, Tuscany, all of Italy; he revels in the fact that their country is desired by Louis XII, the Pope, and Valentino. Nothing good can ever come from the Church or France, but Cesare, on the other hand . . .

This is a man who knows how to fight—and how to win. Does he really have the wellbeing of Italy at heart? Dianora says he doesn't but she could be wrong. Niccolò saw firsthand how his judges execute their roles fairly. Of course, if the duke were on trial they wouldn't dare condemn him, but he is just with his subjects. And the majority of the people hold him in high esteem. Yes, he's a killer, but his cruelty can be used for both good and bad. It's true he had his brother, Giovanni, and his brother-in-law killed, but now he has the strongest army in central Italy and exerts control over a huge territory. Yes, he's unscrupulous—he just can't help himself—but he has a plan.

Hasn't Rome always been ruthless? Hasn't Rome always done far worse, ever since it came into being? The Romans never forgave their enemies. They never hesitated to spill blood whenever necessary.

He enters the study, glances at the window, and thinks of Dianora. He imagines her face, her gestures, the intimacies she shared with him, all her suffering, and he feels ashamed of considering Cesare's aspirations the least bit noble. It's as if he has betrayed her merely with the thought.

He rushes to the window, opens it, and leans out. Dianora's room is dark. He waits for a long time, ducking back in each time someone passes below.

Dianora doesn't come to the window.

Back at the inn, late that night, an exhausted messenger arrives with the gonfalonier's reply. No change in plan, not for now. Niccolò's task remains the same as when he left: propose an alliance with Valentino but do it slowly, while continuing to spy on him.

In normal ink, I-have-faith asks him to pursue the issue of Silvestro de' Buosi, as if he were a very important figure. He does not know that the prisoner will never be freed.

As Niccolò reads the missive, he feels unease and anger building inside of him. He tastes bitterness in his mouth, as if he had been poisoned. It's clear that *Vexillifer Perpetuus* is going to continue with this tactic of delays—although Niccolò isn't entirely sure why—and that he will never consider forming an alliance with Spain.

Night falls and Niccolò can't sleep. He dips his pen in the invisible ink and rapidly composes an epigram that he writes down on white paper. The lines disappear as soon as his words take shape.

La notte che morì Pier Soderini,
l'alma n'andò de l'Inferno a la bocca;
e Pluto le gridò: "Anima sciocca,
che Inferno? Va' nel Limbo tra' bambini."[5]

CHAPTER THIRTY

RES GESTÆ CÆSARIS
The early conquests of Valentino in Romagna:
the siege of Imola and Forlì

A number of great achievements took place at the end of 1499.
In December, Valentino, unifying soldiers from the armies of
the King of France and the Church, marched into Romagna.
The city of Imola surrendered immediately, as did most of
Forlì, although not the stronghold, which Caterina Sforza was
determined to defend, rallying her men for support and rely-
ing on stockpiles of munitions . . .

Niccolò stops writing. The moment he has most been fearing has arrived: he has to write about the fall of the fortress in Forlì. The words don't come easily. Dianora has told him what happened and he doesn't want to betray the painful secrets she shared with him. Anteo Nuffi wouldn't hesitate to do so, but then again, he would stab his own mother with a pen if needed. He would probably even enjoy it. But Niccolò is different.

He also has a clear task to perform, and if he doesn't do it right he won't be able to continue with his mission. What words should he use? He knows that truth can be dressed in many ways, that you can say one thing and that it can be interpreted in an opposite way, but he hesitates. His sense of duty is at odds with his sentiments.

He recalls how Dianora spoke to him in the sacristy; he can't write anything that will sully her. Only through omission can he respect her. He will find something else to write about, and it won't be hard to fill the pages. He thinks back to Caterina Sforza and how he met with her in Forlì when he was sent there as an envoy. He will write about her, Cesare's enemy. There's a great deal to say because she was so many things all at once: vulgar and refined, sensual and erudite. He will describe her greatness while also celebrating Valentino. Dignifying the enemy does not diminish the protagonist, after all.

Niccolò learned this important lesson when he was around ten years old. Before he figured out how to avoid church, his mother, Bartolomea, who always smelled so wonderfully clean, used to send him to Mass. Once, a priest spoke about a passage from the Gospel according to John—or was it Mark?—in which Jesus is questioned by Pontius Pilate. The priest's words stayed with him. The prefect of Judea, who held the power of deciding the prisoner's life or death, asked him if it is true what people say: *Are you the King of the Jews?* To admit to the crime was equivalent to a death sentence as it meant he was contrary to the emperor of Rome. At first, Christ hesitated and then he admitted it: *You said as much; I am King.* It was the Gospel of John, Niccolò recalls. It could have all ended there: Jesus admitted to the crime and condemnation was unavoidable. But then Jesus added that he was born to bear witness to the truth, and that people on the side of truth would hear his words.

The final decision on the matter fell to the enemy, Pontius Pilate. *Quid est veritas?* he asked. What is truth? It is a question that has no answer. In fact, not even Christ could reply.

If an apostle had written about this in a text dedicated to the glory of the Messiah, Niccolò could do something similar for Caterina Sforza—and indirectly for Dianora—without detracting from Cesare in any way.

He's about to pick up his pen and start writing when he hears something outside the door. By now, he has come to recognize the man's footstep and even his way of knocking.

"Rodriguez, is that you?"

"Yes, Envoy. The duke would like to see you."

"Now?" he says, opening the door.

"That is what he said."

The north wind scatters dead leaves far and wide.

Niccolò wonders why he has been summoned at this unusual hour and imagines that Valentino must need something urgently from Florence. He puzzles over what it could possibly be.

He knows that I-have-faith's choice to prolong his strategy of evasion will not protect the city forever. Attacks might be temporarily postponed because of the snow, which normally falls heavily on the Apennines in December. As long as the duke doesn't make his move beforehand . . . As long as the winter isn't a mild one . . .

When he reaches the open space in front of the Rocca, he observes the mountain of scaffolding around the theater. They're busy stuccoing and painting and filling in the fissures in the construction. His thoughts go to Dianora. Maybe he will see her again. Finally. His mood lifts.

With a great show of formality, a servant opens the door to the great hall and steps aside so that Niccolò can enter. He catches a glimpse of Dianora: her skirt and petticoat are in disarray and she looks deeply unhappy. As she slides off the stone table, he notices the blue of her stockings, which have been lowered down to her knees, and the fair skin of her thighs. Borgia is standing with his back to Niccolò, facing the window. He's arranging something under his doublet.

Instinctively, Niccolò backs up to leave, but the servant has already shut the door behind him.

Dianora shuffles across the room, near the wall, her eyes downcast. She coughs repeatedly, her eyes are shiny and feverish. Niccolò feels deep pain for her. If it were possible, he would take her in his arms and console her.

She disappears down the corridor, still coughing. The duke turns to Niccolò.

"Ah, you're already here? I expected you a little later."

"I came as soon as I received your message."

Cesare sits down in one of the stone chairs and indicates the other to Niccolò.

He obeys. They sit face to face. Between them is the table on which Dianora had just been forced to lay. A book of poems rests on the surface.

"Have your people in Florence made up their minds?" Borgia asks, scrutinizing him.

How can Niccolò keep buying time? "You said it yourself, Your Highness. In a republic, the decisions are made by many. This explains why they still haven't let me know anything about your offer of alliance."

"That may be, but I feel obliged to tell you that now Vitelli and the others seek peace and friendship with me . . . "

Niccolò feigns surprise. Valentino goes on.

"They, too, are numerous, so negotiations with them are also taking some time. Everyone has a different opinion and they can't come to an agreement. They have yet to agree on all the details of our accord. Vitelli is giving himself airs, and so is the lord of Bologna. Paolo Orsini is trying to convince them but may not succeed. It would be good if Florence acted swiftly, if your reply arrived before theirs."

"I, too, hope for this."

"What exactly seems to be the difficulty? As I see it, we can be friends in a general way or in a specific way. Generally speaking, I already consider myself your friend and I hope you feel the same way about me. However, we need to become friends specifically . . . "

Where is Borgia going with this conversation? The duke gets to his feet and starts pacing back and forth, talking freely and dramatically. He called urgently for Niccolò because he wants to tell him certain things that he has never admitted to any living soul; he wants to tell him so that Niccolò, in turn, will communicate them to the Dieci and the gonfalonier, so they are fully aware of the situation. In April of the year before, shortly after conquering Faenza, the duke goes on to say, the Orsini brothers and Vitellozzo tried to convince him to return to Rome with his entire army via Florence. He said no; he didn't trust them back then either. He knew that it was all a pretext to try and conquer the Republic of Florence with a surprise attack. Vitelli threw himself at the duke's feet—he wasn't exaggerating—and swore that neither the city nor any towns would be harmed. But Borgia detected betrayal and did not agree to the plan.

Niccolò stares at the duke, no longer shocked in the least by his mendacity. It's not just his boldness, it's something more than that: Borgia seems to enjoy distorting the past, modifying things in a way that pleases him.

Cesare's voice grows louder as he continues. He assures Niccolò that, even then, he cared very deeply about his friendship with the Republic, and that he chose not to listen to Orsini or Vitelli when they suggested attacking Florence where the city was most vulnerable . . .

Naturally he avoids mentioning where that was.

He goes on to add that not only did he reject their plan, but he also threatened to fight them. They, of course, went ahead without him and created all the troubles that Niccolò knew so well, which also upset the harmony that existed between Borgia and the Republic.

"Now, because of our existing friendship, I would like to make a new proposal, and I beg you to communicate it to your lordships immediately," the duke says.

"Of course."

"My soldiers are top notch. Last year, your Republic asked me to be a condottiere for the city, and we even set a price. But then nothing came of it. Tell your leaders that I would gladly fight in the name of Florence. Of course, the offer would have to be appealing, higher than the one made me last year."

Niccolò took his time to answer. "Would you really want to go back to being in service as a condottiere?"

"Half of Italy's noblemen are in service, why shouldn't I be too?"

"Up until now you've always hired your own condottieri."

Borgia laughs. "And that's precisely one reason why it's time to change. I want you to write to the gonfalonier and the Dieci with my suggestion. I hope they welcome the idea. And tell them something else . . . " Valentino's eyes shine with dark amusement. "Tell them that the King of France might actually order you to take this duke," he taps himself on his chest, "into your service. My cousin could easily command you to rely on my men—and then you would be forced to do it. Remind the Lordships that if you know you owe someone a favor, it's always better to offer to do it, rather than to be forced."

Niccolò rushes back to the inn with the image of Dianora's distraught expression at the forefront of his mind, how she darted off when he walked in. Clearly she was unwell and had a fever, but not even that was enough to stop Valentino from taking advantage of her.

The man has absolutely no mercy, just as he would have none for Florence. Borgia had a hard time conquering the Republic of Florence when he acted impulsively and now he actually wants the city leaders to invite him across the border, and even pay him! While it's true that a condottiere has to go wherever his master sends him, and the Dieci and the gonfalonier would undoubtedly send him to attack Pisa, who could ever truly harness a man like that? Once he got his army inside the borders of the Republic, he could do whatever he pleased; it's a short march from Pisa to Florence.

What will I-have-faith and the Dieci decide to do? Valentino is putting them in a bind. It would be dangerous to turn him away, especially after mentioning the King of France. And yet, agreeing to his request is untenable.

What about Dianora? How and when will Niccolò see her again? What is ailing her? Is it only a chill, a minor seasonal

220 - FRANCO BERNINI

illness? Or did the old hag infect her with some kind of sickness of the lungs? If she gets worse, will they send her away from the Rocca? Dianora told her that Cesare doesn't like taking risks . . . Will he isolate her too, as he did with Lucina?

CHAPTER THIRTY-ONE

D*o you have news of the French spearmen? Are they in Faenza or have they moved elsewhere? What are people saying? The woman who guards Dianora Mambelli is unwell and has been taken away. Do you know where she has been sent? Even Her Ladyship Mambelli is ailing . . .*

He stops writing and tears up the message for Farneti. That last line was too direct, it would reveal an excessive interest in Dianora. He starts over.

Do you have news of the French spearmen? Are they in Faenza or have they moved elsewhere? I overheard a soldier say there were rumors of the plague at the Rocca. Anyone who is sick is being sent away. Do you know where they take them, and who they might be? Perhaps someone in close contact with the duke?

He reads it over. That sounds better. This way he will obtain the information he wants without raising suspicions. Why didn't he get it right the first time? Is it wise to lie about rumors of the plague? He has always instinctively known what he can and can't say . . . What has changed? What's wrong with him?

He burns the first message. Then, wrapped in his elegant mantle, he walks out of Porta Montanara.

The tents are all gone. The fields are empty. It is as if there had never been a military encampment there. The soldiers have relocated. But where have they gone?

He walks toward the oak forest, where he leaves the message for his informer.

He returns just as the guards are about to close the city gates.

As he makes his way back to the inn, he sees a man ahead of

222 · FRANCO BERNINI

him, sword hanging by his side. He looks familiar but Niccolò can't recall where he has seen him before. He's with two wiry young men, also armed. He observes them closely and, as he gets closer, he sees that it's Fosco Tinardeschi, the soldier who fights under Vitelli. How is it that he is walking, armed, down the streets of Imola? Niccolò pretends not to see him for both their sakes, but Tinardeschi turns around, salutes him, and waits for him to catch up.

"Why hello again, Machiavelli. They're watching me, of course, but now that we've signed an agreement with the duke, there's really nothing strange about the fact that I'm speaking with the envoy of Florence, is there?"

"Greetings to you," Niccolò says with a puzzled look.

Tinardeschi imagines what he's thinking and offers a reply. "I'm here as an ambassador. I carry with me the agreement signed by my lord as well as those who have joined forces with him. Otherwise I wouldn't dare set foot in the city. Cesare knows me well, as do many others in his circle; it would be too risky to challenge destiny."

"So everyone has agreed to sign the pact?"

"Everyone except Baglioni, who's still negotiating. He wants better conditions for Bologna."

"And His Excellency has signed?"

"Not yet, but he will."

And yet, Cesare had told Niccolò the exact opposite. "When will you stop fighting him?" he asks.

"We've already stopped."

"And what are the conditions of your agreement? May I know?"

"Of course . . . if you buy us something to drink."

The wine that they serve in the osteria is strong and fragrant. Tinardeschi enjoys it thoroughly, as do his two aides-de-camp. One of them has smooth cheeks with a few dark whiskers and a maniacal look in his eyes, while the other one has a heavy jaw, high cheekbones, and greasy brown hair. Both men speak little and listen carefully.

Tinardeschi lists the clauses in the agreement that Niccolò already knows, having read it in the duke's private archive. The terms have not changed. The exchange of hostages that will confirm the validity of the pact has already taken place. Vitelli and the others have each sent one of their own sons to the duke. Many carts of gold are now en route to seal the deal.

"In other words, you have returned to siding with the dragon . . ." Niccolò says.

Fosco stares at him as he takes a sip of his wine, the expression in his eyes contradicting the comment that follows. "Yes, Paolo Orsini managed to convince everyone. My lord was skeptical up until the very end but then he also decided to join the alliance."

"What do you personally think about it?"

"I am merely a soldier; I obey."

"Who will you do battle against now?"

"This I can't tell you. I go where they order me."

No one says a word, but it is clear that thanks to the alliance between Borgia, Vitelli, and the others, they can go wherever they want.

"You should have accepted our proposal to join forces," Tinardeschi adds.

"Unfortunately, it's not my decision to make."

"I know, I know. In your own way, you're just a soldier, like me." He pauses, then takes another sip. "Have you seen the duke much since you've been here? I haven't. I have only spoken with his secretary."

"Monsignor Geraldini."

"Yes, him. I noticed that they transformed a part of the Rocca in apartments—what do they call it? Palazzetto del Paradiso?"

Niccolò nods, while reflecting that the conversation is taking an odd turn.

"Does Valentino sleep there when he's in Imola?" Fosco

asks. He's trying to make his questions seem casual but Niccolò notices that one of the two men, the one with the heavy jaw and greasy hair, sits up in excitement, while the other man, the one with a few dark whiskers, pretends not to care.

"I know very little about his actions; the duke never discusses his routines."

"Yes, of course. From what I've heard, he's the embodiment of secrecy. Some time ago, during the Romagna campaign, I worked closely with him. By day, he was always surrounded by his guards. At night, he kept the door to his room locked from the inside and only his manservant could come in, and only after identifying himself. I wonder if he still does that."

"I can't say, really. I imagine those are precautions that all lords take," Niccolò says, trying to end the conversation. It was getting too perilous for him.

"Yes, of course. I had Vitellozzo adopt the same measures. Exactly the same. The manservant was allowed to knock on the commander's door only when he was absolutely certain that no one had followed him. It's a good habit and usually it's effective."

"You mean sometimes it's not?"

Tinardeschi shrugs. "It all depends," he says, filling his glass. Niccolò turns to look at Jaws, who is following the conversation keenly but then looks away. Whiskers, meanwhile, holds his gaze.

CHAPTER THIRTY-TWO

N iccolò returned to the Rocca four times in two days, each time making his way up to his study and looking out at Dianora's window, but she never reappeared. He thought incessantly about her. He tried to obtain an audience with Valentino, in order to get some news, and when he did not succeed, he cautiously asked his secretary a few discreet questions, but received only the vaguest of replies.

In the meantime he wrote to Florence with all the news he had acquired about the agreement between Borgia and his allies. The messengers galloped off into the mountains, the members of the Dieci met with the gonfalonier, the issues were discussed, and they wrote back to their envoy, who responded with additional information. Messengers came and went.

The Republic still hasn't decided what they want Niccolò to say to the Prince.

On the second day, he finds a reply from Farneti in the hollow tree: the French spearmen have set up camp in the mountains. They could easily invade Tuscany from any point along the road that Niccolò traveled from Florence to Imola, or from a number of other places. The informant writes that the duke will be sending artillery via another route, and he offers a suggestion as to which one.

Farneti also included details about the topic of most interest to Niccolò. There are no cases of the plague at the Rocca. The Spanish woman, Lucina, was sent to a farm on the banks of the Santerno river out of precaution, but it wasn't the much-feared illness that eventually killed her: she died because she had serious problems with her lungs. It would appear that Dianora Mambelli has the same symptoms but in a lighter form, and she is being kept at the Rocca. Luckily, there are no signs of plague here now, Farneti wrote, but if it does arrive, we can only hope that it will beset Valentino.

Niccolò feels encouraged. So Dianora is not seriously ill. He will see her again.

Chapter Thirty-Three

An urgent letter from the Dieci arrives, delivered in great haste by Totto, the messenger. Niccolò has been instructed to communicate the contents of the letter to the duke immediately.

The members of the Dieci, shrewd merchants that they are, know that even spoiled merchandise can be sold when offered in the right way. They suggest that Niccolò pretend not to know about the agreement that has been reached between the duke and the allies. Regarding the duke's proposal to become a condottiere for the Republic, the envoy should say that the Republic would be deeply honored but that such an important condottiere would need to be paid vast sums of money, which they simply do not have at their disposal, and that they would be embarrassed to offer him anything less than what he deserves.

Niccolò hopes to see Dianora in the great hall, but she's not there. Valentino gets up from his throne and strides toward him swiftly and tensely, like a threatening beast. Not a good start. What Niccolò has to say will only worsen his foul mood. He expects the duke to respond with sarcasm and has phrases ready to keep him in check.

"I bring you a reply from the Dieci . . . " Niccolò begins cautiously.

"I'm fed up with their lies. And with yours," Cesare say quickly.

He's furious, but why? Niccolò notices the black leather folder that holds the most recent chapter of *Res gestæ Cæsaris* lying open on the floor, pages scattered everywhere, as if Borgia had thrown it down in disgust. He sees that it has been marked up in red, some sections are underlined, there are notes between the lines, all in an unfamiliar handwriting. Whole passages have been crossed out and rewritten in the margins . . . Niccolò feels like he's been stabbed in the heart.

Niccolò looks at the duke, who stands across from him, and is about to ask him what happened, but there's no time.

"Something in your pages sounded terribly wrong! I just couldn't hold back. I was deeply disturbed by them."

"I apologize. And yet before you were pleased. What changed?"

"Don't interrupt me! I read it over and I know what it is," he says, pointing at the papers on the ground. "In your choice of words I detect that sneaky smile of yours; it's as if you're making fun of me. So I had a famous writer look at the pages, someone who deserves his laurels! And he agreed that you have treated me worse than my own worst enemies!" Cesare points to the libelous and defamatory books that lie on the stone table.

"But no! How can you say that!" Niccolò protests, but wearily. How many times has he seen this happen? Something praised one day is considered worthless the next. How easily those in power change their evaluations when they're poorly advised . . . But who did Borgia talk to? Who did he ask to read it?

"And who might this literary figure be?" he finally asks.

"The name is not important."

"There's always a certain amount of jealousy among writers, maybe that's why . . . "

"You're not even a real writer . . . "

The pain Niccolò feels is transformed into rage. "That's not what you said before! You even compared me to Sallust!"

"I was under an illusion. I simply couldn't see how weak a writer you are."

"And what exactly are my weaknesses? Allow me to prove you wrong."

"It's everything, all of it. It's all weak. And you can't keep asking me to waste my precious time with you!"

Valentino's voice is so bitterly angry it's clear he has taken it personally. His breathing is ragged with rage.

"You're wrong, but as you wish. I'll return the advance you gave me," Niccolò says, knowing full well that this is impossible as he has already spent much of it.

"Keep it! What's that to me? You did what you could, which is to say very little. I will have someone capable rewrite it all."

Niccolò is filled with relief. At least he managed to avoid a dangerous and humiliating situation, the worst a writer can experience. He shrugs, bends down to pick up his pages, and reads some of the words in red: *But aren't we all truly vile? Don't we all find pleasure in our baseness?*

He immediately knows who is behind it: Anteo Nuffi. Hadn't the duke dismissed him? He must've called him back. But when? What did it matter now?

He's about to stand up with the papers in his hand, but Valentino kicks them out of his grasp and they fly everywhere.

"Leave them alone! I paid for them! They belong to me," he says darkly.

Niccolò stares at him long and hard. "You would do well to hold onto them. People will forget about Anteo Nuffi, but my words will live on in perpetuity!" It was a giant risk, but he seems to have hit the bullseye. Borgia squints at him and then shrugs.

"Why do you say such meaningless things?" the duke says, and yet his tone has changed.

"I kindly ask you to formally dismiss me."

"You can go. Leave. Tell your Republic that their time is up. They could have formed an alliance with me but they did not. Too bad for them."

Niccolò nods and heads toward the exit. He weighs the man's final words. The agreement that he came to with Orsini,

Vitelli, and the others has fortified him. Valentino doesn't need to pretend anymore. Neither does Florence.

He feels deeply wounded, as if he had been severely beaten with a stick. People have told me before that I have no future as a writer, that I have no talent, but here I am, he tells himself while leaving the Rocca. He wanders down the main street of the city, his mood alternating between rage and melancholy.

Will he ever be able to express the words that fill his heart?

What if it's true that he really isn't cut out to be a writer? Sometimes he worries about that. All he has ever written consists of a handful of poems, the beginnings of a few historical discourses, the countless letters he's written to and for the Republic, and commissioned writings that he signs *servitor*, servant to the Lords of the Signoria, documents that will end up rotting in the archives.

And what about his women, the loves of his life? There are Marietta and Primerana, of course. Dianora . . . Dianora, whom he will never see again. While other authors and poets had their Beatrices and Lauras, he has whores whose names he has forgotten.

And yet he feels immense gratitude to them nonetheless. While their names may at times escape him, he recalls their faces and other certain aspects of them: the five blond women he met in France, for example, the brunette from Forlì, and Licia . . . Licia who never complains, Licia who would never hurt him, Licia, to whose chambers he is currently headed.

The two of them go directly upstairs and spend the night together. Early in the morning, when he wakes up, it occurs to him that if God actually existed, Niccolò wouldn't be able to praise him enough for having created woman; they show us what life is, not just by bringing us into this world, but simply by existing. And when the world knocks us flat, they help us to our feet.

As he's getting dressed, he realizes that the self-pity he

experienced the night before has been transformed into a renewed strength. He thanks Licia for bringing back his spirit and even makes her laugh.

We are each our own person, he says as he walks out into the street, rain falling lightly. I don't care what others say, I will be myself, and I will continue to write the way I know how.

Unfortunately, though, I'll never be able to see Dianora again.

CHAPTER THIRTY-FOUR

T he following morning a major storm unleashes all its fury on the city. Rivers of rain flow down the cobblestone roads and under doorways, small waves are pushed forth by the wind, everything is flooded.

He tries to play tric trac with Baccino but can't concentrate. He keeps thinking about Dianora and is constantly distracted. And yet he continues to play, even when he realizes it has stopped raining from the sound of voices and footsteps on the cobblestones outside. He rolls the dice, moves his black and white pieces across the triangular spaces, and reflects on the fact that although Valentino may have chased away the writer in him, he can't dismiss an envoy quite as easily. There are certain protocols that need to be respected. And if Borgia finds he needs Niccolò, if there are matters of State to attend to, he won't hesitate to call him back and pretend that nothing ever happened. If that comes to pass, he will ask after Dianora.

Gemma, the innkeeper, comes and sits down with them.

Over time, they have established a relationship of trust with her. Gemma lost three babies shortly after giving birth and her husband died from a mysterious illness. Every so often, under her rough ways, he sees signs of the cheerful woman she once was. Today, however, she is concerned. People say that the plague has come back. Everyone knows the troubles and grief that comes with it, both for those who fall ill and for those who do not. She says she'll start stocking up on dried meat because, if the rumors are true, it will be hard to leave the house for food. She'll also start to wear her medallion of San Rocco again, as he protects those who pray to him.

He listens to her while she speaks. Even though he knows he might have been the one to start the rumor, which Farneti must have involuntarily spread by going around and asking people questions, his own fears of the illness suddenly come to life inside him. Actually, they have never really gone away. The plague has cropped up far too many times, people have been talking about it ever since he was young, often, he noticed, without addressing the topic directly or at any great length, as if merely talking about the malady could bring it to life. He was only ten when the plague first came to Milan. It spread from there, reaching the outskirts of Florence and then vanishing. It returned when he was fourteen, in an even more serious manner. That time, too, it had started in Lombardy and it got even closer. He remembered the initial skepticism, the increasing panic, the constant talk of danger, and the silences, which weighed heavier than the words themselves. He recalled his mother's pale face and his father's fear, which he was unable to hide, and the tangible relief when Florence was spared.

He saw the effects of the plague firsthand when he traveled to France, just two years earlier. It was everywhere. To meet with the King, who kept moving around to avoid coming into contact with the illness, he and the other envoy from the Republic had to travel from town to town. One night, when they were in a dirty and poor village, he fell ill. He thought he was going to die, but it turned out only to be a passing illness of the lungs.

Tric! Trac! The dice strike the wooden table and roll to a stop.

He has lost again. "You haven't tricked the dice, have you?" he asks Baccino in jest.

"You just don't know how to play, I'm sorry to say," Baccino replies. Tric! Trac! His score is so high it's practically offensive.

"That's enough for today, Baccino. Otherwise you'll be the ruin of me."

"Don't get upset now, you need to learn how to lose."

"Unfortunately, I have quite a bit of experience in the matter. Don't remind me!"

Baccino turns to Gemma and smiles at her. "How about cooking up something good so the gentleman's bad mood disappears? And with it, all fears of the plague."

The woman nods. "I've got some goose eggs and greens. I picked up the eggs at the market for the two of you."

"Excellent, thank you, Gemma," Niccolò says and walks outside for a breath of fresh air and to dispel his bad mood.

Before he has time to close the front door behind him, a woman approaches. "Are you Machiavello, the Florentine?"

He turns to look at the woman. Hunch-backed and elderly, she is covered in a large, threadbare shawl, and looks very much like a bundle of wool with two blue eyes.

"Who would like to know?" he replies without identifying himself.

"The prior from the monastery of the Osservanza sent me. Are you Machiavello or not? A skinny man with a pointed chin, that's what Brother Timoteo told me."

He looks around. It occurs to him that it probably has something to do with Dianora. No one is in sight.

"Don't worry. We're alone," she says. "Otherwise I wouldn't have talked to you. I've been waiting a long time for just the right moment," the old woman says, her eyes revealing the pride she feels for executing her task in the best way possible.

"I am the person you're looking for. What does the prior want?"

"I don't know. He'll tell you himself. He's waiting for you in the sacristy. You go on ahead. I walk slowly; you're young."

"Thank you. Good day to you."

Niccolò hurries off. The woman slowly makes her way home.

Taking the usual safe route, but this time as swiftly as possible, he reaches the monastery and peers into the sacristy.

Brother Timoteo, ensconced in the confessional chair, is reading a book with an elegant binding. He looks up and waves Niccolò over.

"Greetings, prior."

"Ah, so Agata was successful. That woman is as slow as a turtle but as smart as a weasel, and trustworthy like few. Also, she's particularly devoted to me. There's no safer messenger."

"You told me we shouldn't meet up anymore . . . "

The prior smiles slyly and closes his book. "If the prophet Jeremiah says that our Lord can change His mind, why can't a humble friar?"

"If it's written in the Bible . . . " Niccolò replies with amusement, indicating the book in the man's hands.

"This? Ah, no, this is the *Decameron*, a marvelous work by one of your fellow Florentines."

"You're reading Boccaccio?" Niccolò, who is rarely shocked, asks with great surprise.

"I've been reading him for years and I find his writing highly instructive. I often say to my fellow friars: if you want to lead people the path to Paradise, show them the road to Hell first."

"Is that the only reason you read it?" Niccolò asks him provocatively.

"Are you hinting at the sins he recounts? If you only knew how many such stories, and even worse ones, I have to hear in confession," Brother Timoteo says, putting the book away in a closet, then opening the door that leads to the garden. "Come, let's go outside and walk a bit together."

The well-planned gravel paths that run between the plants, with their perfect drainage, are already dry, but there's some snow between the beds. There are waxed cloths wrapped around many of the tree trunks, with straw poking out from underneath, and several clusters of branches have been tied together.

"We have to protect the trees from the cold. They're as delicate as humans, if not more," the prior explains, his hands tucked into the wide sleeves of his vestments. "Every night we bring out steaming pots of infusions of valerian, which fortifies them. I even had the north wall that surrounds the garden reinforced to protect the garden from the wind. It's much warmer here than anywhere else in the city. This is altogether a different world."

Niccolò looks at him in puzzlement. He knows that the friar didn't summon him to discuss plants. In fact, he goes on.

"Lady Mambelli will come and take a walk here tomorrow. I do not know if you are aware, but she has been unwell and still now has some difficulty breathing. She can go out for one hour a day, before lunch time. The master physician has advised it. As of this morning, she can spend an hour here, cloaked in furs, like a queen."

"Thank you for telling me as much, but unfortunately I don't have enough money to—"

"You don't have to worry about that," the prior interrupts him to say, pulling a diamond ring out of his wide sleeve. "The duke showers the young lady with so many gifts that he'll never notice if one bauble is missing. It was given to me to facilitate your meeting." The friar weighs the ring in his fat hand. His fingers are so chubby that he will never be able to wear it, not even on his pinky. He admires it then tucks it away and stares at Niccolò. "Of course, we will have to be very careful."

"The young lady will be closely watched."

"And that is part of the favor that has been asked of me. Now I don't want to know why her ladyship wants to see you so badly . . . but be careful not to end up like the past orator from Venice, Alvise Boscolo, may his soul rest in peace."

"Who?"

"Oh, you didn't know? He was found dead in the river a

year ago. He was also very keen on the young woman and did everything he could to see her."

Niccolò tenses up. What is the friar trying to say? "Were you present at their meetings, too?" he asks.

"He wasn't quite as sharp as you and didn't turn to me for help. But I know that he approached her on several occasions when her ladyship went out. It was noticed and . . . "

"What do you think they talked about?"

"This I can't say."

A year ago Venice was openly hostile to Borgia. Perhaps the ambassador wanted to use Dianora against the duke? Or perhaps she turned to him for help from the Serenissima, the way she's doing now through him with Florence? He feels an intense bitterness but then reminds himself that, even if this is so, anyone in Dianora's position had the right to fight with every weapon available to them.

"How did the orator die exactly?"

"They're not sure. His body was in the water for three days so it was impossible to tell. He was an expert swimmer but he had bruises on his cheekbones and his neck was broken, which could have happened in a fall . . . People talked about it for a long time."

"What did they say?"

"You know how it is. Everyone sees things their own way. Some people said, in a whisper of course, that Boscolo's behavior might have annoyed His Excellency." Brother Timoteo shrugs, as if he doesn't want to talk about the subject any further.

Niccolò feels uneasy, as if he has suddenly discovered himself involved in a dangerous game. He's still in time to extract himself but he doesn't want to. He would like to ask what kind of man the ambassador was, if he was handsome, but he knows he shouldn't. The prior would then understand his motivation for seeing Dianora again. "So what's the plan for tomorrow?" he asks.

The friar looks at him with amusement.

The wind has died down, it's bitterly cold, the sky is pellucid, and the sun brings only a hint of warmth.

Niccolò clambers over the garden wall, jumps down, and rushes over to the hiding place that the friar pointed out the day before. In front of the tool shed there's a tall, thick laurel hedge that conceals him from sight of anyone who steps out of the monastery and into the garden.

He doesn't have to wait long before he sees the prior, Dianora, and three guards. Two of the soldiers halt at the edge of the garden, the third walks up the path with Dianora and Brother Timoteo. Even from afar, Niccolò can see how pale she is. She walks slowly. She's wrapped in a fox fur and is wearing a long, dark brown skirt and head covering.

The friar gestures to Dianora and says something to the guard, who nods. The two men stop, lean on the stone well, and begin to chat. She advances on her own. Slowly she approaches the tool shed and looks around. She passes to the left of where he is hiding and then sits down on a bench near the wall. She leans wearily to one side, closes her eyes, and raises her face toward the sun.

He doesn't dare say a thing. He doesn't want to scare her. When she opens her eyes, she sees him but doesn't flinch. Her expression is filled with both surprise and pleasure. Niccolò smiles at her, and gestures for her to be as quiet as possible.

Dianora nods and glances at the prior and the guard, who are at a distance but not that far away that they can speak in a normal tone of voice. She whispers, opening her mouth only slightly. "Thank you . . . "

"I am the one who ought to thank you. How are you?" he replies, also in a whisper.

"A little better, but very weak." Her words float gently from between her half-open lips.

"Stay strong. The worst is past." Why does saying such trivial things, banalities really, bring him such joy? "He has stripped me of the duty of writing for him. I don't know when we shall see each other anymore."

"I heard. That's why I contacted Brother Timoteo." Now her lips barely even move. She's interrupted by a coughing fit.

"Don't force yourself to speak. I am happy just to see you. I, on the other hand, can't be that much to look at, surrounded by laurel like a piece of roast meat."

Dianora hints at a smile. "I've seen worse." She coughs some more, then recomposes herself, moves over a little so the guards see less of her. "How I've missed our conversations . . . I can't imagine not being able to speak to you. I need it! And I don't want to lose you."

"You won't. We'll find a way."

"But how? I'm afraid this will be the last time. I managed to obtain permission from Torrella, the physician, to spend an hour outside; I hope this hour lasts and lasts . . . I want to pretend that I'm not here. Now that I'm certain you Florentines will fight the duke until the very end, I feel—and don't laugh—as if I were from your city."

"Welcome, then."

Dianora smiles again. "Do you have a wife in Florence, Niccolò?"

She used his first name! How sweet it is to hear her say it. "Yes."

"Children?"

"A little girl, born in September. Her name is Primerana and she is beautiful."

"And your home?"

"Oh, it's on a narrow street, it's small, the sun shines in for only two hours a day, but it's enough for us."

Dianora smiles again, as if picturing the house. "I will imagine you there with your ladies. I wish you all happiness with them."

"This is not farewell, Dianora. I am certain of it." Now he

used her Christian name for the first time. They look at each other deeply. Her eyes are sad but luminous.

"I used to be betrothed to a young man not much older than myself. His family was among those who opened the gates to Valentino."

"I can only imagine the pain . . . "

"I had read so many love poems and thought I knew what love was! But clearly I did not."

"And yet you felt it. Never regret what you have felt. It doesn't matter that the young man and his family betrayed you. If we always knew what was going to happen next, we would never do anything."

Dianora looks at him with gratitude. Then she remembers something and looks upset. "In a little more than a month, it will be two years since I lost everything. It seems like forever." She has another coughing fit. "Forgive me, I . . . I still do not have the strength."

"Rest a little."

"No, I want you to know that I haven't had a friend to confide in since then, but when I talk to you, I feel so much less pain . . . "

She keeps talking in a soft voice, sharing her burdens. That night in Forlì, she fought as hard as she could, until the duke grabbed her. Immobilized by the weight of her rapist against the altar, her face pressed down on the stone, she saw, and continues to see to this day, the final moments of her mother's life: her torn clothes, the blood that gushed from her slit throat, the sound of her dying.

When Valentino was finished with her, she saw the bodies of all the other women in the chapel. She expected him to slay her, too, and she tipped her head back and offered him her throat. He looked at her carefully. Maybe he saw the intensity of her grief, or perhaps he was attracted by the challenging look in her eyes. A groups of soldiers came rushing in—Romans, wearing the colors of the pontifical guards, headed by Corella. Borgia pointed at her without saying a word. Corella grabbed her arm and pulled her downstairs. She had to step over countless bodies and even tripped on the corpse of her older brother.

She doesn't have clear memories of the moments that followed, only brief fragments: the courtyard of the fortress, dead bodies everywhere, the surrounding streets, shouting and screaming. A house that the attackers had transformed into a small fortress. Corella pushed her into a room, then closed the door and locked it.

Only much later, at dawn, a woman came in. She was beautiful, slender, and dressed all in black. She had some bread and a pitcher of water.

"Was it—?"

"Yes, Lucina."

Without a word, the older woman made her remove her dirty clothes and bloodied petticoats, and then led her over to one side of the room and washed her.

In the following days, during which time they transported her to the Rocca stronghold in Imola, she learned that Lucina was Spanish, from Valencia, from the same land where that horrible man was from.

Dianora didn't eat for a long time. But then, she gave in from hunger.

She was given new clothes, precious ones. At first, she refused to wear them. Lucina had to dress her. She didn't want to look at herself in the mirror. Every single day, Lucina combed Dianora's hair very carefully, sometimes in long braids that she united on the crown of her head, or else in spirals on either side of her head, like a doll.

One night, about a week later, Valentino came to her wearing his black mask.

He didn't touch her. He stayed with her all night and just talked to her. He wanted to know everything about her, as if he were a friend that she could confide in, which in a way was an act of even greater violence.

She is interrupted by her cough, but then it passes. She carefully takes a breath.

"He abused me with flattery . . . "

For the month that followed, he visited her regularly, deriving great pleasure from his visits but never actually touching her. He told her over and over that he desired her more than he had ever desired anyone, that she was special, that without her he was nothing.

He alternated between kindness and brutality, showering her with gifts. He didn't need to remind her that she was under his control; it was evident. He invited her to speak as if she had come to his chambers of her own will. And then, each time she said something, he would belittle her. Each passing day he stole something from her.

When he looked at her, it felt like she was being struck. When he spoke, it was like she was being kicked.

His words sank into her, left marks on her. She had bruises deep inside, although no signs were visible on her fair skin.

Her body felt filthy. She constantly relived the fear she experienced in Forlì.

Slowly, day by day, she broke down.

Every glance from him struck terror into her, and he derived great pleasure from this.

She felt his eyes on her even when she was alone,.

Soon she started receiving jewels, which she was forced to wear.

Then Lucina tried to win her over. She said that she, too, had been kidnapped five years earlier, in Spain, by Valentino's men, who had raped her before handing her over to their leader. Now she was a prisoner, too. She was also under close watch.

"She dried my tears . . . "

Then, after some time, Dianora was given some books of sonnets and canzones.

Lucina told her that she had been the one to ask for them because she realized how much her ward liked poetry.

After some hesitation, Dianora accepted them. They reminded her of how much she used to enjoy reading at home, how she had started writing poetry and had been encouraged in the endeavor by her father, who had always wanted her to study, like a man.

She would pick up the books, then put them down, then go back to them, consistently avoiding anything that had to do with love.

She knew many of the sonnets and canzones by heart but seeing them in print gave her the sensation, for the very first time, that they represented something of greater importance to her. It felt like she had rediscovered a friend, and that this friend had altered since they first met, but that its presence was still a gentle one.

For the first time in six months, she smiled softly.

But then she burst into tears. The memories of her loss were unbearable.

Lucina observed everything and referred it all back to the duke.

A few days later, Lucina, with an air of great secrecy, confided in Dianora that she had found a way to escape from the prison in which they were being held. They would have to wait for nightfall, for the guards to doze off. The men had forgotten to lock a door; they would need to go down a corridor, descend a staircase that led outside, and then through the fields and across the plains.

How she wished she could return to Forlì! Maybe some of her relatives were still alive. That night she got dressed with both anxiety and joy. She didn't take the medicine that they usually gave her to help her sleep. The two women waited until it was pitch dark, opened the door, closed it behind them, and went downstairs on tiptoe.

It was summer. The night air was filled with the scent of

244 · FRANCO BERNINI

flowers. The breeze felt like a gentle caress. They ran through the fields and down deserted roads, on and on, into the woods. And there, a group of men was waiting for them.

Lucina burst into laughter, greatly amused by the deception. Then he, the duke, that awful man, appeared and without saying a word he grabbed her, threw her down, and raped her.

Afterward, her guardian washed her with water from a fountain.

Then they locked her back up. Valentino came to her chambers whenever he wanted, but always at night.

One day she was given paper and a golden quill pen.

"I didn't touch them for weeks, and then, suddenly, I picked them up and began to write poems."

She never showed the sonnets to anyone. They brought her a few moments of relief from her agony.

When her guardian noticed, she informed the duke instantly.

Lucina took away her poems.

The following night, Valentino returned them to her saying that he liked them. He was pleased with her. None of his other women had ever known how to write poems.

He then handed her a key to her own chambers and opened the door that led to the great hall where he received visitors, the most elegant and largest room in the Rocca, thereby extending the perimeter of her prison.

"Even so, I'll never be able to escape. For that to happen, he will have to die. Only then, and if he hasn't left orders to have me killed, will I be free . . . ."

Saying those words made it feel possible to her, if only for an instant. But then the thought was immediately extinguished. "I'm sorry. I wish I could stay longer, but I'm beginning to feel weak."

Dianora struggles to get to her feet and whispers her farewell. "Who knows if the Lord God will allow us to see each other again. I will pray for it."

"I also hope to see you again, I hope it with all my heart," Niccolò says softly.

Her story leaves him in a state of shock. He knows it was good for her to share her pain but he wishes he could do more to help her. He watches as she makes her way back to the friar and the guard; when they see her approach, they stand up straight. Coughing occasionally, she slowly walks off. She treads lightly, as if not wanting to leave a trace of her existence on earth.

CHAPTER THIRTY-FIVE

L ord God—if you even exist—how can you let all this happen? How can you not see what is going on? Why don't you do something? The world is commanded by those in power and they sit on thrones dripping with blood and tears. Niccolò ponders such questions as he walks slowly back to the inn.

He suffers for Dianora, but he also admires her courage, the dignity with which she faces life. She will never debase herself by accepting what has happened to her or how she is forced to live.

With every passing day the awareness that he is free while she is a prisoner grows more acute. Although he's been forced to do things, he essentially chose his path. She, on the other hand, has to put up with the whims of a tyrant. How can he, Niccolò, possibly set her free? When could he? He feels powerless and it is infuriating, but it is the truth.

Like her, he could write about what goes on, the brazen offenses, the torture; he could do so in both poems and prose. And yet while words can console, they don't compensate for loss, they don't right wrongs, and often all it takes is a gust of wind for them to get blown away. But if you stack them up like an army, they become stone, bronze, iron. Why else would that man and other powerful people like him fear words so much?

Will he ever manage to be as strong as Dianora? Where does all her strength come from? Desperation. Hope. That's what her poems reveal.

And his own verses? They simply don't have that strength.

He's not desperate enough, he doesn't hope hard enough. Will he ever change? If he could, he would be more worthy of her.

He interrupts his reflections and returns to his senses at the sight of an approaching group of riders. At the head are two servants, one on a white horse and the other on a chestnut; neither wears a hat or helmet. Behind them, on a black horse, is a forty-year old man with a beard and curly hair. He's wearing an opulent yellow robe with a brown border, red hose, and a large black and white bonnet.

Niccolò recognizes him instantly. An etching of his face has circulated through Italy; all learned men have seen it at least once. It's Anteo Nuffi. He leans over to say something discreetly to the older man on his left, who wears a blue outfit and a red head covering. This must be the scholar whom Nuffi entrusts with the early phases of research for his writing. Two men around thirty follow behind, one with a weaselly face and frizzy hair, the other balding and terribly skinny. These men, they say, write Nuffi's first drafts, which the poet laureate then edits and signs.

Travelling with them are two attractive ladies. Both have strong features and wear brightly-colored long dresses. Bringing up the rear is a servant who leads two mules piled high with their belongings.

Niccolò wishes he could take a different path and avoid them. He's not worried about being recognized by the man who criticized his writing and stole his job—Nuffi doesn't even know who Niccolò is—but it pains Niccolò deeply to have to look at him. And yet he continues on, much in the same way we are tempted to touch a wound even though it hurts, or root around in our mouth with our tongues when we have a toothache.

The procession halts in front of the Locanda del Sole, the finest lodgings in the city, from which emanate delicious aromas of roast meats. Anteo Nuffi certainly treats himself well. These are the privileges that money can obtain. Everyone dismounts, a stable hand rushes over, and the innkeeper hurries out to welcome the guests with pleasantries. Horses and mules are taken to the stalls, while the poet laureate and his entourage walk toward the main entrance.

Niccolò slips by. He hears the innkeeper showering Nuffi with compliments, who in turn replies with a grand show of modesty. One of the two women asks what they will be having for lunch.

To banish the feeling of powerlessness, Niccolò takes a long walk up and down the city streets and even goes outside the city walls. He walks as far as the oak forest beyond Montanara gate. There are no new messages from Farneti.

The following day a young man dressed entirely in black comes to Niccolò's lodgings. Sent by the duke's secretary, he bears an invitation for the envoy of Florence to attend a performance the following evening; all the orators and ambassadors will take part. The invitation is late to arrive. Perhaps the Duke hoped he already had an engagement. This is not an offense to Florence, but to him personally.

The production will take place in the theater built especially for the occasion by engineer da Vinci. Ah, so this must be the event arranged to celebrate Dianora's birthday, he thinks. Initially, Niccolò is tempted to turn it down but he can't possibly say he is ill; the messenger sees he's in perfect health, and moreover it is one of his duties.

"There will be a performance of *Cupid and Psyche*, written by the famous Anteo Nuffi," the man adds with satisfaction.

"Actually, the story was written thirteen hundred years ago by Apuleius of Madaura, an African," Niccolò clarifies.

"Yes, of course, but Anteo Nuffi has adapted it for the occasion. It will also be interesting because of the machines designed by Master da Vinci, similar to the ones he used in the court of the Sforza in Milan; surely you have heard about them. No? Well then, you'll see, I don't want to ruin the surprise. Even the actors are top notch."

CHAPTER THIRTY-SIX

T he foyer of the theater has been painted in Valentino's colors, with grey columns and a bright red gable above. Garlands of flowers are everywhere. A double row of torch-bearing pages flank the path to the entrance.

Niccolò blends in with the other spectators, all of whom are dressed in their finest clothes.

The theater itself is evenly divided by the stage and the seating area, which is formed by a rising semicircle of wooden benches, also painted in Borgia's colors. Clusters of candles that hang in concave mirrors are positioned at either side of the stage, casting diffuse rays of light onto the stage.

The front row has room for only ten people and, for the moment, is completely empty. The second row, which is longer, is already occupied by the ambassadors and their consorts from various cities. Niccolò sees Agapito Geraldini, who nods at him in greeting. The third row, longer still, seats members of the clergy. Among them is Brother Timoteo, who pretends not to know him. There are still some empty seats there, but Anteo Nuffi's noisy entourage comes in and makes its way over. Sitting in the even longer row above are various military men, some of whom wear the colors of the King of France. They're probably the commanders of Louis XII's spearmen, whom Farneti mentioned.

Niccolò's seat is higher up still—yet another slight—in one of the last two rows, off to one side, and rather uncomfortable. From it, he can only see a portion of the stage and is surrounded by less important people: notable figures from the city and its outlying towns. As he takes his seat, he realizes that some of the orators turn to look at him, commenting on how the Republic has been offended by forcing him to sit so high up. Niccolò ignores them and continues to stare at the heavy gold brocade curtain.

They await the arrival of the duke and soon he makes his entrance, preceded and followed by his personal guards and don Miguel. Dianora walks directly behind him, her eyes downcast so as not to exchange looks with any members of the audience. Her hair has been combed with great care and woven through with fine gold ribbons and pearls. Valentino takes a seat. Dianora sits down to his right; she looks unhappy and coughs occasionally. Valentino's personal executioner sits on his left, while his bodyguards find a place to stand along the walls. With no further delay, from the back of the room comes the music of viols; the concave mirrors in each corner rotate on themselves as if by magic, and the light from the candles vanishes. Darkness falls over the audience. The curtain rises. Hidden lanterns illuminate the stage as brightly as if it were day. The scenery reveals a bare mountain, its pointy peak as tall as the highest seats in the theater. Two paths wend between boulders on each side of the mountain.

The audience mumbles with admiration.

A warm female voice comes from the end of the path on the right. The actress, who slowly makes her way downstage, is dressed like an ancient Greek, in a white tunic tied at the waist with a golden cord and her hair combed in an elaborate manner. Even before seeing her face, just from the way she moves, Niccolò instantly recognizes her. It's Tullia, his former lover from Florence. Clearly she's been working hard, traveling up and down the length of Italy, going from one theater company to the next, to now be able to perform before the son of a pope.

He smiles fondly, recalling intimate details about her, while listening to her song; in rhyming couplets she promises a tale of desperation and love. A king and queen once reigned over a city, she sings, with their three beautiful daughters. While it was easy to celebrate the elder two with human words, it was impossible to describe the splendor of the youngest, whose name was Psyche. Everyone, even in faraway lands, compared her to Venus. She was so beautiful that no man had the courage to ask her to be his wife. Consequently, Psyche was always alone, and convinced she would never know true love.

With a pang of envy Niccolò is forced to admit that Anteo Nuffi's verses, while banal, are deeply expressive. Apparently he's learned a few things over the years. At the same time, Niccolò knows just how strong the myth is on its own. The poet laureate was wise not to alter much of what has worked for more than a thousand years.

Niccolò looks at Dianora, trying to ascertain her reaction. Her face looks pale despite the bright light that shines down on her from the stage. She appears indifferent. This pleases him.

Borgia also peers over at her, scrutinizing her expression.

Tullia, meanwhile, has reached center stage. She points toward the roof, where a bright light suddenly appears. That light is Venus, she sings. Venus is so jealous of Psyche that she asks her son, Cupid, to strike the young woman with one of his arrows so that she will fall in love with an evil man.

A cloud of yellowish smoke appears on the path to the left of the mountain. A figure in a red hooded cape waves his arms and moans loudly.

Is that Cupid, the son of Venus? No, it's the Oracle of Delphi, the high priestess, who declares in a sonorous voice that Psyche must be abandoned at the top of a cliff. A monster in the shape of a serpent will come and take her away and make her his wife. This is what the most high and powerful Apollo wants, and no one can deny the god's wishes. Perhaps Venus has somehow angered him . . . They have no choice but to obey.

The oracle appeared so quickly and distracted the attention of the audience to such a degree that no one, not even Niccolò, saw Tullia leave the stage.

A sad procession makes its way toward the audience from

the path to the right: Psyche, dressed as a bride and weeping, is followed by her parents and sisters, who also cry in despair. The young woman is left on a bluff. Her relatives express the anguish of their farewell in verse and with great sincerity.

Niccolò looks at Dianora again and sees that she is crying. Clearly, this reminds her of her own past. Borgia notices her reaction, too. Niccolò realizes with disgust that the prince chose this story specifically to upset her; yet another form of violence he enacts on her.

Psyche begins her monologue. Her role is interpreted by a smooth-cheeked young man with long, curly blond hair. His soft voice, slender figure, and lithe way of moving make him indeed resemble a girl. Psyche sings with great emotion about her fears for the future.

A sudden breeze makes Psyche's clothes flutter. Where did that wind come from? How did da Vinci make that happen? There's no time to wonder. There's music and Psyche is lifted up high—Niccolò catches sight of a black rope up in the rafters—and the central mountain splits in two, rotates backwards, and opens up entirely so that the two semicircles face the public, revealing the interiors of a sumptuous palace with ivory walls and golden columns. Clearly this is the residence of a god.

Psyche is gently set down in the splendor of the midday sun—the rope falls from her waist and vanishes upward—and mellifluous voices announce that all this now belongs to her: she can have whatever she desires. Trays of fruit, platters of food, and carafes of water are mysteriously extended to her from the walls, all accompanied by music.

The audience is enchanted. Even Niccolò is full of admiration for the set design. He then catches sight of Leonardo standing at the end of one the rows, watching his theatrical machine. Anteo Nuffi expresses his satisfaction loudly. Niccolò glares at him, wishing him a slow and painful death.

The music crescendos, night falls across the scene, and

moonlight shines through the windows. A door in one of the ivory walls opens and a male figure appears, his face hidden by the shadows.

Psyche is lying on a bed, exhausted and depleted. She sits up when the man appears. She starts to get to her feet, but then he is on top of her. The audience can only perceive dark outlines in the moonlight, but it is very clear what is happening. The mysterious man has forced himself on her.

Dianora gasps.

The audience is silent.

Why is the duke allowing this scene to be shown on stage? Those who know Dianora's story will unquestionably recognize the parallel. Niccolò realizes that this is exactly what Borgia wants; he's convinced that revealing his crimes will only make him look stronger.

Daylight arrives and Psyche is alone again. Gentle voices congratulate her because she is now the bride of the god who resides in that palace, an unknown deity who wants nothing more than her wellbeing.

Night falls and the man returns. This time, however, he doesn't take her by force but talks to her gently, professing his love for her. He tells her that she will be his queen and they will be happy, but that she should never, for no reason whatsoever, try to see his face. Their happiness is based on this element of secrecy.

Niccolò recognizes the actor's voice: he has seen him perform in the past. He's about twenty years older than Tullia and has a powerful build. In the shadows he seems much younger. Being the protagonist means that he's also the head of the theater company. So Tullia may well owe her success to that man. One thing's for certain, of all the old members of the troupe that he used to spend time with, Niccolò recognizes only the two of them. Everyone else is new.

Now what's happening? When the mysterious man

approaches Psyche, she does not rebuff him but welcomes him. Once more under the cover of shadow, the couple enacts complicated, fluid gestures, this time revealing a growing amorous understanding.

Dianora gasps even louder and then begins to cough.

Why is Valentino inflicting this pain on her? He already has complete power over her. Isn't that enough for him?

Then, accompanied by the sweet sound of flutes, Psyche and her god of the night announce, with gentle voices, that a child will be born of their union. A son. Violence has generated life.

Niccolò looks over at Dianora. Her eyes are downcast. Valentino stares at her, too.

Why is he subjecting her to watch this? He can't be thinking . . . No, even in Apuleius there's a child. Anteo Nuffi simply retained that part of the story.

The god and Psyche hold each other tightly. She loves him very much now, too, and they're happy, but she also feels lonely during the day, when he does not spend time with her. She asks to see her sisters. She begs him. The god scolds her: old loves must not contaminate current ones, he says. Your sisters want to see you only because news of your good fortune has reached them thanks to Zephyr, the breeze; if they see you here, in this palace of ours, they'll feel deep envy, because that's how humans are. And then they'll say cruel things and bring us grief.

Our peace will soon be disrupted, this is the way of the world, he insists. *Who doesn't want to steal what they like so much? People who envy you thrive on your ruin.*

I beg of you, husband mine, let my sisters come to me. My love for you is great, my lord, and nothing will ever cause me to leave your side, Psyche replies, begging him and crying.

I am moved to mercy for you, and so I shall allow it. I cannot deny that which you beseech me; at the same time I think the mercy I show is a grave error on my part. For when one chooses to see goodness, one sees poorly.

The sun rises, sacred Zephyr carries the two sisters across the sky and to the palace, this time with golden ropes. The girls embrace joyfully and Psyche offers her sisters splendid gifts. The sisters look around, masking their cruel thoughts with good advice. How can Psyche trust someone whose face she has never seen? People say that her groom is the serpent prophesied by the oracle, a monster that will devour her and the child in its need for human flesh. She doesn't believe them? Then, tonight, why doesn't she light a candle when he comes to be with her? But bring a knife, they say, so you can kill the serpent.

Niccolò observes how enthralled the audience is, how willing they are to follow the story wherever it will lead them. This is the magic of the theater, he thinks; it holds as much power over people as the word on which it is based. Suddenly, he is filled with energy and verve. He, too, will do battle with words—his own—and nothing says that one day he won't also write for the stage, and he will be far better at it than Anteo Nuffi.

Night falls. The god comes to lie with Psyche again, this time with passionate fury. As soon as he is asleep, the young woman lights an oil lantern and holds it up with her left hand. In her right, she grips a knife.

Before her lies a handsome man. It is Cupid, the son of Venus.

Incredulous, she caresses his perfect lineaments with the same hand that holds the knife.

She's so mesmerized by him that a drop of scalding hot oil falls onto the god's shoulder.

He wakes up in great pain, his skin burning as if hot lead had been poured on it. He cries out: why did she want to reveal that which the darkness of night should have kept concealed? Why did she betray him? He goes on to tell her how his mother had ordered him to punish her, but how he had been so enchanted by her beauty that he had pierced his own skin with one of his arrows and fell in love with her.

Sad and angry, he rises up in flight—he's a god, after all.

Desperate, Psyche grabs onto his legs so as not to lose him. A strong black rope raises them both up as the set design changes again, rotating once more. The palace disappears, the mountain reappears, this time covered with a thick forest. The actors are suspended over it but then Psyche loses her grip and falls. Cupid flies far away, forever.

What will happen next? The audience waits on bated breath. Even Niccolò, who knows how Apuleius ended the story, is curious. Humans always want to see new things, he tells himself. We fall for it every time, at all performances, in all the theaters of the world. What will happen to the people on stage? Will Cupid fall? Will he fly far away? Who else will arrive to contend for her? Who, ultimately, will win?

When Venus learns that her son is in love with Psyche and will soon be a father, she flares up in a rage against the girl. The goddess summons all the powers of the underworld who appear on stage through hidden trapdoors: there's a Dragon with metallic scales; Cerberus, the three-headed dog, two wondrous machines that seem to move all by themselves; and Charon, the transporter of souls, comprised of two actors, one sitting on the other's shoulders and dressed in a dark, tent-like covering and wearing a ferocious mask. The Dragon, Cerberus, and Charon force Psyche into a corner, where flames of red silk shoot up thanks to hidden bellows. To survive, she has to perform the hardest task of all: steal a phial of porphyry red that contains the essence of beauty from Proserpina, the Queen of Hades.

Initially she succeeds but then commits an error—no one's perfect, after all. She falls prey to curiosity and opens the phial, and in so doing succumbs to the sleep of death. Cupid, now healed from his burns, comes to save her, awakening her—a god can do this—and hands the phial to his mother, who is finally placated. Venus, in turn, calls on Jupiter, who appears in the form of a light that shines down from a hole in the ceiling in the shape of a fleur-de-lis of France, to make Psyche immortal, so that the two can love each other for all eternity.

Tullia reappears on the stage, this time elegantly dressed in a tunic made of a soft fabric that reveals and accentuates her breasts and long legs. She sings a short song about how sweet the night is when you are with the one you love, and she sensually runs her hands across her bosom and belly, down her thighs and up again.

Niccolò feels desire shoot through him. He stares at her as she goes on to sing of the triumph of good over evil. The two cruel sisters will die, consumed by their own envy, the married couple will be happy forever, and a child will be born whom they will call Pleasure.

Pleasure . . .

Tullia disappears into the shadows. The grand finale belongs to the head of the theater company, which is to say to Cupid, who brings the performance to an end with beautiful Psyche by his side. First he thanks Jupiter—the French fleur-de-lis—for its benevolent intervention, saying warmly to his beloved that if he wasn't already married to her, he would do it all over just so the inhabitants of the city—the city where they currently are, he specifies—could see him out strolling with his wife.

Cupid then takes Psyche by the hand, but before leaving the stage, he turns to the audience. "You too, my dear audience, will soon be able to leave. My beloved and I will continue on with our lives, and you with yours. We hope that we have brought you pleasure, because there truly is no better medicine than a good story. Farewell."

As Psyche and her god disappear into the shadows, a great light illuminates stage right from above. While the audience's attention was elsewhere, the set has changed again. It now shows soft, rolling hills dotted with poppies, and a fountain. Real water flows from it into a large grey stone basin.

The audience applauds in delight and awe.

Out of the corner of his eye, Niccolò observes Leonardo, who seems very pleased with his set designs. Will this be the last of them?

Tullia returns to the stage. Wearing a garland of cherries, she goes and sits by the fountain, a pitcher in her hand. The actors who interpreted Psyche's two sisters and mother now come out dressed as shepherds, holding a psaltery and flutes. The actor who played the father carries a lute.

A sense of expectation runs through the room.

Niccolò recognizes the music instantly. It's the Conte Guido song, or it appears to be at first.

The lyrics have been changed. When the introductory music ends, the actor who played Cupid comes out riding a docile horse, wearing Borgia's colors and a large feathered hat. All the other actors follow suit, including Tullia. Together they sing a modified version of the Tuscan ditty that expresses a knight's love for a female knave: *Un cavalier di Spagna cavalca per la via al piè d'una montagna cantando per amor d'una fantina.*[6]

Niccolò is confused. He's never heard this version before. In the meantime, the main actor reaches out to Tullia, who pretends not to see him. *Voltate in qua, mia bella donzellina, voltate un poco a me, per cortesia, dolce speranza mia, ch'io moro per tuo amor.*[7]

People are immediately mesmerized by the tune. Niccolò notices their rapt expressions. Then the chorus begins: *Bella fantina io t'ho donato il cor, Bella fantina io t'ho donato il cor.*[8]

Niccolò is struck by many thoughts all at once. Why did Valentino have them change the lyrics? Why did he have the knight dress in his colors? Is the female knave supposed to be Dianora?

The knight gets off his horse and walks up to Tullia and begins to sing again: *Appresso a una fontana vidi sentar la bella soletta in terra piana con una ghirlanda di fresca erbecina.*[9]

Now he's standing very close to her. *Voltate in qua, mia bella donzellina, voltate un poco a me, lucente stella, deh non m'esser ribella, che io moro per tuo amor.*[10]

Tullia finally turns to look at him, and the chorus begins again: *Bella fantina io t'ho donato il cor, Bella fantina io t'ho donato il cor.*

The knave and knight knit their fingers together as if experiencing love at first sight. The couple then turns to the duke and Dianora and bow deeply. Yes, Niccolò thinks: the Spanish knight is supposed to be Borgia and the song about Tuscan pride has been altered according to Valentino's wishes so that it's a celebration of himself. He doesn't want Dianora to fight him anymore.

But who wrote the new lyrics? Anteo Nuffi? Probably not: he wouldn't have known how to use the Spanish verb *sentar* instead of *sedersi*, as in the original. Unless he did it to please Borgia . . .

A little girl dressed in Borgia's colors steps out of a corner with a large bouquet of white roses in her hand, which she presents to Dianora.

Dianora is caught off guard and refuses them. Cesare whispers to her harshly. She accepts the flowers but doesn't smile. He then asks her a terse question and indicates the stage. She shakes her head firmly, her answer clearly negative.

Niccolò imagines how all the ambassadors, the following morning, will send letters that comment on this turn of events.

Why did the duke want to show off Dianora?

Why did he have them act out that courtship scene around the fountain, which was the very opposite of the horror she witnessed? Was he trying to convince everyone—Dianora first and foremost—that things happened differently than they really did? An oft-repeated lie becomes a fact . . .

The audience jumps to their feet and starts to applaud. Trimmed white roses rain down from the ceiling. People look up, Niccolò included. They hadn't realized that there were other openings in the ceiling, one of which held flowers. The entire theater is a box of surprises.

Some people bend down to pick up the roses, others catch them as they fall, even pricking themselves on some leftover thorns. Dianora stands perfectly still, the bouquet in her arms, lost in her own thoughts, as if she wasn't even there.

After the performance, Niccolò rushes down to the area just below the stage where people have gathered, chatting and commenting with admiration on the show. Surrounded by Corella's guards, the duke welcomes the praise. Dianora stands by his side, her gaze downcast.

She glances around, as if looking for Niccolò. When she sees him, there is desperation in her eyes.

He stares at her in dejection. What can he possibly do?

Valentino turns to Dianora, whispers something in her ear, but she remains immobile. He looks at her angrily. He whispers something else and she smiles artificially, with great effort, which only irks Cesare further.

Dianora glances back at Niccolò. He wishes he could take her by the hand and lead her far, far away from there, but he can do nothing. She coughs. She's clearly worn out.

Then Anteo Nuffi arrives. Looking triumphant, he's ready to boast about his work and the play, but just before he blocks the view, Niccolò sees Valentino say something curt to him, and the poet laureate looks crestfallen. The duke then drags Dianora out of the theater. He's furious. Despite the fact that he dedicated the performance to her, she refuses to be happy.

Niccolò makes his way forward, climbing onto the stage and between the sets. Up close, the theatrical machinery is even more impressive. He sees the trapdoors that concealed the Dragon, Cerberus, and Charon. One is slightly open, inside are wheels, cogs, gears, and ropes that extend down for at least eight arms' lengths. A man is tinkering with something far below.

Niccolò heads backstage, towards voices, skirting other large wheels of both metal and wood, finally reaching a space where the actors are changing out of their clothes. The men, all sweating profusely, are shirtless. So is Tullia. They splash water on their faces and under their arms, dry themselves with rags, and comment on the success of their performance. No one notices Niccolò standing off to one side, observing Tullia with a grin on his face. Suddenly, she sees him and her face lights up with pleasure.

"Niccolò!"

"You were extraordinary," he says going to greet her. He feels the other actors' eyes on him and realizes how eager they are to receive praise, too. "All of you! You were all wonderful."

"Thank you," the head of the troupe replies. "And you are . . . ?"

"A Florentine. I had the privilege of seeing you perform in my city some time ago; you were a superb Creon."

Upon hearing these words, the head actor nods with pleasure. "This evening's performance was particularly difficult for all of us . . . Performing in front of Valentino, dressed in his colors . . . "

"Afraid that the horse would take a shit on stage," Tullia says, laughing.

"No, actually that was not one of my concerns," the head actor says defensively. "I made sure it got a good enema beforehand. We couldn't risk that in front of Cesare Borgia!"

"Well, you never know, it could've gotten diarrhea!" the boy—or girl—with the curly blond hair says. Even up close, it's hard to tell Psyche's gender. The actor goes on to recount how two months earlier they had a sudden attack of the runs on stage but managed to make it look like it was part of the performance. Everyone claps and cheers at the anecdote, and when the actor laughs, Niccolò realizes that she is indeed a woman.

Tullia puts on a shirt, goes up to Niccolò, and takes both his hands. "What a wonderful surprise. It's such a pleasure to see you! What brings you to Imola?"

"I'm here as an envoy for the Republic. How long are you staying?"

"We leave tomorrow."

He looks at her with a warm smile and invites her to dine with him.

Tullia casts a furtive glance at the head of the troupe. "I'm not sure . . . "

Niccolò understands. "Tell me how you are; you're more beautiful than ever. Are you well?"

"Things are good. Finally! I've actually made something of a name for myself, you know . . . "

"I'm pleased. You deserve it. But that final song . . . Were the lyrics written by Anteo Nuffi?"

"Yes, how did you know?"

"Oh, I just guessed."

"It's a silly song that the poet overheard when he got here. We wanted to use something else, but the lyrics came to him quickly. It's nice, isn't it?"

"Very."

"Working for Borgia has been good, he's been generous with us. He even gave us a whole floor of rooms at the inn on the main piazza."

"The Locanda del Sole?"

"You know it?"

"I know where it is but I can't afford to stay there myself."

There's a rustling sound behind Niccolò as someone comes up behind him.

It's don Miguel. He looks ponderously at Tullia. "Milady, I offer you my deepest homage. A knight from Spain, who also appreciated your art, requests the pleasure of your company."

"And who might you be?" Tullia asks, looking at him skeptically.

"A servant for His Excellency Duke Valentino."

"Are you the knight in question?"

"No, I am not. My Lordship is."

"I'm very honored to receive this invitation," the singer replies. "May I extend it to my fellow actors, too?"

"No, it is for you alone."

What Corella does not mention remains unspoken, suspended in the air. Tullia blinks. Niccolò looks away.

"Please be so kind as to wait for me," Tullia says. She then walks over to the head actor and whispers in his ear. He looks at Corella with a mixture of jealousy and greed, calculating how much he might earn from sending his lover to Valentino. Indulging a powerful figure can lead to many things; making the sacrifice will be worthwhile. He nods, then mumbles a few words of encouragement to Tullia, who goes back to Corella.

She says goodbye to everyone and follows don Miguel out of the theater. Niccolò sighs. Will Valentino be satisfied only with Tullia? Or will he force Dianora to join them, and punish her for turning down the bouquet of roses?

CHAPTER THIRTY-SEVEN

. . . I entrust this missive to your Lordships and beseech you to allow me to return. As previously communicated, based on what I have heard, it is no longer necessary to tarry any further. To bring the agreement to its conclusion, an official with a higher level of authority is needed. With regards to my own personal situation, I am compelled to inform you that my expenses are in a state of disarray and I can no longer afford to stay on without receiving additional monies.

Imola, 7 December, 1502
Your Servant

Before signing the letter for the Dieci—a request that I-have-faith will also see—Niccolò takes a breath and smooths down the piece of paper with his fingertips. He wrote impulsively, upon returning from the theater. First he summarized the bits of news he had picked up here and there during the day, essentially providing a reason for the letter, and then closed with that supplication. Will they allow him to return? He doubts it. He knows how the lords and Soderini operate. He's been through this all before. Having him there benefits them: he's the one who's exposed to all the risks. Even so, he must try. It's pointless for him to stay on: he can do nothing further to help Dianora and would truly rather not continue to see her suffer.

He'll ask Baccino to take it the following morning, to do him the favor of leaving Gemma for as long as it takes to deliver the letter personally to Florence. When he gets to the Palazzo della Signoria, he'll know how to describe the conditions in which they find themselves to the Dieci. Maybe he'll be able to convince them. If he can't, no one will.

He signs the letter quickly but then immediately regrets it and tears it up.

He can't abandon Dianora. She needs him.

He's ashamed of what he's just written and quickly brings the piece of paper to the candle flame. Watching it burn makes him feel better.

He knows he will stay on, going against all logic and his personal needs, just to remain by her side, come what may, whatever humiliating experiences he will be forced to undergo.

Suddenly, he notices how quiet it has become.

He goes to the window, opens it, and sees that snow is falling in the dark night. Heavy, thick snow. The cobblestones are already white.

At dawn, he looks out again. The snow is still coming down. Powder, half-an-arm deep, has already accumulated. Up in the Apennines, it will have fallen even heavier. Florence is safe, at least for a few days: the snow will turn to ice and for as long as that lasts not even Valentino's army will be able to attack. He imagines horses slipping on the whitened cobblestones, riders falling. The poor conditions will also make it difficult to move the cannons, which would have to advance through other means. He visualizes the gun carriages sliding backward, crushing the men who struggle to push them forward.

Two merchants outside hurry across the street, seeking cover under the portico of the house across the way. He hears them talking: there's already a lot of snow up in the mountains. Just as he thought.

He goes out, crosses the road, his feet sinking deep into the whiteness. He reaches the portico where the two men stood, leaving their muddy footprints behind.

Walking under the cover of the portico for as long as he can, and in the snow only when he can't avoid it, he makes his way

266 · FRANCO BERNINI

266 - FRANCO BERNINI

to the Locanda del Sole. He's covered in white, his shoes are soaking wet, and the cold travels quickly up his legs. If he can, he wants to speak to Tullia, to find out what happened the night before, to both her and Dianora.

In the piazza near the inn, he sees a few kids throwing snowballs at each other. A man and two young women, elegantly dressed in grey and green, join the antics. In front of the entrance to the inn, the actors are hurriedly piling their luggage into a large, covered wooden carriage with tall wheels. Tullia is nowhere to be seen.

He asks after her and they tell him she hasn't returned yet but that they can't wait any longer. They have to set out on their journey toward the coast, after which they will head north toward Venice, where people are expecting them. They need to leave soon, while the snow is still falling, before the roads turn to slush or ice. They're hoping that the temperatures on the coast will be milder.

But you have to wait for Tullia, he says forcefully to the head actor. The man doesn't reply and continues to issue orders to the others, who keep piling their clothes, costumes, and sets into the carriage. It's like a vast cave, and it swallows everything up. It will be their bedroom and storage room for the coming days.

I'll go look for her, Niccolò offers. The main actor raises his voice in reply: stay out of it, we don't want to bother the duke. At least she's somewhere warm, he says, while we're out here in the cold streets.

Suddenly, there are loud voices from upstairs: Anteo Nuffi and his retinue appear. The two servants drag down their baggage and head toward the stalls. The poet laureate and his assistants look tense; they seem to be bickering about which road to take.

In his anger, Nuffi doesn't even notice Niccolò.

In public, Nuffi never speaks badly about anyone, unless

he's referring to some powerless fool who's the butt of his jokes. Even now, surrounded by his close companions, he doesn't mention any names, but clearly the duke has banished him from Imola. The group discusses whether they should head to Bologna or Rimini, and which roads will be passable. The innkeeper graciously offers them all the information they might need.

Niccolò hides his pleasure, wondering what conspired to convince Valentino to change his opinion so quickly about the poet laureate. While he knows that Borgia often makes rapid-fire decisions, and that he enjoys building people up and then tearing them down, Nuffi must have especially offended him. Thinking back on the evening, Niccolò recalls how, as soon as the performance was over, the prince's attitude had already changed. Perhaps someone criticized the work of the illustrious writer, the same way that Nuffi had torn into his own writing, in a kind of retaliation.

Will another literary figure arrive soon? Perhaps someone even more important? Will that person be able to reach the city before the roads become obstructed?

Niccolò stands to one side and watches with pleasure as the group, shivering with cold in their tabards, gets on their horses—Nuffi is particularly fidgety—and sets off. He watches the horses' legs sink into the snow, their hooves kicking up flecks of white, and, for a few long minutes, he feels deeply content.

The theater troupe is ready to leave. The head actor, assisted by one of the younger ones, climbs up the steps behind the carriage, nervously eyeing the falling snow. The others clamber onto their mules and wrap themselves up in their cloaks.

"But you can't leave without Tullia!" Niccolò exclaims.

"She'll catch up," the man says firmly.

A feeble moan makes them all turn around. It's Tullia, she's frozen stiff, wearing the same light clothes she had on the night before. Her hair is mussed up, she's covered in snow, she's pale, distraught, and can barely move.

Niccolò rushes over and puts his arm around her so she can lean on him for support, just as she collapses with exhaustion. Her hair is soaking wet, she has deep circles under her eyes, and she's trembling hard.

"It beggars belief, Niccolò . . . The poor woman . . . He truly is a devil," she says in a whisper.

She doesn't have the strength to continue and he doesn't have the courage to ask anymore.

The head actor strides over to her. "Ah, my dear Tullia, we were waiting for you," he says to her in a paternal and authoritarian way, seeming pleased with the sound of his booming voice.

She looks at Niccolò with glassy eyes and a lost gaze. A snowflake lands on her face, but a teardrop rolls down her cheek and melts it away.

CHAPTER THIRTY-EIGHT

It snows for three days non-stop. The messengers cannot make their way across the mountain passes. A heavy white light hangs over Imola.

Niccolò wraps himself in his mantle, covers his head with the hood, and goes out. The cold rushes into his nose and mouth, cutting off his breath.

He heads to the Rocca with no other goal than to be closer to Dianora, as if walking around her prison might bring him relief. He knows it's senseless but he goes all the same.

He can barely see the houses on either side of the street. They appear and disappear as the storm blusters and blows, filling all cracks and muffling all sounds. A small cart approaches very slowly, a light grey shadow in the white haze. The driver calls out every so often, warning people of his approach. Niccolò seeks protection under a portico to let him pass.

He moves up the street slowly, like a ghost. When he reaches the open area in front of the Rocca, he dives into it. The vast whiteness is like the infinite ocean he has heard so much about, the one that leads to Western India, from which galleons return laden with gold.

His eyes hurt from the blinding light and he feels confused.

As soon as he sees the fortress through the gusting wind and snow, he stops. He can't go any further.

He stands without moving, losing all sense of time. His clothes are soaked through, his bones are icy cold, he's filled with despair and powerless rage.

The wet cold stings like needles. He yells into the void. A dog howls in response.

Why did he yell? Now someone might come out of the Rocca to see what's going on. He hurries off as fast as he can, running back through the snow drifts, ending up in a street he doesn't recognize. He turns right, then left, at random. He has lost all sense of orientation.

He curses, but softly, worried that someone will hear him.

Then he hears the muffled bells of San Michele off to his right. Another mass, more money for Brother Timoteo. Now that he knows where the monastery is, he understands how to get back to the inn. It stops snowing.

He's on the privy when Baccino knocks on the door.

"Sorry, but one of the duke's guards is asking for you."

When he goes downstairs, he sees Rodriguez dressed in a heavy cloak. Niccolò tries to read his expression, but it's impossible to decipher. He's serious and inscrutable.

Has Valentino decided to chase him out of Imola, too? It stopped snowing a day ago, there's ice on the sides of the roads and muddy trenches in their middle. It's practically impossible to venture out into the countryside. Only the main thoroughfares are viable, and even there, carts sink deep into the slush, feet become clods of wet, sticky earth. Despite all that, will Valentino send him away?

"His Excellency would like to see you," Rodriguez says drily.

"Do you know why?"

The guard shakes his head, no.

It's late afternoon and the sky is clear. They follow a path that's been formed by garrison soldiers, coming and going through the slush and ice. They slip this way and that and are forced to lean on each other for support.

The large dome of the theater is entirely covered in white. Now it really does look like a mountain, one with rounded sides.

Rodriguez leads him into the armory on the ground floor, which is spacious and cold. Only a few torches have been lit.

Borgia, wearing a white shirt, and an instructor are practicing with longswords, using training weapons. Sweat drips off them, they're red in the face. Their swords clash and sparks fly. Nearby, carrying a real sword, is Corella. Leaning against a wall is Torrella, the master physician.

When Niccolò sees Valentino, he feels a knot form in his stomach. He can't express the disgust he feels, but a simple envoy is not permitted to say as much.

The duke has a bruise on his cheekbone where the instructor must have hit him. He fights with some hesitation, retreats, and then raises his sword for a pause. The instructor stops immediately. Cesare sneezes, then presses his left nostril shut with his left index finger, and blows hard. Mucus sprays out his nose. He then throws down his sword, which the teacher immediately picks up, and does the same thing with the right hand and nostril. He sees Niccolò, reaches for a linen cloth, wipes his sweaty brow, and walks over to him.

The duke's eyes are feverish but he wears a cordial expression, as if he had never offended Niccolò.

"Today is a grand day for me. Have you heard the news?" the prince asks in a hoarse, practically unrecognizable voice.

It's not the first time that Niccolò has seen a powerful person suddenly change mood, and he's not terribly surprised.

"No, what happened?" he asks as coldly as he can.

Valentino takes note of Niccolò's distant tone and sighs as though it's inconceivable that someone might be angry with him. Instead he smiles. Niccolò doesn't return the smile, but nor does that upset the duke. On the contrary, he continues to seem cheerful. "Guidobaldo da Montefeltro has fled Urbino. Once again, the city is mine." He blows his nose on the linen cloth then tosses it onto the floor. "I said as much at our first meeting, do you remember? If they take Urbino away from me, it won't be hard to get it back."

Niccolò rapidly calculates the consequences of this news: Borgia is now even stronger; he summoned me to let me know.

Don Miguel hands his Lordship a leather doublet. Valentino slips his arms into the sleeves and fastens it up. He gestures for Niccolò to follow him and he turns down a corridor. It takes Niccolò a great deal of effort to acquiesce.

"Last night I reread what you wrote. I confirm its substance."

It takes Niccolò a second to realize that the duke had addressed him with the informal *tu*. Surely, it was a mistake. In fact, he doesn't seem to be very well. He probably has a fever. He didn't offer an apology—Niccolò knows that's unthinkable and nor does he care to receive one. He's completely indifferent to Valentino's words of praise. The duke realizes this and tries to smooth things over.

"What's troubling you, Niccolò?" Once again, he uses the informal *tu*. He steps closer. "Have I offended you in some way? If so, it was unintentional."

Niccolò never expected to hear him say something like that. Now he is forced to reply. But how? He doesn't want to give the man any satisfaction. He waves his hand vaguely, meaning both everything and nothing.

The prince is aware that Niccolò is cornered and has no way out, and this weakness fortifies him, so he smiles again. "I've decided to print the first chapter of *Res gestæ Cæsaris*. Your handwriting is tiresome to read. I would like to see the text in proper print." His voice grows softer, he takes a breath, and clears his throat. "I will send it to Venice, to Manutius. You've surely heard of him. What do you think of his work?"

Another direct and informal question. This time Niccolò is forced to reply. "He's an excellent printer," he says drily, his choice of words allowing him to avoid using either the formal or informal voice.

"You're right. He's the only one suited to working on our book." The sentence falls flat as Cesare's voice peters out into a sort of rattle.

Don Miguel and Torrella catch up with them and follow at a distance.

"Aren't you happy to hear this?" the duke presses him.

"Thank you," Niccolò says, addressing him with the formal voice.

The duke corrects his sentence, substituting *voi* with *tu*.

Niccolò is forced to repeat the phrase with the *tu* form.

The duke managed to get him right where he wanted and now seems very pleased with himself. He then looks at Niccolò and coughs openly in his face.

Niccolò is tempted to wipe away the flecks of saliva with his hand but stops.

Torrella comes up to his lord. "You need to rest, my Lord, especially if you are certain you want to travel."

"Of course I'm certain," he says, his voice whistling and hissing like an ogre. He stares at Niccolò. "Tomorrow morning I'm leaving for Cesena. I need to attend to some matters there personally. For things to be accomplished well, I need to be everywhere . . . " His final syllables are practically inaudible.

"You shouldn't be using your voice," Torrella says.

"The court will come with me. As will you ambassadors."

Traveling with him will mean spending money, money the Dieci still hasn't sent him, Niccolò thinks to himself.

Valentino, now exhausted, peers at him closely and guesses his thoughts. Or, more probably, his spies told him about the envoy's precarious financial situation. "If it is difficult for you to travel, my court can take care of . . . your needs," he adds.

Niccolò shakes his head. This would bring dishonor both to the Republic and to his own status. It's one thing to be paid to be the duke's writer, but Niccolò's work as an envoy is something else entirely.

Cesare is overcome with a coughing fit.

"My Lord . . . " Torrella insists.

Valentino raises a hand, as if halting something bothersome. He takes a breath and looks carefully at Niccolò. "Go to the great hall. Dianora is there. You can go on your own. You know the route."

Niccolò conceals the excitement he feels. Why is he asking him to go see her?

Don Miguel's eyes reveal dismay. Niccolò notices this and imagines that Corella disapproves of a Florentine walking freely around the Rocca. But his Lordship has spoken and he can't contradict him.

"Talk to her," the duke says. "She grows sadder with each passing day. Maybe you can cheer her up. Dianora writes poems; maybe between you writers there's some sort of understanding," he says, concluding by sneezing in Niccolò's face.

CHAPTER THIRTY-NINE

N iccolò climbs the stairs swiftly, hoping to find her alone. Farneti told him they still haven't found a substitute for Lucina, so perhaps they will finally be able to talk to each other openly, without being watched. But a sudden noise behind him tells Niccolò that someone is trying to catch up. Don Miguel must have sent a guard to follow him, going against the duke's wishes.

When he reaches the entrance to the great hall, an agile, slender servant with dark, wily eyes steps up, opens the door for him, and then moves aside.

He immediately catches sight of Dianora in the warm sunset glow that shines through the window. Dressed in green, her hair in two simple braids, she is sitting at the stone table and staring outside. She doesn't see him right away. When she does, she gasps for joy, tips her head to one side, and all the color returns to her face. But at the same time there's a stiffness about her that is odd.

He quickly understands why. Sitting in a chair next to the fireplace is a Dominican nun. Heavy set, dressed in a white habit, the woman has a tough, peasant face and high cheekbones, accentuated by her white wimple and black veil. In her hands she holds a breviary. The woman looks at him closely.

Niccolò imagines that she's the new guardian, so he introduces himself and explains that the duke asked him to come and talk about literary matters with Lady Dianora.

"His Excellency thinks that we might share a few ideas, since we are both interested in writing," says Dianora.

The Dominican nun nods and declares, as if she is doing

Niccolò a favor, that her name is Sister Sebastiana. Her accent tells him that she's originally from Umbria. She motions for him to enter, then looks back at her breviary.

Niccolò makes his way over to Dianora tensely, certain that the nun will listen to each and every word they say and refer back to the duke. He can't ask her about her health, because he's not supposed to know that she has been unwell.

"What did you think of the performance?" he enquires cautiously.

"The sets and machinery were extraordinary and the actors were gifted. Please, sit down. I didn't much like the story though . . . Yes, it was well written, but I, and this might be my own personal shortcoming, can't stand stories that everyone else seems to like. They bother me. It's something I can't quite explain."

Niccolò looks at her with deep emotion. He is exactly the same way. "You're right, the great mystery that exists between Cupid and Psyche was treated superficially."

"Precisely. The drama in which the protagonist is forced to live was not fully understood." Her eyes dart to his, telling him that she's referring to her own drama, her own imprisonment. She touches the nape of her neck in her usual, delicate way. "As hard as the actors tried, they just couldn't descend into the depths of those emotions. Also, the final reconciliation felt artificial."

So, Dianora was annoyed by the way that Valentino put his feelings on show.

The young woman glances at Sister Sebastiana, afraid she's said too much, and quickly adds, "Then again, one can't expect too much from Anteo Nuffi."

Her words bring Niccolò enormous joy.

"I even said as much to His Excellency, as soon as the performance was over," she continues.

So she's the one who got that peacock kicked out of court. Niccolò feels a sudden warmth inside, but it is short-lived.

"I have started to read the text that you're writing for the duke. It appears to be well thought out," she says but her eyes express the opposite. She is scolding him.

"Thank you," Niccolò says. "How far have you gotten?"

"I'm only at the beginning, at the tragic death of his brother. That's all His Excellency has given me." Her displeasure with it is evident. Luckily, she doesn't have the section about the attack on Romagna.

"It's a piece of writing that corresponds to a specific need . . . " he says in his defense.

"I understand completely, and it's right that you work hard on it. The duke asked me for my judgement and I praised you highly."

So that explains why Valentino called me back, Niccolò thinks. And yet, he is hurt to know that Dianora doesn't appreciate his writing. What can one expect from a commissioned work? "Again, I am deeply grateful, Milady. As long as it is not finished, it can still be improved."

"Of course. But the words we use leave their mark, Envoy. I believe I am in a position to say as much; I write sonnets . . . "

"His Excellency informed me of this. What a pleasant surprise."

"They are trivial things, but even so, when I finish a sonnet I feel devoid of strength, as if I have given birth to something greater than me, something that I will never be free of again."

Suddenly, Niccolò feels weak. He coughs. Will the words he wrote for Valentino remain in posterity? We can't possibly know what the destiny of a work of art will be. Something that seems like it might disappear may actually survive centuries; the things we think important may instead vanish into the void. He tries to banish these thoughts. In any case, he is protected by anonymity.

"The Prince would like me to show you my poems. Might you be interested?"

"It would be a great pleasure."

Dianora picks up a small book bound in red damask and hands it to him. "They are all collected here."

Niccolò imagines that the nun is watching and that the book has already been checked, page by page. He's about to open it.

"Do not read it now. Take it with you. Keep it as long as you need," Dianora says, stopping him, regretting how open she has been. "Form an opinion slowly. Then, once you've read them . . . " She looks intensely at Niccolò, a little hesitant but no longer embarrassed.

He perceives that she's trying to tell him something.

She looks over at Sister Sebastiana, then walks over to the bookshelf and looks for a leather tome, which she eventually finds and pulls out. "I never had any real teachers but I have looked for inspiration in the great writers. Now I'm reading Horace's Epodes, number Fifteen . . . "

Epode Fifteen? "The one dedicated to Neaera?"

"Do you know it?"

"Of course."

"It's incredible how his lines still speak to us today . . . "

What's that glimmer in her eyes? How they twinkle with the last rays of day.

The poem dedicated to Neaera speaks of love. Is she saying . . . ? Is she starting to trust him, a man? No, it can't be. And even if it were so, he wouldn't be worthy of her. She's deeply wounded and will never completely heal, but maybe she feels less pain now than she once did. That must be it. That's why, and not for any other reason, she mentioned it. It's because she finds consolation in Horace.

And yet Dianora continues to stare at him.

Obviously, the nun who's spying on them is not familiar with the poem, but Niccolò knows, even without turning around, that she's observing and listening to them closely. He's reminded of how, when he was a teenager, he once ventured out onto the Arno river when it was frozen over, stopping just in time when he heard a long, dry sound, almost a moan, the sound of the ice about to crack.

He looks down, afraid of showing his feelings. Then he regrets it and looks up again.

Dianora has turned to look outside. She seems distracted.

So, he was wrong. There was no hidden meaning.

He follows her gaze.

In front of them are the plains that lead to Forlì. Only nineteen miles away, yet unreachable. But Dianora is not looking there. She's staring at something specific on the fields below.

Beyond the pane of glass, which does little to protect them from the freezing cold, the sun is setting, illuminating the icy ditch and snowy hillock that Niccolò unsuccessfully attempted to attack with the duke's troops. It all looks so peaceful, suspended in time and space.

"How colorful the snow is . . . " Dianora says softly and warmly.

"Colorful?"

"Yes. See that mound on the far side of the ditch? The part in the shade has hints of blue and grey, and even yellow hues."

Niccolò sees what she means. Even the yellow. He had never noticed it before. It must be from the sunset.

"And over there, where the snow is piled up, around those two trees . . . do you see the pink?"

"Yes, pink, you're right."

"It looks like a piece of fabric that's been left on the ground, like in a painting. Or like a giant wave that has stopped breaking. And there, where the crest of the wave comes crashing down, there's a hint of orange. And even some black in the hollow areas."

They stand looking in silence.

Everything is radiant.

He feels as though Dianora has embraced him but she hasn't even touched him. He turns toward her while she continues to look outside.

Then she turns toward him. Her gaze is piercing.

No, he wasn't wrong. There's a clear request in her eyes.

They are silent.

This heavy silence makes the nun uneasy. She offers up a comment from the other side of the room. "The colors of the snow. I've never heard such a thing. I suppose you can even see colors in the dark of night, now that it's almost here . . . "

"Of course there are colors in the night," Niccolò replies as a kind of challenge. "*Nox era et cælo fulgebat Luna sereno* . . . "[11]

Horace's Epode Fifteen.

Dianora chimes in, " . . . *inter minora sidera.*"[12]

"What's that you're saying?" the nun interrupts them.

"You don't understand Latin?"

"Only the Holy Mass."

"It was night, and a cloudless sky, and the moon was shining among the inferior stars," Niccolò translates for her. "These lines were written 1500 years ago."

"Ah, old stuff."

"Yes, but can you see the colors, Sister Sebastiana? The black night, the white moon, and the distant yellow and pink stars."

The Dominican nun shrugs. "Utter nonsense."

Niccolò has not taken his eyes off Dianora, and although he feels that the ice under his feet is about to crack, he's not afraid. On the contrary, he wants nothing more than to sink into the nothingness. So he continues.

"*Cum tu, magnorum numen læsura deorum, in verba iurabas mea* . . . "[13]

This time Sister Sebastiana doesn't interrupt but listens to those arcane sounds, which remind her of the lulling intonations spoken by the priest when he celebrates mass, not unlike the dirges and prayers she has memorized without even completely understanding them. Surely there's nothing bad in them . . .

Niccolò stops, fearing he's gone too far, that he has

disrespected Dianora, and that the lines that follow might hurt her. He feels regret.

But then she continues, staring at him with eyes full of the evening light: " . . . *artius atque hedera procera adstringitur ilex lentis adhærens bracchiis . . .* "[14]

As if they were kissing. They look at each other and proceed to the vow: " . . . *Dum pecori lupus et nautis infestus Orion turbaret hibernum mare intonsosque agitaret Apollinis aura capillos . . .* "[15]

They stop. They say no more. The nun might understand the next line: " . . . *fore hunc amorem mutuum.*"[16] What is left unsaid remains between them.

Another writer's words have taken them to a place from which there is no return.

CHAPTER FORTY

The darkening sky allows the couple to conceal their emotions from the nun. They're fully aware that any strange comments could betray them. They have to show that nothing between them has changed.

"Forgive me, but now I must bring an end to our conversation," she says, her voice breaking slightly. She wishes she could stay longer but simply can't anymore; it would be too hard for her to keep talking without revealing her true feelings.

He nods dreamily and says that they shall see each other the following evening. He then remembers that, no, she will be traveling to Cesena and they will not meet again until the following day, when he will join them there. He then reassures Sister Sebastiana that they won't speak in Latin again, or if they do, they will translate every word for her.

Dianora dismisses him with a cold nod, the perfect gesture, as if she had grown bored of him. But when her back is to the nun, she looks at him with bright eyes, full of the flickering light from the fireplace.

Niccolò strides out swiftly in order to conceal his feelings. His eyes are bright with excitement too. He's happy she feels a renewed interest in life after having suffered so much. She's suffered a great ordeal, and if meeting him has helped her in some way, then this makes him happy. At the same time he feels unworthy of it: he's burdened by the fact that he has duped her, he's worried that he will have to do it again, he feels all the responsibility of the vow they just made, and he's worried about not being up to her standard. He holds the book she gave him as if it were a delicate, living object. He feels its weight in his hand and strokes the damask cover. He opens it. It's a printed book, not handwritten.

He doesn't begin reading, though, and closes it firmly. She is all around him: in the staircase, in the open space in front of the Rocca, along the roads. A warmth comes over him, a good warmth, which, although he can't say where it comes from, makes him feel like he is capable of achieving anything. He feels certain that everything will go splendidly, but then he reminds himself that he must not lower his guard. He's filled with hope but needs to be careful. They're involved in a dangerous game; he must remain composed and detached.

Late the following morning, he hears horses and carriages pass under his window. The entire court is on the move. He looks out, hoping to see Dianora, but does not. She must be in one of the four or five covered carriages. He gives the order to Baccino to prepare their bags. They will also leave later this morning. We're better off waiting until the following day, the steward suggests, presumably so he can spend another night with Gemma. Niccolò is adamant. Baccino reminds him that messages might arrive that evening and they should wait for them. The messengers can follow us to Cesena, Niccolò says curtly.

He leaves the inn to go speak with Farneti. He needs to talk to him, bring him up to date, find out if he has informers in Cesena, and organize a way of getting news. The shop is closed. He goes back an hour later but the tailor is still not there. He's annoyed. He needs to see him urgently and this is delaying his departure. He walks into the snowy woods outside Porta Montanara and leaves a message in the hollow of the oak tree, getting soaked through with cold and wet. They must meet up soon, he writes, and if Farneti can't meet him before the following morning, Niccolò will have to send someone on his behalf.

As he trudges back into the city, the cold air whips down

the high drifts of icy snow. His bones ache with the cold and he begins to cough.

He discovers that Baccino has still not prepared their bags. Niccolò admonishes him and his manservant defends himself by saying that he doesn't feel very well.

Then I'll do it myself, Niccolò says angrily. Filled with rage, he prepares his own bags so that the following day they won't lose any further time. He goes to bed early and wakes up at dawn feeling extremely weak.

He musters up the strength to get out of bed and drags himself downstairs.

"Do you feel unwell?" Gemma asks, peering at him closely.

I'm just tired, he replies hoarsely and then sneezes. His knees and elbows ache. His throat burns. Illness enters the body through the mouth, his mother Bartolomea used to say. He wants to go see Farneti but doesn't have the strength and sits down heavily in a chair.

When Baccino comes in and asks how he is feeling, Niccolò replies rudely.

He then goes back to his room and flops down on the straw mattress. It feels like he's sinking into an ocean of mud. Now even his muscles ache, as if he had been beaten with a stick. Clearly Valentino has infected him with whatever seasonal illness he had when he coughed in his face. He feels hot, as if on fire, and he coughs incessantly. He shuts his eyes.

In his wakeful, feverish state, he sees evil faces of people he doesn't know. Then he has visions of da Vinci's theater crumbling under the weight of the snow into an empty abyss.

A jolt runs through his body. He opens his eyes. He's sweating heavily now and has no strength to speak. He surely has a high fever. He tries to call Baccino but the only sound he can make is a throaty rattle. No one can hear him and this pains him deeply.

He starts dreaming again. He sees Dianora walking off, he wants to call out to her, he begs her to turn around, but he can't, he has lost all his strength. His colleagues in the Chancery laugh at him: why, he's not even a *notaio*! Just the son of a second-rate lawyer, strapped with debt. How on earth did he even manage to get a job in the Palazzo della Signoria, they ask, sneering at him; did his ass belong to someone? To whom? Or is he kept like a dog on a chain, to be sent in to attack or hunt someone down? An animal to be kicked around, a cur that's content with a rotten bone, a howling mutt . . . He sees his old teacher, Marcello Adriani, dressed in a sumptuous robe; he's frowning at him. Greek, he says, you'll never learn Greek, you just don't have the head for it, he says. You'll have to get by on your faltering Latin. You'll never amount to much.

Niccolò hears mice scurrying around the room, up and down the walls. He knew there were mice, disgusting creatures, and now that he can't defend himself they have come to take advantage of him.

Baccino leans over him and rests his hand on Niccolò's forehead.

Niccolò looks up at him through heavy-lidded eyes. He coughs so hard it feels like his chest is going to explode.

"It's this fever that's going around," his steward reassures him.

"Could it be . . . poison?" He is overcome by a convulsive cough, interrupting his painful questions. "Did they . . . find out . . . about us?"

"Silence, watch what you say. Rest now."

Gemma peers in from the doorway. Baccino turns to her. Niccolò hears him say something about hot broth, and he thinks back to what his mother used to make when he was sick, strong enough to even heal the wounds of Christ. He sees the iron nails planted in the feet of Christ, he feels the weight of the cross that he carried when he left the church to avoid Duccio Del Briga. The killer stares at him with triumph in his eyes. He sees a body float by on the river, face down, dressed in elegant clothes, soaked through: it's Alvise Boscolo, the orator from Venice.

He hopes the broth arrives soon but no one comes. He wishes he had the strength to call for help. He knows his fever is rising, even the straw feels hot. He coughs and coughs. The King of France looks down at him with a weary expression. The plague is at the palace gates.

Hot water flows over his dry lips. No, it's broth. But it has a strange flavor. Is it poison? No one knows what kind of poison the Borgia family uses because no one has ever survived it. How many cardinals have they killed to possess such massive wealth? All those grand palazzi and vast holdings, transformed into armies. Why does he feel so ill? Maybe it's not a winter malady, maybe it really is the plague. He recalls the dead infected bodies, the wounds and sores.

"We should let him sleep."

Don't leave, he would like to say. I have no one except you. I'm all alone, I have always been alone. That man gave me his fever, he says to himself again. Yes, that's what it is, nothing more than that, just an illness due to the cold. Every winter brings its share of maladies, but I've never been this sick in all my life.

He hears a man and a woman talking about calling a doctor. I'll go, the man says. Niccolò starts coughing again, he can't hear them. When he goes back to breathing normally again, they're gone. Who were those people? My father and mother? No, they're dead. My father died when I was in France; I couldn't even go and say a final farewell to him. Why do we think that the final moment of life is so important? While surely it is for the person who is dying, it's far less important for those who are left behind . . . And anyway, my father still talks to me. When was the last time he came to me? Every cough feels like a raw wound.

Someone pours some liquid into his mouth. It has a sweet flavor and is as thick as oil.

"No, Gemma! What're you doing?" he hears Baccino say. That's what the man's name is: Baccino.

"It's a cough syrup I found on his desk."

The steward takes the bottle out of the woman's hand. "It's not for that kind of cough."

Niccolò understands. It's the invisible ink. He tries to spit it out, but he's already swallowed it. Will it hurt me? He doesn't even have the strength to ask. It's December and rain is falling on the Arno. He watches from Ponte Vecchio, his black tabard pulled tightly around him. He wants to go home but can't find the way.

Niccolò wakes up. A man with a scent that he recognizes places a cold hand on his chest.

It's just a winter cold, Niccolò says, trying to wriggle free.

Allow me to decide, the master physician says and, with help from Baccino, he rolls Niccolò over to auscultate his back.

Exhausted, Niccolò sinks into the straw. He hears them talking about his lungs. He can't find the words to describe the depth of pain he feels.

They have him drink something that tastes like rusty iron.

Is it the invisible ink again? No, this has a different flavor. The idea of picking up a quill pen seems impossible, as if it were an enormous iron club that not even a giant could raise. A blank piece of paper seems like a tangled forest, impossible to make his way through, not even by striking out with a sword. Gone is his strength to write, it will never come back. The stories that he could have written have disappeared, like water on sand. Words that could have become houses or cities for so many people are lost forever.

He feels sad for the words that he never managed to breathe life into; they were like bold children who could have made people laugh or incited anger or brought consolation or provoked thought.

I'm sorry, Dianora. Those words will belong to someone else. They will belong to people like Anteo Nuffi, who always manages to find success. Conte Guido will no longer ride for

Tuscany. No, he never even existed. Neither him, tall and proud, nor his elegant horse. I didn't even find time to read your poems. Forgive me.

He hears someone dragging a chair over to the side of the bed. It's Baccino. He's staring at him.

"Did you go into the mountains?" Niccolò asks him.

"Quiet, Niccolò. Don't worry about anything. Don't say anything."

Even in the haze of his fever, he understands what his steward is trying to tell him. He remembers that he's there as a spy and must be careful of what he says.

"Sleep. Drink water. Do as the doctor ordered."

Water brings life, he knows that much. It generates life, the way women generate us. But what does water represent to people? It is the things they believe in. The things we have them believe, isn't that right, Baccino?

The man looks at him in silence. He places a hand on his shoulder, as if to tell him to be strong, and then stands up and leaves.

Niccolò shuts his eyes. He feels his chest rising and falling but has a hard time breathing because of the cough. He needs air. He looks around for it with determination. That's when he finally sees Dianora's face again. She is smiling at him.

Day turns to night. Gemma brings in a new candle each time the wick burns down. They have to keep it lit so that she can see if Niccolò, may God protect him, has gotten worse.

When the sun rises, Torrella, the master physician, returns. Baccino helps him raise Niccolò up to a seated position so the man can visit him quickly and ably.

His lungs have not been compromised, the fever will vanish in two days, but he may be weak for much longer, he says. Even His Excellency was ill for some time but now he's feeling better. He sends his greeting and expects to see you soon in Cesena; he is counting on it.

Dianora's waiting for me too, Niccolò thinks and nods in reply. I'll be happy to join him there, Maestro, he then says.

Torrella glances around the room, noticing the uncomfortable conditions. We shall requisition the finest home for you, he adds.

"Thank you, but the Republic will pay for me . . . "

I must insist, the doctor says. You need warm lodgings, an adequate place. Write to your Republic, explain the situation, I am sure they will not stop you from accepting the duke's kind offer. He cares about your wellbeing, which is also that of Florence.

I agree, Baccino says.

Niccolò understands what his steward is implying: with their limited means, they could never afford lodgings in another city without dipping into their own personal funds, which they do not have.

"We'll provide you with a covered carriage to transport you there as soon as you are capable of moving."

Torrella looks over at Baccino. You, as his steward, need to tend to him, and travel with him in the carriage. He then turns back to Niccolò. Now rest, he says.

Niccolò closes his eyes with gratitude. While he lets himself drift off to sleep he hears Torrella prescribe some medicines that will also be paid for by the prince.

CHAPTER FORTY-ONE

Gripping his reddish mantle tightly around him, his bones and lungs still aching, Niccolò climbs into the covered carriage decorated in Borgia's colors. Inside, it's more or less like a wooden-paneled room with small windows, seats, and even a daybed made of interwoven leather strips and covered with cushions and rugs. He no longer has a fever but still feels weak. The snow on the roads is almost entirely gone. Has it been six days, or more? He can't say.

Baccino stands on one side, helping him in, and Gemma on the other.

He asks what day it is.

The twentieth of December, they reply.

Cold air sneaks in between the folds of the mantle and he shivers as he settles down in a corner of the carriage.

In a fog, he watches as Gemma sadly says goodbye to Baccino: even though his steward says he will be back soon, they both know it is farewell.

The carriage lurches forward, there's the clatter of the wooden wheels on the cobblestones. Niccolò wishes he were lying warm in bed but knows it's pointless to resist.

The carriage makes its way toward the city walls. Baccino hands him the letters that have arrived from Florence while he was unwell: three from the Dieci and one from the gonfalonier. Niccolò puts them to one side. He's not strong enough to read them now and will only be able to decipher Soderini's message when he arrives in Cesena.

The steward whispers into Niccolò's ear things he hadn't

been able to say with Gemma present. It's hard to hear and the wheels rattle loudly on the cobblestones. The French are still camped out in the villages at the foothills of the mountains and the townspeople are annoyed by their presence because the men are depleting all their provisions. The roads leading into the Apennines are now passable.

Niccolò's weary mind is filled with thoughts and questions that move faster than his sick body. He needs more information, everything possible. Is it worth going to Farneti's shop before they leave Imola? No, it would be too risky.

A crowd has gathered outside the gates. People look up at the walls. The duke's soldiers are conducting executions, hanging people from the ramparts.

Baccino leans out a window of the carriage to see. Niccolò is also curious. Two middle-aged men's bodies already hang dead. A younger man is still kicking.

Farneti, a rope around his neck, is forced to walk to the edge. His skin is a sickly white, he has bruises on his cheeks, and his mouth is caked with dried blood.

Niccolò gasps. So they managed to catch him and torture him. Did he talk? Are those other men his spies?

The soldiers give Farneti a push. He falls hard, his body twists, his neck snaps, his corpse swings back and forth. Niccolò didn't hear if he said any final words. The people who have gathered below cheer with satisfaction as a noose is placed around the neck of the next convict, a man of about thirty wearing a soldier's jerkin.

Niccolò clenches the mantle that Farneti made for him and stares at the swaying body of the tailor.

Baccino observes him carefully. He asks if Niccolò feels ill, if the fever is coming back.

Niccolò shakes his head.

Who do you think they're hanging? Baccino wonders out loud.

I don't know, he says.

The crowd cheers as the soldier falls to his death.

I wonder what it feels like to be killed like that, Niccolò wonders. How much did Farneti suffer? When did they discover him? How long had they been watching him? Did they know that he had been meeting with Niccolò? They can't kill me for talking to him. It's normal for an envoy to spy.

If Borgia's men knew about Farneti and his spies, did they manipulate them? Did they feed him information that was useful to them? No, impossible: Baccino confirmed what Farneti had told him about the soldiers. Maybe the duke's guards didn't catch all of them. If any survived, they will contact the Republic.

Did Farneti leave a final message for him in the oak tree? Best not to collect it. Only a madman would risk going to look now.

They're surrounded by fields. Baccino opens a wooden box lined with velvet. Inside are the medicines that Torrella prescribed. Niccolò recognizes them; he started taking them immediately after the doctor's visit. He takes a few sips, always fearing that they might be poison. But he does feels better, this much is true.

The fields are still covered with snow, mainly under the trees, in the shade. Before they reach Forlì, he's overcome with fatigue and dozes off, his head rolling forward onto his chest. He looks up, then dozes off again, over and over.

He wakes up with his shoulders and neck aching. Baccino is fast asleep across from him.

Outside, the air is clear and he can see far into the distance. He recognizes the road. They're nearing Cesena. He sees the house of the farmers who generously fed him while he was traveling. No one is outside, but a wisp of smoke rises from the chimney.

He is warmed by his gratitude to them. He remembers their

faces and the taste of those olives, the vegetables, that bread. It
occurs to him that he could ask the carriage driver to stop, that
he could pay them for their kindness. He knows, though, that
they would be offended by the gesture.

He thinks about Dianora, now captive in Cesena. Feelings
of regret weigh heavily on him, pain mixed with bitterness. He
had been unlucky; his illness impeded him from spending time
with her just when he received permission from Cesare to do
so. Will he be able to see her again? Or will the duke forbid it,
as a way of punishing him from having been in contact with
Farneti? "Go ahead and try—if you can," Valentino had said
about spying at their very first meeting in Imola. Maybe he will
allow Niccolò to see her again.

He wishes he had her book of poems; it's in his travel bag, in
a distant corner of the carriage. The time and effort it takes him
to reach it is immense.

He strokes the soft damask cover. Remembering how Dianora
stood in the light of the setting sun, he feels his strength return
to him. He hesitates before reading, as if he's afraid to bring
her presence into the hardship of the current moment. But he
needs to feel her closeness, so he opens the book.

He skims the pages, stopping here and there to take in a
few words, not unlike how one looks at a landscape, initially
attracted by the stronger marks of color, the tallest trees, the
most striking shapes.

And then he randomly stops on a passage.

Re del cielo che di tutti hai pietà
che l'ampio mondo riempi di vita,
che di tanto dolore mi hai nutrita,
dove io non vedo dammi libertà.[17]

He looks out at the plains, notices how endless they seem,
and is struck by her curtailed freedom. He feels the burden of
her imprisonment as if it were his own. He aches with her; it
feels like there is no way out for them. He wishes he could see

her, smile at her, confide in her, console her, save her. He goes back to reading her words.

Fa' ch'io non tema quanto accadrà.
Portami nei sentieri di pianura,
e nelle selve, là dove ovunque dura
la tua voce, o Signore che dai pace.
Conducimi lì dove più ti piace,
consola questa mia anima errante
ed io sarò per te una fida amante.[18]

He looks away, moved by her lines. He can't handle reading anymore. He bows his head and closes his eyes. He sees her in his imagination.

The walls of Cesena, which he recalls as being yellowish, are blood red in the sunset.

The house where they will stay is three stories high, has a loggia, and looks out onto a small piazza.

Ennio, the head steward—a bulky man of around fifty with a big nose—welcomes Niccolò and Baccino to the home. He makes no effort to hide his irritation at their presence. The family he serves, descendants of the noble Falchi family, are not likely to be among those who favor Valentino.

They walk down a long, cold corridor lined with portraits. Ennio carefully names them one by one, beginning with a knight who took part in the first Crusade, explaining so that it is exceedingly clear that members of the Falchi family were already traveling the world long before anyone named Borgia was born in a small provincial town of Spain.

Valentino probably derived great pleasure in requisitioning rooms in this house for them, Niccolò thinks. With some malice, he asks the servant how they managed to make portraits of so many Falchi family members who had been dead for centuries. Perhaps the painters traveled back in time?

They based their works on written testimonials that have

been passed down from generation to generation, Ennio replies curtly.

The family members are in the house but do not come out to greet them. Niccolò hears their voices from behind a closed door that surely leads to a grand hall.

The rooms prepared for the envoy are spacious: the furniture is made of walnut, the ceilings are high and paneled with wood, the central beams have been painted with a floral motif, and a fire has been lit for him.

A room next door has been prepared for Baccino.

Ennio announces that he will have their baggage brought up and leaves them alone.

"I should probably go and get some food for us," Baccino murmurs as soon as the man leaves. "These people are capable of poisoning us just to offend the duke."

Niccolò nods, he's exhausted, and he goes and lies down on the bed.

He wakes up not long after; he needs to get to work. With some fatigue, he reads and deciphers the letter from the gonfalonier. In normal ink, I-have-faith updates him on how Guidobaldo da Montefeltro escaped, destroying several fortresses in the Duchy of Urbino before leaving so that they wouldn't fall into Cesare's hands yet again. In invisible ink, the gonfalonier urges Niccolò to send news soon; he very much wants to know Borgia's intentions.

The Dieci also ask him to write with news.

So Niccolò sits down at a table and, with great effort, writes. He may be weak, but events continue to unfold, and he has to stay on top of them. He uses all his strength and discipline to write a few clear lines. And then he signs off, exhausted: *servitor.*

He lies back down on the bed. Tomorrow. Tomorrow he will go. Tomorrow, whatever it takes, he will go to the court to see Dianora.

CHAPTER FORTY-TWO

A gapito Geraldini climbs the stairs, panting, out of breath. Behind him is a page who carries a heavy, dark brown bear skin fur over his arm.

Ennio leads the way. He behaves much less rudely when Valentino's first secretary is in the house.

Niccolò is sitting in a chair at a window of his room. He can't stand lying down anymore but still doesn't have the strength to go outside. He looks down at the people in the small piazza below and the sight of them rouses him. He holds Dianora's book of poems in his hands and rereads a few of them. His eyes go from the page to the piazza and back again in a constant flow of sensations, images, thoughts.

It's as if she were there with him, speaking to him, as if he could ask her questions and she could answer them, every line revealing new meanings and interpretations of the subject at hand.

Ennio stops outside Niccolò's door, indicating to the secretary that they have arrived, and announces Agapinto's presence.

Niccolò jumps to his feet when he hears Geraldini's name. He doesn't want to greet him in his bedchamber and certainly can't let him see his unmade bed or the pissoir on the floor. Luckily he had gotten dressed; despite the huge effort, he had forced himself to resume certain daily routines.

He hurries out of the room, closing the door behind him. The secretary smiles and extends a cordial welcome. His Excellency would like to know if he has regained his strength, if he had a good trip, and if he is well enough to come and see him.

Why does the prince want to see him? Judging from Geraldini's expression, it would seem as though his intentions were good.

"Before receiving you, the duke asks that you meet with lady Dianora again. He said that you were better than any medicine for her, although I confess I don't understand exactly what that means."

Niccolò is tired but feels a surge of joy regardless. Worried that his eyes might betray him, Niccolò conceals his pleasure with irony. "I wasn't aware I had that power, but I'll gladly act as a cure if it pleases His Excellency."

"What illness does she have that you can heal?"

"You know how we Tuscans enjoy good conversation; I suppose that for her ladyship I am something of a toy or companion animal."

Niccolò brings her book with him.

Night is falling fast. They walk down roads that Niccolò has never seen before. The secretary insisted that he wear the bear fur, under orders of Torrella, who told them all about the envoy's illness. Niccolò duly obeyed. He must have looked like an odd animal: short, with skinny legs, wrapped in that enormous fur. It did keep him warm, though, and the air was bitterly cold.

A large stately home sits at the end of the road: the façade is under construction and two new lateral wings are also being built. Everything is covered by a tangle of scaffolding. So this is the construction site that Ramiro de Lorqua pointed out to him from high above. It will be the future royal palace, where Cesare intends to bring his court. Seen from the ground, it is far more impressive than from the stronghold above.

Geraldini explains to Niccolò that one wing is already livable and His Excellency has moved into it; he wants to keep an eye on the work personally, convinced that the men need to watched carefully, every single day, and that only by living in the palace will he discover what needs to be modified and how. To make the palace even larger, the duke purchased thirty adjoining buildings to the loud jingle of coins. All of them were consequently demolished. The duke is now having his workers move walls and open up a courtyard in the palace where before there was an intricate warren of rooms on different floors.

In the vast foyer, support poles hold up the vaulted ceilings and the scaffolding is teeming with workers. There's rubble on the floor, dust in the air, and it feels like they're entering a forest thick with fog.

They come to a slight clearing: the ambassadors of Ferrara and Mantua sit waiting in a corner. Also with them is a fifty-year-old man with a pockmarked face that Niccolò doesn't recognize.

He asks Geraldini who the man is.

Geraldini tells him it's the ambassador from Pisa.

Pisa? What's he doing there?

The secretary is silent.

The three ambassadors are annoyed at having to wait for an audience in such conditions. Valentino must be enjoying this thoroughly, Niccolò thinks. The workers definitely are: they shout and yell from high above and make bits of paint and plaster fall just to see how those snooty, well-dressed gentlemen react.

The ambassadors take out their irritation on Niccolò and his fur coat. As he walks by, the Pisan ambassador comments loudly that the envoy from Florence looks like a furry animal that has come down from the mountains.

On the second floor, men are busy painting the walls. On the third, women are scrubbing the tiles. After climbing the stairs to the fourth floor, they make their way down a long corridor with a window at the end, through which Niccolò sees even more scaffolding. It's warm, so while they are walking, Niccolò removes the heavy fur and folds it over his arm.

A young pageboy, practically still a child, with long straight red hair, appears out of nowhere and asks if he can carry the fur. Niccolò gladly hands it to him.

The secretary stops in front of a door on the right that leads to a large room that is being decorated as a study. Two husky carpenters are building a bookshelf that takes up an entire wall. "His Excellency would like you to do your writing in here. The room will be ready by this evening."

Niccolò nods. "Where is the duke's study?"

Geraldini points to a room a bit farther on. "He wanted you nearby."

And where is his private archive, Niccolò wonders to himself. Will it be in the prince's rooms, not far from his bedchamber, as it was in Imola? Dianora will surely know.

They continue to the end of the corridor and stop in front of a large door on the left. Geraldini nods to the pageboy, who knocks on the door.

Dianora turns to look at him and smiles widely. Perhaps too widely. She is clearly pleased to see him. Dressed in crimson and white, she sits on a large chair in front of a broad window, her hair gathered at the nape of her neck. "You're better! What a relief. The duke and I were so worried about you."

"Thank you, Milady. I am indeed now well. Greetings, Sister Sebastiana . . ."

The nun steps out of a small room on the left, in which he catches a glimpse of a bed. "Salutations, Envoy," she says irritably and suspiciously.

Niccolò is aware that their secret may be more evident in the light of day. He feigns interest in the room, the rugs, and the pieces of furniture. He feels Sister Sebastiana's eyes on him.

He makes banal comments to reassure her and speaks at length about the construction of the imposing palace. The Dominican nun does not reply.

Dianora does. She also offers vague and general thoughts on the building that's going up around them, where, as usual when

His Excellency is involved, the work is accomplished swiftly and well.

Sister Sebastiana remains silent; she watches them closely and then sits down nearby.

Dianora realizes that Niccolò has brought her book of poems with him and so she gestures at him to take a seat across from her.

"Did you read any of the poems?" she asks, her hand automatically reaching up to the back of her neck. She's happy because they're about to enter a space that is theirs alone. All the same, she fears Niccolò's judgement.

He nods. He has reflected at length on what to say so the words come easily, so that his comments are clear and strong. He praises her work not with flattery but by analyzing it carefully. He uses terms that comment on the qualities of her writing without ignoring its weaknesses, because both share the same creative force.

He opens the book, runs his finger across the words of the poem he's talking about, and it is as if he's touching her skin. They look at each other now and then; the conversation carries them forward and yet they are also careful not to reveal their emotions. They feel closer than ever before, they're sharing something much greater than both of them, something that Dianora has evoked in her writing and which now exists outside of her, in her words, which have also taken hold of Niccolò.

Sister Sebastiana stares at them. She realizes that an understanding exists between them but she is not suspicious. After all, they're only talking about poetry, an innocuous subject; she doesn't think for a minute that they might feel the same explosion of passion that she feels when she thinks about the Lord, how she gets drunk on prayer, both when she's alone and also when she is with her sisters. Actually, she even starts to get a little bored of all their talk about technical aspects and rhyming schemes.

Consequently, Dianora and Niccolò are free to worship the

god that unites them. It's not her Christian one, nor his doubtful one, but the power of writing. It hides itself in what it seeks to show, and makes that which is invisible apparent.

Trusting in this power, Dianora looks at Niccolò, bows her head gracefully, and tells him that two days earlier she started composing a new sonnet but that she hasn't gotten beyond the first lines. She asks if he might help her with the rhymes.

Her request, which comes as he is handing her back the book, is a surprise. He enthusiastically agrees, although he confesses that he doubt he will be much help.

"I think you will. After all, you too are a poet," Dianora replies.

"I try to be," he says lightly, holding back the emotions that her words have triggered inside.

She smiles and is both moved and unsettled, realizing that it is lucky that she is seated with her back to the nun, otherwise she would have given herself away.

"Come, let us go sit at the desk together. I started with a memory of my home in Forlì," she says by way of invitation.

He takes a seat next to her, breathing in her perfume and feeling the warmth of her presence.

Dianora picks up a piece of paper that rests with others on the table and reads four lines that rhyme in -ordo and -ura. They express how memories take her back to her life within those walls (*mura*), how she was born into a safe and protected world (*nacque sicura*), and how strong and indissoluble those memories are (*più non scordo*).

The sound of her voice overwhelms him. No other music could touch him quite as deeply.

That's as far as she got, she says. She would like to continue recreating the sense of tranquility that existed in those rooms but does not know what to write next.

He looks at her calligraphy, so orderly and harmonious, and feels a burst of shared emotion. He knows that words offer a direct path to her soul and he wants to tread carefully.

The pain. Those lines were born of pain. Is he able to her offer some consolation? Of course that's not the purpose of writing. Writing is not meant to hide the hardship of things. But if he created lies for Valentino, why can't he offer her words of comfort?

He does not want to let her down but he's not entirely sure he can go through with this. The friction he feels generates a line with an *-ura* ending: in her father's house there was no sense of fear (*paura*).

What feelings and memories do his words waken in Dianora? The same ones that he imagined when visiting her home in Forlì? It would appear so, because her eyes fill with a veil of tears as she thinks back to those chambers and the great hall where she spent her time, coming up with a new line to add to the preceding ones, this time with an *-ordo* ending ... *A voi ripenso in questo gel ch'io mordo* (I think back to all of you in this biting cold).

He notices how devastated she is. How can he possibly compensate for what she has lost? He chases back the knot he feels in his throat and decides to oppose the biting cold she has mentioned with a warmth (*la calura*) that banishes the cold, how the energy of life can overcome all tragedies.

Dianora nods.

He has reminded her of how important it is to hold onto life. She goes back to feeling hopeful. She smiles. She recalls how, in the thick of night, when everyone else was fast asleep, she would listen to the gushing fountain outside her window. Back then the city was calm, everything was peaceful, and night was her friend.

Niccolò looks at her and imagines that fountain, he imagines himself with Dianora in that gentle night, and wishes he could laugh gaily with her.

While the lines of the poem may soon end, while they may speak lies, while their consolatory power may merely be a deception, for as long as they have a hold over the two of them, they are welcome.

The voice of the nun stops them short. What's the matter? Why do you have that expression on your face? Is there a problem? Is something wrong?

That's just how writing is, Sister Sebastiana, Niccolò says. People experience emotions that do not really exist as if they were real. Is there nothing to drink here? Some water? So much talking makes a person thirsty.

The nun points grumpily at a pitcher and glasses. Niccolò fills two and hands one to Dianora. While they drink, they return to the composition and reread what they have written; they are no longer two separate people, a woman and man, but one unit.

The peaceful rooms in Forlì become—without saying as much explicitly—the very room in which they find themselves. Here, too, night can be a gentle friend.

So they write about the glow and serenity of the beautiful moon and the silence that surrounds them.

Che molto in alto va liberamente
Sopra ogni cosa dove più le piace.[19]

They, like the moon, wish they could go wherever they wanted, they wish they were free to love each other.

Together they come up with the final two lines of the sonnet, which express both the hope and an assignation.

Ogni dolore cancella dalla mente
la notte e dona la sospirata pace.[20]

At night. They will see each other at night. When that wretched man and the nun are fast asleep. They're certain of it, even without saying as much. They do not know how or when, but they know they will.

He is deeply moved by her sigh, and a shiver of joy overcomes him. He feels as though he's on the verge of tears. He stops himself. A man cannot cry. He looks away and crosses the astute gaze of Sister Sebastiana.

Has she figured out what's going on between them?

"Forgive me, but I don't feel well. It may be that my illness has not completely passed. I must take my leave," he says in a hurried voice.

The nun relaxes.

Dianora nods and looks at him with bright eyes. She understands.

CHAPTER FORTY-THREE

N iccolò closes the door slowly behind him and takes a deep breath. He looks up and down the corridor in confusion, then sees the young page with the red hair get up from a chair down the way and come toward him, bear fur over his arm. He was waiting to accompany Niccolò to the prince.

Niccolò wishes he didn't have to see anyone, not now at least, but he can't refuse. He readies himself, concealing all the emotions that run through him.

Valentino is in the great hall, in perfect health once more. He strolls contentedly between tall architectural model buildings, two arms' high, that have been built to reproduce an entire neighborhood of a city. There are buildings, churches, and cupolas. Walls are dark in color while building cornices are lighter. There are doorways, windows, and balcony parapets. The prince beckons Niccolò over, saying how pleased he is to see that he is well again. This is how Cesena will be, he explains with pride. It will take years of work, but this is how it will be.

Niccolò recognizes the fortress high on the hill. The light wood model version is surrounded by bastions that are stronger than the existing ones and the road uphill that connects it to the city is dotted with bulwarks of varying sizes. The buildings below are laid out in an organized manner on a grid of perpendicular streets to be built in the future. A few churches will remain where they are but many will be demolished.

Borgia points to a long boulevard that will lead to the royal palace and begins to walk up it. It was designed by him personally; he told the architects what to do. No, not Leonardo da Vinci, because he's busy with other things.

With evident pleasure, Valentino lifts up the roof of the model of the royal palace and reveals the minute details within. There are endless rooms, miniature pieces of furniture, and even a theater with sets.

"These are my wife's chambers, and these are my daughter's, who will one day be Duchess of Romagna."

The rooms set aside for his daughter are substantially larger than those of his bride.

Luisa Borgia, future duchess of Romagna. The Pope might have granted his son the lands that once belonged to the Church, but the prince is already thinking about future generations, Niccolò observes.

"I recently received a portrait that depicts how she looks now. She will not be a great beauty," Valentino says.

Niccolò wonders why the duke feels the need to tell him that.

Borgia stares at him closely and continues. "I know you saw Dianora. How did you find her?"

"It would appear that her dark mood is passing."

"Good. Did you read her poems? What do you think of them?"

"I found her work excellent."

"So, she's a real poetess. Might she aspire to some fame?"

"She has all the necessary qualities to go far," Niccolò says. Even in a world that accepts and idolizes writers like Anteo Nuffi, he thinks.

Cesare hints at a smile and stares off into the emptiness. Niccolò has never seen him with such a keen expression.

"My mother was—and still is—very beautiful. My sister Lucrezia resembles her very much," the duke continues, somewhat to himself.

What does this comment have to do with the previous one about his daughter? What is he thinking but not saying? He mentioned Dianora, then spoke of the beauty that a mother transmits to her children . . .

Does the duke intend to get her pregnant? He already has illegitimate children spread out across Italy, at least eight of them, they say, but no one knows who the mothers are. Perhaps they were important for building alliances, or merely to widen his circle of influence.

Niccolò tries to think of something to say that will prompt him to share further intimacies. He struggles to find the words without revealing what he is thinking, so he remains silent and waits for Valentino to continue.

But it's too late. The prince has already turned back to the architectural model of the kingdom. "You can't see it here, but I'll knock down some buildings around the court to create gardens. Not immediately, though. I don't want to make too many enemies out of the townspeople; my most recent requisitions have caused some to protest. Does the family you are staying with ever mention me?"

Is that why he placed him there? To spy for him? "No, not directly anyway."

"Have you noticed any unpleasantness?"

It wouldn't be wise to deny it all together. "Nothing specific."

"The head of the household does not like me. But his children are starting to side with me . . . "

How does he know that? Who is his informant?

" . . . Just like many others who are starting to realize that it's worth their while to side with me. Things are getting better. Soon I'll sign an agreement with Bologna. Bentivoglio has agreed to a pact. I hope your Republic will soon do the same."

"I have only just started replying to letters . . . "

"I imagined as much. Have you heard anything about Ramiro de Lorqua?"

The duke is like a fish, darting this way and that; suddenly he is where you least expect him, wherever his interests may lead.

"No, this is my first time outdoors in some time."

"Yes, but I mean in the house where you're residing."

Niccolò shakes his head.

"I must leave now," he says. "When will you return to see Dianora?"

"We didn't make any plans."

"Do it soon. You are good for her."

CHAPTER FORTY-FOUR

Niccolò needs to set up a new network of informers. Farneti may have had people in Cesena, but they've probably been discovered and killed, or, if they managed to get away in time, they're in hiding.

As soon as he returns to the Falchi home, he asks Baccino to take a walk with him. He needs to make plans but does not want to risk someone overhearing them. Before they go out, he removes the bear fur, which he is embarrassed to be seen wearing. He has already decided that he will sell it as soon as possible—and will surely get good money for it.

He wraps his reddish mantle around him and they set out. Because he still feels weak, not strong enough to wander up and down the streets like they did in Imola when they didn't want to be overheard, they go into a large, empty church. Sitting in a pew confabulating, they look like two men deep in prayer.

Thoughts of Dianora mix with his obligations and duties. It's as if a flood has swept over him and dragged him off. He feels out of control and yet he is unafraid. On the contrary, he feels stronger than ever, full of an energy he wasn't aware that he had.

You're right, Baccino, Niccolò says. We can only rely on ourselves. You start exploring the roads and paths that lead up into the mountains in the direction of the border with Tuscany with the excuse of delivering our missives, and we will write to Florence to ask for men who can scout around for us. We need Ardingo because he's as fast as lightning; we can train him to be

310 · FRANCO BERNINI

an informer, not just a messenger, and then we'll send him all around Romagna.

Oh, Dianora, you make me a better person. I've always been so careful, always acting so judiciously, measuring my actions. But now, with you in my life, everything seems to be within reach. We managed to trick the duke and together we will do it again.

Something else we need to do, Baccino, now that the road to and from the Republic is longer, is to ask for more messengers. We will also need to ask Falchi to give us more rooms to host the additional riders.

And don't you forget, Dianora, that just like Valentino's star rose up into the sky, so it can fall. Louis XII will not protect him forever. Perhaps Spain will beat France, its army is strong, in which case the situation in Italy will change. Also, sooner or later, the Pope will die. And all the people who were wronged by his crimes will seek retribution. And we will be free.

What's that, Baccino? Yes, it might still be snowing in the mountains. You're right. I'm quite certain that the duke will wait until it has all melted, or at least until the roads and paths through the forests are easy to cross.

Where are the French spearmen? Are they still up in the mountains? We must send Ardingo to find out what's happening.

I would gladly ride out myself if I were strong enough but I should probably stay here in Cesena and try and gather more information at the palace.

I'll return to you soon, Dianora. They're giving me my own study and it is not far from you. You see? Writing for that awful man has turned out to be useful.

I need to find out where his private archive is located. Will you help me like you did last time?

Oh, Dianora . . .

We'll see each other again tomorrow. Cesare has asked me to spend time with you. But that nun, she's a sly one. She's already seen enough. We need to be careful. All it would take is one affectionate glance between us and she will understand how we feel about each other.

We need to see each other at night, just like we promised each other. I will try and come to you. First I need to understand the layout of the rooms. I do not think it's impossible. You mentioned sleeping medicine; do you want to try and drug Sister Sebastiana?

Baccino glances at Niccolò sitting next to him in the pew.

Niccolò realizes that he has gotten distracted, absorbed in his own thoughts for too long. He shakes himself and says they should return to the house.

"We'll have to risk dining at the Falchi home tonight," Baccino says as they start to walk back. With the meager funds that come from the Republic they can't afford to keep eating in osterias. Thankfully, Baccino has become friends with Ennio and explained to him that the Florentines are not on Borgia's side, that they only pretend to be. That was enough to melt Ennio's hostility, who said that if this is the case, they were welcome to dine with them as their guests.

Apparently, they have excellent cooks.

Standing in front of the entrance to the Falchi home are three men with swords and daggers. From afar they look threatening, but as they get closer, Niccolò recognizes Tinardeschi and his two assistants, Jaws and Whiskers.

"I heard you were in the city, so I came to say hello," Fosco says jovially.

He's been in Cesena for two days and will stay a while longer, acting as an intermediary between the allies and the duke. He invites Niccolò to dine with him at the Locanda al Cervo, where he is staying.

Niccolò wishes he could return to his chambers and lie down. He's not even hungry. And yet he goes. After all, it's his duty.

A few steps down the road, Tinardeschi nods at the two guards, Valentino's men, who have been by his side ever since he arrived. "They're quite good at following me, but let's have some fun and lose them."

Fosco turns down a narrow alley, then another, goes through a doorway, crosses a courtyard, and comes out in another alley. In the meantime, he asks Niccolò if he's seen Valentino at the palace.

He speaks casually, as if they were out for a stroll, but his eyes are alert and dart this way and that.

Niccolò has a hard time keeping up and asks for news of the allies.

"I'm pleased with the agreement they've signed," Tinardeschi says. "From now on, they'll all be condottieri for Borgia, and he pays well."

"What about the lord of Bologna?"

"He's also going to sign a pact with the duke. In exchange for peace, he's promised to give him money and soldiers."

"Even more soldiers? How many does the man want?"

"It's hard to say. Did you know that he recently dismissed the French spearmen?"

Niccolò peers at him carefully. How can this be true? "Are you sure?"

"Yes, he ordered them to return to Milan in two days' time."

That's odd, Niccolò thinks. Why deprive himself of his best troops now? "Why did he do that? Does the King of France need men in Lombardy?"

Tinardeschi shrugs. "I think Valentino wants to reassure my lord and the Orsini brothers that he's retracted his claws."

Yes, that must be it. He clearly has something else in mind, Niccolò thinks.

"The maneuver has confused everybody," Fosco says with some concern, "but he still has more than enough cavalry. Moreover, yesterday, six thousand infantrymen arrived from Val Lamona, and also a thousand Swiss pikemen."

"In other words, he can do whatever he wants," Niccolò comments drily.

"As usual, he will never be caught unprepared."

"Do you trust him?"

"Paolo and Francesco Orsini do, my lord sometimes does, but I do not. What about you Florentines?"

"Luckily I'm not the one to decide. I merely report what I see."

They walk down a narrow arcade that connects two streets. There's the stench of urine and a small devotional niche with a statue of the Virgin Mary.

"Here's some news for you, Envoy: the Pope has excommunicated Senigallia."

"Senigallia? In the Marche?"

"Yes, an important city," Tinardeschi comments.

"Did the Pope excommunicate it to make it available to the duke, as he did with Cesena, Forlì, and Faenza?"

"Yes, probably."

"How did the lords from the city react?"

"The Della Rovere family members have swallowed their pride and are now desperately seeking a way out but they won't find one."

"Is that where you're headed now? Senigallia?"

"I can't say. I await orders."

Fosco pushes open a door and the four men step into a dark room with low ceilings.

"Is this the Locanda?" Niccolò asks, who has no idea where they are. Fosco shakes his head, smiles, and gestures for him to be quiet.

A few seconds later they hear the footsteps of the two guards walk swiftly past.

Tinardeschi and Niccolò look at each other in silence. Then Tinardeschi orders Jaws to go out and have a look. The coast is clear.

"I wanted to talk to you without having those meddlers around," Fosco says smugly, sitting down at the table. They didn't enter the Locanda al Cervo but instead went to an osteria at the end of a narrow street. Tinardeschi has known the owner, a distant relative, for years, and they were seated in a private dining room.

They're served hot, tasty roast pork. Whiskers asks his leader with some curiosity if it's true that two years earlier, at the fall of Acquasparta, a few members of the Vitelleschi army ate the flesh of their massacred enemy, and if it tasted like pork, which is what he heard. Apparently, the Vitelli adore pork.

With his mouth full of food, Tinardeschi explains that things didn't happen quite that way. Yes, they conquered Acquasparta after four days of battle, losing many courageous soldiers on the field, but eventually the head condottiere of the enemy army, a man by the name of Altobello da Canale, was hacked to pieces. The local peasants hated him so much that they chopped him up and ate some of the flesh, but most of it got thrown out. And yes, they did indeed say that the meat tasted something like pork, only slightly more bitter.

Tinardeschi burps, takes a swig of his drink, and wipes his mouth with the back of his hand. There are lots of stories like that, he goes on to say. He once heard a rumor that Vitellozzo, following the siege of Capua, the year before, sprinkled poison on the open wounds of an enemy in order to kill him. Actually he stabbed him with a dagger, and he did well; Vitellozzo wasn't one to forget a wrong and the man he stabbed, Ranuccio da Marciano, had been involved in the death of his brother.

Fosco leans over and asks Niccolò details about the part of

the building where Valentino has his chambers. He himself has only been on the first floor, where they receive the ambassadors; what is it like upstairs?

He is trying to make his questions seem casual but they are not, Niccolò thinks. He, in turn, reveals the information easily, noticing how Fosco and his two men sit up and listen carefully. He never says anything specific about Valentino, but he does describe where the duke's study is located.

Tinardeschi nods, then says that the man's study must be close to his chambers. Niccolò agrees and, as he speaks, he hesitates, because he realizes that there could be consequences in sharing this kind of information; it's like watching a small white pebble roll down the side of a mountain, bumping into other rocks, and generating a landslide that crashes down to the valley below. In actual fact, he's not doing anything wrong. On the contrary, he knows he is in the right.

If they were to attempt to take the life of Valentino, he thinks to himself, would he be considered an accomplice for having this conversation? It would be hard to prove. He would deny it. This gives him a thrill. He hopes that their attempt is successful, and that they do it soon: for Dianora, for Florence, and for himself it would be equivalent to liberation.

He is silent. Tinardeschi's eyes are on him but his gaze is unfocused, he's thinking of something. The man frowns and grips the handle of his dagger.

Niccolò watches Tinardeschi's strong hand closely, feeling once more just like that skilled archer in the war against Pisa.

CHAPTER FORTY-FIVE

A t night. They will see each other at night. But how? He remembers the suspicious looks the nun cast in their direction. They have already risked too much. They mustn't make a single mistake. It's up to him: he can move around freely, so he needs to find a way. By talking about the night, perhaps Dianora was trying to let him know that the nun is a heavy sleeper. While that may be the case, Valentino, whose rooms are also nearby, surely is not, nor are his guards. They will have to wait until Valentino leaves the city, but no one knows his plans except him.

Under the cover of darkness and despite his fatigue, Niccolò returns to the palace. He says to the guards at the entrance that he has to go to the study that has been reserved for him by His Excellency.

A page he's never seen before escorts him along the route he already knows. When he reaches the fourth floor corridor, he sees Borgia's two guards standing at the far end. He doesn't even glance at the room where he met with Dianora so as not to raise suspicion. All it would take are a few steps, a simple knock on the door. He would like to do it but refrains from it.

The page takes his leave. The study is larger and better equipped than the one in Imola. There are pens, ink, and a stack of paper on the desk, as well as various documents from the ducal archive that have to do with the war in Romagna.

He walks back to the door, opens it a crack, and peers out into the corridor. To reach Dianora's room, he would have to walk directly in front of Valentino's study. And if his study is near his private chambers, as Tinardeschi suggested, then it will be difficult, as surveillance will be even stricter.

He walks over to the window that looks out onto the street. He sees candles flickering in the houses across the way. The scaffolding that wraps around the entire building is empty at that late hour. He looks both ways: wooden ladders that function as steps connect one floor of scaffolding to the next, all dirty with flecks of cement. He looks up: the builders' structure extends high overhead, like a castle to the sky.

Could he climb across the scaffolding all the way to Dianora's window? It wouldn't be hard to identify where her room is: it's on the other side of the corridor, at the end, and so around the corner of the building, about twenty arms' distance. Yes, that's how he will do it. It can be done.

He is excited by the idea and eager to set out. He's about to make his first move but realizes that an elderly bald man is watching him from the window of a building across the way. He closes the window. He has to wait.

To reign is to have people believe, Valentino once said to him. He will pretend to be writing, there in that study, until late at night, busily describing the duke's achievements, when actually he will make his way over to her.

How long can he realistically stay there? Hours and hours, because the task of writing has no set rules. But he will also have to produce something to justify all the time he spends there. Valentino will ask to read what he has written, and he's only gotten as far as the siege of the castle in Forlì. He now has to deal with the most difficult section.

He sits down at the desk and tries to muster up the strength, but it's not easy. What Dianora once said about the power of words had a strong impact on him, and he almost feels ill.

She was right. What you write marks you forever, even if you don't realize it there and then. He decides that when he finishes the account for Valentino, he will only write for himself—in addition to the letters for the Dieci and I-have-faith, of course. But that's another story altogether.

I will no longer feel ashamed to stand before you, Dianora. I will be the man that you desire, I promise you.

But in the meantime . . .

In the meantime, if I want to have an excuse to see you I have to continue with *Res gestæ Cæsaris* and write about those events that brought ruin and death to you and your family. I know how I will do it. You told me the truth, but I won't write about that now, not here. In your defense and out of respect for you, I will write about something else. I will write line after line about the troops in the field, the alliances that were struck, how many cannons there were, how many foot soldiers there were, how many knights took part, who conducted the sieges, who handled the defense, how they broke through the wall, Caterina Sforza's movements as well as Valentino's.

And then I'll move on.

So be it.

He has already written three pages when there's a knock at the door. It's one of the duke's guards: he saw the candlelight flickering under the door and came to check on him. Niccolò explains what he's doing and the guard nods. He knew that he might find a scribe at work.

Behind the guard, out in the corridor, he sees two other men dressed in armor, standing watch outside Valentino's study. This means reinforcements are sent in at night.

He has to let Tinardeschi know. It will be useful information to him. What point are they at in their preparations, he and his two assistants? When will they strike? And how? He knows that Tinardeschi is a skilled mercenary, he's certainly capable of the undertaking. But Valentino is always suspicious. It will be hard to surprise him.

The possibility that Fosco might make an attempt on the

life of the duke, something that Niccolò had avoided thinking about too much, overshadows all other thoughts, and Niccolò realizes how critical it would be. He supposes Tinardeschi will use a dagger, he will probably stab him in the heart, or maybe he will cut his throat, the way they did with the Duke of Gandía. It could happen any night, even tonight; that's why Tinardeschi asked what kind of precautions they usually adopt. Where will they enter the building? Through a back entrance? Or will they also make use of the scaffolding?

Niccolò mulls over these thoughts for a long time, examining all the possibilities without the slightest hint of remorse.

He then returns to his own projects. Quietly, he goes to the door, peers out at the movements of the guards. They're still there. It's clear that they will stay at their posts all night, a sign that Borgia is in his chambers. It's too risky.

When he returns to the Falchi house, everyone is still awake. The door to the main hall is open. Niccolò sees the head of the family, a sixty-year-old man with longish dark hair and a beard flecked with white. He's arguing with his son, a man of around thirty. Niccolò hears them mention Ramiro de Lorqua.

He cautiously enters the room. They barely glance at him and keep on talking. Clearly, the matter they're discussing is so important that all other concerns fall to the wayside.

The governor. Valentino had him arrested. He's been thrown into a dungeon.

This is big news indeed. What has happened?

The father shakes his head, he thinks it's all theatrics, that de Lorqua will soon be freed. The younger son says nothing. The older son is pleased, he hopes de Lorqua receives just and rapid punishment. Now that the governor has fallen into a state of disgrace, the older son is bold and explicit: everyone in Romagna hates Ramiro the Ogre for his dishonest and cruel ways. No one has forgotten how he once threw a young pageboy into the fire merely for having spilled some wine.

The boys' mother makes a gesture that suggests prudence; things could always return to the way they were.

Ennio stands in the doorway with a stunned expression on his face. Although he doesn't say anything, Niccolò realizes that the head servant is starting to reassess Borgia.

That's exactly what the duke wants, he says to himself. By sacrificing de Lorqua, he is fortifying his own position and satisfying the people. De Lorqua was essential for conquering Romagna but now he's more useful to the duke in chains. What will his punishment be? Cesare knows how much hatred the governor generated; he can use the man to purge the soul of Romagna and win the people over by making it seem like he wants to settle the score.

CHAPTER FORTY-SIX

Niccolò returns to the royal palace early the following morning for more news. He sees close to twenty knights riding out the front entrance. They're in a hurry and they quickly pick up speed. Swords hang by their sides and they're dressed in light armor.

He's forced to step back against the walls like the other passerby, so as not to be knocked over. He recognizes some of the duke's soldiers. Even Rodriguez is among them. Then, on a black steed, comes Cesare himself, wearing an iron chest plate but no helmet. He's talking rapidly to Corella, who rides alongside him. He has a resolute air about him and looks angry. What has happened? Does it have something to do with the arrest of de Lorqua?

No one notices Niccolò.

He watches as they go by, disappearing as quickly as they came.

As soon as he enters the palace, he seeks out the duke's secretary.

Geraldini greets him cordially. Did the envoy come to gather news about the newly deposed governor? He's been accused of corruption, extortion, and kidnapping. He starved the people, increased taxes in an arbitrary manner, and made vast profits by stockpiling and then selling enormous quantities of grain that belonged to the State.

But they already knew that, Niccolò thinks to himself. What changed? Is Geraldini hiding something from him?

He will be tried immediately and justice will be served, the secretary goes on to say. The fact that he has been imprisoned shows, yet again, how the prince, in his great wisdom, can both make and unmake men as he wishes, according to their merits.

The pockmarked ambassador of Pisa rushes over, out of breath, for information. He stops short when he sees Niccolò and glares at him coldly, as if there were some kind of personal dispute between them and not just the age-old hostility that exists between their two cities.

Geraldini notices, understands, and smooths all feathers. Ah, the ambassador from Pisa. You're probably wondering, Machiavelli, why he's been invited to court, seeing that we care so deeply about our friendship with Florence. You should know that it was Pisa that came to us, and we simply could not refuse to meet with them. I can tell you this, though: they came to ask advice from His Excellency after being contacted by the King of Spain, who has every intention of supporting them and reinforcing their military presence . . .

So Spain wants to build another front against France in Tuscany. It would have been better for the Republic if they had found out sooner, he thinks. How did the prince respond? Niccolò asks.

Oh, he considered such an alliance dangerous, Geraldini replies. So many Italians stand with the French; Louis XII is powerful in Italy and an enemy of Spain. But His Excellency also took advantage of the opportunity to build a relationship with the Pisans, in order to help Florence. In fact, if the Prince creates an alliance with the Pisans, he will have an easy time of bringing the two cities to the table to negotiate, with the help of France.

Not a chance, Niccolò tells himself. What a great number of intriguing plots get woven in this court! They're playing at so many tables all at once.

You're amused by it all, Geraldini says. That smile of yours gives it away. It's not the first time I've noticed it. Believe me, you Florentines should welcome someone helping you with

Pisa, to end the fighting and bring about peace. And that's what the duke wants, after all. A long-lasting peace. He has shown it by dismissing the French spearmen. What else can he do to show his good intentions?

Do you want to go up to your study? How long will you stay? You don't know yet? I understand, the work of the writer is never done. Sometimes I think that we writers are like miners, who toil far from the light of day: life goes by and we don't even realize it.

He longs for the night, but it seems to take forever to come. He can't write, he can't concentrate, he can't think coherently. But nor can he leave. The workers climb down from the scaffolding just before dark, at the sound of a whistle.

He barely touches his food—steak, some vegetables, bread, dessert—that a pageboy brings him. He pretends to review his papers. He drinks some wine for courage.

He peeks out into the corridor. As usual, two guards stand watch at the far end, even now with the prince away. Surely the level of surveillance is less stringent. Maybe he can risk it. He goes back into his study, opens the window, and looks out at the scaffolding, which is barely visible in the darkness. In his mind he sees the layout of the rooms around the corner. There's the room where he met with Dianora, which has two windows. Sister Sebastiana came out of a doorway that probably leads to the chambers where they sleep, a little farther down the corridor. One window, then another, and he will have arrived.

He sees a fire burning in the hearth across the way, a distant glow. He decides to go all the same: the darkness will protect him. He extinguishes the candles and leans out the window. The wind is picking up, he feels it on his face.

From the chimney across the way comes a gust of smoke, carrying with it the smell of roasted meat. He realizes he is hungry, so he crawls back to his desk and nervously bites off a morsel of meat. He wipes his mouth and fingers on the napkin, then hurries back to the scaffolding, leaving the window slightly open. He's not sure why, but he is reminded of that October night when he snuck out of his house to get away from the men he thought had been sent by the money-lender. That's when all this began.

He makes his way forward, sliding his hands across the wooden structure and the stones of the façade, feeling his way. He heads to the left, as planned. He reaches the corner and goes around it. After three arms' length, he comes to the corridor window. He then makes his way over to the windows of the main hall. Peering in the lead-paned windows, he sees the room is empty, but there are embers in the fireplace and their weak glow illuminates the furniture.

He reaches the next window and looks inside without pressing up too closely to the glass, so he remains hidden. A stub of a candle on a night table sheds light on a cot where someone is lying. The Dominican nun's habit rests on a chair. Suddenly, he sees Sister Sebastiana sit up and blow out the candle.

He stays still for a long time, waiting for her to fall asleep. The wind picks up, blowing harder and colder. He hears two dogs barking in the distance.

He moves on to the next window. It's pitch black. Is this Dianora's room? Did he calculate it correctly? He taps ever so softly on the glass with his fingertips.

He's afraid that the nun will wake up, and yet, at the same time, he knows all will go well. He feels warm inside, despite the cold air outside. He taps again. Softly. Even softer.

He's about to give up. It's too risky. He taps one more time.

Dianora emerges from the darkness with a look of alarm on her face. Niccolò brings his face up to the glass, smiling, imagining what he might look like to her, with his cheek and nose deformed by the glass. Dianora looks surprised and happy. She opens her mouth but doesn't say a word.

There's the light sound of the window being opened.

He leaps inside, his heart racing. They embrace without

hesitation. He's afraid of holding her too tightly, but she pulls him close. She's trembling. The world ceases to exist; it has disappeared entirely. There is only silence and the sound of the wind.

Dianora glances back over her shoulder as if struck with a sudden fear, her arms loosen her grip around his neck. Then she squeezes him even tighter and brings her face up to his, crying with joy.

He caresses her head, kisses the salty tears that fall from her eyes, and feels the warmth of her body close to his, her breath on his neck.

Dianora lets herself go, as if a long period of suffering had come to an end. A shiver runs through her. "I knew you would come. These past few nights, I've being lying awake, waiting for you," she whispers almost imperceptibly.

He feels her heart beating rapidly in her chest. He rests his cheek against hers, smooth and cool.

"Your beard is scratching my face."

He forgot that he hadn't shaved that morning. "Forgive me."

The contact they lose through their cheeks is reinforced through their hands, both of them still so incredulous that they are actually together.

A sudden noise makes them jump. Has the nun woken up next door?

Dianora steps back, gripping Niccolò's hand tightly.

Another sound. Footsteps. A light passes by under the door.

Niccolò kisses Dianora's hand, goes toward the window, and climbs out onto the scaffolding.

Sister Sebastiana says something that's hard to decipher. Dianora replies, "What noise? I didn't hear anything. Hush now, let me sleep."

The nun doesn't come in. If she had, she wouldn't have been able to see him. He's already back in the darkness. He smiles. He will remember that night forever.

CHAPTER FORTY-SEVEN

He returns to the Falchi house. He doesn't even try to sleep. The hours pass quickly. He sits at his desk, goes and lies down, gets up again, strides around the room in a state of feverish excitement, without seeing what's in front of him, feeling only Dianora's embrace, warmth, and breath on his skin.

He knows that she, too, is probably lying awake and thinking about him. For the first time in a long time, she probably feels like she can dream again. Perhaps she is fantasizing about the duke's death, hoping that life will smile on her once again. With her trust in her God, she surely feels lighter; she probably feels as though everything she's been through will soon be resolved. He imagines her eyes bright with tears, luminous after all these years of hardship.

You'll see, Dianora: Tinardeschi's knife will take care of that monster of a man. Hopefully, it will be soon. He's astute and will find a way of killing him. You'll soon regain your freedom.

We'll live together in Florence. We'll manage somehow. I'll leave Marietta. Yes, she'll suffer, but she'll get over it. And I will raise Primerana, I'll stay by her side.

Time will heal your pain. Everything you have suffered and that is part of you now will gradually be transformed into a scar that aches only from time to time.

CHAPTER FORTY-EIGHT

C hristmas Eve arrives, bringing with it the scent of wood burning in fireplaces and cakes baked in kitchen ovens. It's bitterly cold. Valentino is still away and Niccolò has no idea where he is, but hardly even worries about it anymore.

He knows that he cannot return to the palace until the holiday has passed without raising suspicions. What commissioned writer would work on such an important holiday?

He imagines that Dianora will go to midnight mass at the Duomo. The duke tried to show her off in the theater in Imola, and if he knows him at all—which by now Niccolò thinks he does—he will try showing her off again.

When Baccino sees him getting dressed for church, he looks at him in surprise. Although the steward is not devout, he goes to church once a year, at Christmas, just in case God exists. But Baccino knows that Niccolò has always stayed far away from anything even remotely connected to the church.

"Have you become religious?" Baccino teases him.

"It's a question of duty," Niccolò replies mysteriously.

The central nave of the duomo is full. The women sit on the priest's left and the men to his right, the side that is closer to God.

Niccolò pushes his way forward with Baccino close behind, until he sees her. She is seated in the first row under the careful watch of Sister Sebastiana, close to the central aisle. Her guards stand nearby, the only men in the women's section, because even the Heavenly Father must obey Borgia.

Just like the first time he set eyes on her, he can't actually see her face, only the nape of her neck and hair. But what is out of view, he remembers well: her gentle gaze, the way she often touches her neck, the delicate way she tips her head to one side, the way she walks—which he would recognize instantly, even in a crowd of people. The church is filled with her. And yet, he is also intensely aware of himself all of a sudden, his straight back, his tense muscles, the way he breathes in deeply, the air around him filling him with nourishment.

It feels like he is embracing the world in its entirety. When the gathering sings a hymn and he sees Dianora singing along with them, he feels certain that she knows he is there; she not only turns to her Lord but also to him. He lets himself be carried along by the sound and tries to follow the words, as a way of being with her.

To his amazement, he feels the strength of the people enter into him, both the younger folk and the generations that have yet to be born. The great force of it all makes him feel invincible.

The eventuality that Valentino will be stabbed to death by Tinardeschi becomes, in his mind, a certainty. He sees it as if it has already happened, with extraordinary clarity. He feels content with the role he has had. All it took were a few words to indicate the best route to take to reach him; he likes thinking that he had a part in it. It was an act of justice, which must exist somewhere. Dianora will forever be grateful to him, as will his own city. He will be able to tell her about his role right away; he will inform the Republic one day, perhaps, when the right occasion presents itself.

Singing along with everyone, he is filled with exultation and feels as though he is in a dream.

But, suddenly, when the hymn ends and the priest goes back to saying Mass, this state of elation vanishes, and he feels weak. He realizes that both he and Dianora are suspended over an abyss. They will be either the happiest or the unhappiest people

in the world. Happiness is within reach and they will either encounter desperation and pain or great joy.

When the Mass is over, he stands outside and waits for her
to walk by. And when she catches sight of him, her face lights
up, and although the light fades immediately, he is filled with
glee. Her face is both a confirmation and a promise.

But then she moves off, surrounded by the nun and the
duke's guards.

Niccolò pushes Baccino behind a column and orders him to
exchange cloaks, taking advantage of the bustling crowd to do
so.

"What's going on?" the steward asks.

Niccolò doesn't reply but gives him instructions to lead the
guards who will surely follow him on a long, roundabout walk.
In the meantime, he exits the church and mixes with the crowd,
filled with an excitement and anxiety that makes him both incredibly lucid and swift.

He sees her up ahead, a street away, and follows her. He
hears someone talk about her, what a great beauty she is. Her
appearance in public did not pass unobserved. The woman so
many people have mentioned finally has a face.

Soon the crowd diminishes. Dianora, the soldiers, and Sister
Sebastiana are the only ones directed toward the palace.

He decides to follow them.

One of the soldiers turns around to look at him.

He stays behind them.

Then the nun turns around.

He twists away quickly, facing a wall. Did she see him? He
realizes that he's being foolish. Why risk everything just to see
her face one more time? Reason returns to him and he quickly
turns down a side street.

When he returns to the Falchi home, Baccino is waiting for
him.

"It was that woman, wasn't it? You followed her . . . "

Niccolò waves vaguely as if to say that there's a reason but he can't explain it.

"Niccolò, I saw how you stared at her. I have to warn you against it."

"Against what?" Don't even think about interfering in this, he thinks to himself; no one has the right to do that.

"You know."

"Baccino, she holds precious information." If his steward refers anything back to the Republic, this will be the line of truth he will uphold. Niccolò looks at Baccino calmly. No one would ever suspect a thing from his words or tone. No one except for his trusted manservant, who knows him so very well.

"Don't try that with me, Niccolò. Nothing good can come of this."

"I have nothing to say to you," he retorts swiftly.

"I beg you, keep your head," Baccino says again. Niccolò has never seen him so concerned. "I won't denounce you, of course. But, at the same time, I can't just stand by and watch you fall to your ruin."

Bothered, Niccolò denies everything and says it's time for bed. He hands his steward his cloak and takes back his mantle, secretly hoping that Baccino will continue talking about her and yet, at the same time, fearing what he might say. If he keeps talking, Niccolò feels like he might even admit everything. He may even try and share some of the concerns he feels. But Baccino doesn't say a word. He just sighs and walks off.

CHAPTER FORTY-NINE

Niccolò can safely return to the palace only on the day after St. Stephen's. He is so eager to see Dianora that he leaves the house very early in the morning.

As he crosses the main square, he realizes it is market day. The vendors are setting up their stalls and tables, moving about with difficulty because of the bitter cold.

A number of the duke's guards come out, dragging a heavy object wrapped in cloth. Niccolò is struck by the absolute silence and tension in the air, and by the frigid cruelty that the armed men emanate.

He slows down to watch, instinctively cautious. The guards stop, bend down, and remove the cloth. They dump something on the ground. Two merchants walk over to it and look, then retreat immediately.

Other people slowly and carefully go and see what it is. Among them is a middle-aged woman bundled up in heavy woolen clothes. Niccolò decides to go look, too, trying to hear what people are saying as he does. Everyone is silent. A few people mutter in hushed voices. A woman peeks at it, then quickly turns away, pale, wavering unsteadily on her feet.

Niccolò pushes his way through the merchants to see. It's a body that has been decapitated and cut in two lengthwise. Lying next to the corpse is a long saw with a wooden handle and a knife covered in blood. A nauseating odor of freshly-butchered meat hangs in the air.

The head is farther off, sitting in a puddle of dark blood. He recognizes the face despite the deformed features and disturbing grimace. It's Ramiro de Lorqua, his mouth and eyes wide open.

332 · FRANCO BERNINI

Niccolò looks away, disgusted, and walks up to a guard.

"What was the man's crime?"

The guard looks him up and down; his accent says that he is a foreigner and his mantle says that he is wealthy. "Corruption and theft. He was executed on orders of His Excellency the Duke."

There is a murmur from the crowd. Some people look satisfied. A young man with a fleshy mouth, hard face, and high temples looks downright pleased. An adolescent shudders with horror. Other people come and look, curious but hesitant. Niccolò imagined the man would be punished but never in such a cruel manner. Borgia certainly doesn't do things halfway.

"Was he sawn in half alive?"

"We decapitated him first; we're not Turks!"

The town crier appears, drum tied tightly to his chest and drumsticks in hand. He's been sent to proclaim the news. He glances uneasily at the cadaver and proceeds with a drumroll. At first hesitant, he calls out the news, gradually becoming more certain of himself: His Excellency hereby delivers to the loyal people of Romagna the corpse of the most vile de Lorqua, whose crimes and abuses of power, including ribald methods of tax collection, corruption, and depraved cruelty, as well as an attempt to deceive the prince, warranted his swift execution; all the grain that the criminal had stored away will be distributed to the good people; the magnificent duke will now and forever make certain that the hard-working and peaceful people of Romagna receive the fair and just governance they deserve.

A guard spears de Lorqua's head with a lance and drives the long pole into a crevice in between two rocks. Everyone looks up at it. Niccolò notices both their satisfaction and shock at the ferocity of the spectacle; he shivers with the same deadly excitement he felt when he watched the joust. Suddenly, he feels very weary, as if the fever has come back. It occurs to him that Valentino will be both loved and feared at the same time.

How skilled he was at spilling blood and inventing a convenient reason for it. The people from Romagna will believe him and, moreover, all the crimes that were committed in the region will be attributed to someone who is no longer alive.

Now, before he can return to the palace, he has to go back to the Falchi house and write to the Republic, informing them of this recent event. As soon as he has finished, he wakes up Totto, the messenger on duty, and entrusts him with two missives. These actions manage to dull some of the memory of the violence done to de Lorqua's body.

Eventually, Ennio arrives with a message from the owners of the house; they heard about the execution—word gets around quickly—and they've decided to celebrate with a lunch and would like to know if he, as their guest, would like to join them.

He excuses himself with a smile; an envoy can't participate in such events, he is obliged to follow protocol, but he would gladly send his steward in his place. It's a show of courtesy to the Falchi family, as well as a way of finding out more. He would gladly send Ardingo too, if he were there, because four ears are better than two, but he is out patrolling the land in the direction of Rimini to discover where Borgia's troops are headed.

In the meantime, Niccolò continues to reflect on all aspects of the execution. Was the goal only to offer something to the people? Or did Ramiro de Lorqua commit some other crime? Was he guilty of treason? Was his death a message to someone specific? Perhaps to other condottieri? If so, why? And what did that mean for Niccolò if it was?

Obviously, the execution mainly benefitted Cesare: after conquering Romagna with great cruelty, he now brought about peace with the same ferocity. In this he was far more decisive than Florence, who, in order not to be considered cruel, chose not to punish the leaders of Arezzo, which only led to further revolt and general disorder, killing, and kidnapping that continued to harm entire cities; the prince, by killing de Lorqua, harmed just one man.

Although this is what Niccolò truly thinks, he realizes that he will never be able to say as much to Dianora. He is ashamed to admit it but he realizes how important it is to see the coherence inherent in Valentino's actions. By analyzing the oppressor's actions, Niccolò is not hurting anyone, he says to reassure himself. He is merely fulfilling his role as writer.

Chapter Fifty

He rushes back to the palace. The duke's guards block the entrance to the palace one hundred steps away from the main entrance. Security has been reinforced. Surely this has to do with de Lorqua's execution. What hornet's nest has been tipped over?

Niccolò identifies himself, the soldiers unwillingly allow him to pass, and he makes his way over to the main entrance, which a number of highly armed soldiers are securing shut.

He says he needs to go in and up to the study that has been reserved for him by order of His Excellency.

A soldier he doesn't recognize scowls at him. "All visits have been suspended until we receive further orders."

"May I speak to the First Secretary?"

"I will tell him that you're looking for him. He will contact you."

"I insist. I need to see him now."

"Impossible."

"But I have to see Milady Mambelli, on the duke's orders."

"Silence, Envoy."

He walks away, conscious that he will have to wait to see Dianora until this period of alarm has passed. Surely she's thinking the same.

What is going on? Perhaps Tinardeschi can tell him something.

He rushes over to the Locanda al Cervo.

The innkeepers looks at him oddly when he asks about Fosco. Apparently he and the two men he was traveling with paid their bill and left in a hurry early that morning. They even left behind many of their clothes, and nice things too; does Niccolò know when they will come back to get them?

He replies that he has no idea. In the meantime, it occurs to him that their hurried departure is somehow connected to the death of the governor.

CHAPTER FIFTY-ONE

T he celebratory lunch in the Falchi household goes on until nighttime. Baccino returns to the room drunk and with much to report. The cook, he says, prepared her specialty, blanc-mange—an amalgam of lard, chicken breasts, egg whites, rolled in flour and baked in a very hot oven—which went perfectly with the decades-old red wines they brought up from the cellar.

Even more than the food, the Falchi family savored the details of the execution that had been relayed to them. Ramiro the Ogre was dragged before the executioner in his best clothes and sumptuous cape. He was decapitated near the fortress. His clothes were divvied up between the soldiers present. All his possessions—thirty thousand ducats, vases, silverware, and horses—were confiscated.

The Falchi sons praised Valentino for his actions. Their father, who had been skeptical of the man in the past, has since changed his mind and also raised his glass in the duke's honor, suggesting that perhaps even his own lands, which de Lorqua had appropriated, might now be restored to him.

The people in the farmhouse where Niccolò stopped for a meal also surely rejoiced at the news that Ramiro the Ogre had been executed. Maybe now they will receive some of the grain that he had stockpiled. Even a small quantity would restore hope to them: they could start farming again, and when the prince eventually asks their sons to go to war for him, they will willingly oblige.

An hour after sunset, Ardingo returns from Rimini. He heard about the execution of the governor along the way, which was met with praise all around, the people saying that de Lorqua was punished for the irreverence he showed to Lucrezia Borgia when, at the beginning of the year, she traveled from Romagna to Ferrara to be married to Ercole d'Este.

Why wait so long to punish someone? Niccolò wonders skeptically. The more he thinks about it, the less convinced he is that the governor was truly killed for his thieving ways. And this makes Tinardeschi's swift departure even more suspicious. There must be a link between the execution, Vitelli, and the others. Where are those men now? And what about Valentino? How many soldiers does he have with him? Ardingo says that Borgia is on his way from Rimini to Pesaro. He has about a thousand men with him. Senigallia has fallen, Oliverotto's troops broke through the city walls. Other condottieri will arrive soon. The fortress still stands but the castellan has announced that he's ready to surrender, but only to Cesare in person.

That evening, around the same time that he held Dianora in his arms the night before, he shaves his beard carefully. It makes him feel close to her.

CHAPTER FIFTY-TWO

N o one can enter the palace for two days, the guards remain on high alert. Niccolò has just completed a chapter of *Res gestæ Cæsaris* when he receives a letter from Soderini that is deeply disturbing. Apparently, Vitellozzo and the other condottieri have suggested to the prince that, now that it's no longer necessary to do battle in the Marche region, they should lay siege on Tuscany as a united front.

Apparently, Borgia has also started negotiating with Florence's neighboring enemies: Pisa, Lucca, and Siena. The circle around the Republic seems to be tightening, I-have-faith concludes, without much faith at all.

Because of the critical situation, the gonfalonier for life has decided to send an ambassador to His Excellency: as soon as a man is chosen, he will set out.

Niccolò begins to fret. He has worked long enough in the Chancery to understand that he will soon be definitively dismissed. Florence needs someone with more authority than he has to try and stop the disaster, if this is even possible. When they will have chosen the person they want to send—Soderini and the Dieci are probably vetoing each other's choices at this very moment—he will communicate the news to the duke's court and then return to Florence.

Niccolò feels his chest constrict, it becomes hard to breathe. Yet again, they have used him and now they are ready to discard him. He imagined as much, he knew it. Sure, there was even a moment when he wanted it, but that was when he wanted to avoid seeing Dianora suffer. Now things are different. He would give anything to stay longer.

He grabs what he has written for Valentino and walks swiftly out of the house, fearful that a knight with the title of ambassador is already on his way.

It's bitterly cold and feels like it might snow. The remains of de Lorqua's body have been removed from the piazza where they hold the market. People walk by as if nothing had ever happened, but Niccolò knows that the image of that slaughtered body will remain in their minds for as long as they live, that they will go on to tell the story to their children and grandchildren.

He strides boldly toward the palace. He will do whatever it takes to gain entry. There are still a number of soldiers on duty at the front door but, as he approaches, he realizes they are more relaxed, as if the state of emergency had dissipated. They allow him to enter.

The secretary welcomes him obsequiously. Niccolò tells him that he came to do some work in the study. Geraldini nods in approval.

He climbs the stairs quickly, feeling protected by the thick walls around him. For as long as he is there, the news of his dismissal can't reach him, so he can legitimately continue in his role.

The guards in the third-floor corridor block the entrance to both the duke and Dianora's rooms, but they do not stop him from entering the study.

The evening passes excruciatingly slowly. He stares at the fire. He paces back and forth. He sits down at his desk and makes corrections to the manuscript of *Res gestæ Cæsaris*.

He despises everything he has written. He pushes the text away and is quickly filled with a sense of tranquility. Some lines dedicated to Dianora come to mind: *Oh dolce notte, oh sante ore notturne e quete* . . . [21] He realizes that they are the cornerstone for something. He doesn't have to ponder the following lines because they come on their own: *ch'i disiosi amanti accompagnate* . . . [22]

They appear in front of him, as if they were precious gems laid out on a velvet cloth, and seeing them united together, other lines follow: *In voi s'adunan tante Letizie, onde voi siete . . .* [23]

Even though it's not a perfect rhyme, the sound is beautiful, simultaneously bitter and sweet. Other words spring forth that instead rhyme well: *sole cagion di far l'alme beate.*[24]

He has never enjoyed the act of writing as much. It feels like the lines are deeply his, they resemble nothing else he has written; they are his and Dianora's together. It feels as though he has entered a happy, new world, as beautiful as a field in the month of May.

As soon as it gets dark, big flakes of snow start to fall, drawing a curtain between them and the rest of the world, muffling all sounds. He's glad: no one will venture out in this weather and it will be easier for him to make his way across the scaffolding. Then he stops short when he realizes that his footprints will be visible until fresh snow falls. But who will see them up there, at this hour of the day?

He has to wait until Sister Sebastiana goes to sleep. How will he know for sure when that is? What if she wakes up all of a sudden? These careful considerations fill him with joy, not anxiety. He opens the window. The light from his fireplace brightens the surrounding whiteness. He is watching the snow cascade down and reveling in the cold air on his face when he hears a sound on the scaffolding. He perceives movement in the darkness. A shadow approaches.

It's Dianora. She's barefoot and wearing a shawl. Her hair is tied back with a green ribbon.

He grabs her and pulls her inside. Her skin is icy cold but her breath is warm.

"I slipped the nun some of the sleeping medicine they give me," she says softly but not so quietly that he can't hear. "Finally, we have light. Now I can see you."

Under her shawl she's wearing only a light gown. She's

trembling, the hem of her dress is wet with snow, and her feet are freezing.

"Why didn't you wear shoes?"

"I wanted to make as little noise as possible."

He embraces her and notices that she's carrying something, a parchment scroll. She removes it from under her shawl and drops it on the floor.

"I didn't want it to get wet."

"What is it?"

Dianora throws herself into his arms and kisses him hard. Her face is cold but her mouth is warm. He takes her in his arms and leads her over to the fireplace. Holding each other, they lower themselves down onto the rug, the warmth of the fire enveloping them in its glow. He rubs her feet quickly and delicately.

No borders exist between them; her skin feels like his own.

"Thank God I've found you," she says.

They embrace.

Dianora's cheeks shine brightly in the warm light from the fire. They hold each other tightly, their breaths mingling.

"Oh Niccolò . . . "

He kisses her forcefully. She reaches up to her hair and tears off the ribbon that holds it back; her long locks fall around them like waves. She looks at him with big bright eyes.

"Love me; it is what I desire most."

Afterwards, Dianora lies on the edge of the rug, facing the wall, her hair mussed, in a state of total abandon. Niccolò caresses the curves of her hips. He listens to her deep breaths and then realizes she has begun to weep. Worried, he props himself up on one elbow to see her expression, but sees that she's crying with joy. She raises her face to his, searching for his lips.

Her tears flow onto his face. Dianora reaches up and dries them away with the tip of her finger, then writes something with them on the floor, something meant just for the two of them.

She turns back and smiles at him through her tears, communicating all her radiance to him. They don't say a word and yet they understand each other perfectly. Their silence is filled with meaning.

Then Dianora sits up, caresses him, leans over him, and kisses him again. She is both frightened and happy. He perceives what she is feeling as if they were his own emotions; she is so at peace that she is afraid something inside of her will break. But gone is the sense of despair and grief. On the contrary, she feels a joy greater than any she has experienced since the tragedy, and her imagination leads her to envision a future that causes her heart to race.

She brings her two hands close to his face but doesn't touch him. Niccolò feels the warmth in her hands and is deeply moved.

What's this? Is he crying too? Only old men cry.

He tries to hide his embarrassment, but she holds his face still, firmly and sweetly. Then she kisses him again.

"I wrote the beginning of a canzone while I was waiting to go to you. It is for us," he says and holds out the piece of paper.

"I brought you a map; I took it from the archives," Dianora says, pointing to the parchment scroll on the floor near the window.

Niccolò picks it up and examines it. It shows the walls of Florence as seen from above. It does not reveal the maniacal precision for details or pictorial skill of the map of Italy that Cesare showed him. Leonardo didn't draw this one, and yet it is still very precise. It is also marked with notes that were clearly written by Valentino.

"It shows our weak points, where cannons could break through the walls . . . " Niccolò intuits quickly.

"Which is what happened to my city," Dianora says softly.

"Now we know where he'll try and attack us. Thank you for this, from the bottom of my heart."

He continues to pore over it as she begins to read his poem.

The corner wall one hundred and fifty arms' distance from Porta San Giorgio; the old wall at the beginning of the hill that goes down to San Piero Gattolino; the part of the wall that looks out from San Friano toward the Arno. He tries to memorize it all. And while he's doing that, he thinks about what kinds of reinforcements will need to be sent to these points. They could place large artillery on the towers to defend themselves better.

He has to let the Republic know immediately. A parting gift from the humble envoy to His Lordships . . . Will they feel a bit ashamed when they substitute him? As this thought runs through his head, he feels a sensation of both fear and challenge. Even if they do call him back to Florence, he thinks to himself while looking at Dianora, he doesn't actually have to go.

She, in the meantime, has read his poem. Her face is filled with deep emotion. "This is unlike any poem I've ever read before . . . You have found your voice."

Where does all this joy come from? It is as if the world is only now beginning. Everything from this moment forward will be possible and easy. The two of them will find a way. They will survive, together.

Dianora tips her head to one side. She has heard something. She scrambles to her feet in a hurry.

"What's wrong?"

"Can't you hear?"

There's a noise outside, still distant, but rapidly approaching.

It's the sound of horses' hooves, first sinking into snow, then crossing the cobblestones. Their fear causes them to imagine sparks flying up from the iron horseshoes and warm air steaming from the horses' nostrils.

"At this time of day . . . with this weather . . . it can only be him."

They quickly get dressed, there's a flurry of clothing, the sound gets louder. They kiss and embrace tightly. Then they let each other go and she makes her way to the window.

"Your ribbon!"

It had fallen to the ground, she rushes back, picks it up.

"The map! The map!"

He hands it to her, she slips it under her shawl, and starts to climb across the scaffolding.

He watches as she disappears, then stands staring out at the emptiness. He hears the heavy lock turn downstairs, followed by the sound of voices welcoming back the duke. Niccolò looks at Dianora's footprints on the scaffolding. It will be some time before they are covered by fresh snow.

He leaves the window open so that all traces of her scent disappear.

CHAPTER FIFTY-THREE

H e recognizes the approaching footsteps, rushes to close the window, sits down at the desk, and spreads out the papers of *Res gestæ Cæsaris*. The door opens and Cesare strides in. He's dressed in his riding clothes, he still has his gloves on, he looks weary and bitterly cold.

"Greetings, Niccolò."

"Greetings to you."

"They told me you were hard at work. Bravo."

"Was it a tiring journey, with this snow?"

"Ah, I wish it were only that."

He reaches out his gloved hands toward the warmth of the fire and looks with curiosity at the papers that Niccolò has spread out in front of him.

"Is that new work? Did you finish the chapter?"

The duke takes the pages, grabs a chair, drags it over to the fireplace, and starts to read. Slowly, as he makes his way through it, he returns to his usual self, his vitality returning to him from some hidden source.

Niccolò thinks about Dianora's footprints. They're surely still visible, they won't have been covered by fresh snow yet. He observes Valentino carefully, he's completely taken with his reading. Niccolò is certain that those pages—written in a hurry, unwillingly, and incomplete at that—will displease the duke.

Instead, Cesare looks satisfied. Maybe he envisions himself projected through those words and into the future, centuries ahead, as if already there, elsewhere. When he puts down the pages, his gaze remains lost in the distance.

"Superb. You have managed to capture the essence of my soul."

"I'm pleased you think so," Niccolò answers using the *voi* form.

"Why do you address me with such formality?" Valentino says curtly.

He made a mistake, it's his nerves, he can't do it again. "I'm sorry but your compliment took me by surprise."

"You explain everything perfectly. It's concise. Not one mistake. This is exactly what I need. When will you be able to complete the final chapter?"

"One week. At least."

"That long?"

"It's a complicated subject."

"It is indeed." He holds the papers on his lap but leans toward the fire, talking without looking at Niccolò. "I want you to write the Republic and tell them that I will chase Pandolfo Petrucci out of Siena and take charge of the city."

Now he wants Siena? Wasn't it enough that he had forged an alliance with Pisa? I-have-faith was right to inform him that the duke was plotting with all of Florence's enemies.

"It will be both to my advantage and your own. I would expect the Republic to send in some of its soldiers to fight alongside mine in this undertaking. I imagine that you'll want to punish the city that has been your enemy for so long. If you don't take advantage of this moment, everyone will think you are weak. Either we beat Pandolfo together or Siena will continue to be a safe refuge for everyone against you."

"I will communicate it to them immediately."

"And tell them that, in so doing, you will also be doing a favor for the King of France."

"For His Majesty? But Siena is under his protection."

"Louis protects the community, not Pandolfo; I will wage war against him, not against the people. I have already started to spread the news there. I expect that the people will be the ones to chase him out. But if this does not happen, I will bring my artillery unit up to their walls."

Niccolò recalls the map of Florence, the secret that he now possesses. In that very instant, he sees a strand of Dianora's long, blond hair on the desk. He is reaching for it when Valentino turns around and looks at him with an amused expression on his face.

"Once we have Siena under our control, then I will feel safe."

Niccolò's hand stops mid-air. He looks up, blinks, and glances elsewhere. The oddness of his movement attracts Cesare's attention, who looks in the direction of Niccolò's gaze, then puts the pages down on the chair, and approaches the envoy.

"After which I'll lead my men to fight Louis in Lombardy and the Kingdom of Naples."

Valentino halts.

The blond hair shines brightly on the dark wood surface.

The duke sees it. He picks it up. Niccolò sits perfectly still. The duke looks at him and understands instantly. He gets up, goes to the window, opens it, and peers out.

Dianora's footprints are still visible, only partially covered by the snow and the sweep of her gown.

What should Niccolò say? That he approached Dianora on behalf of the Republic, and then lie and say she revealed nothing? It still wouldn't save her, and might just make things worse, because while Valentino might be able to put up with a personal betrayal, his reaction would be ruthless if he suspects her of interfering in matters of state.

Valentino turns around and storms out, slamming the door behind him.

Niccolò stays seated, incredulous, for a few moments. He can't believe that they have been discovered. Then the awareness arrives all at once, and he feels his energy drain away. He puts his head down on the desk. It would be pointless to attempt escape. What will become of him? He will certainly be punished. He imagines poison, a dagger, a rope around his neck. Valentino will want to keep it quiet, no reason to make an enemy of Florence. He will probably end up like the ambassador of Venice, face down in a canal. A pretend suicide, an attack by some brigands along the road. Even Dianora will disappear, she has no one besides him and he is worth less than nothing. He can only hope, for both of them, that death comes quickly.

After a long while, he gets up to leave. Whatever destiny holds in store for him is better than waiting. He opens the door, intending to leave, but two of the duke's guards turn and glare at him and block his path, gesturing for him to remain in the room.

At the first light of dawn, he opens the door again and looks out. Corella comes striding toward him.

He retreats into the study and goes to the window. The duke's executioner bursts into the room but doesn't approach Niccolò. He gathers up the pages of *Res gestæ Cæsaris* and places them under his arm.

"Come with me," he says in a low, flat voice. He doesn't even turn around to see if Niccolò obeys.

CHAPTER FIFTY-FOUR

They walk down corridors and descend staircases. Two covered carriages stand waiting in the street. Both are made of oak and have strong iron reinforcements. A cluster of riders surround them, about twenty men in all. The snow has stopped falling.

Don Miguel pushes him toward one of the carriages. Then the front door of the palace opens and Dianora comes out, escorted by Rodriguez. She's pale and her hands are tightly tied with her emerald green ribbon.

They look at each other and communicate without saying a word; neither of them regrets it.

Rodriguez leads Dianora to the second carriage. Impulsively, Niccolò marches over to her and takes her hands and holds them tightly. She squeezes his. Rodriguez is taken by surprise and looks at don Miguel, as if waiting for his orders. Niccolò expects Corella will hit him or yank him away but he does nothing. For a few brief moments, their fingers intertwined, the couple looks into each other's eyes, transmitting a fragment of what they could have spent a lifetime saying to each other.

Then don Miguel grabs Niccolò's arm, separates them, and murmurs something to Rodriguez, who unties Dianora and has her climb the two wooden steps into the carriage. As soon as she's inside, he slides a heavy slat across the door. Rodriguez mounts a strong chestnut horse, issues his orders to the carriage driver, and trots off, the carriage and ten of the horsemen following behind.

"Where are you taking her?" Niccolò asks. Corella doesn't reply but his expression is different than usual, as if Dianora's fragility had, for some mysterious reason, touched him. But then his vulnerability disappears and he orders Niccolò to climb into the carriage.

There are two seats and the windows have irons grates on them. He realizes the door has been shut securely behind him. With a jolt, the carriage departs.

He notices that he is being taken in a different direction than Dianora.

The roads are passable, but not without their difficulties, and the ride is uncomfortable and bumpy. He can barely see outside. He sits hunched over, worn out, and yet clearheaded.

If that strand of hair hadn't been there, if he had seen it earlier, if they had been more careful . . . His many regrets only amplify the pain.

How long will it take Baccino to realize that Niccolò has been taken away from Cesena? A day at least, too long to raise the alarm, to think of some counterattack. But it's pointless now anyway.

Even though he's frightened, he notices that he feels something entirely new, as if he were far removed from his life, as if his life didn't belong to him anymore. That's it, he says to himself darkly: he is not in control of anything anymore. And while on the one hand it feels like he is elsewhere, he is still inside his own skin, and that is where all the pain will be played out.

He, like Dianora, is at the mercy of Valentino. The fact that they share this destiny feels almost like a consolation to him. He hopes he can see her once more and that they will be dealt with in the same way. Together they can withstand anything.

The carriage travels across the snowy countryside. Sometimes the wheels get stuck in the mud and they have to be freed. They travel for a long time. Finally they stop. The guards open the door for a moment and offer him something to eat; he doesn't accept, he only drinks some water.

Later they pass a monastery. He hears singing, men's voices, which fade quickly. The day after tomorrow will be the last day of the year. There will be celebrations, even in Florence. When night falls, Marietta and Primerana will think of him. Will he still be alive?

At sunset they stop in a post house but they keep him shut inside the carriage and under close watch. Once more they offer him food, which he refuses yet again. He doesn't sleep. He tries to imagine where Dianora is but he cannot.

At dawn, they set out again, this time on a smoother road.

The hours pass. They cross fields and towns. He's exhausted, his muscles and back ache but he can't fall asleep. He has nothing to cover himself with, the cold gets into his bones. He lies down on the floor of the carriage and falls into a state of extreme debilitation, neither asleep nor awake, and the hours go by. Night falls, they continue by torchlight, the light of day returns, they continue to travel.

There's whinnying and the sound of hooves arriving from behind. Someone gallops up to them, shouting at them to stop.

He looks through the grate.

A group of knights in armor is fast approaching. They're escorting Valentino.

The soldiers that surround the carriage start to murmur. Everyone salutes the duke respectfully. He calls to some of them by name. Then, Corella, who is by the Prince's side, orders them to bring out Niccolò.

They're in the middle of the countryside. Niccolò is exhausted from the journey and has a hard time standing on his own two feet. Don Miguel helps him climb onto a mule. The three men make their way to the front of the procession, the other horsemen follow behind.

Niccolò considers asking Valentino about Dianora but knows he won't get a reply. He thinks about escaping, but knows it would be impossible: the other riders would catch up right away. He looks at the dagger that Corella wears on his belt, perhaps he could try and take it away and kill himself with it. He realizes that don Miguel is watching him carefully; Niccolò would never be able to surprise him. And even if he did, he would never be able to kill himself. Let them do it.

The duke drives his heels into his horse's sides. Corella calls out to Niccolò to follow them. The guards bring up the rear. The carriage stays where it is.

Cesare turns to Niccolò. "We're going to Senigallia. Vitelli and the others are waiting for us there. They suggested meeting, and I reassured them that together we will take possession of the fortress to show that we are friends once again."

The duke's words are of no interest to Niccolò anymore. They're meaningless and vulgar. He sees an expression of satisfaction on Borgia's face and is forced to look away. But Borgia doesn't let up.

"Even so, they brought many soldiers with them, as if they don't trust me. But I forgive them." He pauses. He stares at Niccolò, who returns the look. "Just like I forgive you and Dianora. Do you believe me?"

Something deep in his guts forces Niccolò to reply. "No."

The duke nods and looks at Niccolò approvingly.

A messenger comes galloping toward them. He communicates some news to Valentino in a coded language. The prince looks meaningfully at Corella, then stares at Niccolò.

"After I dismissed the French spearmen, Vitelli and the others felt safe. They gathered their armies together and now think they can control me. But I anticipated this and, over the past few days, I moved my men around, divided them up, and had them travel on different roads so that no one would be able tell how many there are."

"Why are you telling me this?" Niccolò finds the strength to ask. The duke had never revealed anything in advance.

"I'm talking to my biographer, not to the man who betrayed

me," Borgia says, looking at him decisively. Then his face lights up with amusement. "The only soldiers I will reveal to Vitelli are the ones we'll meet up with in a few hours. All the others have been in hiding for days near Fano. Two thousand knights and ten thousand infantrymen."

Without intending to, Niccolò retains the information.

"The road from Fano to Senigallia is not long and completely flat; my men are travelling it as we speak, and with great haste."

They stop in the late afternoon in a meadow that is crowded with infantrymen and riders. A river runs nearby, and an icy wind blows down on them from a damp, thick forest nearby.

Now, when he thinks of Dianora, he feels responsible for having led her into the worst possible situation. She could have survived her imprisonment if he hadn't interfered. This awareness causes him great despair.

Cesare dismounts quickly, gestures for Niccolò to follow him and, without waiting, goes and speaks with his soldiers. Niccolò hesitates but Corella urges him to get off his mule and accompanies him to where the prince is speaking in Valencian to a dozen of his personal guards. They listen attentively. At the duke's command they break up and get back on their horses.

Valentino goes toward a different horse than the one he had been riding. He stops, opens his arms, and helpers suit him up with armor of burnished steel. He tells them, in Italian, to pull the ties tighter. They hand him a sword.

"Soon we will see Senigallia," he explains to Niccolò. "Everyone is there. Apparently Vitellozzo, they tell me, was skeptical. He said it wasn't a good idea to offend a prince and then trust him, but Paolo Orsini convinced him with both words and gifts, gifts that I gave him."

His armor now securely fastened, Borgia gets into the saddle, takes up his helmet and places it over his head. His guards surround him.

Don Miguel pushes Niccolò back toward the mule, gets up

onto his own bay, takes the reins of the mule, and leads him over to the duke.

"I sent the weapons carts ahead," Cesare says turning slightly toward Niccolò, "to show that we're not moving in formation."

There's the sound of drums: the advance guard moves off, about a mile ahead.

"There are five hundred riders," the prince adds. "The troops belong to Lodovico della Mirandola and Raffaello de' Pazzi, and they're the best I have."

A fifer pipes an order. The infantrymen begin to march. There are probably more than a thousand men, including Swiss guards and Gascons. They follow the horses in closed ranks.

Borgia starts to ride along the road, surrounded by his guards. Corella hands the reins of the mule to Niccolò, glares at him, and orders him to ride along with them.

Behind them come the other soldiers.

"All my other men are already in position over there," Cesare gestures to indicate the foothills of the mountains not far away.

Is he truly sharing these details so that Niccolò will write about it? So he doesn't want to kill him after all? Or will he do so at a later time?

A rider approaches the troops. He brings news that the condottieri are waiting to pay their respects to the duke nearby, just beyond a small woods outside Senigallia, with only their personal guards. Oliverotto has stayed in the city with a thousand infantrymen and a little more than a hundred knights.

Valentino nods. He looks around at his personal guards, silent and tense. He digs his heels into his horse. The others do the same.

They ride to a field where Paolo Orsini is waiting for them. He wears light armor and has two knights by his side. He raises his hand in a salute and smiles.

Francesco Orsini comes riding up behind him. He is also wearing light armor and only has a few guards to protect him.

Someone approaches from afar on a mule. Niccolò recognizes the man, he had seen him once before during the siege on Pisa, but he has lost all the ferocity he had back then. It's Vitellozzo. He is unarmed and wears a tattered, black robe that is too small for him. He's pale and dazed, his large eyes are bulging. He has the appearance of being unwell: one leg is bandaged, undoubtedly to lessen the pains of the French illness. He looks nothing like the man who only a few months earlier spread terror through the Republic.

Tinardeschi, riding proudly by his side, is the one who looks like the real condottiere.

Valentino and the Orsini brothers greet each other by squeezing each other's wrists in a sign of friendship. Vitelli watches as if in a dream and then he salutes the duke, too.

Niccolò, who is nearby, hears the exchange of courteous words—finally they are reunited, they will do great things together—and notices that Borgia's guards have casually spread out around the condottieri.

"Why isn't Oliverotto here?" Cesare asks.

"He chose to stay in the city with his men," Paolo Orsini replied.

"To do what?"

"A drill."

Valentino casts a glance in don Miguel's direction, who promptly rides off toward the city. The cavalry follows him.

"Shall we proceed?" Borgia asks.

The walls of Senigallia are decked out for a celebration. Flags with the Borgia colors and flags with the colors of his allies hang from the bastions. On the left with respect to the north wind is a gate, bolted shut, and on the right is a larger gate with a drawbridge and several defensive contraptions. It is the only one open. From it extends a road that leads into and through the city.

In front of the gate is a small cluster of houses and a piazza, one side of which looks toward the river.

Valentino's knights stop just before the drawbridge. Half of the horses stand with their hindquarters pointed toward the river, the other half pointing toward the countryside, allowing the rest of the army to parade down the middle.

Advancing on horseback down the center of the road are Corella and Oliverotto Euffreducci, a dark-haired, robust man with a bold air.

When Valentino approaches, Oliverotto salutes him. "Welcome, Cesare."

"Greetings. Have you finished your drills?"

"I convinced him it was time to stop," don Miguel says calmly.

"Does this seem like the right moment for drill work? Aren't you pleased to see me?" the duke asks Oliverotto.

"Of course I am."

"Good, then let's enter the city together so the people see us united."

They all move forward around Valentino. Vitelli is still surly, but the other condottieri are in a good mood: they have known each other for a long time and this is evident.

The hooves of the horses echo loudly as they cross the wooden drawbridge, followed by the steady marching sound of the Swiss guards and then the Gascons, who bring up the rear.

"We will dine together in a house that I requisitioned," Borgia announces, as they move forward between the crowds who line the street, watching with curiosity.

The building is three stories high and made of dark stone.

In the courtyard, Rodriguez stops to speak to another military guard.

Maybe Dianora is here, too. Maybe they sent her via another route. Where could she be now? The chance that Niccolò might see her again, even if it may be for the last time, fills him with energy.

Niccolò tries to intercept the gaze of Rodriguez, who looks elsewhere. While they are getting off their mounts, he realizes that Vitellozzo is staring at him.

"I recognize you," the condottiere says. "You came to Pisa while my brother Paolo and I were attacking it on behalf of Florence."

Vitelli comes limping over to him. "You had my brother tortured and killed because he wasn't able to conquer the city. You unjustly accused him of betrayal. I was saved purely by good luck." His face has turned crimson, he seems to have returned to the height of his fame as an angry drunk.

Why bother replying? In the despair Niccolò feels, he can do nothing but offer a few simple words. "It was not I who made that decision."

Standing behind the condottiere is Tinardeschi, who looks at Niccolò as if to say, don't mind him.

Vitelli steps even closer to Niccolò. "But I found out that you justified his death sentence by writing that Paolo didn't take Pisa either because he was colluding with the enemy or because he wasn't capable of it, and therefore deserved to die. You are a vile man!"

"That is an unjust accusation. I only did my duty as chancellor by writing out those motivations."

Borgia steps between the two men. "Tame your language, Vitelli. These are things of the past. Machiavelli could do nothing to influence the events which were decided upon by his superiors. Now come with me."

They climb a wide staircase. Rodriguez steps out of a small doorway and joins them. Niccolò peers at him closely, but the man's expression is indecipherable.

They reach a grand hall. From a room nearby—through a semi-shut door—comes the sound of plates and utensils and the smell of roast meat. His hunger pangs are strong. His body wants to live.

"Is the Florentine staying? Does he get to listen in to our conversation?" Vitellozzo asks bitterly as he sits down at the table.

"No, he is here merely to watch," Cesare replies.

"Watch what?"

Everything happens very quickly. With a nod from Valentino, his guards, who stand in pairs behind Vitelli and the others, grab the men.

Vitelli pulls out an estoc and wounds one of his attackers. Oliverotto wriggles out of their grasp, reaches for a short dagger from his boot and tries to kill himself, but they manage to stop him.

There's screaming, punching, the sound of chairs being knocked over. There's a tangle of interlocked bodies.

Tinardeschi strikes an enemy, but then another man comes toward him and beats him hard, forcing him to retreat.

Francesco Orsini doesn't even react. Immobilized by two soldiers, he falls to the ground, stunned, his face on the floor. One of the men goes to help his fellow guards.

Niccolò watches with incredulity. Without even realizing it, he carefully logs all the details. Rodriguez remains standing by his side. For an instant Niccolò thinks he will also be thrown down on the floor, but Rodriguez doesn't move.

Corella is forced to step in to help the guard fighting with Tinardeschi.

Vitelli, taken from behind by one of the duke's men, kicks out in desperation. They grab him and his estoc falls to the ground.

One man cries out in pain louder than all the others. It is Tinardeschi, he's been stabbed in the heart by don Miguel and collapses to the floor.

Cesare watches everything unfold as if it were a performance. The surviving four condottieri are now all his prisoners.

"Take them away," Valentino orders.

As they're dragging Vitelli away, he calls out that his men

will free him. They quickly gag the man. The others are dazed and silent.

The prince turns to Niccolò. "So, what do you think?"

"A beautiful display of deception," he replies and immediately wishes he hadn't but it was truly what he thought. It was as if someone he had no control over had spoken in his place.

Cesare stares at him with pleasure, kicks Fosco's cadaver, and nods knowingly at Corella.

They leave in a hurry. Rodriguez grabs Niccolò by the arm and pulls him away.

The room into which he is locked is small and cold. There's a table and chair, nothing else. There are bars on the window.

He hears shouting and fighting in the street: Valentino's troops are doing battle with Oliverotto's men. At this very moment the rest of Borgia's soldiers are probably attacking Vitelli and Orsini's armies at castles nearby.

He imagines Valentino leading his troops into battle and hopes that something goes wrong. Fighting on city roads is never easy; perhaps he will get wounded. That would be enough to change the course of things. Furthermore, Vitellozzo's infantry are known to be strong and they certainly won't let themselves be taken by surprise.

This is what he hopes, but cold reasoning tells him the opposite. Valentino was ready for everything, he'll win out, the condottieri will be killed the following morning, and so will he and Dianora.

The noises outside increase in intensity. He sees a fire blazing in the night sky some streets below. Did something catch fire unintentionally during the skirmishes? Or did Oliverotto's men create a diversion?

He recalls the nightmare he had in Forlì: in the destruction of Florence, he saw fires, heard screaming, and felt all kinds of imaginable pain.

Where is Dianora now? Is she also being kept prisoner

there? Is she reliving the fall of her city? Surely she is in agony, if she's still alive . . .

He hears a man screaming, long howls at regular intervals. Are they torturing someone? Who? Surely not the Orsini brothers, as their families are too powerful. Perhaps Euffreducci, or maybe Vitelli.

Two hours later, maybe three, don Miguel opens the door. His clothes are covered in blood. He gestures for Niccolò to follow him.

They enter a room. Valentino stands there alone. He is no longer wearing his armor, but a black doublet. He looks out the window at the flames that light up the city.

"Oliverotto's troops have been vanquished. Some of my soldiers lost control and started sacking and burning houses. I will have them killed," he says without turning around when he hears Niccolò and Corella enter. Then he places something in the pocket of his heavy jacket and wraps a black scarf around his neck.

He turns around. He's glowing with pride at his success. "We didn't manage to surprise the Orsini and Vitellozzo troops and they escaped, but they won't get far. Euffreducci and Vitelli are dead."

"I strangled them both with a viol string," the executioner says softly, as if offering an important piece of information.

"They wanted to kill me," Borgia continues. "They had an agreement with that traitor, de Lorqua. They swore they would kill me with a crossbow when I was out riding and secretly promised Cesena to de Lorqua . . . "

Kill him with a crossbow? Once more, Borgia has clearly invented something to justify his actions.

"They died without dignity: Oliverotto screaming that it was all Vitellozzo's fault, Vitellozzo begging for mercy, asking my father to absolve him for his sins."

Who knows if it truly happened that way. It's easy to speak

ill of the dead, who no longer have a voice. Is Cesare telling Niccolò this because he wants it to be remembered that way?

"The last two men alive are the Orsini brothers, an important family . . . I will respect good form and will have them strangled in a matter of days." Suddenly, he seems ecstatic. "If, one year ago, I had done what your Palazzo della Signoria had asked and killed Vitellozzo and crushed the powerful Orsini, I would have received a hundred thousand ducats. Now I've done it at no expense to them, with no effort from them, and without even being asked. You should be pleased." He points at Niccolò. "But ours is a tacit agreement; it is as if it had been written. Florence is now indebted to me and needs to pay up. I say this without any ingratitude."

He nods at Corella, who pushes Niccolò over to a table on which lie—he hadn't seen it—paper, pen, and an inkwell. "Write to the Dieci and your gonfalonier. No more delays. Now that I've freed myself of the traitors, I will focus on Siena, as I mentioned already. And on Perugia. Either you are with me or against me. They need to send an ambassador in your place if they want to conclude this pact. Or else there will be war."

Should he refuse? No, it is still his duty to communicate these requests to the Republic. "Who will deliver the messages?"

"We will have them brought to your servant in Cesena. He is looking for you but won't suspect anything because we will have the letters delivered to him by a Florentine merchant. This man, who works for us, will tell him that you followed me to spy on me, and that all is well."

Niccolò doesn't have the strength to ask what his destiny will be, nor that of Dianora. And he doesn't ask mainly because he is afraid of hearing the answer. He feels like he is a boulder sinking to the bottom of a river, the water closing over him. No one will ever know that he and Dianora ever existed.

CHAPTER FIFTY-FIVE

The fire that continues to burn two streets down casts a glow across Dianora's face, her eyes, her temples, and her thick hair.

She sits with composure in a chair beneath the window, breathing softly. Her hands are once again tied at her wrists with her hair ribbon. The rest of the room is pitch black.

The screams that she heard rising from Senigallia as it was being sacked reminded her of Forlì. New grief adds to existing grief. She stands up and turns away so as not to see anymore.

That's how Valentino, Corella, and Niccolò find her when they walk in. Niccolò is flanked by the two men; don Miguel holds one of his arms tightly and a lantern in the other hand. No one says a thing.

In the dim light, Dianora looks at Niccolò as if the other two men weren't there. He perceives what she is feeling from the expression in her eyes and her face. They are closer than ever. Whatever happens, they will face it together. Don Miguel rests the lantern on the table and blocks Niccolò from moving by twisting his arm behind his back.

Cesare slowly walks toward Dianora in the darkness without saying a thing.

Niccolò understands. "Stop! Kill me, not her!" He tries to break free. Valentino turns to look at him for a brief instant, his eyes glassy, feeling like the master of all things, of life.

Dianora stares at Valentino and does not cower or retreat. She has the same dignified look on her face as when she challenged him in Forlì. She tells him with her eyes that she is not afraid. Soon she will be reunited with her father, mother, and other dear ones.

He walks up to her.

She spits in his face.

Niccolò feels don Miguel tense up: he would like to step forward and punish that affront, but that would leave Niccolò free, so he does not.

Cesare takes a step forward and wipes his face with his gloved hand. As if indifferent to the offense, he pushes Dianora onto a nearby bed and forces her to lie down on her side. She obstinately stares straight ahead. With his left hand, he holds her head down. With his right hand, he caresses her cheek and hair. Then, again with the right hand, he takes a short, squat, two-headed iron hammer out of the pocket of his doublet, pulls off his scarf, and twists his hand so the hammer is well wrapped in the fabric.

Niccolò tries to step in but Corella holds him back. The noise from outside seems to vanish, as if it were far, far away.

Cesare raises the hammer high up and brings it down hard onto Dianora's temple, between her eye and ear, close to her hairline. The sound echoes drily through the room. Her mouth drops open, she doesn't scream, and yet it is as if a scream runs through all three of them. Her body quivers in an ungainly manner.

Valentino strikes her again. Dianora's body moves jerkily, she gasps, looks one last time at Niccolò and then her head tips back. Her irises slowly turn white. Her eyes are empty. There's not a drop of blood on her skin.

Cesare breathes heavily, more from the excitement of having committed a crime than from the effort itself. He returns the hammer and scarf into the pocket of his doublet, removes the ribbon from Dianora's lifeless wrists, and turns her body over so that she is lying on her back. He then stands up straight.

It looks like she is sleeping. Her hair flows around her face, her mouth is slightly open, her white teeth are barely visible, her palms face upward as if she were floating in clear, cold water.

Niccolò feels a sharp pain deep inside and a long lacerating feeling in his chest. His eyes are moist with tears. The weight of all the most tragic moments in his life come crashing down on him.

Borgia bends down and kisses Dianora and then walks over to Niccolò. "She was my weakness and now she is no longer," he says and is silent for a moment, imperial and yet visibly moved by the words he just pronounced. "Not even a physician could discern how she died. Do you understand who I am? Now do you understand?"

Niccolò nods. To his dismay, the awareness has entered into him like a sword. He is horrified and devastated. "I understand. But I will never write about you again. Kill me."

Cesare shakes his head. "I have taken my vengeance." He removes his black gloves, first one and then the other. His hands are covered with boils, some of which are covered with scabs while others are still fresh.

The French sickness. Niccolò understands why he often wore gloves but he's too distraught to feel any horror.

Valentino pushes aside part of his beard to reveal wounds on his face, too, near his jawline. "Dianora didn't know about it, but she surely got infected. Perhaps you have been, too, now. Who knows? So much depends on luck. I myself wasn't very lucky with the illness."

Niccolò stares at him, his anger growing more intense by the minute. Even if he dies, as he imagines he will, choked now by Corella or at some future time by the French illness, he tells himself that he will never beg for mercy. He will die with the same dignity that Dianora showed.

Cesare puts his black gloves back on, waves to Corella to let Niccolò go, and immediately the executioner's grip disappears. "Leave immediately for Florence. Tell your gonfalonier that I sent you back because I want to sign the treaty of alliance with one of your ambassadors," he orders. "You will finish our book. Now that I know you can write it the way I want, I will let you live. I will send someone to come and get it when you have completed it."

"I will never write another word for you."

Valentino looks at him with a strong sense of possession. "Yes, you will. Even if you don't care about your own death, you know that I can reach deep into your city and kill your wife and child whenever I want. Anyway, soon it will all be mine," he says, his eyes shining. "I will become King of Tuscany."

Niccolò feels weak. He realizes that any life he has left to live will be difficult, painful, and pointless.

Borgia then comes even closer and speaks in a less threatening, almost kind, tone. "But you will not write out of fear. You'll do it because you now understand what power truly is. The discovery has spread through you like poison. You are a true writer, and you feel compelled to write about what you know of the world. You belong to me, forever."

Niccolò lowers his head in defeat.

The prince walks quietly out of the room, while the fires continue to rage through the city. Corella grabs Niccolò's arm and the lantern and starts to leave.

Niccolò tries to turn around to take one last look at Dianora but don Miguel pulls him away.

FLORENCE, ELEVEN YEARS LATER

EPILOGUE ONE

FEBRUARY 12, 1513

Not a day has gone by that Niccolò hasn't thought about her. Sometimes the memory comes to him softly, like a whisper, but more often than not, it screams out from deep within.

He never told anyone about Dianora and yet he speaks to her constantly. She is a wound that time cannot heal, a sadness that helps him survive life.

He is at home, he sits at the window that looks out on the street below and stares at the blank pieces of paper before him. His face is now lined with wrinkles. His hair is thinning and grey at the temples.

He hears the sounds of everyday life around him: the voice of Marietta, their two sons, and the babble of little Guido, who's only a year old, sounding tragically similar to the sounds that little Primerana used to make. She succumbed to a fever when she was still in her infancy.

Bernardo and Lodovico giggle and run to him on their strong, little legs. Their mother chases behind them. "Let your father write," she says, pulling them away.

He's grateful to her for saying those words, even though surrounding noises never bothered him. When he holds his pen in his hand, he is transported elsewhere, to a place where the noises of the world fade far away.

But now he is not writing. Marietta thinks he is, and he continues to pretend in order not to delude her, out of a sense of discipline, and due to the fear of emptiness. It is the only activity that is truly his and he can't give it up, even if his role has been diminished to the degree that he only goes through the motions. With utmost care, he sharpens the tip of his feather pen and dips it into the inkwell. And then he hesitates with uncertainty as he has done thousands of times.

He has no one left to write to.

He can't write to the Dieci or to the gonfalonier, he misses having to constantly write letters. Back when he needed to, it sometimes felt like a burden, but now it would be a pleasure. The city's leaders have changed, the Republic was defeated by the Medici family with the help of Spain one year earlier, during the summer. The new people in power have isolated him from all public duty; they simply couldn't forgive him for having served their predecessors. Other men were given a second chance: Pier Soderini is comfortably ensconced in Dalmatia, for example. Niccolò was not given an opportunity simply because he does not come from a powerful family. They took away any money he had and now he gets by on loans from friends and acquaintances.

He could always write poems . . . as he had always wanted to do.

"You've found your voice," Dianora once said to him.

If he had indeed found it, he lost it that same night. He has not composed anything as strong as that poem and he is now over forty.

If Dianora had never met him, she might still be alive. He can never forgive himself for that. If it were possible, he would change the way things came to pass. Over and over, he imagines the early moments of their fall: the initial glances, their first tacit looks that held a reciprocal promise. No, no, he says to himself; he wouldn't do it again.

Then again, maybe he would. He often thinks back to the sense of danger that united them.

He was never as happy as when he was with her.

In fact, a part of him died with Dianora. He had already changed that very night, after Valentino killed her, when Corella pushed him out the front door and into the icy cold, which was punctuated by blasts of heat from the fires that raged throughout the city, the flames reaching high above the rooftops, sparks flying every which way.

Some people tried to put out the fires with pails of water, others wavered unsteadily on their legs, drunk on the wine they had stolen. Screams of terror came from near and far, as did frenzied laughter and the sound of women calling for help.

Don Miguel led him to a group of soldiers on horseback. They would accompany him to the border of the duchy, he said, going on to inform Niccolò, who struggled to comprehend what he was hearing, that everything that he had written up until then would be sent to him in Florence so that he could complete the task. He then placed a heavy wad into his clothes: the remainder of what he was owed.

Corella threw a shabby, old cape over him. Niccolò was reminded of Holy Friday processions he had seen when he was young; Roman soldiers had thrown the same kind of cape over Christ.

He recalls struggling for breath, hoping that some sudden illness would strike him dead, but that did not come to pass.

Don Miguel had then whipped Niccolò's horse across his hindquarters and the animal had bolted, carrying him off, soldiers by his side.

A single thought came to Niccolò. It was senseless but it filled him with fear. It was January, the same month that Julius Caesar crossed the Rubicon on his way to attack the Republic. Valentino would do the same with Florence.

And indeed the prince tried to do so the following year, after conquering Perugia, Assisi, Siena, and becoming protector of Pisa, thereby surrounding the Republic. He was stronger than he had ever been, he had a powerful and faithful army, he had erased all imminent danger, and he was ready to launch the final attack when the King of France intervened. Louis XII had started to suspect the Borgia family, both father and son. He knew they were trying to negotiate with Spain.

Niccolò followed the events from Florence, listening carefully to all the talk that circulated within the Chancery. Valentino was still their mortal enemy and they continued to keep an eye on him. Niccolò knew him intimately, unfortunately, and was well aware that he would wait until the French were stripped of the Kingdom of Naples by the Spanish to become Lord of Tuscany.

He imagined—like someone who can't wake up from a nightmare—what the duke's next moves would be: as soon as he no longer feared France, he would side with Pisa; Lucca and Siena would surrender immediately, partly because they disliked the Florentines and partly out of fear; the Republic would have no way out. The prince would win them over by acquiring so much strength and such a strong reputation that from then on, he would be able to survive on his own, without depending on anyone else's fortune or strength, including that of his father.

But before all this could unfold, on August 17, 1503, the Pope and Cesare went to a dinner hosted by the wealthy cardinal Castellesi.

The following morning the Pope died and his son fell gravely ill. People said that poison had been put in the wine destined for the cardinal and drunk by mistake in abundance by the pope and to a lesser degree by Cesare. Or perhaps it was due to a fever, a frequent occurrence in the malaria-infested Rome of those days.

When the news reached Florence, Niccolò suspected that this time Valentino was in grave danger, and he was right. The man had spent his whole life preparing for the moment when his father would die, but he never imagined that he would fall ill too.

The people of Rome were overjoyed to come out and see the black and swollen corpse of Alessandro VI. Cesare was young and regained his strength with doses of strong medicine, but from that moment forward committed one mistake after the next, as if the death of his father had stripped him of his true strength. Dianora had been right, she had foreseen it. Her great ability to feel allowed her to understand things in ways that had nothing to do with reason. She had seen farther off into the future than Niccolò or anyone else.

During the conclave, Valentino sought out alliances with cardinals tied to France as well as Spain. In so doing, he made enemies of both. A pope was elected that he favored, but the man fell ill and died less than a month later, perhaps with a little help.

Valentino made even more serious mistakes during the following conclave. While he could no longer get one of his candidates elected, he could have easily blocked a cardinal that he had hurt in the past, or one he feared. Instead he cast his vote for Giuliano, from the powerful della Rovere family, who were deeply hostile to the Borgias. In exchange for being named pope, he promised Borgia the position of Captain General of the Church. Valentino trusted the man. He, who never trusted anyone. Or perhaps he had no other choice.

When, in October, della Rovere was named Julius III, he didn't carry through on his promise and asked Borgia to surrender all his fortresses in Romagna. Cesare refused and was taken prisoner.

Romagna remained faithful to Cesare and refused to abandon him, a sign that, at least there, he had sown his crops well.

Because Cesare no longer had an army, he tried to ingratiate himself with the Spanish, who, in the meantime, had beaten the French and controlled all of southern Italy. Ultimately he surrendered Romagna to the Pope in exchange for safe conduct to Naples.

Yet another mistake. When Niccolò heard the news, he was pleased: Valentino was heading towards his definitive ruin.

Naples was home to all the relatives of Alfonso d'Aragona, including Sancia, his sister, who wanted vendetta.

Also eager to get back at him was the widow of the Duke of Gandía, the brother he had had killed. Over time, she had become very influential in the Spanish court and wanted justice.

Valentino knew very well that one cannot offend the powerful and pretend they will not exact their revenge, but apparently he forgot this rule, or else he overestimated his own strength. He was placed on a ship, taken to Catalonia, and imprisoned in a fortress.

There were great celebrations in Florence at this news. Even Niccolò raised his glass, both for himself and Dianora.

Two years later, when people stopped talking about him, Cesare managed to escape. His wife had abandoned him when he fell into a state of disgrace, or perhaps she had been forced to do so by Louis XII, who had come to despise him. Valentino's brother-in-law, the King of Navarra, offered him a safe harbor in exchange for his help in a small local war against a rebellious count. During a night-time skirmish near a castle, Valentino was isolated by his own men. Some people said he had advanced on his own, which was unthinkable for a soldier with so much experience. Others said it was destiny. His enemies surrounded and then killed him.

When Niccolò found out—it was a bitterly cold March, and the rooms of the Chancery were biting cold—he felt deep joy, and yet he was also surprised to feel an element of pain for the loss of that sharp mind.

Cesare's corpse was stripped of his weapons and armor by his enemies and left naked until someone came to retrieve his remains. His bones were left to rot in a church somewhere. The year was 1507.

The Republic of Florence was constantly at battle with its neighbors, the Medici family, and the Pope.

Niccolò made every effort to assist the Republic by

organizing and building up troops. He remembered how Valentino had successfully trained peasants, and he tried to imitate the duke in this, convincing the leaders of the city that Florence would be stronger if it could rely on its own men for soldiers, just like the ancient Roman armies. He started to recruit foot-soldiers and traveled through the hills around the city. Mostly he looked for peasants who were used to hardship, to toiling under the hot sun, people who knew how to handle iron tools.

Even though many years had passed, he often thought back to the time with Borgia when he had been incapable of commandeering those four troops, and for this reason he sought to hire the best condottieri.

His armies managed to conquer Pisa, their eternal rival.

They were incapable of defending Prato, however, where they suffered a disastrous defeat to the Spanish. This tragedy proved to be the definitive end of the Republic. And of Niccolò.

The weight of Niccolò's sorrow had a paradoxical effect on him: the end of a dream gave him ample time to think rationally about things. And yet that was also a treacherous gift, one which he would have rather gone without, but which he could not refuse.

Over time, he came to realize that the Republic fell because of its own limitations, that he had also made many mistakes, and that not everything that Valentino did was completely wrong, but that actually, while he was still in command, he had behaved far better than many other princes, both past and present.

Rational thinking can, and often does, take us down surprising paths. While Niccolò's hatred and disgust for Valentino remained intact, he was forced to recognize a voice inside his head that told him he had learned a great deal from the man. He thought back to the days when Cesare smugly confided his most intimate thoughts about war and power to him. Niccolò knew that Valentino had not lied to him in moments like that.

Or, at the very least, he was aware that the duke had shared some truths about the world with him.

Over time, the teachings that Niccolò garnered from Cesare came back with greater frequency and growing intensity. The passing years purified the lessons and washed away the blood that stained them.

If he were a different person, he might have been able to ignore them. But he was not.

He has a vague recollection of the pages he wrote for the prince while he was in Imola and Cesena. As soon as an envoy delivered them to his house, as Corella had promised, Niccolò burned them. The mere sight of those mendacious words filled him with disgust.

Without realizing it, when he wrote them, he relinquished all sense of personal dignity. He regained it when he offered his life in exchange for Dianora's in Senigallia. Perhaps this was why, now that he was entirely powerless, he felt he could distil new words out of the memory of those old and impure ones. He could write about what he knows. By taking new paths, he could reflect on the essence of power. But would it be worth it? Who would even publish it?

The ink on the tip of the pen is drying. His hand rests mid-air. The page is still white.

Writing takes willpower, energy, and desire.

He no longer has any of these.

He tells himself that they'll come back to him one day and that things could be much worse. He was not stricken down by the French illness and Borgia's money allowed him to pay off his debts to the money-lender.

These thoughts bring him some relief. But then he thinks back to Anteo Nuffi, how widely venerated that man was, and he is subsequently filled with a sense of disgust and dismay.

The midday church bells ring, the ink is drying again. And at what it costs . . . In order not to waste it, he writes a letter to an acquaintance. He would like to start a small business, make a little money, build a henhouse, sell chickens, but he needs a man to oversee it.

Outside someone walks by singing "Il Cavalier di Spagna." The tune has gotten around, the new words have officially taken the place of the old ones, Conte Guido has been swept away. Cesare is dead, but continues to ride at the foot of a mountain. Hearing Anteo Nuffi's lyrics bothers and weakens him, they're like leeches sucking his blood.

The song stops, which alarms Niccolò. He detects an unnatural silence. All conversation has ceased and tension fills the air.

Someone knocks at the door, but not urgently. Marietta looks out the window and then over at him, her face filled with concern. Niccolò hurries to the window.

The men are dressed in the same leather jerkins that the Gonfalonier's guards once wore, but instead of the lily of Florence they display the Medici family crest with its six balls.

Dino Gherardi still heads the unit. Without saying a word, he looks up at Niccolò, the expression in his eyes both firm and somber.

For an instant, Niccolò considers running out the back but he's no longer a young man, and besides, he knows that someone would be there waiting for him. He embraces Marietta quickly and rushes downstairs, while the children huddle around their mother's skirts.

As soon as he opens the door, an officer throws a black hood over him. A second man ties his hands.

"No!" he hears Gherardi shout, sensing that the captain has stopped a third man from striking him.

The hood is rank with the foul smell of sweat.

"What's going on? What do you want?" he hears himself say, mostly because they expect him to say something. He knows that they won't reply.

He perceives their movements around him. They have rushed into his home and are now searching it.

They drag him away. He imagines his wife watching without being able to do a thing as drawers are emptied and furniture is overturned. His children cry, his neighbors are surely watching through cracks in the shutters.

He moves his feet mechanically, stumbling every so often. They have to hold him up as they go. In the silence he detects not only the footsteps of the officers nearby but those of people who step out of the way. It makes him mournful to think about other people's very normal lives, how they are on their way home for lunch, or about to sit down with their loved ones. He is aware that he has entered a terrible parallel world, one which he has long known existed but which he has always avoided thinking about, never having been forced to until now.

Weak and frightened, he lets himself be pushed along.

E ven from under the hood, he realizes the direction they're headed. They have crossed the river and they're leading him to the Bargello. His intense yet perceptive anxiety, which has long been his condemnation, leads him to think the worst.

What will they accuse him of? He no longer has any debts, so it must be something related to matters of State. He hasn't been involved in anything for a year and he has always been careful not to speak with anyone. He has been keeping his ideas to himself with even more care than usual. They certainly can't accuse him of plotting to bring back the Republic because he has never been in contact with any of the people who were sent away. Will they accuse him of being paid by those in exile? His poverty is proof of his good faith.

When Gherardi takes off the hood, he finds himself in a large, dark room. Small patches of light shine through narrow fissures in the wall high above. The room is damp, he can feel the moisture in the air.

They shut him in a cell without windows or furnishings, just a grate on the ceiling for air. His stomach growls with hunger but he is certain they won't give him anything to eat. They're probably already reading through the papers they took from his home, they have surely handed them over to the judge, he thinks.

He sits down, back up against the wall. All he can do is wait. Whatever is going on will have some logic to it, but it will be up to him to decipher what that is.

Three hours pass, possibly more, before they come for him.

They conduct him to a wood-paneled room with long shadows. Two men sit at a desk. A lantern hangs overhead: arcs of light illuminate their faces. One of them is a well-known judge who does everything that the people in power tell him. The other is a chancellor; he dips his pen in ink and smooths down the pages of the register in which he will soon write everything that transpires.

Behind them, in the shadows, is a narrow wooden aperture. Is someone watching from behind it?

"Are you Niccolò di Bernardo Machiavelli?" the judge asks him flatly.

They know who he is but he must reply.

"Do you sometimes frequent the house of Lenzi, on Borgo Ognissanti?"

He has been there before, yes, but a long time ago; why are they asking? He knows that he has to be very careful of everything he says. It's easy to take innocent words and use them to build an accusation. All of his words are being transcribed in the chancellor's register, where they become as if engraved on stone.

"Are you aware that relatives of the exiled Piero Soderini often go there?"

"I was not aware of this." He was.

"Do you know Pietro Paolo Boscoli di Giachinotto, who also frequents that house?"

Pietro Paolo is a handsome, blond, string bean of a man, around thirty years old, with barely a hair on his chin. Yes, he has seen him there. When? Probably in November.

"What did you talk about?"

"About my land. I tried to sell him some wood but he didn't want any."

Lucky for me, Niccolò thinks. If he had bought the wood, they would have seen it as some kind of deal. He recalls Boscoli's face, how bored he looked when Niccolò had made his offer.

Pietro Paolo is a descendant of an old family and considers himself superior to purchasing wood.

The judge holds up a piece of paper, which had previously been folded up, gauging from the creases. "Do you recognize this piece of paper?"

"No."

"And yet your name is on it."

And there it is, in fact. Niccolò Machiavelli, black on white, together with twenty or so other names.

"I do not know why it is there."

"Do you recognize the handwriting?"

"No."

"Do you frequent any of the other people on the list?"

"No."

"Are you certain?"

"Yes."

The judge nods and stares at him. He then leans forward. "Do you know His Excellency Giuliano de' Medici?"

Until that point, the judge had been speaking in a monotone. Now his voice has changed. Niccolò realizes that he has to tread even more delicately. The ground is getting slippery underfoot. Giuliano is the leader of Florence. Why are they asking him this question?

"I saw him pass by once from afar."

He recalls his hook nose, the strong jawline—so typical of his family—and how he rode into the city in victory, surrounded by his guards and festive crowds.

"When?"

"On his return to the city. I saw him from a window."

"Of which house?"

There's no reason to hide it. They probably already know the answer.

"Sandra di Pippo's house. I spent two days there."

Sandra is a well-known prostitute. He had gone there at the fall of the Republic, in a kind of funeral rite.

"What sentiments do you nurture toward His Excellency?"

"I think he is capable of doing great things. He could unite all the Italian forces against foreigners. Moreover, he is a poet, as was his father, and therefore he understands deeper—"

"I didn't ask you that. Do you hate him?"

"Absolutely not. I even wrote him to ask if I could keep my position in the Chancery."

"We know that. Why did you write him?"

"Because I thought that Florence still needed me." He was still *humilis servitor* after all. He had done it out of love for his city. He had even surprised himself by the act.

"So you're still interested in public affairs . . ."

Put that way, it sounded suspicious. "I thought I might still be useful."

"To whom?"

"To the State."

"The Republican State?"

"To the existing State. A person needs to learn to accept things as they are, if you know what I mean." Mistake. He had not displayed sufficient enthusiasm for the Medici family. On the other hand, anything else would have sounded artificial. He does not love the new leaders, but now that the Republic no longer exists, if the people in power called for him, he would run, because facts are stronger than desires. That's why he wrote to Giuliano, who never replied to his letter.

The judge holds up a letter that was taken from his home. It is the one he had been writing when they came to arrest him. The judge asks him what Niccolò meant by needing to find someone to oversee the henhouse. What was he alluding to?

Nothing, he replies. Someone to take care of the chickens, roosters, chicks, eggs. That's what he was thinking about. He was trying to make some money.

"Why are you smiling?"

"I'm not smiling. Why would I smile?"

"It looked like you were."

"I'm not smiling, I assure you."

The judge nods, puts away the letter, holds up the list with his name on it again. "Do you recognize the handwriting of the person who wrote this list?"

Niccolò shakes his head, no.

"The list was written by Pietro Paolo Boscoli, who swore to kill the lordships Giuliano and Lorenzo de' Medici and Cardinal Giulio, and has confessed as much. It would behoove you to do the same."

What kind of hell was this? He can't breathe. He realizes that he is in grave danger. Boscoli is nothing more than a braggart, as far as he knows; he probably was never a real danger, but they want to make an example of him . . . Or perhaps there is something to the conspiracy. Boscoli often used to make remarks about Brutus and Cassius, and that was the main reason that Niccolò spent as little time with him as possible. He was also the heart and soul of a group of young men, and had many friends . . .

"I know nothing of this conspiracy."

"Boscoli wrote down all the names of the people he could count on."

"It must have all been in his head. I never said or did anything to encourage him."

"You served the Republic."

"I served Florence and, as I mentioned, I would do it again if the Medicis offered me the chance."

"You're intelligent; you must have realized that they have isolated you because they don't trust you." The judge has gone back to his usual monotone voice.

"There is no reason to think that."

"Perhaps there is. Boscoli wanted to bring back the Republic."

"That's his problem."

"Not yours?"

"No."

The judge taps his finger on his name on the page. Two words on that piece of paper are like nails on a cross. "So why did the traitor think he could count on you?"

"You'll have to ask him."

"He won't reply. Do it for him."

"He wrote my name down without me knowing about it. I would never plot against the Medici family. I challenge you to find a witness that has heard me say a single bad word about them."

Niccolò knows that they could easily invent witnesses. But he's such a small fish that they won't bother going to the trouble.

"So you refuse to reply."

"I do not refuse. I did reply."

"But you do not admit anything."

"I cannot confess to a crime I did not commit."

Epilogue Three

They take him to the same torture chamber they have been using for decades. Many of the jailers are the same, too; they have gone from working for the Republic to working for the Medici family, except for one, who chose to go into exile. The head executioner has not changed: he's a fifty-year-old man chosen by the lords of the city from among their most trusted men.

A physician has him undress, examines him to make sure that he has no wounds, palpates him to verify there are no hernias and to avoid the risk of his intestine coming out. Niccolò feels the man's cold fingers on him and knows there's no escape. His breaths come short and fast. He is troubled by the fact that his beloved city now has their hands on him—hands that are actually claws.

The physician finds him fit for the rope.

The judge asks him again if he wants to confess.

He doesn't reply.

With a nod from the head executioner, a jailer grabs his left hand and holds it firmly behind his back, then uses his free hand to grip Niccolò's shoulder. With help from a second jailer, he then grabs Niccolò's right arm and yanks it behind his back, too, at which point he ties the two wrists together.

"Don't fight it; just let yourself go," they advise him.

Niccolò hopes that the executioner knows how to do his task well, otherwise he will be maimed for life.

"How long have you been doing this?" he asks the man.

"Twenty years. I have a great deal of experience," the executioner replies.

He feels the man come up behind him. His wrists are positioned so that one is on top of the other. They are then wrapped with a strip of leather. He then feels the men tying some ropes around the leather in a ligature. He starts to sweat, despite the fact that the room is freezing cold. He is at the complete mercy of a power that is far greater than him, but he must force himself to rely on reason. He has nothing to confess and yet, under that kind of torture, people often admit to anything. If he doesn't speak, they won't be able to condemn him to death. That's the first step he must take. He needs to get out of the labyrinth into which he's been thrown. Will he succeed?

A thick rope descends from the ceiling and hits him in the back.

Even if he can't see, he perceives what's going on: they're wrapping it around the ligature and tying it in a knot.

"Pull him up slowly," the executioner says. He has a Roman accent.

The jailer who tied Niccolò's wrists together now grabs his thighs and lifts him up, while the other man secures the rope to his wrists. He is yanked high off the floor. He hangs in the void: a pain the likes of which he has never felt before rages through his shoulders. The weight of his body pulls his arms out of their sockets.

It's even worse when they let his body swing back and forth. With every single movement, the pain gets more acute, always increasing. It's a lacerating pain and it makes him tremble and shake. He yells, screams, and pants. He, who always used irony and reason to separate himself from the rest of the world, now lacks both. All his thoughts are reduced to brief, disconnected flashes. His entire history, memory, and feelings are gone. They no longer exist. All he understands is that he is mistreated by the city of Florence. He cannot ignore or detach himself from this aggressive act. If he had something to confess, he would; not having anything is now the worst condemnation. He screams louder and urinates on himself.

"Will you talk now?" the judge calls out from below.

He hears himself scream but says nothing.

They lower him and place him face down on the ground.

He feels the icy pavement on his chest and cheek.

The physician slaps his arms back into their sockets. "You can go again," he says.

They lift him to his feet.

Once more, a jailer wraps his arms around Niccolò's thighs so his feet do not touch the floor. Before he is raised up again, the executioner asks the physician, "How long can we go on?"

"No more than an hour. If necessary, we can continue tomorrow."

An hour. Tomorrow. Quantities of time that seem impossible to tolerate.

L arge black insects crawl between the cracks in the cell wall. Lice chew on his scalp. Niccolò lies curled up on a dirty and hard cloth. He has no strength. He has lost count of how many days it has been. At least twenty. His shoulders, dislocated six times and six times pushed back into place, hurt a little less. He can at least move them now.

Senza pietà Fortuna qui mi serra . . . [25]

Now I really know what you meant, Dianora, for I have experienced it on my own flesh. They've been violent with me, as they were with you, and now I'm in prison. And like you, I have no way out. How strong you were to write poems in this condition! I will never be able to do so again. Will I ever fall lower than this?

That'll be hard, a little sprite says from somewhere deep inside him. You've already fallen far.

A person can always sink further, he replies darkly. The fetid air in the cell, the foul smell of his urine and excrement fills his nose. And to think he was once afraid that Valentino would have tortured or killed him . . . when actually it was Florence that reduced him to this state.

It stinks down here like the gully of Roncisvalle, full of putrefying cadavers of Palatine dukes and counts, the sprite says with a smile, or like parts of Sardinia where the brambles are full of guano and boar feces.

He imagines the places that the sprite suggests, and for some unknown reason he starts to laugh wildly, the way people in great desperation often do.

It's nighttime, but the prison is wide awake. There's the sound of slamming and banging on the railings from cells nearby; he hears locks bolting and keys turning in rusty keyholes.

Jupiter spews its lightning bolts and Etna erupts, the sprite says with amusement.

That's when Niccolò realizes what this little voice is trying to say: reality must be dressed with images and words to make it tolerable.

The sprite is irony, which abandoned him when he was afraid but which has now returned. Dianora sent him the sprite, as a kind of medicine.

He laughs again and feels his strength begin to return. He gets on his knees and then to his feet, tugging on the leather cord that ties him to the wall, knotted like the jesses used by falconers to tie off their birds' talons. He can only take three steps but his mind moves both far and fast. They won't kill him, but they could keep him in prison for life. Does he know of anyone who could intervene on his behalf with the Medicis? No one comes to mind, no one he knows would take such a risk. He can only beg for mercy. Giuliano? He didn't even reply to his letter. But what if Niccolò sent him a poem? Giuliano's a poet, too, after all. And there's a shared feeling between poets. He won't beg; he'll write a sonnet. A light caudate sonnet, born out of this filth. A-B-B-A. He thinks of some early rhymes: *poeti, geti, Giuliano, io, ho io . . .*

Io ho, Giuliano, in gamba un paio di geti con sei tratti di fune in su le spalle . . . [26]

The tone is right, I'm not commiserating, nor am I hiding anything . . . *-eti, -alle . . .*

L'altre miserie mie non vo' contalle, poiché così si trattano è poeti! [27]

A cry of pain and the sound of chains clanking come from the cell next door. "Stay down!" one of the jailers screams.

Luckily they didn't chain me up. But they could if they wanted to. The noises are making it hard to concentrate. I need to think: *-alle, -eti*

Menon pidocchi queste parieti . . . [28]
Now something that rhymes with *alle*.
Bolsi spaccati, che paion farfalle.[29]

There's the deep, dark sound of chanting from outdoors. It comes to him through the metal grill, which has the shape of a wolf's mouth and leads to the inner courtyard. He stops composing the poem to listen. It's the friars from the Confraternità dei Neri, they're leading a condemned man to his death. He raises his head and sees the light that precedes dawn, the glow of torches. The gallows is in the courtyard. Whose turn is it today?

He hears a voice. It's Pietro Paolo Boscoli. He sounds more desperate than he recalls and yet also firmly resolved; he refuses to kiss an image of the Redeemer. Someone, the confessor probably, urges him to repent, to say he believes in the rules of the Church.

There's whispering. He can't hear what the condemned man and priest say to each other.

There's silence.

Niccolò visualizes the executioner raising his axe.

There's a heavy thud.

Then more silence.

And finally, the sound of the friars chanting their psalms.

He confessed, but I will not. I am alive and a poet. A poet! Niccolò holds onto this word with all his strength.

When they open his cell door, he fears they are going to take him back to the torture chamber. At the mere thought of it, he feels a sharp pain in his shoulders.

Two officers place a bucket of water and a dirty rag on the floor.

"Wash up, and do it quickly."

"What?" That's all he can say.

"You're being released," Dino Gherardi says, entering the cell. "You will now go home, pack up your things, and by the end of the day you must move your family to your farm in Sant'Andrea in Percussina. You are not allowed to leave the farm. If you need to come to Florence for some important matter, you will have to ask permission. You may never leave the Republic; it is a crime punishable by death."

The sunlight that shines through the grating in the ceiling of the prison is blinding. He is forced to shut his eyes and wavers unsteadily on his feet.

Gherardi grabs him and has him sit down.

"It will pass," he says. "Stay seated until you get your strength back. You haven't been maimed and that's what counts."

The road home is inconceivably long. He's exhausted, he has to walk slowly and stay close to the wall so he can lean on it now and then. He helps himself along with his hands, step by step.

He notices how people in the street look at him and move away. Everyone has heard about what happened to him.

After what seems like an endless amount of time, he reaches the street where he lives, or rather, where he used to live.

Bernardo and Lodovico are playing with other children near the front door.

Bernardo notices him first. "Babbo! Babbo's home!" he says, running toward him, followed by his brother. But then the boy stops and hesitates, as if he's afraid of him, as if something obscure and dangerous has taken his father's place. Lodovico does the same.

Niccolò smiles to reassure them, but they keep their distance.

Marietta rushes out of the house and to his side. Her eyes are shiny with tears and she hugs him. Niccolò flinches with pain but holds her tight.

He's wearing a used black tabard that he bought at the market after haggling over the price. It's old but warm enough to protect him from the first chills of September. He wanders between the trees on his farm in the afternoon light, noticing how his neighbors have started to encroach on his land.

He smiles to think that he, just like the city of Florence, has enemies at all cardinal points. His neighbor to the west worries him most. Spacagna is a slimy delinquent who, with each passing season, has been trying to carve out more space for himself with his hoe. I will plant oaks to stop him, Niccolò thinks. But the bitterness remains. Even if he manages to block Spacagna, others will follow suit. "A man who has land has war," his father used to say.

He will fight them all, day after day. When he was first released, he could do nothing. After the rope torture, everything scared him, and for a long time. He couldn't deal with even the smallest problems. Things are better now but still not perfect.

He bends down, picks up a clod of earth, crumbles it, and lets the soil spill between his fingers, testing its consistency. He notices it needs fertilizer. He will have to find a way of obtaining some because the few animals he owns simply don't produce enough.

He goes into his woods and looks around, choosing new places to spread moss so he can capture thrushes. He can catch from two to six a day but needs more than that: he uses them to barter for food and to give as gifts when someone does him a small favor.

The cords of wood are all there, stacked in their place. When the north wind starts to blow, buyers will step forward. He has already spoken with Batista Guicciardini, Filippo Ginori and . . . one other person. Who was it? Why can't he recall names as quickly as he used to? The cousin of the priest; Giovanni, no, Jacopo. Jacopo del Bene. The extra money will help them through the winter. Will it be enough?

He leaves the woods, looks at his small stone house, faded amber in the evening light, and walks toward it slowly.

Niccolò's desk, once an old dining table, measures three arms' length by two. He has pushed it up against a window and piled it high with his papers and books. He closes the door behind him. The sound of his children's voices fades until it is just a background noise.

He hangs his tabard on a peg and puts on the only decent clothes he has left. It is already cold indoors, and sitting still for long periods of time makes him even colder, but he has to save the wood until real winter comes.

He sits down and rubs his hands together. The sun sinks down even further. He thinks of Dianora and she appears before him. He is glad to have put on his best clothes to receive her.

She often comes and visits with him, and always does so with tenderness, though she comes to him less frequently than she once did. Today she smiles at him warmly. It looks like she is glowing. The passing years have not diminished her beauty or the light in her eyes.

She reminds him that Borgia is dead and that the two of them are still together. One day, she says, he will be known as a poet, it's only a matter of time. She repeats the lines he recited to her on their last night: "*Oh dolce notte, oh sante ore notturne e quete, ch'i disiosi amanti accompagnate . . .*"[30] If he managed to write those, he will write others.

He repeats the words out loud and feels the warmth of her

hands and cheeks; he is moved to tears, something that happens ever more frequently. He never completed that poem.

A sound at the door makes him jump. It's just the children playing outside, Bernardo pushed Lodovico against the door. They bicker and run off.

Dianora has disappeared but she will be back, he's certain of it.

He reaches out for a piece of paper. The suffering he experienced at the hands of the authorities have led him, almost as a kind of reaction, to rediscover hope. He has started writing again. This time it does not feel like it will be for naught. He's finishing a pamphlet that he would like to dedicate to Giuliano de' Medici. Niccolò is almost certain that he was released from prison thanks to him; perhaps he was moved by Niccolò's sonnet. Maybe Giuliano will allow him to return to service. If Niccolò is given the chance, even if only for some menial task at the beginning, he knows he will be able to prove his worth. And if he can get the pamphlet that he has almost completed into Giuliano's hands, the leader of the Florentine State will surely realize the wealth of experience that Niccolò has, and it won't matter that he acquired it when Florence was a Republic. Niccolò needs to get back to work, he needs it desperately. His family is falling into the most ignoble poverty imaginable.

He has given the pamphlet the title *De principatibus*. Valentino was right: a Latin title lends gravitas to the writing. Niccolò has poured everything that Cesare taught him into those pages. He was never as close to real power as he was in the months he spent with Borgia, excluding when he was given the rope six times.

What the duke confided in him about leadership provided him with a framework for this new piece of writing: by understanding how you can fall into the depths of hell, you can also avoid ending up there.

The next time Dianora returns to him, he will explain why it is neither bad nor wrong of him to write about these things. On the contrary, showing people what hides behind the deception of power, stripping away all the gold crowns and laurel wreaths, opens people's eyes to the truth. She, a victim of power, ought to understand that better than anyone. And he, a victim in his own right, has it carved in his flesh.

He knows he will never be compensated for the suffering he experienced and he will never come to terms with the torture, but he can at least defend himself. Dianora taught him the importance of this. You must never be afraid to understand; you must always write about things the way they truly are.

Niccolò chose to write the pamphlet in prose because these kinds of subjects are not well suited to poetry. Perhaps, one day, if he has the strength, he will try and put it in verse. Writing about Valentino came easily after spending time with him the way he did. Now, after so many years have passed, he sees things differently, as if the events that took place never actually pertained to him. Niccolò is forced to admit that, before Cesare's fall from power, he offered a strong example of how to occupy a throne: how important it was to have good fortune and good weapons; how to protect yourself from enemies, gain friends, and conquer others, either through brute force or deception; how to have soldiers revere you, love and fear you; how to shape an era.

But was that what really happened? Now and then he wonders as much. It seems to Niccolò that Borgia was not that different from other bold figures who managed to capture the public's attention for some time and then disappeared. The more he writes about Cesare, even if the man invented things, the more the hazy figure of Cesare takes on consistency. He has been transformed into an ideal prince. Niccolò can't help but admit to himself that this is exactly what Valentino wanted from him. He wanted to have his story told, and in so doing, live on.

Niccolò is also obliged to recognize that he owes his survival to the duke. The cornerstone of the palace of words that Niccolò has written so far came from Cesare. After completing the sections that regarded Borgia, Niccolò added examples from both ancient and recent history, putting absolutely everything he knew down onto the page. The book has become a treatise on what a prince truly is, how many different kinds of princes there are, how power can be acquired, seized, maintained, lost. The topic has allowed him to express himself and has kept his mind busy. Now that the book is substantial and just the right length, he's certain that a prince, especially a new one like Giuliano, will appreciate it.

He rereads the pages, corrects a sentence here and there, continuing to reflect on their subject.

How can he be sure Giuliano will read it? Even if he had read Niccolò's sonnet, it's very possible that such a lengthy piece of writing as the treatise will annoy him. Niccolò also wonders how he will get the book into Giuliano's hands: he can't deliver it personally because he's an outlaw. He needs an intermediary, but who could that be? Ideally it would be someone who understands books and writing. He must choose carefully; when writers are short of ideas they don't hesitate to copy. Someone might appropriate the ideas in his pamphlet, change things around a little, alter the title, and pawn it off as their own. Then it would be gone forever.

The fear of being deprived of the little he has managed to make for himself with such enormous effort is discouraging. He puts down his pen and sighs. When faced with such mammoth enemies, he feels weak.

Fortunately, Dianora returns to him and sits down by his side. No, she says to him, we are not defenseless. The work we do remains in perpetuity. As long as you remember me, I will not die. No one will ever take from you that which you have experienced firsthand.

Yes, but after us is nothing, he whispers to her. I don't have much time left, he says with a sad smile, his eyes filling with tears.

Time does not exist, she says.

He hears the door creak open and recognizes Marietta's step. He knows exactly what she is going to say: let's eat dinner now while there's still light. That way we will save the candles for when it is deep winter.

He blinks away his tears, gets to his feet, and walks toward his wife. Dianora comes with him. They leave the room together.

The last rays of sun fall at a slant on the manuscript, the long shadows dividing it in half. Motes of dust dance in the light and then settle slowly on the pages he has written.

TRANSLATOR'S NOTES

[1] "Mouth, for kisses, was never the worse: like as the moon reneweth her course." Boccaccio, *The Decameron*, Day II, Novel VII. tr. J. M. Rigg, A. H. Bullen, London, 1903 https://www.brown.edu/Departments/Italian_Studies/dweb/texts/DecShowText.php?myID=nov0207&lang=eng

[2] https://penelope.uchicago.edu/Thayer/E/Roman/Texts/Plutarch/Lives/Caesar*.html

[3] Trapped by Destiny's merciless hand,
with no one nearby to lessen my distress,
I'm shaken by the deepest unhappiness;
peace is nowhere to be found in this land.

I am a lady, and so is Destiny
and yet her cruelty has clawed
and whipped and unshod:
now despair and grief reside within me.

To escape I turn from this barren knoll
To dwell in memory, and revisit what was mine:
Father and mother, and many a good soul

That the heavens took before their time.
And yet I rise up against these offenses;
no one can erase what I have seen: the crime.

[4] Life on this earth is very short, many are the pains that, living and struggling, each person sustains—that is why we, following our whim have left the daily world of noisy strife to pursue the life of shepherds and nymphs, passing and using up the years in frivolities, in play, because he who deprives himself of pleasure to live in anguish and breathless despair in the ordinary world must either somehow be insensible to the anguish he suffers himself, and the evils the strange events by which almost all mortals are oppressed.

Machiavelli, *The Mandrake*, Opening Song, tr. Wallace Shawn, Dramatists Play Service, NY, 1978

[5] The night when Pietro Soderini died,
His soul for entrance into Hell applied.
But Pluto shouted: Hence, thou simple soul!
This is no place for you. Go to the infant's Limbo, fool!
The editor's introduction to *The Historical, Political, and Diplomatic*

Writings of Niccolo Machiavelli, tr. from the Italian, by Christian E. Detmold (Boston, J. R. Osgood and company, 1882). Vol. 1. History of Florence. https://oll.libertyfund.org/page/machiavelli-niccolo-1469-1527#c_lf0076-01_footnote_nt007

[6] A Spanish horseman rides at the foot a mountain singing of his love for a young girl.

[7] Turn this way, my lovely damsel, turn this way just a little, please my beloved hope, because I am dying for your love.

[8] Lovely young girl, I gave you my heart, Lovely young girl I gave you my heart.

[9] I saw the beauty sitting on the ground near a fountain, wearing a garland of fresh flowers.

[10] Turn this way, my lovely maiden, turn towards me just a little, bright star; do not fight me, for I am dying for your love.

[11] It was night, and a cloudless sky, and the moon was shining. (This translation of Horace's *Epode 15* [see notes 11—16] is by A.S. Kline [https://www.poetryintranslation.com/PITBR/Latin/HoraceEpodesAndCarmenSaeculare.php#anchor_Toc98670063].

[12] Among the inferior stars.

[13] When you, about to offend against the great gods' power, Swore words of loyalty to me.

[14] Clinging to me more tightly, with your entwining arms/ than ivy to the towering oak.

[15] Swore that while wolves threatened the flock, while Orion, the sailor's/ Enemy, stirred the wintry sea,/ That while the breezes should flutter, in Apollo's unshorn hair.

[16] Our mutual love would endure.

[17] King of Heaven who shows mercy to all
Who fills the wide world with life
You have raised me on such great pain
Grant me freedom where I see none.

[18] Give me courage to face what will take place
Lead me down paths and across meadows
And through the woods, to the place that is filled with
Your voice, o Lord who brings peace.
Lead me there, to the place you favor,
Console this errant soul of mine
And I will love you forever.

[19] That rises high and freely/Above everything and to the place she likes best.

[20] All pain is canceled from the mind/ At night and grants the sigh of peace.

[21] "Oh sweet night, O holy hours (from Macchiavelli, *The Mandrake*, as above).

[22] That lie with desirous lovers.

²³ In you are joined all joys.

²⁴ You alone know the secret of making hearts glad.

²⁵ From Dianora's poem, note 3: "Trapped by Destiny's merciless hand".

²⁶ I have, Giuliano, on my legs a set of fetters, with six pulls of the cord on my shoulders . . . This translation of Machiavelli's Sonnet 5 "To Giuliano, Son of Lorenzo de' Medici" (see notes 26-29) is by Allan Gilbert [*The Chief Works and Others*, Vol. II, Duke University Press, 1989, p. 1013–14, https://www.jstor.org/stable/j.ctv1220h92].

²⁷ my other miseries I do not intend to recount to you, since so the poets are treated!

²⁸ These broken walls generate lice . . .

²⁹ . . . so swollen that they look like flies.

³⁰ See note 21.

ABOUT THE AUTHOR

Franco Bernini's screenplay for *The Grey Zone* won the Grolla d'oro Prize for Best Screenplay at the 50th Cannes Film Festival. He teaches screenwriting at the Italian National Film School. He has written three novels and a collection of short stories. *The Throne* is his English-language debut.